THE BOY WHO STOLE
FROM THE DEAD

ALSO BY OREST STELMACH

The Boy from Reactor 4

THE BOY
WHO STOLE
FROM THE
DEAD

OREST STELMACH

Text copyright © 2014 Orest Stelmach
All rights reserved.

Printed in the United States of America.

Published by Thomas & Mercer, Seattle

www.apub.com

ISBN-13: 9781477809488
ISBN-10: 1477809481

Library of Congress Control Number: 2013908438

For Ihor

AUTHOR'S NOTE

Chernobyl and Odessa are located in Ukraine, but these popular English spellings are derived from the Russian language. The proper spellings for these cities based on the Ukrainian language are Chornobyl and Odesa. Beginning with this novel, I will utilize the proper English spelling for all Ukrainian words. Thanks to all the fans of *The Boy From Reactor 4* who wrote me and suggested this change.

CHAPTER 1

"WATCH OUT," ROBERT JR. SAID.

Robert Sr. slammed on the brakes. The jacked 4x4 skidded to a stop in the snow. Lauren Ross looked up from the front passenger seat. A reindeer stood in the middle of the deserted road, twenty feet away. It didn't have that deer-in-the-headlights look. Instead it looked sweet, goofy, and regal, with a two-tiered crown of antlers.

"You thinking what I'm thinking, Papa?" Robert Jr. said.

"This is as good a place as any."

Lauren heard a rustle behind her. Robert Jr. lifted a rifle from the rack on the back wall. His side window was open. She turned toward the windshield. The reindeer hadn't moved.

"Oh, no," Lauren said. "Please don't."

"You folks from the lower forty-eight," Robert Jr. said. "How do you think that venison gets in your grocery store?"

"I'm from New York," Lauren said. "We don't have venison in our grocery stores. You can't do this."

"I understand what you're feeling," Robert Sr. said. "When I was a child I had the same emotions. But we rely on subsistence in this part of Alaska. In Kotzebue, a man's got to hunt to survive."

Robert Jr. slid the rifle's bolt handle forward and locked it down. He handled the rifle as though he'd been born firing it twenty-something years ago.

It was 15°F outside but Lauren was sweating. She understood what Robert Sr. was saying. They weren't idiots with permits hunting defenseless animals for sport, an oxymoron if there ever was one. Still, she couldn't help herself. A single thought kept coming back to her, as it did whenever her colleagues at the Sports Network boasted after a hunting trip. It bothered her less when a random person was killed than when an innocent animal was slaughtered. Maybe it shouldn't have, but it did.

"Locked and loaded," Robert Jr. said.

Robert Sr. said, "All right, then."

"Shit," Lauren said. She averted her eyes. "I can't watch this."

"It's not what you think," Robert Sr. said.

"You mean you're not going to shoot the reindeer?" Lauren felt something hard press against the back of her head.

"No, dear. We're not going to kill the caribou."

She'd arrived via Anchorage yesterday. Kotzebue was a three-mile long gravel spit at the tip of the Baldwin Peninsula, twenty-six miles north of the Arctic Circle. The locals pronounced it "Cots-a-byoo" but called it "Cots." The population totaled 3,201. Neat rows of modular homes packed a narrow strip of land, some more ramshackle than others. Spare tires, rusty gasoline drums, and snowmobiles filled the yards. Kotzebue malamutes wandered among them, tethered by long chains to their doghouses.

Lauren checked in to the Bayside Inn, a no-frills bed and breakfast. She ducked into the inn's restaurant for lunch, and was ecstatic when she saw the menu featured comfort food, albeit at exorbitant prices. She'd read up on the local cuisine. The last thing she needed was herring egg salad or peeling ptarmigan eggs. She inhaled a burger, wiped the ketchup off her plate with a French fry, and washed it down with a Diet Sprite.

Her first appointment had been at city hall at 1:30 p.m. Her second one had been at the June Nelson Elementary School an hour later. She introduced herself as a reporter from the Sports Network doing a background piece on a seventeen-year-old prep school hockey phenom named Bobby Kungenook. Neither one provided any new information. No one in city hall or the school knew the Kungenooks or a son named Bobby.

When she was finished, she took a cab to the neighborhood where the Kungenooks lived prior to their deaths in 2000. Lauren went house-to-house knocking on doors asking about their deceased neighbors. The doors closed quickly, in most cases before Lauren was finished asking questions. No one knew anything. No one could help.

When she got back to the inn at 4:00 p.m., two men were leaning against an old Ford pickup truck at the curb by the entrance. They looked like father and son. They wore matching parkas and fur hats. The younger one looked to be in his mid-twenties. The older one closer to fifty. He introduced himself as Robert Seelick. His son shared the same name.

"I'm told you're looking for me," Robert Sr. said.

"Who told you that?"

"Mayor Schroeder."

"Funny. He didn't mention you."

"And Principal Coffey at the elementary school. You met with her after you left the mayor's office."

"She didn't mention you either."

"I'm sure they didn't want to volunteer me."

"To do what?"

"Help a stranger from the lower forty-eight."

"I'm guessing that's me."

"You're the only one in town."

"How can you help me?"

"My wife and I were best friends with the Kungenooks."

"Holy crap. I mean, that's incredible. Do you have a minute to talk now?"

It was her first break. Their son had come to New York from nowhere, beaten the NHL's fastest skater in a race, and lit up the record books at Fordham Prep. The Jesuit priests at Fordham said he was from the Arctic Circle but he spoke Ukrainian and Russian better than English. His guardian in New York wouldn't let Lauren near him. Something was off about the whole story. Lauren was as sure of it now as when she'd seen the kid play for the first time.

She pointed to the restaurant at the inn. "Can I buy you both a beer? Or two?"

"Thanks, but we have an errand to run. We thought you might want to come along."

"What kind of errand?"

"We need to pick up dinner," Robert Jr. said.

"You're going to the grocery store?" Lauren said.

"Something like that," Robert Sr. said. He told her their destination. "Coming?"

Robert Sr. drove them out of the residential area toward the southern end of the peninsula.

"What do you do for a living?" Lauren said.

"I'm a civil servant," Robert Sr. said. "Junior works for Rotman's."

"Rotman's?" Lauren said.

"The general store," Robert Jr. said. "Serving Kotzebue since 1932."

Robert Sr. said, "On his off days, he writes music. Boy's got a natural talent for rhyming. As you can see."

"Serving Kotze-boo, since 1932." Robert Jr. swayed to his own beat in the back seat.

"We hunt, too," Robert Sr. said. "Not much luck today."

"You work for the Sports Network?" Robert Jr. said.

"I do," Lauren said.

"They let you come out here on your own?" Robert Sr. said.

"Usually there's a cameraman too, but this was a special project. It took a lot of convincing to get my boss to let me go, and he wasn't willing to spend the extra money."

"Why did it take a lot of convincing?" Robert Sr. said.

"It's a bit of a fishing expedition," Lauren said.

"It sure is."

Robert Sr. took a right turn onto a snow-covered access road. Two minutes later he was parked in front of Kotzebue Sound. Robert Sr. pulled a fishing rod the shape of a gas grill lighter out of the trunk. Robert Jr. grabbed an axe. They attached rubber webs with spikes to the soles of Lauren's boots. Then they marched onto the Chukchi Sea.

The ice shimmered beneath an orange sunset. A gust of wind brought tears to Lauren's eyes. After a hundred yards they stopped walking. Lauren looked around. They were so far south the fishermen along the northern shore looked like ants circling their holes. She was alone. Alone with the Seelicks, the Arctic Ocean, and the secrets beneath the surface.

Robert Jr. drove the axe into the ice. It barely cracked.

"Why are you here, dear?" Robert Sr. said.

"I'm doing a piece on Bobby Kungenook. He's a hockey player at Fordham Prep in New York City. A once in a lifetime, can't miss prospect. Thing is, he just appeared out of nowhere. Supposedly he was home schooled by someone in Alaska but no one knows by whom. How old was he when his parents died?"

"Couldn't say. Best of my recollection, the Kungenooks sent Bobby away to be raised by another family when he was two. That would have been 1994. They told my wife and me what they were doing and we never spoke about it again."

"What family?"

"Don't know," Robert Sr. said.

"Why did they send him away?"

"Bobby's father, John, lost his job. And his mother—Jackie— was ill. She suffered from a spinal condition her whole life. They both struggled with depression. This isn't an easy place to raise a child during the best of times, let alone the worst. They decided to give Bobby a better life. They decided to send him to a better place."

"What place?"

"Don't know," Robert Sr. said. "Like I said, it wasn't something anyone wanted to talk about."

Ice cracked. Water sloshed to the surface. Robert Jr. stepped aside. Robert Sr. dropped the line into the hole and handed Lauren the rod.

"You take it," he said.

"I don't want to mess up your dinner," Lauren said.

"Don't worry. We won't let you."

Lauren squatted down and held the rod above the hole.

"When Bobby arrived at Fordham, he didn't speak English," Lauren said. "Were either of the Kungenooks of Ukrainian descent?"

"No," Robert Sr. said. "They were both Inupiaq."

"And their relatives?"

"Inupiaq, too. Cousins, mostly. You knocked on their doors today."

"I'm sure I did. And none of them speak Russian either."

"Not that I know of."

"Then it doesn't make sense."

"But I'll tell you who did speak Russian," Robert Sr. said.

Lauren looked up.

"Otto von Kotzebue."

"Who?"

"Otto von Kotzebue. He was an Estonian navigator working for the Russians. He discovered Kotzebue in 1818. You know who else spoke Russian?"

Something pulled on the line. Lauren looked down into the hole.

"His father, August von Kotzebue. He was a famous author. He was murdered by a theology student who didn't like his politics. You know what they did to that theology student?"

Lauren looked up.

Robert Jr. stood beside his father, axe on his shoulder.

"They decapitated him," Robert Sr. said.

The line tightened more.

"Something's biting," Lauren said.

"Why do you care about this kid's story so much?" Robert Jr. said. "Don't you have more interesting things to write about?"

"Once I start digging, I never stop until I'm first with the story and the job is done."

"Why?" Robert Sr. said.

A vision of Lauren's mother, carefree and smiling, flashed before her eyes. She took a deep breath and willed the image away. "That's the way I'm wired."

The Seelicks pulled a fish out of the hole. It was sixteen inches long.

"Alaskan whitefish," Robert Sr. said. "See. Your fishing expedition was a success after all."

By the time they returned to the truck it was dark. As Robert Sr. drove them back, Lauren contemplated her next move. It was as though the Kungenooks had sent their son to be raised by a family in Ukraine, which was preposterous. But why else would he speak Ukrainian and Russian fluently but not English?

"You ever cover the Iditarod?" Robert Jr. said.

"No," Lauren said. "One of the other reporters does."

"But you know what it is," Robert Jr. said, sounding impressed.

"Sure. Four hundred mile dog sledding race that starts in Nome. One of the world's last great races."

"Cool," Robert Jr. said. "You know, for someone who asks a lot of dumb questions, you're pretty smart."

Then the reindeer crossed their path.

Breathe, Lauren told herself. Focus on your breath. Take yourself inside. Breathe.

No one had ever pointed a gun at her let alone pressed one against her head. She sensed this was going to be a binary event. Either they were going to kill her or she was going to win a Pulitzer. If two local yahoos were protecting the Kungenooks by intimidating a reporter with a hunting rifle, this had to be more than a sports story. The only question was whether she'd survive the night to pursue it further. If she did, the first order of business would be to make the Seelicks pay.

"The way you said that makes it sound as though you're going to shoot me instead," Lauren said.

She glanced over her shoulder. Robert Jr. had shifted away from her in the back seat to accommodate the length of the rifle's barrel. It rested on the seat back behind her.

"In the old days," Robert Sr. said, "when an Inupiaq family decided it couldn't take care of another child, it would put the baby on a sled with a sign around its neck and leave it in the open. The sign would have the name of a nearby village written on it, and people who found the sled would push it along in the right direction. Eventually the sled would arrive at its destination, and if it survived, some new family would adopt the baby."

"What are you saying?" Lauren said. "The Kungenooks put Bobby in a sled and he ended up in Ukraine?"

"No. Bobby was a boy. Inupiaq would never give up a boy. They would only give up a girl. That's why Bobby's such a mystery. It was sacrilege in our culture to give up a boy. That's why everyone pretends he never existed. That's why no one will talk about him. Do you understand now?"

"Yes," Lauren said. The story kept getting better and better, she thought. That's what she understood.

"Good," Robert Sr. said. "Because if you keep disrespecting the dead by digging into their past, if you keep disrupting this community, it's going to end badly for you. When are you leaving town?"

"Tomorrow morning."

"Good. Let me ask you this: Who's taking care of the boy in New York?"

"He has a guardian."

"She must know his story, right? Why don't you talk to her?"

"I tried. She won't return my calls."

"Did you try saying 'please'?" Robert Jr. said.

"Please take me back to my hotel," Lauren said.

"We understand each other, right?" Robert Sr. said.

The rifle pushed harder into her neck.

"Yes. We understand each other."

"All right then," Robert Sr. said.

He drove back to the Bayside Inn. Lauren's feet kissed the pavement before Robert Sr. could apply the brakes. She held the door and glared inside.

"You point a gun at me? You threaten me? And you think you're going to get away with it? I'm going to have a camera crew down here tomorrow. I'm going to make you national news. But first I'm going to go inside, make one phone call, and have you both arrested."

"For what?" Robert Sr. said. "You came looking for us. You told the mayor you were looking for someone who could tell you about the Kungenooks. We took you ice fishing as a friendly gesture. Then we drove you home. You think something else happened?"

"Do you have any idea who you're dealing with?"

"It's your word against ours."

"Exactly."

Robert Sr. shrugged. "All right then. Make sure you spell my name right." He unzipped his parka to reveal an olive shirt. It boasted a pair of gold stripes on each collar and a gold Kotzebue police badge with a turquoise centerpiece. "That's *Captain* Seelick," he said. "With a *C.*"

When Lauren got back to the room it was 6:35 p.m. She poured herself a Scotch from the flask in her suitcase and knocked it back with a trembling hand. She decided to keep the day's events and her discoveries to herself. She didn't want to get scooped by anyone at the sports station, or heaven forbid, one of the news networks. Besides, she had a lead now. Seelick had referred to Bobby's guardian as "she." Lauren had never told him the guardian was a woman. Seelick knew Nadia Tesla.

It was 10:35 p.m. in New York. Too late to call. Lauren pulled up the contacts on her cell phone and dialed Nadia Tesla's number on the landline anyway. Nadia had agreed to give Lauren an exclusive if she waited until June. It was only April. Waiting, however, was not one of Lauren's virtues. Perhaps if she saw the 907 area code she'd answer, Lauren thought.

The call rolled to voice mail. Lauren hung up and called her assistant. Laughter echoed and glasses clinked in the background. Her assistant sounded excited.

"Have you heard the news?" she said.

"What news?" Lauren said.

"Bobby Kungenook was arrested two hours ago."

"You're kidding me."

"No. Isn't it awesome?"

"What's the charge?"

The word rolled off her assistant's lips in a husky whisper. "Murder."

CHAPTER 2

N ADIA TESLA KEPT HER EYES GLUED TO THE ELEVATOR OF
New York City's Sixth Precinct Police Station in Greenwich
Village. When a man in a checkered sports jacket emerged and
locked eyes with her, Nadia sprang from her seat near the front
desk. His hair was the color of coffee but his moustache was
gray. He held a clipboard in his hands. He introduced himself as
Gregson, the detective who'd called to tell her Bobby had been
arrested.

"How's Bobby?" Nadia said.

"He's fine."

"Is he hurt?"

"No. He's fine."

"I want to see him."

"You can see him in criminal court when he's arraigned."

"When will that be?"

"Probably tomorrow. Eighteen to twenty-four hours in most
cases."

"Tomorrow? That's unacceptable. I'm Bobby's legal guardian. I demand to see him now."

"You can't. Bobby's in police custody."

"I have a right to see him."

"No, ma'am. Actually, you don't."

"He's seventeen, for God's sake. He's a minor. I must have a right to see him."

"If he was sixteen or under, you'd have a right to see him. But he's not. You'll be able to see him at arraignment."

"That's unbelievable." Nadia studied Gregson. She forced a smile. "Look, the police must have discretion in cases like this, right? Can't you let me see him for a minute?"

Gregson shook his head.

"What if you were in the room with me the whole time?"

"I'm sorry—"

"So I can see he's okay. So he can see that I'm here."

"Your boy is being charged as an adult."

"He's actually going to be charged? This can't be happening. This must some sort of misunderstanding."

"I doubt it."

"What makes you think he did this thing? What evidence do you have?"

"I can't discuss that with you, ma'am."

"He must be scared to death. You have children, Detective?"

"Yeah, but not in police custody on a murder charge."

"Who did he supposedly—Who's the victim?"

Gregson shook his head. "I'm sorry."

The station doors swung open. Johnny Tanner burst inside. His golden ponytail shone against his black pinstripe suit. As a man, he was too crude and too much a showman for Nadia's tastes. As a friend, he was too thoughtful and reliable for her to live without.

"They won't let me see him," Nadia said.

"Why not?" Johnny said.

Nadia looked at Gregson. "This is Bobby's attorney."

"I want to see my client," Johnny said. "Now."

"The suspect hasn't asked to speak with an attorney."

"I don't care what he did or didn't ask for. I'm his attorney. Take me to him now, or those reporters out front—I saw the *Post* and the *Daily News* out there—they're going to hear about how the NYPD denies minors their constitutional rights. Have you seen this kid skate on YouTube? He's got a following, you know."

Gregson considered Johnny's comment. "Can I speak to you in private?"

Johnny put his hand on Nadia's shoulder. Her pulse slowed. "Wait here," he said. "And don't worry. I'm here now."

Johnny and Gregson spoke for a moment and disappeared into the elevator. Nadia paced. A uniformed cop behind the front desk spoke quietly on the phone. Two men in plain clothes sat at their desks working. The rest of the workstations were empty.

The depth of her fear for Bobby surprised Nadia. It shouldn't have. He was her cousin, not her son, and she'd only known him for a year. But they'd shared a harrowing journey when she'd helped him escape from Chornobyl to New York. The experience had created a bond of such depth that here, in the police station, she wished she could swap places with him. For he was all she had, just as she was all he had.

Johnny returned ten minutes later. Too soon, Nadia thought. He was back too soon.

"Did you see him?" Nadia said.

"For a minute."

"And?"

"He looks okay. But he wouldn't talk to me."

"What do you mean he wouldn't talk to you?"

"Gregson asked him if he wanted his attorney present. Bobby said no. He didn't want me present."

"He said that?"

Johnny sighed.

"That doesn't make any sense. He knows you. Maybe he was scared because Gregson was in the room. Why couldn't you de-mand to speak with him alone?"

"Because it's his fifth amendment right to request counsel during police interrogation. But he waived that right with me in the room."

"This is insane."

"Have you had dinner yet?" Johnny nudged her toward the exit. "Let's go find a diner."

Nadia didn't budge. "I'm not leaving him here alone."

"Nadia."

"I'm not."

"They're going to take him to Central Booking at Centre Street. He's going to get fingerprinted and interviewed by CJA—the Criminal Justice Agency. They make recommendations to the judge on bail. He'll spend the night there. He'll be arraigned tomorrow. There's nothing we can do about it."

Nadia lowered her voice. "Johnny, he's got issues."

"He's allowed three free local phone calls. He used one of them. And no, I have no idea who he called. But he has two calls left. I left my card on the table in front of him. If there's an emergency, he can call either of us."

They dodged a pair of reporters and took a cab to the Manatus Diner on Bleecker. They sat in a private booth. Johnny asked for a beer. When Nadia didn't join him he changed his order to coffee. Johnny chose the hot open turkey sandwich. Nadia tried to order the Greek salad but succumbed to the baked ziti.

"Where was Bobby supposed to be tonight?" Johnny said.

"After he finished his homework he was going over to his friend's apartment on the Upper East Side."

"What's his name?"

"Derek Mace. He goes to Fordham Prep. He's a defenseman, too. He's Bobby's personal bodyguard on the ice."

"Well, according to the cops he ended up in the Meatpacking District in an alley on Washington between thirteenth and fourteenth instead, where he supposedly stabbed a British businessman to death. Then he walked to the precinct house and turned himself in."

"You mean he actually admitted he killed the guy?"

"That's what it looks like. We'll get more details tomorrow."

"That's so preposterous, I don't even know how to respond. Bobby doesn't know any kids from England, and he certainly doesn't know any British businessman. And what would he be doing in the Meatpacking District?"

"He was carrying the murder weapon when he turned himself in."

"Bobby doesn't even own a knife."

"It wasn't a knife. The victim was stabbed in the throat multiple times with a screwdriver."

Nadia felt herself blanch.

"What?" Johnny said.

"A screwdriver?"

Johnny nodded.

"What color?"

Johnny frowned. "What color?"

"Yeah. What color was the handle?"

"I don't know. Why?"

"Bobby carries a screwdriver and a flashlight on him at all times. The screwdriver has a translucent yellow handle. The penlight is black."

Johnny stared at Nadia. "Why does he carry a screwdriver and a flashlight?"

"I don't know. It's worse than that. He can only sleep if they're under his pillow."

"You never told me that."

"I didn't know myself until I found them there one Saturday morning. He was eating breakfast. I was stripping the bed. I never noticed them when I met him in Ukraine last year. But then, we were on the run from some determined people who thought we had something very valuable. I was more concerned about our lives than his possessions."

"Did you ask him about it?"

"Of course. He said he doesn't want to talk about it, but then, he doesn't like to talk much about anything. That's why I'm so worried about him. I know it sounds nuts, but I'm concerned how he'll get through the night without the screwdriver and flashlight."

"He's a tough kid. He's been through worse and then some, right?"

"That's for sure."

"There's something else."

"What?"

"He was wearing only one shoe when he turned himself in."

"That's strange. He wears high top basketball shoes. Laced tight. He's obsessed with protecting his ankles. For hockey. How could you lose a high top that's laced to the top?"

"You couldn't. You'd have to unlace it and take it off on purpose."

"Why would he have done that?"

"Who knows? He must have had a reason. Has he been acting different lately?"

"In what way?"

"In any way. He seem preoccupied? Like something's worrying him?"

Nadia thought about the question. "No. Not that I could see. But the truth is I only spend time with him on the weekends, mostly Sunday. Between my work, his schoolwork, his commute, and hockey—that reminds me. Robert Seelick called. He saw Lauren Ross today. She's in Kotzebue. And someone called me on my cell from a hotel in Kotzebue but didn't leave a message. Had to be her."

Johnny's eyes widened.

"It's okay. She was just fishing. She doesn't know anything. He said she's going home tomorrow. I liked her when we met at one of Bobby's hockey games last year. I told her I'd give her an exclusive in June. It's only April. She couldn't wait. Had to start nosing around at what turns out to be the worst possible time. When Bobby's been arrested. I wish she'd stuck to her word." Nadia looked around to make sure no one could hear them. "Will Bobby's story hold up through this?"

"He's got a valid birth certificate, and now a driver's license, too, right?"

"Right."

"The district attorney's worried about the crime. He's not going to go digging that deep into a suspect's past for no reason. He's too busy. The criminal justice system is overloaded. I wouldn't worry about that."

"No?"

"No. Trust me. Whatever else happens, no one is going to find out who this kid really is."

CHAPTER 3

B OBBY ENTERED THE COURTROOM FROM A SIDE DOOR. HIS arms dangled in front of him, wrists cuffed. He wore a red t-shirt and jeans. Long black hair covered his ears.

A sheriff guided him toward a table facing the judge. Nadia stood up. Bobby's eyes fell on hers. Nadia smiled. She'd prepared for this moment since waking up. She nodded and channeled all the positive energy she could muster. Bobby's expression remained blank. He gave her nothing. No hint of recognition. No acknowledgement of her presence. Instead, he continued scanning the courtroom as though hers was another face in the crowd. He took his place beside Johnny and turned toward the judge.

Nadia sat down. Someone was speaking. She knew she should be listening but she couldn't shake Adam's blank stare. An eerie sensation gripped her. She'd lost her connection to him. And now, in this courtroom with this murder charge, Nadia wondered if she'd ever really known Adam. No, no, she reminded herself. He was no longer Adam. She'd forbidden herself to use his real name. That's how mistakes happened. That's how the wrong name got blurted out to the wrong person. He was Bobby. Now and forever, no matter what else happened, he had to remain Bobby.

"Docket number 12728. People vs. Aagayuk Kungenook."

Inupiaq choose an Anglo name based on someone they admire. Adam had chosen his Anglo name after meeting his uncle in Kotzebue. His uncle Robert had provided him with his false identity, and Adam had adopted his Anglo name. Since then, everyone had called him Bobby.

"Mr. Tanner, nice to see you," said the judge, an elegant amazon with fair skin and a firm jaw.

"And you, Your Honor," Johnny said.

"What brings you here today?" She glanced over the bridge of her cat eye glasses.

Johnny pointed to Bobby with an open palm.

The judge glanced at Bobby and then studied the papers in front of her. "Waive the reading?"

"Yes, Your Honor," Johnny said.

The judge turned to the assistant district attorney at the desk opposite Johnny. He looked too young to be enforcing laws.

"Notices?" the judge said.

"Yes, Your Honor," the prosecutor said. "7-10-31-A."

Johnny's neck snapped in his direction. The judge extended her hand. The prosecutor gave the judge and Johnny copies of his report.

The prosecutor read from the second page. "'We bumped into each other accidentally on the street. We got into an argument over whose fault it was. He came at me with a knife. Luckily I managed to catch his wrist with my left hand and grab my screwdriver with my right. I couldn't bring myself to stab him in the eye so I stabbed him in the neck instead.'"

"I don't understand, Your Honor," Johnny said. "Doesn't sound like a confession to murder. Sounds more like a textbook application for self defense protection under Article 35."

"Except there was no knife at the crime scene," the assistant district attorney said. "And the state has an eyewitness who will testify the victim had no weapon. That the defendant attacked him. The eyewitness is a former police officer."

"This is the first I'm hearing of this, Your Honor," Johnny said. "The police must have extracted this statement before I had a chance to confer with my client."

"The defendant waived his fifth amendment rights," the prosecutor said.

"Because he was scared and confused," Johnny said. "He's barely seventeen."

"He was calm, cool, and collected when he told his story. Ask the detectives."

"There's an impartial bunch."

"That's enough, gentlemen," the judge said. She looked at the prosecutor. "Bail?"

"Given the severity of the charges, Your Honor, the people ask for remand."

The judge turned to Johnny.

"Your Honor, my client has no priors," Johnny said. "He's a student at Fordham Prep School in the Bronx. He has an excellent academic record and he's a star hockey player. He has strong ties to the community. His legal guardian is here today."

Johnny glanced over his shoulder.

Nadia stood up and raised her hand. All eyes turned to her. She didn't smile, nod, or channel positive energy. Instead, she seethed. There was no way Bobby had killed a man. In fact, there was no way he'd lifted a hand to another human being unless his life had been threatened. He wasn't temperamental or violent, and he'd worked too hard to get to America. He was living his dream. The probability he would throw it all away in a fit of rage was zero.

"Given the severity of the charges—murder in the first degree—I'm inclined to agree with the prosecution," the judge said. "Defendant is remanded into custody."

The sheriff whisked Bobby out of the courtroom.

This time, Bobby didn't even bother to look at Nadia.

CHAPTER 4

NADIA BOUGHT THE WEDNESDAY PAPERS ON THE WAY HOME from the arraignment to her apartment on East 82nd Street. She feared the murder might be the cover story on either the *Post* or *Daily News*. But a prostitution ring catering to wealthy financiers and politicos had been busted in Manhattan. Speculation about the names in the madam's black book dominated the press. Also, New York City still averaged more than five hundred homicides a year. Not every one could make the cover of the papers. And the victim wasn't anyone particularly important or sympathetic. He was a random young businessman.

The murder was reported on the *Post*'s and *Daily News*'s seventh and eleventh pages respectively. Johnny had warned Nadia that sometimes reporters paid cops for a copy of a mug shot. Nadia held her breath while she turned the pages but neither paper featured one. Instead, they showed two different action shots of Bobby during a hockey game. Nadia recognized them from the Fordham Prep website. Both columns reported that Bobby had been charged with the murder and mentioned his epic race against New York Ranger star Márian Gáborik in Lasker Park during Hockey Night in Harlem last year.

The victim's name was Jonathan Phillip Valentine. He was a thirty-two-year-old associate at a real estate development firm in

Manhattan, originally from England. According to his employer's website, he'd earned his MBA from Columbia and his undergraduate degree from the University of Nottingham. The articles referred to sources close to the investigation. They said Bobby allegedly stabbed Valentine with a screwdriver near his home in the Meatpacking District under mysterious circumstances.

Nadia wanted to discuss the entire event with Bobby in person immediately but that wasn't possible. After his arraignment, he was taken to Rikers Island. Prisoners whose last name began with letters A-L were permitted visitors on Thursday and Sunday. Nadia would have to wait another day before she could see him.

Johnny called late Wednesday afternoon.

"The assistant district attorney called me back," Johnny said. "Our preliminary hearing is in three weeks. If the judge thinks there's enough evidence for the prosecution to proceed—and he will—then a grand jury will be convened. Grand juries meet only with the prosecution. They almost always indict and put the burden of proof on the defense. If they indict—and they probably will—a trial date will be set."

"When do we get to see their evidence?"

"I filed a motion for discovery this morning. But the way this generally works, we won't see jack until after the trial date is set. We may get dribs and drabs, but the prosecution will do everything possible to protect their witness, and give us as little chance as possible to prepare."

"So we need to find out what happened on our own."

"Basically."

"Then that's what we'll do. When you saw him at Rikers yesterday, after he was processed, he wouldn't talk about that night at all? Not a word?"

"Nope. Not a single word. I told him about the process, like we discussed. He listened. I told him you were putting money into his Department of Correction account so he can buy food and other stuff, and that you'd be by after work tomorrow."

"And he said . . ."

"He said to tell you to forget about him. That you weren't his guardian anymore. And that you were not to try to visit him under any circumstances."

"I don't know what he hoped to achieve by telling you that, when he knows me well enough to know nothing is going to stop me."

"Maybe that's his way of making sure you do visit him."

"That may be the first thing I've heard in two days that actually makes sense."

"You'll find out tomorrow," Johnny said. "How's your business doing?"

"It's doing okay." After a steady stream of work since she'd opened her shop as a forensic security analyst last June, she hadn't landed a client in three months. But she was too proud to admit it to Johnny or anyone else. "Why?"

"If I found something and the judge changed his mind and granted bail . . ."

"How much collateral do I have?"

"Exactly."

"Not much," Nadia said. "All my income goes toward expenses. With the apartment and Bobby's tuition, I've used up most of my savings. But I would come up with it somehow."

"Let's worry about getting him out first. A couple of things I found out from the ADA."

"What's that?"

"The screwdriver that was used as the murder weapon?"

"Yeah?"

"It's a cheap-looking thing. He said the handle's a see-through yellow."

"Bobby made it himself in shop class in his prior life. That's not the kind of news that's going to get him bail."

"And they found a black penlight in his pocket."

"Like the screwdriver, it never left his possession."

"But no shoe."

"No shoe."

"The question is why he kept those things on him at all times."

"No, that's not the question, Johnny." Nadia shivered. "The question is how he made it through a night in prison without them."

CHAPTER 5

LAUREN GLANCED OUT THE WINDOW. FROM THE AIR, THE storage and processing plants of the Red Dog Mine resembled the American flag. Long red buildings stretched horizontally, while a cluster of smaller blue ones filled a corner. The mine itself was an open pit. It looked like an amphitheater being carved out of the ground. A dedicated fifty-five mile asphalt road connected the mine to port and barge operations on the Chukchi Sea.

The prop plane lurched and dropped among the mountains. Lauren was glad she'd skipped lunch. When it landed at the airstrip beside the mine, she darted ahead of the twelve workers commuting from Kotzebue to be the first off the company plane. Outside, the manager of public relations introduced himself as Prince Hall and escorted her to a plain office.

"This is all spur of the moment, isn't it?" Hall said. "The home office called this morning to tell me you were coming. They said you're doing a piece for the Sports Network. I didn't quite get the context."

"We've been covering the Iditarod for years," Lauren said. "But now we're thinking about adding the Kobuk 440, too."

"Why, that's fantastic."

"Since the race starts in Kotzebue, I'm working on a background piece about the local area. The Inupiaq, their culture, their lifestyle. Given you're one of the biggest private employers in the region —what are we, a hundred miles away?"

"Less. Only eighty."

"Only eighty. You're even closer than I thought. You're vital to the local economy. Your track record for environmental responsibility seems beyond reproach. At least from what I've read."

"And everything you've read is true. The Arctic is a national treasure. We're the world's largest zinc mine. We hold ourselves to the highest standards where emissions and waste management are concerned. I would love to give you a tour of our facilities and tell you all about it."

"That would be great. And perhaps I could meet an employee or two."

Lauren suffered through a tour of the mine, zinc processing plant, residences, and even the cafeteria. She pretended to care about the difference between drill and blast mining, and grinding and sulphide flotation methods. She even studied an ISO 14001 environmental certification report. It was torture.

"You mentioned meeting an employee or two," Hall said, when he was done with his dog and pony show. "I thought you might enjoy meeting one of our plant managers. She's a woman, like yourself."

"That sounds interesting, but I had someone else in mind. You have a musher on staff who placed third in the Kobuk 440 five years ago."

"Really? I didn't know that. I was rotated in from Anchorage eighteen months ago. What's his name?"

"Dave Ambrose. He writes a blog on dog sled and snowmobile racing. He's good. I'd like to get his perspective on a few things. And see if he's interested in doing some writing online for us. Nothing that would interfere with his career here, of course. Just a hobby."

"Let's see if he's working today. Workers in the mine work four days on, three days off. On account of the exposure to lead. If he's in, I'll ask the supervisor."

The laws of probability prevailed. Twenty minutes later, Ambrose walked into a conference room with a gray respirator hanging below his chin, and matching pads strapped to his knees. He appeared to be in his late twenties. Lauren repeated what she told Hall when she met him.

Ambrose's eyes lit up. "You're going to cover the 440?"

"We're considering it."

He thrust his fists over his head. "Awesome. That would be so awesome." He dropped his hands and slumped. "But I'm not going to be of any use to you."

"Why do you say that?"

"You want to follow a team up close and personal, right? My racing days are over. The mine's tough on the knees. Tendonitis. It never goes away. I know some of the other fellows, though. I know Jimmy Hines. He placed third in the Iditarod last year. I can introduce you."

"Dave, I didn't ask to speak with you because I want you to race. I asked to speak with you because I read your blog last night."

"You read my blog?"

"You're a good writer. You know the sport and you have a good sense of humor. What's your blog called? *Plains, Strains, and Snow Machines*?"

He nodded.

"I wanted to see if you're interested in working with me on this."

Ambrose blinked a few times. "Work with you?"

"Yeah. With the Sports Network. Be a local resource. Provide us with introductions to the people you know. And most importantly, be our reporter online. On the Network's website."

"Me?"

"Yes. You."

"Are you kidding me? That would be—That would be unbelievable. But the job. I couldn't give up my job."

"I would never ask you to. This would be more of a hobby. An extra gig that supplements your income. I'm sure you could arrange your schedule to take some vacation time around the actual race. Couldn't you?"

"I do it every year."

"So there's no problem. Apart from the race, you can write wherever, whenever you want and post your articles online anytime."

"Oh my God. I won't let you down, I promise. I have all sorts of ideas already. I could start with the origins of the Iditarod. It commemorates the 1925 serum run from Nenana to Nome. An outbreak of diphtheria threatened Nome. A hundred dogs ran relays for 674 miles to deliver the serum. The lead dog's name was Balto. He ran ninety-one miles in a blizzard. Complete whiteout conditions. There's a statue of him in Central Park. In New York City. You're from New York, right? Have you seen it? Have you seen it?"

"I've probably walked by it a hundred times but never paid attention to it. Before you get too excited, Dave, I need you to help me with something else first."

"Okay. Name it."

"I'm working on another story. It's about a boy from Kotzebue. His name is Bobby Kungenook. Does that name ring a bell?"

"No."

"He's seventeen years old and he lives in New York, too."

"And he's from Kotzebue?" Ambrose laughed. "Get out of town."

The phrase caught Lauren off guard, even though it was just an expression. She remembered the rifle pressed to the back of her head. She really did need to get out of town.

"I can't seem to find out much about him," she said. "You know how people guard each other's secrets in a small town."

"In a small town, sometimes secrets are all you have. Why are you interested in this kid?"

"He's a hockey player at a prep school. He's good. A can't miss prospect. You guys follow hockey up here?"

"Sure. Scotty Gomez is from Anchorage. He played for the Devils when they won the Cup."

"I'm doing a background piece on him. That's all. Seems he was born in Kotzebue but disappeared."

"Disappeared?"

Lauren shrugged. "Supposedly he was home schooled around here but I can't seem to find any trace of him. Maybe you can do better."

Ambrose considered her question. "And that's all this is? A routine background piece?"

"That's all."

"Okay. I can do that. I can make some calls for you."

It was a lie, of course. Lauren's assistant had stayed up half the night trolling the Internet on her behalf, reading the online archives of the *Arctic Sounder* and checking local links looking for an angle that Lauren could leverage. Then she found Ambrose's blog and read his bio. Ambrose was from Kotzebue. If he didn't know the Kungenooks, he knew someone who did. And his passion for dog sled racing and writing could be leverage. It was Lauren's best chance to cajole a local into revealing a secret.

The only place in Kotzebue with Internet access was the Arctic Blues Espresso coffee shop. Lauren had been there at 7:30 a.m. when it opened. After studying Ambrose herself, she'd called the folks at Red Dog and told them she was working on a story that might cast the company in a favorable light. She'd emphasized that the Sports Network was considering covering the Kobuk 440, but didn't promise it would happen.

When they were finished touring, Hall accompanied Lauren to the cafeteria for coffee at 3:00 p.m. Afterward, Ambrose was waiting for her in the conference room.

"Here's the bad news," Ambrose said. "No one's going to talk about a boy who went missing at age two. Not going to happen. But here's the good news. My cousin works at OTZ. She said you should be asking questions about the boy who appeared, not the boy who disappeared."

"What do you mean?"

"You should ask her that. You flying back to Kotzebue today?"

"Yes."

"Good. She'll meet you."

"Where?"

"At OTZ."

"What's OTZ?"

"Kotzebue Airport. It's one of the biggest employers in town."

Ambrose was a good man doing his best in a harsh place. He didn't deserve to be used, lied to, or given false hope. But that's exactly what had happened.

Too bad, Lauren thought. Life was a race. She wasn't delivering a serum or saving humanity and there would never be a statue of her in Central Park, but she had to be first with this story. She had to be first with every story.

Still, when she said good-bye to Ambrose, Lauren saw the spark in his eyes and the bounce in his step, and for that fleeting moment, all the joy seeped out of her.

CHAPTER 6

O N THURSDAY, NADIA PACKED TWO SHOPPING BAGS WITH clothes and books. She took the Q101 bus to Rikers Island. It was located on the East River between Queens and the Bronx near LaGuardia Airport. Visiting hours ran from 1:00 p.m. to 8:00 p.m., but people started lining up earlier. Nadia arrived at 12:05 p.m. She was twenty-seventh in line but some of the visitors in front of her were children accompanying a parent. By 12:45 p.m., the line stretched farther than she could see.

A huge young man with a shaved head cut to the front of the line. Two women stuck their fingers in his face and screamed at him in Spanish. The young man shouted back. Their threats grew louder until four security guards emerged from the jail. The guards tackled, cuffed, and dragged him inside, all without saying a word. The crowd cheered. Word spread that he was a recently released felon who'd returned for his personal possessions. Nadia was reminded that she was not in Manhattan anymore, and neither was Bobby.

At 1:35 p.m., Nadia entered the visitor's center. An efficient guard checked her driver's license and took down her information.

"You got to be announced," the guard said.

"Excuse me?" Nadia said.

"The prisoner has got to want to see you."

"Oh."

"Prisoners only get one set of visitors per day. If someone they don't want to see comes in, then they can't see their families later, is why. Sometimes reporters try to get in. Sometimes enemies. You see it all here. You the boy's mother?"

"Legal guardian. Can you tell him if he sees me then a young woman by the name of Aline Kabaeva will visit him Sunday?"

The guard frowned. "Who?"

Nadia wrote the name on a piece of paper and gave it to the guard. Aline Kabaeva was a former Olympic gymnastics champion, current lawmaker, and rumored paramour of Vladimir Putin. Nadia had duped a cop into believing she was a reporter interviewing the Russian sex symbol during her escape from Russia on a train with Bobby. She'd been so convincing Bobby had believed her, too, until she admitted she'd made up the story. Nadia hoped Bobby would get a laugh out of the message, and that the memory would remind him of the bond they'd formed to survive that trip.

The guard left and returned five minutes later. "He's in the infirmary."

"What happened?" Nadia said.

"I don't know. You got to go to the hospital at the North Infirmary Command. They'll tell you."

"Will I get to speak with him?"

"Depends on if he wants to see you and if he can speak."

"What does that mean?"

"Exactly what it sounds like. He's in the infirmary for a reason."

Nadia got directions and hurried to an adjacent building. She had to wait an hour and fifteen minutes in line. She spent most of that time fighting images of Bobby being beaten to a pulp. Once inside, she stored her cell phone in a coin locker per regulations. She identified herself to another guard and repeated her request regarding Aline Kabaeva.

An ambivalent guard escorted her to a small room with two chairs and a table. There were no windows in the room. The air smelled of mold. A gaunt man in a white coat came in and introduced himself as Dr. Champion.

"We had to remove him from the general population," Champion said. "For his own protection."

Nadia felt faint. "Why? What happened?"

"Does Aagayuk have problems with anxiety?"

"No."

"Is he prone to panic attacks?"

"No. Why? Did he have one?"

"Actually, he had several. When the lights went out. He had great difficulty making it through his first night. And he didn't make it through his second night. I've prescribed an anti-depressant—"

"You gave him an antidepressant? Without my approval?"

"Aagayuk is in the state's custody now."

"But common courtesy—"

"It's my responsibility to keep him functioning properly."

"It would have been common courtesy to call his guardian, don't you think?"

"I treat hundreds of prisoners, ma'am. My job is to keep them healthy. Keep them alive. Phone calls to loved ones are just not realistic."

The notion of Bobby taking an antidepressant wasn't as disturbing as a doctor at Rikers Island writing the prescription. "What was the catalyst for all this? Did something happen?"

"He had an altercation with some of the other inmates."

"What kind of altercation?"

"The unfortunate kind. He cost his neighbors a bit of sleep. They made him understand how unhappy they were about that.

He's going to have to go back in one week. Seven days. That's the prescribed time for the antidepressants to get into his system. That's the longest I can keep him. His other wounds will certainly be healed by then."

"What wounds?"

"If the medication works, it will cut off the extremes of his behavior. He won't get too happy. He won't get too sad. It'll neutralize the panic attacks and he'll be able to sleep at night."

"What wounds?"

"More importantly, the other inmates will be able to sleep. Maybe they'll leave him alone. Though I'm told they've seen his ears. Half-ears, I should say. With jagged ridges like some sort of genetic mutation. I've never seen that type of handicap before."

Bobby was born with abnormal ears because his mother had suffered from radiation syndrome. "I'd like to see Bobby, please," Nadia said.

"Who?"

"Bobby. Aagayuk. His Anglo name is Bobby. I'd like to see my boy. Now, please."

Champion left.

A guard escorted Bobby into the room. Bobby limped. Bruises shone around both eyes. A large bandage covered his forehead.

"Oh my God." Nadia stood up to hug him.

Bobby raised his hand for her to keep her distance.

Nadia stopped. The sight of his palm in her face wrenched her heart. But she didn't want him to read her emotions so she erased the disappointment from her eyes. This was no time for sentiment.

Bobby grimaced as he sat down. He wore a gray jumpsuit and orange flip-flops. The guard stood against the wall. Bobby and Nadia spoke in Ukrainian.

"How are you?" Nadia said.

"I told Johnny to tell you not to come. Why didn't you listen to him?"

"Why would you say something like that? You know I'm going to come no matter what. I asked you a question. How are you?"

"It doesn't matter anymore."

"What do you mean it doesn't matter? Why are you acting this way? Why won't you tell me what really happened that night? It can't possibly be like you said. A man doesn't walk up to you and try to stab you for no reason. Not even in New York. Especially not in Manhattan."

Bobby let a few seconds pass. "Do you remember what you said to me when I opened the locket?"

After evading mobsters and government agents halfway around the world, Bobby had opened the locket to reveal its treasure. "No more lies," Nadia said.

"That's right. No more lies. And I haven't lied to you since."

"You're saying you killed that man in self defense. He came at you with a knife first."

"Yes."

"And you never saw him before that night."

Bobby didn't answer.

"He had no reason to want to kill you."

He remained mute.

"You didn't expect to see him that night. This wasn't a planned confrontation. Was it?"

Bobby looked at her with the same dead eyes he'd shown her in the courtroom.

"Why were you wearing only one shoe when you turned yourself in? It was a basketball shoe. It couldn't have slipped off or been pulled off. You had to unlace it for it to come off. Where is your left shoe? Why did you take it off?"

Bobby turned his head away.

"Are you going to answer me? You know, I'm sitting here worried to death either someone's going to kill you here or they're going to convict you of murder, but if you keep acting so rudely to me I'm going to come across this table and smack you." She had no intention of actually hitting him. Since straight talk wasn't working, she was hoping to provoke a reaction.

Bobby sat still looking as though he was calculating something. Then he leaned across the table. "You want the truth?"

"Yes, please."

"Okay, here's the truth. I don't like you. I never really liked you from the minute I first met you. You think you're smarter than everyone else. And you don't know how to have fun. That's why no one wants to be around you. The only friend you have is Johnny and that's only because you pay him. You'll never get married. You're going to die alone."

His words stung. They brought tears to her eyes. She'd risked her life to bring him to America. She spent every penny she had to feed him, shelter him, and send him to prep school. And yet, she didn't believe a word he was saying. He knew her vulnerabilities. He knew where to hit. For some reason he was trying to push her away.

Nadia leveled her chin at him.

"There are two bags outside for you. There's a coat, sneakers, and four sets of underwear, socks, shirts, and pants in one bag. There's six pencils, two notebooks, all the Harry Potter books, and four hockey magazines in the other. Everything is permitted. I checked. One of the hockey magazines is old. There's a hole in one of the pages inside. That sound familiar?"

Bobby blinked. It was the magazine he'd brought from Ukraine. It had special sentimental value.

"Good," Nadia said. "Nice to see you're still human."

"No, I'm not still human. I'm a machine. I've left your world. You mean nothing to me. I don't ever want to see you again."

Bobby stood up. The guard opened the door. They disappeared down a corridor. A second guard came by and escorted Nadia out of the infirmary.

Nadia walked outside, waited for the bus, and boarded it. When it crossed the bridge off Rikers Island, she looked back at the jail.

Bobby was emphatic he hadn't lied to her. When he'd made that point, she'd looked into his eyes and seen truth. Nadia believed him. The kid had a sense of honor. He said he'd never lie to her, and he was determined to live up to that promise. When Nadia asked him if he'd ever seen Valentine before Tuesday night, Bobby didn't answer. When she asked if Valentine had a reason to want him dead, he remained quiet. Same as when she asked if he'd expected to see Valentine that night. Bobby refused to answer those three questions because he didn't want to lie. By Nadia's logic, her conclusion was unimaginable yet necessarily true.

Bobby and Valentine had known each other. Valentine had a motive for killing Bobby.

And they'd met Tuesday night knowing one of them might kill the other.

CHAPTER 7

For seven years Nadia walked home from work along Madison Avenue and dreamed of owning a townhouse on one of the side streets of the Upper East Side. They defined charm, privacy, and success. The fantasy fueled her fourteen-hour days at the Monroe private equity firm. After she was fired last year, however, she avoided Madison altogether. But when she started her own business and landed her first two clients, she returned. Now, on the verge of stepping inside one of them for the first time, owning them once again seemed like nothing more than a fantasy.

The townhouse belonged to Trent and Meredith Mace. Nadia cheered with them during Fordham Prep hockey games. They'd gone out to dinner together after a couple of games.

Meredith opened the door, invited her in, and gave her a huge hug. She guided Nadia to a sitting room beyond the foyer. A glossy Old Masters portrait of a mother and her two sons hung on the wall. The boys sat at their mother's feet.

"How is he?" Meredith said.

"I just got back from Rikers Island. He's in the infirmary."

"Did he get sick?"

"He had some issues with anxiety. And then he was beaten."

Meredith let out a cry, covered her mouth. "That's awful. I'm so sorry this happened to Bobby. And you. Trent and I know it's a misunderstanding. When we saw the address . . . Trent was the general contractor on loft conversions a block away from where it happened. We couldn't believe it. It's as though it happened in our own back yard. We're sure it'll get straightened out."

"I'm trying to straighten it out. But I need your help."

Meredith's eyes widened as though Nadia had asked for a limb. "Of course." She swallowed hard. "Anything we can do. Anything."

"The night of the murder, Bobby told me he was coming here."

"And I told you on the phone he didn't come here."

"But was he supposed to come here?"

"No. I asked Derek and he said they hadn't planned anything."

"Would you mind if I spoke with Derek?"

Meredith shifted in her seat. "Forgive me for saying this, Nadia. But if Derek already said they didn't plan anything, how else could he possibly help?"

"I'm hoping Derek might have some insight into Bobby's state of mind, if not his whereabouts that night."

"Why would Derek know anything about his whereabouts?"

"He's Bobby's friend. He might know something and be completely unaware of it."

"Nadia, Trent and I love Bobby to death. You know we do. And we love you, too. But we don't want Derek distracted from his schoolwork."

"It'll only take a couple of minutes. I promise."

Meredith grasped for words.

"We can talk right here," Nadia said. "You'd be in the room with us."

"Obviously I'd be in the room with you. I'm not sure you understand . . ."

"Of course I understand. Bobby's been arrested for murder. You want to protect your son. You want to distance him. You don't want him involved. You don't want him talking about it or even thinking about it if you can help it."

"Exactly. I'm so glad you see. It's not personal—"

"No, it is personal. Everything that matters in life is personal. Bobby's in jail, Meredith. He's already been beaten once. In a week they'll release him from the infirmary. I'm trying to find something, anything that might help us understand that evening."

"I wish we could help you."

"Before he gets beaten again."

"I really do."

"Bobby didn't kill anyone in cold blood," Nadia said. "You know that. You see how he plays hockey. He doesn't have a mean streak. He doesn't have any violent tendencies."

"As opposed to who, my son?"

"No, Merry. As opposed to the person who's really responsible for that poor young man's death. As opposed to the thugs who beat Bobby and might kill him next time."

"You have a lot of nerve showing up here and comparing my son to the criminals your boy is in jail with."

"What are you talking about?"

"I think it's time for you to leave."

"I did no such thing."

"Please leave, Nadia."

Nadia felt her composure slipping. All she wanted to do was talk to the kid with his mother present. Was that unreasonable? Funny how you never really knew a person until you suffered through adversity with her. Nadia took a quick breath to steady herself.

"I didn't compare Derek to anyone," she said. "This conversation has gotten a little—"

"Get out."

"Merry. Please. I'm just trying to find out if Derek knows anything that might help."

The floor creaked. Meredith turned toward the door.

"Help with what?" a man said.

Trent Mace filled the doorway. A spoon protruded from a pint of Ben & Jerry's Chocolate Therapy. He bounded into the sitting room and hugged Nadia with his free hand. She'd spied him watching her in the Fordham stands on more than one occasion. Nadia guessed she might have better luck with him.

"Help with what?" he said.

Nadia explained.

"Honey, go ask Derek to come in for a few minutes."

Meredith bristled. "May I speak with you in the kitchen for a minute?"

Trent excused himself and followed his wife out of the sitting room. Meredith's fury echoed down the corridor, but Trent's reply didn't. A minute later they returned with Derek. He sank into an upholstered chair.

"I don't know why he said he was coming over here," Derek said.

"You didn't make plans earlier in the day?" Nadia said.

"Nope."

"Is it possible he was going to pop over unannounced?"

"Huh?"

"Did Bobby ever come over unannounced, or did he always make plans ahead of time?"

"I don't know. I guess there was always a plan. I mean, Bobby's a planner, right?"

"Is he?" Nadia said. She'd never thought of him that way.

"Sure. He draws up plays for the coaches sometimes. And he knows what he's doing every day for the next week."

"Did he mention what he was doing the night he got arrested?"

"Nope."

"Nothing at all?"

"Nope."

"Did he seem different?"

"What do you mean?"

"Did he seem upset or depressed or concerned about anything?"

Derek shrugged. "I don't know. You can never tell about Bobby. That's his thing. He's poker face twenty-four-seven. If anyone should know what he's been thinking, it should be you, shouldn't it? I mean, you're his guardian, right?"

"Hey," Trent said. "Watch your mouth." He turned to Nadia. "I'm sorry about my son's manners." He turned to Derek. "What about the girlfriend?"

"Girlfriend?" Nadia glanced at Trent, Meredith, and Derek. "What girlfriend?"

Meredith looked surprised. She glanced alternately at her husband and son.

Trent commanded his son with a nod of the head. "Speak."

"There's a girl in Brighton Beach," Derek said.

"What?" Nadia said. "Since when?"

"I don't know. About a month ago."

"What's her name?"

"I think it's Iryna."

"You think?" Trent said.

Derek stared at his father from the roofs of his eyes. "Okay, her name's Iryna. She's Russian."

Nadia blushed. She could feel Meredith's eyes all over her, judging her for not being intimately familiar with every aspect of Bobby's life. And Nadia agreed. She thought she'd known about everything Bobby did, but clearly she'd been kidding herself.

"How did he meet her?" Nadia said.

"I don't know," Derek said.

Trent pointed a finger at Derek. "Son, you think you're helping Bobby by keeping a secret? You're not. It's time for you to man up. Speak."

Derek took a deep breath. "She's a model."

"What type of model?" Nadia said.

"Lingerie and swimsuits and stuff."

"How old is this girl?"

"I don't know. Maybe sixteen or seventeen."

"How did Bobby meet her?"

"She friended him on Facebook."

"Facebook? Bobby's on Facebook? That's impossible." Bobby had agreed to stay away from social media to minimize the risk of someone recognizing him and revealing his true identity. "Since when?"

"I don't know. A couple of months. He's got fans."

"He does?"

Derek nodded. "On account of the Gáborik race. The YouTube videos."

"And how did this girl find him?"

"A friend of hers showed her his home page. They had a lot in common."

"What friend?"

"Another girl. A friend of mine."

Meredith frowned. "What friend of yours?"

"Someone I met. She goes to St. Mary's in Flushing. We play them twice a year. She goes to the games."

"And you've been seeing this other girl?" Shock registered on Meredith's face.

"She friended me after one of the games this past season. We've gone on a couple of double dates. She's a model, too. It's nothing serious."

"Who is this girl? Who are her parents?" Meredith turned to her husband. "Did you know about this?"

Trent shrugged.

"The apple doesn't fall far from the tree," Meredith said.

"Did Bobby go to see Iryna the night he was arrested?" Nadia said.

"Couldn't tell you," Derek said.

"Son, if you're lying . . ."

Derek glared at his father. "I'm not lying."

"Do you know her full name and address?" Nadia said.

"Her last name is Arshun. I don't have an address. We never went to anyone's house."

"How about a phone number?"

"Nope. I never called her. She's Bobby's girl."

"But you have your girlfriend's number."

"I wouldn't call her my girlfriend."

"Call her whatever you want," Trent said. "But go get your cell phone, and call her now."

Derek stood up.

"No, no," Nadia said. "I just need a look at her Facebook page. If I can get a last name and a look at her picture, that'll be plenty."

"You don't want her phone number?" Meredith said.

"No. I'll find her," Nadia said. She caught Derek's eyes. "I'd rather her friends not warn her I was coming."

CHAPTER 8

THERE WERE THREE ARSHUNS LISTED IN THE PHONE BOOK AS living in Brighton Beach. All were listed under men's names. Nadia called them sequentially. A different woman with an Eastern European accent answered each time. Nadia identified herself as Cynthia Moss, Vice President of the Lauder Modeling Agency in Manhattan. She asked to speak with the promising young model named Iryna. Each time she was told no such person lived there. Nadia asked if they knew a teenage model by that name that lived in Brighton Beach. The first two women said no and hung up. The third one, however, kept talking.

"Is this about modeling?" the woman said.

"No," Nadia said. "Super modeling."

The woman gasped. "Iryna lives with my daughter's friend. Please hold. I give you phone number."

Nadia called and left a voice mail. Iryna called back three minutes later. She spoke good English but with the same accent. They agreed to meet for drinks at 8:00 p.m. After Nadia hung up, an investment banker called with a job proposition. His client needed a forensic securities analyst fluent in English and Russian. He wouldn't reveal his client's name. They set up a lunch for tomorrow. The prospect of a paycheck energized Nadia. She called

Johnny, told him what she was up to, and took the subway to Brooklyn.

There was a saying that Brighton Beach was conveniently located near the United States. Immigrants arrived en masse from the Soviet Union in the late 1970s. In the 1980s Brighton Beach became headquarters for the Russian mafia. A man named Marat Balagula was its leader. He had a kind heart with a soft spot for educated immigrants who couldn't find jobs in America. He also made a fortune through shell companies that distributed gasoline but kept taxes for themselves. When word got out he was in business with the Italian mob, Russian hit man Vladimir Reznikov put his 9mm Beretta against Balagula's head at a nightclub and demanded $600,000 for not pulling the trigger. Reznikov returned to the club the next day for payment. A Gambino crime family associate shot him dead.

Much had changed in Brighton Beach since then. The ghetto was torn down and replaced with luxury condominiums. Afghans, East Asians, Mexicans, and Pakistanis joined the mix. If there was still a Russian mafia presence, it never made the papers.

Nadia marched from the subway stop toward the Atlantic Ocean. The wind whipped her hair. The air smelled of salt. Nadia wasn't worried about her safety but she still felt as though she was entering enemy territory. She was the daughter of Ukrainian immigrants walking into a Russian enclave. Ukraine had suffered for centuries under Russian oppression. The Soviet Union was a Russian creation. Stalin did his best to starve Ukraine. Brezhnev tried to eradicate all traces of its culture.

Nadia learned to speak Ukrainian before English even though she was born in Hartford. When she was recommended for Russian language classes in junior high school by the Spanish teacher, her parents were initially reluctant for fear it would pollute her Ukrainian. They hailed from Western Ukraine, where nationalist pride ran deep. The further East one travelled, the more Russified the Ukrainian population. In Kyiv, Russian was still more prevalent than Ukrainian even though the country had been independent since 1991.

Bobby was from central Ukraine. His Facebook page said he was fluent in Russian. That infuriated Nadia as it hinted at his past. It was an exercise in mindless self-indulgence. His Facebook page didn't mention he spoke Ukrainian. That irked her. If he was boasting he spoke Russian, why didn't he mention he was fluent in his native Ukrainian? It was as though the latter didn't matter.

His girlfriend's Russian ethnicity also troubled Nadia. That ethnic bias, in turn, disturbed her. The end result was a continuous loop of distrust, apology, and acceptance. In Iryna's case, however, Nadia seemed stuck on the distrustful part. She feared the girl was an opportunist who figured out Bobby might become a professional hockey player. She also worried Iryna might be older than seventeen.

The name of the restaurant was Gogol-Mogol. Nadia expected an elegant dining room that morphed into a rowdy scene at midnight. Instead she walked into a small café serving coffees and pastries. Pink walls featured elegantly stenciled recipes. Macaroons, Baba Au Rhum cakes and chocolate bombs filled the display cases. Crumbs littered the shelves behind the counter. They were empty except for four loaves of bread.

An old man sat reading a paper and drinking coffee at one table. A middle-aged couple shared an éclair at another. Music accompanied dessert. It arrived in muted bursts from speakers in the ceiling. Rap music. With Russian lyrics. Something about diamonds and disrespect. Sung by dueling women.

A lithe girl stood behind the register in a pink shirt and white pants. Nadia recognized Iryna from her picture. She was about five foot seven with an oval face, enormous blue eyes, and perfect alabaster skin. She wasn't the Russian girl next door. She was what the Russian girl next door aspired to look like.

"Iryna?" Nadia said.

She spoke so softly Nadia barely heard her. "Yes."

Nadia introduced herself and extended her hand. Iryna smiled, shook it, blushed, and dropped her head. The sequence was so sweet and genuine it took Nadia's breath away. In the time it took to say hello, Nadia found herself questioning her preconceptions about the girl, her ethnicity, and her motives.

"Would you like to talk in the kitchen?" Iryna said. "More privacy."

Nadia followed Iryna through a door into the kitchen. Four stainless steel ovens lined one wall. A matching stove, refrigerator, and sink filled another. A heavyset woman wearing an apron was rinsing utensils. The center island contained a mixer and various pans covered with flour and remnants of dough. The appliances looked new, except for the microwave oven elevated on an old wooden table near a pantry. It was a child's toy, made of red plastic.

A woman with pronounced cheekbones entered from a back room. Her skin suggested she was about thirty but the wear around the eyes said the years hadn't been easy. She wore a chef's uniform and carried herself with an air of authority. She stopped beside the toy oven.

"Galina, do me a favor and take the register for a few minutes," she said. She spoke perfect English.

The heavyset woman shut the faucet, grabbed a hand towel, and left.

"I'm Tamara," the young woman said. "Iryna's roommate. And cousin. You must be Ms. Moss."

"No," Nadia said. "I'm not. My name isn't Cynthia Moss. And I'm not in the modeling business."

Tamara reached inside the toy oven and pulled out a gun. She aimed it at Nadia.

"We know you're not. There is no Lauder Modeling Agency. Who are you and what do you want?"

Nadia stepped back. She'd miscalculated. She was expecting a verbal confrontation once she admitted she'd lied. Not a gun.

"My real name is—"

"Usually it's men who try to take advantage of Iryna. They say they run their own modeling agency or they're film producers but they're really after one thing. You're the first woman ever. Why did you lie? What is it you want? I got robbed last month. I could shoot you right here—"

"Don't." Nadia raised her hands in the air. "Please. Let me explain."

"What do you want from Iryna?"

"I want to ask her some questions."

"About what?"

"About a boy she's been seeing."

"What boy?"

"His name is Bobby Kungenook. Iryna knows him."

"Of course she knows him. I know him, too."

"You do?"

"Sure. He's been here four or five times."

"He has?"

"He's a fiend for my fruit tart. How do you know Bobby?"

"He's my . . . I'm his . . . I'm his guardian."

Tamara's eyes bugged out. "Oh my God. You're Nadia Tesla?"

Nadia nodded.

Tamara put the gun back in the oven. She rushed to Nadia and hugged her. When they parted, they laughed. Nadia's laughter was more a function of relief than any sense of humor in the situation. Iryna stood to the side looking more grateful than anyone.

Tamara insisted they start over. She and Iryna brought in three cups of coffee and three raspberry-chocolate macaroons. Nadia hadn't eaten dinner yet but she didn't care. There were only two chairs in the kitchen so they stood at the center island.

"Why did you pretend you were someone else?" Tamara said.

"I was afraid Iryna wouldn't talk to me," Nadia said.

"Why did you think that?" Iryna said.

"It was a mistake," Nadia said. "I have a tendency to expect the worst from people. It's my profession. I'm a forensic financial analyst. I tear companies apart and look for something wrong. And I always find something. It's made me cynical."

"It's not that," Tamara said. "It's not a professional thing."

"It's not?" Nadia said.

"No. It's a Uke thing. You're Uke, right?"

"Yes. Bobby told you?"

Tamara nodded.

"Wait. Only a Uke uses the phrase 'Uke.' You're Ukrainian, too? What's your last name?"

"Shevchuk."

"Born here?" Nadia said.

"Passaic, New Jersey."

Nadia glanced at Iryna.

"She's half and half," Tamara said. "Her father was Russian but her mother was Uke. She came over from Ukraine . . . How long has it been, sweetie?"

"About six years," Iryna said.

"Has it been that long?" Tamara shook her head.

Nadia sipped her coffee. "So did you go to Uke school in Passaic on the weekends?"

"It was Monday and Friday nights for us. Through eleventh grade. I never made it to *matura*." *Matura* was the name of the high school "maturity exam" administered at community Ukrainian schools across America. "What about you?"

"All the way through high school," Nadia said.

Tamara rolled her eyes sympathetically. "Christ. We missed out on all those school dances. The things normal kids did. That used to bother me when I was growing up. But now when I look back at it . . ."

"It was worth it," Nadia said. "Two languages, two cultures, richer life."

"You're right," Tamara said. She raised her cup of coffee. "To a free Ukraine," she said in Ukrainian. "And new friends."

They clinked their cups.

Nadia glanced at Iryna. "How did you meet Bobby?"

"Through a friend of mine," Iryna said. "Another model. She's dating Derek, Bobby's friend. She goes to prep school. Hockey is big in prep school—"

"Where do you go to school?" Nadia said.

"I graduated last year," Iryna said. "Abraham Lincoln High School."

"Oh," Nadia said. "So you're how old?"

"Eighteen. Just this January."

"That makes you what . . . five months older than Bobby."

Iryna blushed.

Tamara shrugged. "Not so bad, huh?"

"It rounds to zero," Nadia said, especially given she was half Ukrainian.

"I saw Bobby play hockey before I met him," Iryna said. "I went to the game with my friend. Fordham Prep against Holy Cross. In Flushing. He was so beautiful on the ice. The way he moved. With the black hair under his helmet down to his shoulders. He looked like . . . he looked like the Dark Knight."

"That's very sweet," Nadia said. "When did you see Bobby last?"

"I tried to see him yesterday but he wouldn't come out."

"You went to Rikers?" Nadia said.

Iryna nodded. "He was in the infirmary. I had to wait in two lines. It took me forever but when I gave my name to the guard at the hospital he came back and told me Bobby said to go away. He said to forget about him, that he never wanted to see me again."

Tears welled in her eyes. Tamara patted her shoulder.

"He said similar things to me," Nadia said. "Don't believe it. He's convinced he's going to be convicted for something he obviously didn't do and he's pushing us away so we don't suffer. Some sort of honor thing."

"I'm going to go back this week," Iryna said. "I'm going to keep going back until he sees me."

The girl's determination impressed Nadia. This was clearly more than a passing acquaintance. But they were teenagers, Nadia thought. She should have expected this.

"How often have you been seeing each other?" Nadia said.

Iryna shrugged. "Once a week. We mostly text. Lately we'd started to talk on the phone more."

"Was Bobby with you the night he was arrested?"

"We were supposed to meet in the Meatpacking District," Iryna said. "A friend was going to sneak us into Soho House Screening Room. Ethan Hawke was screening *Dead Poets Society*. I waited in front of Soho House but Bobby never showed. And then he called me on my cell phone to tell me he'd been arrested and he wouldn't make it."

"Did he sound different leading up to that night?"

"I don't think so." Iryna considered the question further. "There was this one thing, though."

"What thing?" Nadia said.

"It was weird. We ordered some takeout for dinner. We were eating here at the outside table in front of the café. Just him and me. We'd gone to see a movie with Derek and my friend but they'd gone their own way after the show. Bobby insisted on taking the subway home with me and walking me to the door. He always does that, even though I tell him it's safe. All of a sudden he got a phone call on his cell. He listened for a while, like almost a minute. And all the time he's turning white. Like he's going to pass out. And then he hung up and acted like nothing happened."

"He never said a single word?" Nadia said.

"Nope. Not a single—No. That's not true. When he first answered the phone he said 'Yes,' like you do if someone says your name. 'Hello, is this Bobby?' 'Yes.' That kind of thing."

"And that was the only word he said?"

"That was it."

"Could you hear the other voice on the line?"

"Yeah, I could hear a voice."

"Man or a woman?"

"I couldn't tell you. With the music and the other customers…"

"Did you ask him who it was?"

"Sure. He said it was one of those automated messages trying to give you a free cell phone for changing your service plan. But I could tell he was lying."

"When was this?"

"Last Friday," Iryna said.

Four days prior to Valentine's death, Nadia thought. She wondered if that phone call set a chain of events in motion that led to Bobby killing Jonathan Phillip Valentine.

"He's such a sweet boy," Tamara said. "We know he didn't kill that man. If there's anything I can do to help, please let me know."

"That's kind of you," Nadia said.

Nadia realized she was famished. She bit into the macaroon and looked around the kitchen. The appliances were top-of-the-line and brand new, too.

"Your café is cute and this is a beautiful kitchen," Nadia said.

"Thank you," Tamara said. "I didn't know my father most of my life and it's been a happy discovery. He spoils me. With stainless steel ovens and gold jewelry."

"And this macaroon is to die for, Tamara," Nadia said.

"Thank you, Nadia," she said. "But please. Call me Tara. All my friends do."

CHAPTER 9

NADIA GOT HOME AT 10:30 P.M. SHE STRIPPED HER CLOTHES and jumped in the shower. When she got out, she put on her favorite robe—the one with the pink elephants—and poured herself a glass of chardonnay.

Bobby's cell phone wouldn't help Nadia identify who called him. It was locked away with his other personal possessions in prison. Nadia logged onto her wireless phone carrier's website. Bobby's cell phone usage appeared under her account as part of her family plan. She knew her ID and password by heart because she paid her bill online. She also monitored Bobby's usage. The exercise provided unexpected satisfaction. It wasn't the product of spying. It was a function of responsibility. It was a family plan. She was the head of the family. The title secretly thrilled her, though she never would have admitted it to Bobby. He held things inside. Acted as though discussing emotions was a weakness. Outwardly Nadia disagreed, but deep down she knew she was just like him.

The phone calls and text messages Bobby had received during April appeared under current usage. Nadia studied the phone numbers. She recognized most of them: Derek, Iryna, her office, her cell, their apartment, the Fordham hockey coach, and three other hockey teammates. Iryna's number appeared more often as time passed. The first of the month she texted him twice. The day Bobby was arrested she texted him twelve times. That bothered her less than it would have before she'd met the girl, but Nadia's blood pressure still spiked.

Five phone calls were placed to Bobby on the day Iryna said he'd answered the phone and turned white. One was from Nadia, the other from the hockey coach. Nadia didn't recognize the other three numbers. The first had a 718 area code. Nadia searched the Internet.

Brooklyn.

She dialed the number.

A woman with a Slavic accent answered. "Hello, Café Glechik, how can I help you?"

Nadia entered "Glechik" into the computer and searched. "Are you a restaurant?" she said.

"Yes." Annoyed now. "How can I help you?"

"Do you do a big takeout business?"

"Yes. What would you like?"

"Thank you." Nadia hung up.

The search brought up a supposed Ukrainian restaurant in Brighton Beach. The sour cherry dumplings looked tempting, but half the dishes were Russian. The owners were from Odesa near the Black Sea. That explained the Russian influence. That must have been the takeout Iryna and Bobby ate for dinner.

The next number had a 551 area code. Northern New Jersey. Nadia dialed the number.

It rang five times. A man with a gruff voice picked up.

"You called Bobby Kungenook's cell phone on April eleventh," Nadia said. "Who are you?"

"Who am I?" He paused. "Who the hell are you?"

"I'm Bobby's legal guardian. He's a minor. Do you want to tell me who you are or do you want me to—"

The voice mellowed. "Ms. Tesla?"

"That's right."

"This is Tom Dowd. The NHL hockey scout. We met after the game in Coney Island this year."

Nadia remembered. "Why are you calling Bobby without my knowledge?"

Dowd mumbled an apology. Nadia warned him not to call Bobby without asking her permission first.

"How's that thing going with his arrest?" Dowd said.

"It's a misunderstanding," Nadia said. "We're looking forward to our day in court."

The third number had an area code of 713. Houston, Texas. That made no sense. Nadia dialed the number and got the automated answering service for the parks and recreation department. That made even less sense.

Nadia checked the log again. The number 44 was printed to the far left of the entry. The country code for England. She searched for international call information on the web. A call from a landline contained ten digits and two to five more for an area code. A call from a mobile phone contained only ten digits. There was no area code. That meant it was a call from a cell phone.

Nadia dialed the number.

"The number you have dialed is no longer in service."

She cursed under her breath. Prepaid cell phone, she guessed. This was the call that Iryna had described. The one that made Bobby blanch. Valentine was from England. The call came from London. It was too much a coincidence to be anything else.

Afterward she checked his outgoing calls. She found nothing suspicious, leaving her with one logical conclusion based on her previous discovery.

The answers to her questions were in London.

CHAPTER 10

L AUREN SAT BESIDE THE PILOT IN THE HELICOPTER'S COCKPIT. The engine droned. Blades whirred. Headphones muffled the noise. A microphone mouthpiece extended from the side of her headgear to her lips. She'd met with Ambrose's cousin at the Kotzebue Airport. That woman, in turn, had given Lauren a hot lead on Bobby Kungenook. Now she was en route to Anchorage in pursuit of that lead.

The pilot's name was Dan Garner. He had the complexion of a leather bomber jacket.

"My father was a bush pilot, and my granddaddy was a bush pilot before him, " Garner said. "Yes, ma'am. Before he became a pilot, my granddaddy worked for Wyatt Earp right around the turn of the century. During the Nome Gold Rush."

Lauren flashed him a look of disbelief. "*The* Wyatt Earp?"

"The one and only. That was around 1895, about fifteen years after he and Doc Holliday shot those cowboys in the parking lot outside the O.K. Corral. Tombstone was a silver-mining boom town, you see. And Wyatt Earp had business interests in mining and gambling."

"How did he end up in Alaska?"

"The Klondike Gold Rush in the Yukon triggered a stampede in 1880. He came with the former mayor of Tombstone."

"How'd they do?"

"By the time they got there the beach gold was gone. You needed sophisticated equipment to mine what was left."

"So they struck out."

"Hardly. They opened a saloon, catered to the miners with food and prostitutes and the other basic necessities of life, and went back to California four years later with a hundred grand."

Lauren had never heard of anyone referring to prostitutes as one of life's basic necessities. She cast an uncertain glance in Garner's direction. "How about that."

"The smart ones don't gamble. The smart ones supply the gamblers with their basic needs."

"Is that what a bush pilot does?"

"I don't follow."

"Bring supplies to remote areas of Alaska? Bring whatever the people need?"

"That's right. Living in Alaska is a gamble. That means everyone's a gambler in Alaska. It takes an adventuresome heart to live here. Plenty of gamblers in Nome back then. Jack London, the writer. And Swiftwater Bill Gates, the fortune hunter."

"Bill Gates? No relation, I'm sure."

"No, but William H. Gates I, grandfather of Mr. Microsoft, was at the gold fields in Nome at the same time as Swiftwater Bill."

Lauren couldn't tell if he was serious or not. "I'm going to have to look that one up."

Garner nodded as though pleased she couldn't read him. "The Nome Gold Rush was pretty much a bust, too. Then the Eskimos got bent out of shape because the white folks hunted their moose and their caribou, and the smaller game, too. They said the white man made it harder for them to survive. Can you believe that? Truth is it was time for them to learn they're part of America, and America is the white man's country."

Lauren paused to make sure she'd heard him correctly, then fantasized about kicking the door open and sending him flying into the rotors. "How much longer to Anchorage?"

"About half an hour. What brought you to Nome, if you don't mind my asking?"

"I'm a sports reporter. I'm working on a story about a high school boy in New York. He's a promising hockey player, a once-in-a-lifetime prospect. And he's from Kotzebue."

"You're kidding me. What's his name?"

"Bobby Kungenook." Lauren eyed Garner. "Ever hear of him?"

He pursed his lips, then shook his head. "No. Sorry. If he was that good you'd think we'd have heard about him in Nome."

"Exactly. No one knows anything about this boy. He was given up for adoption at an early age but there's no record of it. It looks to me as though he was born in Kotzebue, went to live with someone who speaks fluent Ukrainian, and showed up in New York City at age seventeen."

"Ukrainian?"

"And Russian."

"Plenty of Russian history in Alaska, that's for sure. If he's an Inupiaq, his parents might have tried to find a home for him with another Inupiaq family. If they failed, no white American family would take one of theirs, so it makes sense it would be some sort of Russian."

Lauren shuddered. "Hopefully I'll get some clarity in Anchorage."

"You meeting someone there who knows the boy's story?"

"I got a lead in Kotzebue. I'm not sure this man knows the whole story, but I think he's met him. I think he knows something about him."

"Good for you. Is this going to be a television story or a newspaper story?"

"Both."

"Hot dog. I can't wait to read it. And see it. By God you've got me curious. I need to know how this ends."

They sat quietly the rest of the flight. Garner landed the helicopter at the Campbell Heliport near the Anchorage airport. A blue sedan idled by the runway.

"Is that your man?" Garner said.

Lauren handed him the headphones. "No. Those are agents of the ATF, the Bureau of Alcohol, Tobacco, Firearms, and Explosives. Anchorage field office."

The creases in Garner's face deepened.

"You're my man, Dan. You know that."

Garner's lower lip twitched.

"Last May you flew a boy and a woman into OTZ. They were met at the airport by police Captain Robert Seelick. They stayed in town for a couple of days, and then you flew them out."

"I don't know what you're talking about."

"Then let me explain. There are one hundred twenty-nine dry communities in Alaska, where it's illegal to sell or consume alcohol. That creates opportunity for bootleggers. A bottle of liquor that costs ten dollars in Anchorage may cost a hundred fifty in a dry town like Point Hope. You, Dan, are a bootlegger. How did you put it? Oh, yeah. You supply the people with their basic needs. And since alcoholism is a huge problem among the Native Americans, obviously it's a basic need. Am I right?"

Garner blanched.

"In fact, alcoholism is such a huge problem that in a wet village, homicide is six times more likely than in a dry one; assault is four times more likely; and sexual assault is three times more likely. The end result is that a lot of people don't like you, Dan. A lot of people blame you for their family's problems, hence one person's willingness to rat you out to me. Now, you have two choices. Either you tell me everything you know about the boy and I tell those agents I have the wrong man, or they're going to turn your life upside down. Which is it going to be, Dan? Do you want to go home, or do you want to go to jail?"

Garner regarded her with contempt. "I want to go home."

"Good. I want you to look at this picture very carefully. And I already know the answer so don't waste my time lying. This is just a warm-up for the important questions." Lauren pulled a photo of Bobby Kungenook from her briefcase. "Is this the boy you flew into Kotzebue last year?"

CHAPTER 11

N ADIA ARRIVED AT GLOBAL REAL ESTATE PARTNERS IN Midtown to meet with Valentine's boss at 10:00 a.m. on Friday. She'd implied she was an aunt looking for closure in Jonathan's death. She'd promised to be brief and thanked the man profusely for agreeing to meet with her even before he'd said yes. By the time she was done pleading, he couldn't say no.

"Jonathan wasn't your usual Brit," Austin Russell said. "In fact, if it weren't for the accent, you'd have guessed he was a good old boy himself. They would have loved him down in Texas."

The morning sun poured through the open blinds in Russell's modest office. When Nadia squinted, he apologized, hoisted himself to his feet, and closed them.

"What do you mean he wasn't your usual Brit?" Nadia said.

Russell wheezed from the exertion. When he returned to his seat, his torso spilled onto his armrests. "Not the reserved, stiff upper lip type. Life of the party, that one. Not afraid to show his emotions or let people know what he thought, either. Not necessarily the best personality to have if you want to climb the ladder at Global Real Estate Partners but he will surely be missed."

"He was the life of the party?"

"That's an understatement. He had that larger than life attitude. Bigger, better, more. That was his motto. We have a holiday party for the New York office every January. Used to be in December but everyone's schedule is so loaded . . . and the rates go down after New Year's. Well that wasn't enough for Jonathan Valentine. He said there had to be a true Christmas party. So he hosted his own for the other associates. Paid for the entire kit and caboodle on his own dime."

Nadia decided to play along with the prevailing sentiment. "He was a kind soul, that Jonathan," Nadia said.

"Even hired a band. Some hot European club act touring America." Russell shook his head with admiration. "You know, he wasn't the smartest analyst here. And I don't mean that as an insult. He was plenty smart. But we recruit from Columbia and Wharton here. Still, he would have been a heck of a promoter. He would have brought us a lot of business through sheer personality."

"What was he working on recently? If you don't mind my asking."

"He was part of the team working on a project in New Jersey. New outlet mall outside of Atlantic City."

"Nothing international? In London perhaps?"

"No. We're strictly Eastern Seaboard. We have offices in twelve foreign countries. London deals with London."

"So Jonathan didn't travel much."

"Atlantic City and back. If you call that travel."

"Did he have any vacation recently?"

Russell frowned as though it was a strange question for her to ask.

"I'm just trying to understand his last days," Nadia said. "I don't know why. It may be my way of dealing with the grief. Would you indulge me? Please?"

Russell stared at Nadia for a moment, then shrugged. "Just the day of his . . . just his last day."

"He took that day off?"

"Personal day. And of course, there was his father's funeral in England. He was gone for almost a week. So tragic, both of them dying within a two-week time frame."

"Yes, it was," Nadia said.

Valentine was in London when the call was made. Valentine had made the call to Bobby himself, Nadia thought. And he'd made it on a prepaid phone so it couldn't be traced to him.

"I'm sorry," Russell said. "I didn't catch whether you were his aunt on his mother's or father's side."

In fact, Nadia had never said she was Jonathan Valentine's aunt. It was actually Bobby who called her "Auntie," a title she manufactured during their escape from Russia. Whenever she perpetrated a ruse, Nadia liked to stick as close to a truth as possible.

"Yes," Nadia said. "Thank you for your condolences, and thanks so much for taking the time to meet me. I know how busy you are."

Russell appeared confused by her answer but when he saw her hand extended the gentleman within him burst into action. He pushed off against the desk and rose to his feet. He smiled sympathetically and shook her hand. As Nadia turned to leave, his eyes narrowed again.

"I don't think you mentioned your name," Russell said.

"Thank you, Mr. Russell," Nadia said. "I'll be sure to extend your condolences to the rest of the family when I see them in London."

When she got home, Nadia called the Stern School of Business. She asked to speak with the director of the placement office. She knew that Valentine had earned his MBA at NYU. Global Real Estate Partners's website said so. Tens of thousands of students had earned their MBAs from NYU in the last few years. There was no chance the placement office would know Valentine was dead.

Nadia identified herself as a forensic security analyst, discussed her background, and said she was looking for an understudy. She told the director that Valentine had applied for a job and she wanted to verify his graduation. The director did so. To confirm they were speaking about the same Jonathan Valentine, she asked to verify his current and previous addresses. Nadia offered Valentine's most recent address in the Meatpacking District. Johnny had procured it from the police report. The director verified it. Then she asked the director for Valentine's previous addresses. He gave her the address for the University of Nottingham, and for a secondary school called Felshire. Nadia thanked him, hung up, and jumped on the computer to buy a plane ticket.

Maybe they would have loved Valentine in Texas, but they knew him in London.

CHAPTER 12

NADIA SAT AT A CIRCULAR TABLE IN THE LOUNGE OF THE Four Seasons Hotel on East Fifty-Seventh Street. Her potential client had arranged for an investment banker to meet her. Nadia presumed it was some form of an interview to measure her qualifications.

At noon, the Four Seasons became one of the hot spots where financiers gathered to discuss deals. This was ironic because the hotel itself was a monument to the peak of the Japanese real estate market and poor financial planning. The owners finished construction in 1993 at a cost of $477 million, or $1.3 million per room. They promptly went bankrupt and sold the hotel at a 60% discount. More than two decades later, the average cost for new luxury hotels was still less than $600,000 per room.

As Nadia watched the foyer, discount was not a word that came to mind. On the contrary. When a banker chose the Four Seasons he was sending a specific message. His client wanted to hire the best and was willing to pay top dollar. Oh, she'd have to work for it, there was no question about that. The days of mediocrity being rewarded were over. The market collapse of 2008 saw to that. But Nadia wouldn't have had it any other way. She enjoyed earning her money and she desperately needed the gig.

Lunch was scheduled for 12:30 p.m. The banker showed up at 12:29 p.m. That was another promising sign. Deal oriented professionals usually raced from meeting to meeting and inevitably ran late. Punctuality implied the client demanded it. Such adherence to the client's demands meant a lucrative revenue stream was at risk.

When the man in pinstripes carrying a black valise saw Nadia, he sighed with exasperation. He headed straight toward her as though he'd studied her website. He was tall and slim with a weak jaw and a slippery complexion. He introduced himself as T. Bradley Ehren. He dumped his briefcase on the table. He didn't offer his hand or a business card. He didn't sit down, forcing Nadia to look up at him.

"This is a complete waste of time," he said. He flipped the briefcase on its end and worked the combination locks.

"Nice to meet you, too," Nadia said.

He grunted. Popped the valise open. Pulled out a stack of papers and closed it.

"Like I told you over the phone," he said, "I'm conducting due diligence on behalf of my client. My client is contemplating certain transactions and he's looking to hire someone."

"What kind of transactions?"

"Obviously that's privileged information. He's interested in hiring the best financial analyst in the business but he needs a very particular set of skills. You come highly recommended. To him. Not to me."

"Then it's a good thing he's making the decisions."

"He's looking for someone with a thorough understanding of financial accounting. An experienced analyst who can scrub the books."

"Yes."

"And someone who can speak Russian fluently. Passing knowledge of Ukrainian would be helpful, too."

"Yes," Nadia said, though some technical vocabulary would be a challenge.

"That reduces the candidate pool somewhat, though this is a global search. There are several excellent candidates in Europe."

"I'm confident I can compete."

Ehren laughed. "Industrials," he said.

"I beg your pardon?"

"Industrials. The last requirement is that the analyst must have an intimate knowledge of global industrial companies. Your background is in energy, isn't it?"

"Yes."

"Then you see why this is a waste of time. I asked around. You have a good reputation and if you say you're fluent in these languages I have no doubt you are or you'd be found out quickly. But the industrial expertise . . . "

"Is of secondary importance," Nadia said. "Financial statements are financial statements."

"Really? Let's see about that." He organized his documents into three stacks and dumped them in front of Nadia. "These are audited financial statements for three industrial companies. You can see the black magic markings at the top. The names of the companies have been redacted. All you have are the balance sheet, income statement, and statement of changes in financial position for the last five years. One is in English. Two are in Russian."

Nadia frowned. "Is this a homework assignment?"

"No, Nadia. This is a test."

"A what?"

"A test. A real time, live test."

"I'm a professional. I haven't taken a test since interviewing for my first job."

"Great. I'll tell my client his exercise was beneath you." Ehren reached for the papers.

"Wait," Nadia said. "What exactly do you want? A statistical analysis? Fundamental ratios? My assessment of—"

Ehren raised his palm and grimaced. "Please. Don't insult us. I can get a girl fresh out of B-school to give me a ratio analysis and blow me at the same time."

"Then what?"

"Name the companies."

"Excuse me?"

"You have to name the three companies. You have their financials. If you can understand financials and read Russian, and you know the industrial world, you should be able to name the companies."

Nadia knew she had no chance. None whatsoever. But her father had taught her survival skills in the Litchfield Hills when she was a child. Among the lessons: never underestimate your resourcefulness under pressure.

"You see," Ehren said. "It wasn't personal when I said this was a waste of time. Shall we call it a day?" He started to collect the papers.

Nadia slammed her hand on top of them. "Not so fast."

Ehren frowned.

"How much time do I have?"

Ehren checked his watch. "It's twelve thirty-four. You have one hour. We'll make it one thirty-five. Don't say I'm not generous."

"What are the rules?"

"Rules?"

"Yes. Are there any rules?"

"The rules are to name the companies in one hour. You can use any and all resources at your disposal with one exception. You can't discuss the financials with any other person."

"Understood."

"You sure you want to embarrass yourself?"

"Yes. It's a hobby of mine. It keeps me grounded."

Ehren shook his head. "Fine. Then I'm going to go meet my client as planned and leave you to it. If you come to your senses and realize the futility of the matter, feel free to order up some lunch."

Ehren started to leave.

"How many other candidates have you seen?" Nadia said.

"Nine."

"Anybody name all the companies yet?"

"No. But my sister—she worked at Goldman for five years—got two of them."

Ehren turned and walked toward the front desk. A fresh-faced woman bustled to him out of nowhere. She looked like a recent college graduate. Probably an associate. She appeared to be vomiting information to him.

Nadia pulled her computer tablet and financial calculator out of her bag. Fired up the computer, stuck the modem into the port, and turned to the financials. The two Russian companies had sales of $22.3 and $3.2 billion respectively. The American company had sales of $575 million. Nadia ran some ratios. The smaller companies were profitable but the bigger one had tiny margins.

And it dawned on Nadia. Perhaps there weren't three owners. Perhaps the smaller companies were owned by the larger company. Or, perhaps the smaller American company was a target of the man who owned the two Russian companies. The latter argument made sense. That would explain why Ehren's sister identified the two Russian companies but not the American one. He didn't own it yet.

She needed to focus on the owner, Nadia thought. Not the financial statements. If she discovered the owner, she might be able to name at least two of the companies. Ehren said she could use all the resources at her disposal as long as she didn't share the financials with anyone.

Those resources included her eyes, ears, legs, and the Internet.

Ehren also said he was going to meet with his client.

His client might be the owner.

Nadia checked her watch. It was 12:51 p.m. She had forty-four minutes left. She kept her tablet running but stuffed it in her bag. Left her calculator beside the financials. Tossed down a pen for good measure to make it obvious someone was still sitting at the table.

Nadia signaled a waiter serving a table. He ignored her. She ran over to him and asked him to bring her an iced tea and a grilled chicken salad. Told him she'd be right back.

Nadia knew the layout of the Four Seasons from several hundred company presentations. Executives pulled up in their chauffeured cars near the back entrance on Fifty-Eighth Street. The back entrance opened onto a stairwell that led downstairs to three meeting rooms. Companies looking for financing hosted presentations for professional investors in those rooms.

Nadia bolted past the front desk and out the back door. A long line of shiny black cars idled by the curb. A driver chatted with the doorman. A police cruiser was parked farther up the street. No sign of Ehren.

Nadia went back inside. A woman bustled down the stairwell. As she rounded the corner, Nadia caught a glimpse of her hair and face. Ehren's fresh-faced associate. Nadia followed her to the basement.

The corridor teemed with investors. Ehren's associate disappeared into one of the meeting rooms. Nadia walked the length of the hallway three times, pretending to be waiting for a friend. Each time she stole a glance inside the meeting room. On her third try, she spotted Ehren's profile. Her spirits sank. The company making the presentation might have been the client Ehren had referred to. If so, she was out of luck. It was an American bathroom parts supplier. Not a Russian conglomerate.

Nadia walked to the back of the corridor and waited. Six minutes later, Ehren steamed out of the room, raced up the stairs, and exited via the back door. Nadia followed at a safe distance. Made sure Ehren wasn't lurking before stepping outside the hotel.

Ehren stood beside a Maybach farther west in front of Tao, a restaurant. A chauffer with granite shoulders opened the rear passenger door. A man in a gray business suit emerged. He was tall and athletic with boyish looks. He appeared to be in his forties. He waved his finger at Ehren as though scolding him. Ehren bowed his head and took the beating.

An investment banker was yielding to another man. This client didn't represent a lucrative revenue stream for Ehren, Nadia realized. He represented the mother of all revenue streams.

They disappeared into Tao.

Nadia pulled her New York City library card from her wallet. She slung her bag over her shoulder and carried her tablet computer in her other hand as though taking notes. She hustled over to the Maybach. The driver was reading a Russian newspaper.

Nadia rapped on the window. The driver jumped. Glared at her. Nadia rapped again. He rolled the window down.

"Nadia Tesla, *New York Chronicle*." She flashed her library card and made it disappear just as quickly. "I'm doing a story on Russian oligarchs," she said in Russian. "My cameraman just took a picture of your boss and I want to make sure I get his name right. If I get it wrong and he calls me on it, I'm going to tell him to speak with his driver. You see, this is a piece about the Russian oligarchs' favorite charities. It's about all the good their money is doing around the world. Now your boss, the man who just walked into Tao is Mikhail Prokorov, owner of the New Jersey Nets—"

"No, no, no. Not Mikhail Prokhorov. Simeon Simeonovich. That is Simeon Simeonovich. How can you not know that? What kind of reporter are you?"

"An incompetent one, I'm afraid." Nadia fished her real business card out of her wallet. "Give this to Mr. Simeonovich. Tell him I look forward to working with him."

Nadia rushed back to the hotel lounge. An iced tea and a field green salad topped with grilled chicken awaited her.

She found the Wikipedia page for Simeonovich. He earned a PhD in quantum physics at age twenty-five. He used his profits from trading metals on the Russian market to become the country's first corporate raider. His first purchase was a smelter. He slept near the furnace for the first six months to prevent criminals from ransacking the factory. After expanding his holdings in commodity businesses, he diversified into industrials.

He consolidated his businesses under the umbrella of the Orel Group. Orel, which rhymed with "propel", was the Russian and Ukrainian word for eagle. He was the majority owner of eleven companies. Six traded publicly on the Russian stock exchange. A seventh traded on the Ukrainian exchange. Nadia subscribed to a global database of financial statements. She checked the most recent financials for the publicly listed companies in his portfolio. Nadia was certain he would never share private company financials with an outsider, let alone use them to test analysts. The two Russian companies had to be public.

She was right. The small Russian company was a specialty steel manufacturer. The large Russian company was the consolidated corporate entity. That left the third company. The American one.

The other candidates' inability to identify the American industrial company perplexed Nadia. They were industrial analysts. They knew the American marketplace cold. If they couldn't recognize the company, that meant it either wasn't American, or it wasn't an industrial. But it had to be an industrial. Ehren had emphasized his client's obsession with industrial expertise. And if Simeonovich was looking to acquire an American industrial, it made sense to craft a test accordingly.

That meant the company wasn't American. It was a Russian company whose financials had been re-stated according to United States GAAP standards. That's why no one could identify it. The company itself existed but its American financials were manufactured for the test.

Nadia converted 2010 revenue numbers for the remaining company into rubles. She scanned the income statements of Simeonovich's other companies. She checked five of them. None matched. She converted the sales numbers for the last company in Orel, a mining equipment manufacturer. Compared it to those of the third company. They were close, but didn't match. The sales number on the Russian financials was higher. Then Nadia remembered they probably shouldn't match. American accounting standards were notoriously strict. The Russian accounting system allowed sales to be recognized earlier. Revenue numbers might be higher under the Russian system.

Close only mattered with horseshoes and grenades, Nadia thought. And Russian accounting standards.

She scribbled the names of the three Russian companies on top of the financials. Stacked them together, flipped them upside down, and set them to the side. Sipped her iced tea and dug into her salad.

Ehren arrived. When he saw her eating, he smiled. He nodded at the stack of financials and donned a sympathetic look.

"You shouldn't feel bad," he said. "You were put in an impossible situation."

Nadia flipped the financials upright and slid them across the table. Ehren froze when he saw the first name. His jaw dropped when he read the other two.

"This . . . this is impossible," he said. "You couldn't have . . . You . . . you cheated. You called someone."

"The best industrial analysts in the world couldn't identify those three companies. Whom exactly do you think I called?"

A cell phone rang. Ehren stood oblivious.

Nadia speared a chunk of grilled chicken. "It's yours."

Ehren fumbled with his pocket.

"It's Mr. Simeonovich," Nadia said. "He's calling to tell you to hire me."

Ehren's eyes widened. He answered the phone. Stared at Nadia. He listened and interjected a few "yes, sirs."

After he hung up, he slipped into the chair across from Nadia. The dazed expression never left his face.

"He wants to meet you as soon as possible," he said.

"I have some urgent business in London. I'm leaving tonight."

Ehren's expression brightened. "How long will you be there?"

"Today is Friday. I'm returning home Sunday. We can set something up for Monday."

"No. Mr. Simeonovich is based out of London. He's only in New York City for the day. Let me see what his plans are. How is your schedule on Saturday? Could you meet with him there?"

"I have some meetings in the afternoon but I'm free in the evening."

"Let me talk to him. Now, about your compensation."

CHAPTER 13

JOHNNY TANNER WAS IN THE MIDDLE OF HIS SATURDAY morning workout at the gym when his cell phone rang. His workout took an hour. Not fifty-five minutes. Not an hour and five minutes. One hour. The faster he worked, the more he revved up his metabolism. He'd been fat as a kid growing up—to ease the pain of his father's beatings he hid in his room and ate. Sky-bars and salt water taffy, mostly. He never wanted to look that way again.

He did a thirty-minute circuit of weight training, followed by twenty minutes on the treadmill at seventy percent of his maximum heart rate, and finished with ten minutes of stretching. He always checked the phone number when someone interrupted but he only answered if a judge or an ADA was calling. Or a certain woman.

"Uh-oh," Nadia said. "You sound out of breath . . ."

Johnny's heart skipped a beat as soon as he heard her voice. "You caught me mid-workout."

"I'm returning yours. It sounded urgent. You want to call me back?"

"Nope. I got a call from a friend in the NYPD. There's been a new development in Bobby's case."

"Why does this sound like bad news?"

"The cops went to Fordham and interviewed a few teachers and the hockey coach. Standard procedure. Everyone said good things, without exception. No worries about his background. One thing, though. The Fordham hockey coach? He said there was an incident this past season after a game. Bobby got into a brief altercation with a random guy outside the locker room."

"Altercation?"

"A shoving match. Nothing serious."

"What guy? He never told me about this."

"They showed the hockey coach a picture of Valentine. He confirmed it was him."

"What?"

"There's more. They interviewed the security guard at the rink. He said the same guy, Valentine, was hitting on a real cute Russian model in the stands during the game. Wouldn't take no for an answer. The guard swears he heard her say number four for Fordham was her boyfriend and she wasn't interested."

"Iryna."

"They found her name on Facebook and interviewed her this morning. She confirmed the altercation."

"She didn't tell me she'd met the guy Bobby supposedly killed when I spoke to her at the bakery the other day."

Johnny let a moment go by. "Is that a realistic expectation? She just met you. You expect her to bare her soul? Besides, don't you think Bobby told her to keep her mouth Ziplocked about everything? He doesn't want to talk to you. You think he wants his girl talking to you?"

"No. You're right. Bobby must have told her not to say a word about that to anyone."

"But the district attorney has motive now. Protecting his girlfriend's honor, his own honor, whatever."

"How did Bobby and Valentine meet that night in the first place? The odds they bumped into each other on a Manhattan street is zero. One of them called or e-mailed the other to arrange it. My guess it was Valentine." Nadia told Johnny about the call from London. "And it turns out Valentine was in London visiting his father on his deathbed."

"So he calls Bobby from London to set up a meeting because of a spat over a girl? That doesn't jive."

"That's why I'm in London. I took the red-eye."

"London? What the hell—"

"I don't think this was about Iryna. Bobby's too levelheaded. He grew up turning the other cheek. And Valentine had too much to lose. The job, the lifestyle. All over a girl? It's more likely this had something to do with his father's death."

"Which makes no sense whatsoever."

"Which is why I'm here."

"I'm going to see Bobby this morning," Johnny said.

"Are you going to ask him about his brush with Valentine at the hockey rink?"

"Yeah, but if he's not talking it's not going to get me anywhere."

"All you can do is try."

Johnny cleared his throat. "Yeah, right. Trying is not going to make you feel better if there's a guilty verdict. There're plenty of bigger names that will take this case given the publicity it might get."

"No—"

"We talked about this before. Reputation matters with judges and prosecutors. I graduated Rutgers, not Harvard. I've got no pedigree, and I've got no shame. I'll represent anyone. I don't play basketball with any judges. The bigger names do. Bobby might be better off with one of those bigger names."

"No. You know everything that happened last year. Everything. You're the only one I trust. And I don't want to discuss this again."

They discussed logistics and hung up.

Johnny did the rest of his resistance workout without pausing between sets. He imagined two scenarios. In the first, the judge dismissed the case because of a legal maneuver. In the second, a jury found him innocent after Johnny delivered a stirring closing argument. In both cases, Nadia expressed her gratitude by kissing him, and what was supposed to be a gentle thank you turned into something more.

Something much more.

CHAPTER 14

SEABIRDS CIRCLED LITTLE DIOMEDE ISLAND, AN AMERICAN territory in the Arctic Circle off the northern coast of Alaska. They nested in the cliffs that surrounded the village. The early morning sun shimmered on the snow-capped sea.

Lauren followed her tour guide along the rock walkway. The village consisted of four rows of houses, thirty buildings max. She'd seen the Native Store, Washeteria, and clinic, bingo hall and the armory. It was 10° outside. Lauren was wearing a parka but never stopped shivering.

Her tour guide's name was Karen Kuvalik. The trail of clues from Kotzebue had led Lauren to Karen and her husband, Sam. They knew Bobby Kungenook and his real story. Lauren was sure of it. Convincing them to part with the truth, however, was going to take some persuasion. Lauren was prepared to do whatever was necessary. If the locals were protecting Bobby Kungenook, the story had to be about more than hockey. It could be a simple matter of illegal immigration, but her gut told her otherwise. Cops didn't point rifles at reporters' heads to protect an illegal immigrant. Lauren suspected this was the type of story that created international headlines.

"So you know Ricky Wells?" Karen said. She spoke in a monotone.

"No. I don't really know him. I'm producing a show on the Kobuk 440. And Ricky's a top competitor. I know he comes out to Diomede once a year to hunt polar bears, and I thought that would be interesting to our viewers. I asked if he wanted to come out with me but he couldn't take time off from work." That was true, but the entire exercise was an excuse to meet with Karen and Sam.

"That's too bad. I never met him. I've seen him from a distance but I never met him. He's still single, isn't he?"

"I don't know. I didn't ask. I thought you were married, Karen."

"I am. But my sister isn't."

"Ah. I see. I imagine the pickings are slim on the island."

Karen shot her a look. "What does that mean?"

"No, no," Lauren said. "I didn't mean it that way."

"What did you mean?"

"Literally what I said. There are one hundred thirty-five people living on your island. How many age appropriate single men can there be?"

"It's even worse than that."

"It is?"

"Yeah. There's basically four families in the village. Pretty much everyone's related."

"Yikes. That is a problem."

"Yeah. I was lucky. I got my Sam when I was eighteen. No sense wasting time, you know? When you see something you want, you have to go get it."

"Tell me about it. So if you want to get married and live on Diomede . . ."

"You have to go find a boyfriend on the mainland and bring him back. You have to go find a man who loves you so much he's willing to live on Inalik."

"Inalik?"

"Diomede Village is called Inalik. Diomede Island is called Ignaluk. A Danish navigator by the name of Vitus Bering found

81

the island in 1728. It was the same day the Russian Orthodox Church was celebrating the day of their martyr, St. Diomede. That's how the island got its Anglo name. He was beheaded."

"Who was beheaded?"

"St. Diomede."

Lauren remembered the Seelicks talking about beheadings in Kotzebue. An eerie sense of foreboding washed over her. "I heard something like that before. How did your mother find your father? Did he live in the village or did she have to go outside?"

"He lived in Wales. It's the westernmost town on the mainland. She used to go to Wales with my grandmother to get supplies. For ivory carving. He was helping his father out in the store. He carried supplies to her taxi. One time, she slipped and fell on the ice, and he was there to help her up."

"I bet she didn't slip."

"No. I don't think so. How about your mother?"

"Excuse me?"

"How did your father meet your mother? Was she a reporter like you?"

"My mother?" Lauren stumbled on a protruding rock. "I haven't seen my mother in a long time."

"But how did your father meet your mother?"

"My mother was an actress. My father was her manager." Until she stopped getting work, Lauren thought.

They arrived at the front door to a small wooden home tucked into the side of the cliff. The front of the house rested on stilts to remain level.

The inside was clean and simple. Lauren met Karen's sister. She was watching over Karen's two children, a boy and a girl. They played in the living room. Karen served coffee in the kitchen. A folding door provided privacy.

Lauren could sense she was on the verge of the biggest break of her career. She reminded herself to be patient, let the conversation come naturally.

"You owe me fifty dollars," Karen said.

"I do?" Lauren said.

"Yeah. It's the fee for entry into the native corporation. The village is incorporated and charges visitor fees to help pay for the basics. I should have collected it when I met you at the helicopter but I . . . I don't know. It seemed a little rude, you know? Hi, how are you, give me some money." She opened a folder and removed a pad full of official receipts. "Can you spell your name for me?"

Lauren spelled her name and paid the fee. She folded the receipt and put it in her bag.

"Is your husband here?" Lauren said. "I need to get back to New York as quickly as possible. I was hoping I could interview him right away."

"Sam's not home."

"When do you expect him back?"

"Hard to say. He left on a hunt yesterday. Usually takes them five to ten days to find a bear."

"But I was told he'd be available for an interview," Lauren said. "He's the master hunter. That's why I came here."

"Don't worry. There's another hunter who can talk to you. He couldn't go out on account of a sprained ankle. I can call and get him over here now if you like."

"No, don't do that." Lauren sighed. "You seem like a nice person, Karen. Your kids are beautiful. I would have rather had this conversation with your husband, but I'm afraid I have no choice."

"What do you mean?"

"I didn't come here to research polar bear hunts."

"You didn't?"

"No."

"Then why did you come here?"

"Last April you and Sam hosted a young boy for three nights. Do you remember that boy?"

Karen's expression tightened. "No."

"The pilot who flew him out, Dan Garner? He told me he flew out a boy and a young woman to Nome last year. Said it was done on the QT. Said Sam snuck them onto the helicopter."

"I don't know what you're talking about."

Lauren showed Karen a picture of Bobby. "This is the boy who stayed here with you. Probably sat in this very kitchen. He calls himself Bobby Kungenook but I'm guessing that's not his real name."

Karen glanced at the picture and turned her eyes away.

Lauren showed Karen a picture of Nadia. She'd taken it during one of Bobby's hockey games. "This is the woman who was with him. Her name is Nadia Tesla."

"Never met her. Never seen her. And she's never been in my house, that's for sure."

"You didn't even bother to look at the picture."

"You should go now."

"Okay, Karen. I can do that. I can leave right now. But I'd ask you to reconsider. I'd hate for this to get out and for you and Sam to be arrested."

Shock registered on Karen's face. "Arrested? For what?"

"Aiding and abetting illegal immigration. That's a felony. And if the boy you helped is a felon himself for any reason, aiding and abetting a felon."

"Why would you think the boy's a felon? I mean, if there were a boy. Why would you think that?"

"I'm not saying he's a felon. I'm suggesting that he could be one. After all, how much did you really know about him?"

A child's laughter filtered in from the living room. Karen glanced at the door.

"Garner is in federal custody on bootlegging charges," Lauren said. In fact, she'd let him go after he told her everything to stay true to her word. Apologized to the Feds and told them she was mistaken about the bootlegging. "Illegal distribution of alcohol in dry communities. The ATF agents haven't asked him about Bobby yet. Why should they? They don't know anything about them. But if they somehow found out he helped sneak a boy in from Russia or Ukraine . . . That is what happened, isn't it?"

Karen glanced at Lauren.

"I just want to know where the boy came from," Lauren said. "I have no doubt you and Sam meant well. No doubt. I'll do everything possible to protect you."

Tears welled in Karen's eyes. "We got kids. We can't go to jail."

"You're not going to go to jail if you tell the truth. You helped a stranger. No one goes to jail for that. It's the lies. People go to jail for covering up the truth."

Karen stared at Lauren for a moment. One of the children squealed with delight. Karen sighed.

"Okay," she said. "But if we're going to talk about this, I need a drink first."

Karen went to the pantry and brought back a bottle of molasses and two glasses. At least that's what the label said. She poured two doubles of what smelled like bourbon.

"I thought Diomede was a dry village," Lauren said.

"It is."

"Then what is this, for medicinal purposes?"

"No, for baking. I make bourbon cookies." She slid a glass toward Lauren.

"It's nine in the morning, Karen."

"Yeah but it's midnight in Eastern Europe."

Karen knocked back her entire drink in one gulp. She stared at Lauren as though waiting for her to do the same. Karen's reference to Eastern Europe wasn't random, Lauren thought. She downed her bourbon. Savored the burn in her throat. She was about to get the scoop of her life.

"Are you ready for the truth?" Karen said.

"Yes."

Karen nodded. "The truth is . . . Sam's not on a polar bear hunt. He's working on his snow machine at the launching dock. He can tell you everything. Put your coat on and follow me. You can leave your bag. No one will touch it. We'll be right back."

They climbed down a path along the cliff to the edge of the frozen sea. A man kneeled before a snowmobile, right glove off, tinkering with the track. His round face was flush from exertion.

He smiled when he saw Karen. "Hey. What are you doing—" He froze. Lauren spied fear, not anger in his eyes.

Karen introduced Lauren to her husband. Sam questioned Karen with an earnest expression.

"Dan Garner's been arrested," Karen said.

"What?" Sam said.

As Karen explained the charges, her sister emerged from their house above. She shouted something incomprehensible. Sam nodded at Karen for her to go.

Karen glanced at Lauren. "One of our kids banged his head." She turned to Sam. "She won't stop asking questions until she understands what happened. Don't lie. People go to jail when they lie."

Karen left. Sam resumed his tinkering.

"Why is this so important to you?" Sam said.

"It's my job."

"It's your job to ruin people's lives?"

"No. It's my job to reveal the truth."

"Even if it ruins people's lives? Why would you want a job like that?"

"We all have our calling. Mine is to dig."

Sam stood up. "I'm almost done here. Do me a favor. Take a seat. Hold the handlebars as though you were riding it so the weight is distributed like it would be. I just put in new shocks in the rear suspension. I want to make sure they're on right. You ever been on one of these?"

"Yes, I've ridden a snowmobile." Men and their assumptions. She slipped onto the snowmobile and grabbed the handlebars. "When the boy who calls himself Bobby Kungenook showed up on this island, where did he come from?"

A shadow appeared on the snow in front of her. A hand reached over her shoulder. It was a man's hand with calluses like scallops. It flipped a red switch, turned the key, and pulled the starter cord. The engine hummed.

Robert Seelick Sr. appeared at her side. "Before you ask a question, you should be sure you want the answer." He yanked a lever beside the steering column.

The snowmobile surged.

Lauren's neck snapped back. She teetered. Grasped the steering wheel. The snowmobile accelerated. The wind whipped her face. She lowered her head beneath the windshield. The throttle, Lauren thought. She pulled the throttle to the left. It wouldn't budge. She pulled harder. It didn't move. She squeezed the brake handle. Nothing. She squeezed again. It didn't work.

Snow flew. Shards of ice stuck to the windshield. The engine sang. Lauren clung to the handlebars. She yanked the throttle, squeezed the brake again. Still nothing. She tried to turn the ignition off. The key wouldn't budge. She turned harder. It wouldn't move. It was stuck in the on position.

Tufts of fog obscured the horizon. Lauren couldn't brake. She couldn't cut the power. She was going too fast to turn—how fast was she going? Didn't these things go more than a hundred miles per hour? She didn't heed Seelick's warning in Kotzebue. She'd taken one risk too many to find the truth about the boy. Now she was going to die. Alone. In the middle of the Bering Strait.

But what choice did she have? She had to dig. It's what she did. The memory that persecuted her asserted itself. If she dug hard and fast enough, she might save her mother yet. Her mother was waiting for her help. All she had to do was get there in time—

The engine sputtered. The snowmobile slowed, lurched, and resumed its pace. Another ten seconds passed. The engine burbled, quaked, and died. The snowmobile coasted into the fog. Lauren wiped snow off the fuel gauge. It was empty. They'd forgotten to fill the gas tank.

Euphoria gripped Lauren. She was going to survive. She wasn't going to die after all. She'd only been gone for what— ninety seconds? Two minutes at most. There had to be a border patrol of some kind. Someone would see her—

An alarm sounded.

They'd found her already.

Ask and ye shall receive, Lauren thought. She could see only twenty feet through the fog but she could hear human voices and the sound of a motor. Coming at her. Sam Kuvalik and Robert Seelick had aimed the snowmobile away from the island, but the initial thrust must have changed her trajectory. She'd probably travelled on a diagonal from one side of the island to another side. Everyone had heard the engine, and someone in the watch-tower had seen her.

There had to be a watchtower, right? Hell, this was the Arctic tip of the American frontier.

Lauren climbed off the snowmobile. Her back stiffened. Her legs trembled. As the fog rolled, the island came in and out of view, about a mile away. Strange, Lauren thought. Somehow, it looked bigger.

Four men with rifles burst through the fog. They wore white uniforms and fur hats. One of them shouted something but the wind swept his words away. The men aimed their rifles at Lauren.

She raised her hands in the air. "Are you guys the border patrol?"

The soldier answered but this time an engine drowned out his voice. A jeep emerged from the fog. It stopped on the ice beside the soldiers. The engine idled. Four more armed soldiers piled out. They aimed their rifles at Lauren.

Several soldiers spoke. The island loomed even larger in the background. There were no settlements on the lower ridge.

This time Lauren understood. She understood that Sam Kuvalik and Robert Seelick had made no mistakes. They'd aimed the snowmobile in the perfect direction. She'd run out of gas at the precise spot. Karen Kuvalik hadn't made any mistakes, either. Lauren had left her purse and wallet behind. She had no passport. She had no ID. And her breath reeked of whiskey even though it was still morning.

What Lauren could not understand was a word the soldier was saying.

The island in front of her wasn't Little Diomede. Lauren remembered the Alaskan guidebook. It was another island, two and a half miles away called Big Diomede.

And on Big Diomede the soldiers spoke Russian.

CHAPTER 15

PRISONERS AT RIKERS WERE ALLOWED UNLIMITED VISITS from their attorneys. When Johnny arrived ten minutes before noon, he did a double take at the line forming in front of the prison. A striking young woman with a perfect oval face stood first in line. More than an hour before visiting hours started. Now that was devotion, Johnny thought. She stood a few steps apart from the rest of the line, closer to the lot where Johnny had parked.

She looked familiar. At first Johnny thought he might have seen her in a Victoria's Secret ad or in *Sports Illustrated*. Then it hit him. It was Iryna. Bobby's girlfriend. She caught him staring at her. She soured and looked away. Men must have stared at her all the time. She probably thought he was leering at her. Instead of looking away, Johnny smiled and approached her. In her modeling shots, fully made up, she looked like a mature vixen. Up close, in person and *au naturel*, she looked like a kid. A sweetheart.

"Iryna?" he said.

She looked horrified a strange man was speaking to her.

"You're Bobby Kungenook's friend, aren't you?"

She frowned as though confused.

"I'm Johnny Tanner. Bobby's attorney."

Relief washed over her.

"I'll tell him you're first in line," Johnny said. "I'm sure that'll cheer him up."

"But I'm not first."

Johnny looked at the door to the visitor's center. No one stood in her way. "What do you mean?"

"You're first."

Johnny laughed. "Attorneys can go in whenever they want. They don't count."

"They're the only ones who count." A shadow fell on her face. "Is Bobby going to be okay, Mr. Tanner?"

"Call me Johnny. I'm going to do everything possible to help him."

"He's not going to stay in jail the rest of his life, is he?"

"Not if I can help it."

"I want to give you my card. In case there's something I can do."

Iryna picked and probed inside her bag but couldn't find one. She blushed. Then she fumbled with her wallet. She was trying so hard—she wanted to help so badly, Johnny thought—the entire situation became awkward. Johnny felt his own temperature rising. When she found a business card, they both exhaled. She scribbled a number on the back of it.

"My cell is on the back. If there's something I can do to help Bobby."

Johnny took the card. "Iryna Stasiak. Elite Modeling Agency."

"He didn't do this thing, Mr. Tanner."

"You seem certain. How long have you known each other?"

"About two months."

Johnny smiled. "But it doesn't take long when you connect with someone, does it?"

She blushed. "No. It doesn't."

"Did you know the victim?"

Iryna blanched. "Excuse me?"

"Did you know the victim, Jonathan Valentine?"

"No."

"Did you ever see him before you saw his picture in the paper?"

Iryna froze.

"Like at a hockey game, for instance?"

"Bobby told me not to tell anyone but the police came by. I couldn't lie to the police. I love this country. I don't want to be sent back to Ukraine."

"No one's sending you back anywhere. You did the right thing."

"I did?"

"Absolutely. Can you tell me what happened?"

Iryna repeated her story. It matched the version he'd heard from his friend in the NYPD.

"And you never dated Valentine?"

She looked horrified. "No. I didn't date him. I didn't know him. I never spoke to him except for those ten seconds in the stands."

"And Bobby?"

"He never mentioned him."

"Not once?"

She set her jaw and locked eyes with Johnny. "Not ever. I know it looks bad. But he didn't do it. He couldn't have done it. He's too sweet to hurt anyone. When he sees a bug in his room, he won't even step on it. He says every living thing matters."

"You guys sound like you have a special connection."

"We have a very special connection."

"Why?"

"Why do we have a special connection?"

"Yes."

"We're both damaged goods."

"How so?"

"We were both raised by strangers. Neither one of us ever knew our mothers. Did you know Bobby carried a screwdriver and flashlight everywhere he went?"

"Yes."

"Did you know he slept with them under his pillow?"

"I heard about that."

"Do you know why?"

"No. Do you?"

"No. I asked but he wouldn't tell me. He doesn't like to talk about his past."

"He's not the only one."

"But I think his past may have something to do with all this."

"Why do you say that?"

She shrugged. "When a girl gets to know a boy, she has a feeling about him."

Johnny thought of Nadia. Wondered what feelings she had for him, if any.

He thanked Iryna, said good-bye and entered the jail. A guard escorted him into the private room where Johnny was waiting. The bruises on his face appeared lighter. The first time they'd met, Bobby didn't say a word. Didn't make eye contact. He just sat in his chair the entire time staring at the wall. Looking as though he'd given up on life.

"How do you feel?"

Bobby didn't answer.

"You sleeping better?"

Bobby ignored him.

"There's been a new development in your case. Actually, it's old news to you." Johnny told him the police had learned about his previous confrontation with Valentine. "Tell me what happened that night after the hockey game. Did you have words because he hit on Iryna? Is that why you guys met up in the Meatpacking District? To fight it out once and for all?"

He said nothing.

"How am I supposed to defend you if you don't communicate with me?"

Bobby stared at the floor.

Johnny stood up. He paced back and forth in front of the table for twenty seconds.

"Okay," Johnny said. "Here's how I see it. You won't talk to Nadia, the person who cares more about you than anyone else. You won't talk to me, your lawyer, the person between you and a life in prison. There're only two explanations. First explanation, you're an idiot and a moron. We know you're not stupid. So that's out the window. Second explanation, you're protecting someone. Most likely Nadia. Your thing with Valentine wasn't about Iryna. It's something else. Something much more dangerous than a fight over a girl. Something so dangerous that you don't want Nadia poking around in it, the way you know she will. So you go deaf and mute on us, for fear you might put her life in danger, the way yours was that night with Valentine. How'd I do?"

Bobby's lips tightened a fraction of an inch. If Johnny hadn't been staring at them he wouldn't have noticed the kid's reaction. It struck fear in Johnny's heart. It meant a threat of some kind was still out there.

And his girl was alone on the other side of the ocean.

CHAPTER 16

G RAY SKIES COVERED LONDON BUT NADIA COULDN'T HAVE
cared less. She had a special fondness for England, as did
most Americans, even if they didn't care to admit it sometimes.
Although the Corvette trounced the Jaguar around the track, it
was forever searching for the elegance in the rearview mirror.
She sat opposite the headmaster of Jonathan Valentine's secondary school. Rain drizzled against the window of his office. The
headmaster wore a gunmetal and brown patterned suit. The
seams were fraying.

"I love your pottery collection, Mr. Darby," she said, nodding at the bookcase filled with ceramic figurines.

"Why thank you."

"Toby mugs?"

His eyes widened. "Yes."

"Royal Doulton."

He brimmed with delight. "Do you collect?"

"My mother does. Or rather did until it became fashionable.
Once other collectors started hoarding new releases for specula-
tive purposes, she gave up."

Darby came alive. "So did I. What a shame, I tell you. One of
the great joys of my life ruined by opportunists. They're not true

collectors. They don't appreciate the craftsmanship or the whimsy."

"I see your Alfred Hitchcock has a pink curtain. Not a gray one, which is the common variety. That's rare, isn't it?"

"It's the jewel of my collection."

Nadia stood up to take a closer look. "It's spectacular."

Darby blushed. "Why thank you, Ms. Tesla."

"Call me Nadia, please. I've heard they exist but I've never seen one. I appreciate your giving me a glimmer of joy during what is sure to be a grim visit to London." She sat back down.

"We heard the news about young Mr. Valentine. It's a tragedy. The faculty—the entire institution—we're all devastated."

"Thank you, Mr. Darby. I hope it wouldn't be too painful if I ask you some questions."

"Questions? About what?"

"About Jonathan."

"Forgive me for being so blunt, Ms. Tesla, but what is your connection to Jonathan?"

"I was referred to you by the Office of Alumni Relations at the University of Nottingham. A kind lady there confirmed Jonathan was a graduate of Felshire. I thought he was because I found an old article online, from the school newspaper. It mentioned Jonathan Valentine was named Most Valued Player in a football match against Westminster. Was Jonathan a great athlete?"

Darby squirmed. "Yes, but you haven't answered my question—"

"Was it just football for him, or did he have other interests beyond scholastics?"

Darby started to answer but stopped himself.

"You do get to know your students fairly well, I suspect," Nadia said, "given how small the classes are. What did I read? Seventeen students on average per class at Felshire?"

"Yes, that's about right—"

"Gateway to Oxbridge. I never heard that term before in America. I've heard of Oxford, of course. And Cambridge. But never the term 'Oxbridge'. Was Jonathan's family disappointed when he didn't get into either and ended up at Nottingham?"

"Please, madam . . . Please stop talking for a moment and answer my question."

"What was the question?"

"Who are you?"

"I told you. My name is Nadia Tesla." Nadia had considered using an alias but decided against it. A lie would have to be perpetuated. That could become a problem if Darby led her to a person with whom she needed to be honest. The closer she stuck to the truth the better off she was. Besides, the odds Darby knew she was guardian to Valentine's alleged killer were low.

"Yes. No. I mean, what is your connection to Jonathan? You're an American. I suspect you're not related."

"No. And any such dream is dead now, isn't it?"

Darby frowned. "I'm afraid you have me at a constant loss, Ms. Tesla."

"Nadia."

"Very well, Nadia. Please tell me why you're here."

Nadia thought of the time her father asked her if she'd be willing to take the Ukrainian Girl Scout survival test at age twelve. The thought of revealing her true feelings and saying no terrified her. But she felt compelled to do so. She needed to channel the same reluctance and sincerity. She'd concocted the story she was about to tell Darby on the plane to London. Rehearsed it countless times in the hotel. She knew the script. Now it was a matter of delivery. Reluctance and sincerity.

"I was Jonathan's lover," Nadia said.

"Oh." He blushed. His tone eased. "I see."

"We were going to get married."

"He always did like older . . . I'm so sorry."

"Until Jonathan found out I was pregnant with his child. Then he threw me out of his apartment in the middle of the night."

"He did what?"

"He said he never wanted to see me again. Said I couldn't be sure the child was his given I was a whore, and if I tried to sue him to get a DNA test I'd regret the day I was born. I'm just trying to get to know the father of my child a bit, in case he or she asks me about him down the line."

Darby digested her comments. "Bastard," he said under his breath. He stood up and closed the door to his office. Collapsed back into his chair. "May God have mercy on my soul for saying this. I know he was the father of your child but you're better off with him gone. I hate to say it, but the world is better off with Jonathan Valentine dead."

It was Nadia's turn to be taken aback. "Why would you say that?"

"I've been headmaster here for thirty-two years. During that time I've seen some five thousand young men pass through these halls. Jonathan Valentine was the worst of the lot. And whoever the runner up is he's a distant second."

"You're kidding me."

"No, I am most assuredly not kidding you." Darby opened a drawer. He pulled out a bottle of single malt Scotch. "Will you join me?"

Nadia patted her stomach. "I'd love to, but under the circumstances . . ."

"Oh. Something else, perhaps?"

Nadia declined. He fixed himself a Scotch on the rocks.

"In what way was he the worst of the lot?" she said.

"In every way. He was a sociopath. Society's norms meant nothing to him. He had no morals whatsoever. It would have been bad enough if he were merely a pathological liar with criminal tendencies. But no. He was a rogue, a cheat and a scoundrel, too. And he was charming. So charming. As you know. Or rather, as you knew."

"Yes. Too well. What were some of the worst things he did, if you don't mind my asking?"

Darby considered the question. "It's not that I mind your asking, it's more that you may mind my answering."

"How so?"

Darby's eyes drifted toward Nadia's stomach.

"He got a girl pregnant," Nadia said.

"My dear, this is a senior boarding school for boys only. There are no girls."

"Then I don't understand."

"Women, my dear. And note that I'm using the plural case. Women. One was a maid and the other was the music teacher."

"And he got them both pregnant?"

"At the age of seventeen. Within the span of two months."

Nadia sat speechless.

Darby nodded. "He ran a gambling operation out of his dormitory, stole gold from the chapel, extorted money from the weaker boys, and beat up the biology teacher."

"And he wasn't expelled?"

"He should have been. But he wasn't."

Nadia studied Darby. His face was the color of eggplant. The straight line drawn by his lips suggested it was a function of embarrassment and resentment.

"Parental influence?" Nadia said.

Darby shrugged. "Parental influence, a man's instincts for survival. Sometimes they're one and the same."

Nadia let a moment go by. "I'm sorry. I can see you were put in a bad spot."

Darby sipped his Scotch. "Damn Russians."

"I beg your pardon?"

"Damn Russians, I said."

"What about them?"

"They came here because England offered legal sanctuary and a fair due process of law. Hypocrites. I've had men walk in here with bags of cash offering to build swimming pools, classrooms, and gyms in exchange for admission. One man landed his private helicopter on the cricket field. Asked if he could build his personal landing pad there. You can't imagine the gall of these people."

"I'm confused," Nadia said. "What did the Russians have to do with Jonathan?"

"You mean he didn't tell you?"

Nadia feared she was about to be found out. Her gut was telling her she was supposed to know something she obviously didn't.

"Tell me what?" she said.

"That his parents were Russian. That he was born in Russia. That he was Russian."

Nadia sat dumbstruck. "How can that be? He didn't have a Russian accent. And his last name—"

"His father changed it. Legally. Used to be Valentin. He added a letter. That's all it takes to go from Russian immigrant to English gentleman. One more letter at the end of a man's name."

"Why did the father change the family name?"

"When he immigrated, Jonathan was a baby. Oh, and his first name was Ivan, by the way. Ivan Valentin. His father wanted Jonathan to have every possible advantage. He didn't want him labeled a Russian. It may be that he didn't want him burdened by his own past, though I don't know any details in that regard. That's me speculating."

"Is there a large Russian community in London?"

Darby appeared shocked. "You must be joking."

"No."

"There's a long history between Moscow and London. Lenin was here six times between 1902 and 1911. The collapse of the

Soviet Union led to several waves of immigration. The early wave in 1991 was mostly professionals looking for a better way of life. Work permits were scarce and visas were hard to obtain so their numbers were limited. The second wave in 1994 was a nastier mix of people. They started showing up to burn money on the weekends. Kremlin insiders, ex-KGB, Russian-based criminals. Then John Major created the investor visa. Anyone who invested 750,000 pounds in UK government bonds could apply for English citizenship after a five year wait."

"Let me guess. That led to the third wave."

"In 1991 there were a hundred visas granted to Russians. In 2006 there were two hundred and fifty thousand. The super rich poured in. We became the official bag carriers for the world's financial elite. We can offer what New York and Hong Kong cannot—a superior tax haven. In England, a person can claim to be domiciled abroad and not pay taxes on income earned outside the U.K. Add to that London's perfect location—five hours from Moscow, and its top boarding schools for the children, and you have . . ."

"Runaway property values," Nadia said.

"And the headmaster to Moscow-on-Thames sitting humbly before you."

"I had no idea."

Darby glanced at her midsection again. "No, I dare say you didn't. Again, I'm so sorry about your predicament. Better days ahead, I'm sure."

"What can you tell me about Jonathan's father?"

"Not much, I'm afraid. Secretive sort. All of them are, to some degree. Said he made his fortune in the lumber business in Russia. Only spoke with him a few times. The entrance interview, of course. And then commencement and graduation. His wife did visit the boy now and then. I'm sure it was a struggle for young Jonathan to keep his hands off her."

Nadia recoiled. "I beg your pardon?"

"No, no." Darby laughed. "Second wife. He divorced the first wife, Jonathan's mother, here in London. It was amicable. She got a generous settlement. The second wife is a former page three girl."

"Page three girl?"

"One of our newspapers, the *Sun*, publishes topless pictures of glamour models on page three. This one was of Russian extraction. Natasha. Wayward girl. He was sixty-eight, she was thirty-six when they married. What does that sound like to you?"

"New York City."

Darby drank.

"I understand the funeral is tomorrow morning," Nadia said.

"Yes. You're not planning to attend, I hope . . ."

"Why? Do you think that would be a bad idea?"

"There's only Natasha and her baby. A girl. I don't think there are any relatives in Russia. If she finds out you're with child, she might consider you a threat."

Nadia savored the moment. Darby had provided a quantum leap in her investigation. Valentine's Russian heritage gave her hope there was a deeper connection between Bobby and him.

"Then we'll have to keep it our little secret, won't we, Mr. Darby? In fact, let's agree on this. As far as the rest of London is concerned, I'm not pregnant at all."

CHAPTER 17

THE MOURNERS CHANTED PSALMS. THE CHOIR SANG HYMNS.
The priest swung his censer and filled the air with incense.

The funeral service for Jonathan Valentine was held at the Cathedral of the Dormition of the Most Holy Mother of God and Holy Royal Martyrs, a Russian Orthodox Church. Nadia arrived early with Darby and stood in the back. When she went to use the ladies' room downstairs, she was surprised to see the steps to the church overflowing with mourners.

Nadia was raised Ukrainian Catholic. Still, there were enough similarities between the two churches to transport Nadia back to her father's funeral. The final hymn, *Vichnaya Pamyat—Eternal Memory*—could coax tears from the devil. Nadia remembered sobbing with the rest of the church, while wrestling with the guilt of having felt relief when she'd learned of her father's death. He'd pushed her so hard to be the perfect child in school, church and the community. His death had lifted a burden from her shoulders which in turn had spawned guilt.

Luxury cars lined the winding access road to the cemetery. Bentleys, Jaguars, Range Rovers, and Mercedes sedans. Cliques of heavyset men smoked, chatted, and eyed each other warily. The crowd from the church seemed to have grown exponentially. It surrounded the burial site twenty rows deep.

Nadia stood beside Darby on a knoll overlooking the funeral procession. She searched for the widow Valentin but didn't see a woman near the casket. A former glamour model who was thirty-two years younger than her deceased husband might not be overcome with grief, Nadia thought. She might, however, possess a wealth of valuable information.

"Why does this look like some head of state died?" Nadia said.

"Tribute," Darby said. "From the old country. As are the arrangements here, at gravesite. The proximity of the Russians to the bereaved family is dictated by hierarchy. The more powerful the man, the closer they are to the mother—stepmother, I should say."

The knot grew larger in the pit of Nadia's stomach. She wondered whose son Bobby had killed.

"I'm shocked there are so many of them here," Nadia said. "I assume that's a reflection of the deceased's family's power."

"Not necessarily. This is the customary community turnout for anyone of a reasonable social standing, which is to say a reasonable amount of wealth. Most of these men derive their income from the former Soviet states. Many of them are at war with each other, in a corporate sense. Their cumulative word is notoriously meaningless. There's more *schadenfreude* than sympathy here, I'm sure."

"That's a relief. I'd hate to offend the wrong person."

"Unless you hold the promise of untold fortunes, you don't have to worry about these men pursuing you."

Nadia thought of the locket, and the priceless formula she mistakenly thought it contained. She thought of the mobsters and government agents who'd pursued her around the world last year.

Darby nodded toward the grave. "Natasha, on the other hand, is quite the quarry. The widowers and recently divorced are already making their power moves."

Natasha walked to the front and sat in the front row. She wore a somber expression but her eyes weren't puffy or tear stained. Her black dress didn't hide her curves. She was a woman who insisted on maximizing her sex appeal in all situations. Always hoping to make an impression. Even at her husband's funeral. There was information there, Nadia thought. Information she could use to secure the meeting she was hoping to arrange.

Men in Savile Row suits had already formed a line to offer her their condolences. A group of fifteen to twenty people sat at a ninety-degree angle to the rest of the crowd, close to Natasha and the grave. They were older and appeared more formal in attire and posture.

"Who are the people off to the side?"

"Lesser royals."

"Royals? As in royalty?"

"Yes. The Dukes and Duchesses of Ancaster, Kesteven, and beyond."

"Who?"

"Exactly. Some of the Russians with money are obsessed with integration into British society. The older Valentine—the older Valentin—was one of them. They're transfixed by a royal title, however obscure. I better go pay my final respects before the priest arrives."

"I'll do the same," Nadia said.

"I thought we discussed this. What can you possibly hope to gain by meeting Natasha?"

"An invitation to afternoon tea."

Darby frowned. Nadia pulled out a business card. She slid her arm through the crook in Darby's elbow. They walked together to the grave.

They waited in line. After Darby offered his condolences, Nadia stepped forward. Natasha looked more like a queen holding court than a bereaved parent. She appraised Nadia with large brown eyes. Nadia extended her sympathies. Then she handed Natasha her business card and whispered two words in her ear.

"I'm flying back to New York tomorrow," Nadia added. "There's no time to waste."

Nadia got the call on her cell phone two hours later.

Tea was at 3:30 p.m.

CHAPTER 18

L AUREN SAT IN HER BRA AND UNDERPANTS ON THE COLD
metal chair wondering how a story about a teenage hockey
player could have landed her in a Russian jail cell. It wasn't a
story about a teenage hockey player, she thought. There was no
doubt whatsoever. It was so much more.

Hard plastic cuffs dug into her wrists. Leg irons bound her
feet. They'd shuffled her into the little man's office as though she
were a trained assassin. Her teeth chattered. She tried to stop
them but couldn't. Lauren wondered if the little man could hear
the clicking noise behind his desk. She prayed he couldn't. It was
a sign of weakness. Whether they tortured, imprisoned, or eventually killed her, one thing was certain. She'd be damned if she
showed any weakness.

He said his name was Krylov. Deputy Director of the FSB,
he said, the Russian federal security service. He looked like the
passive-aggressive type. Soft voice and proper manners, even
poured her a cup of tea and cut her a piece of coffee cake, though
he didn't loosen her restraints. What would he be like when he
didn't get the answers he wanted? Based on her ample experience, not so nice. Short men were the worst when they didn't get
their way. A short Russian man? That had to be a nightmare.

They had searched and blindfolded her before shoving her in the jeep. Removed the blindfold once they got to the prison. Everyone wore a uniform as though the island housed a military operation. A man with several gold stripes on his collar tried to speak with her in Russian. Once he realized she only spoke English, they brought her back to her cell and fed her dinner. Soup with cabbage and meat. No surprise. The entire place smelled like boiled cabbage. She didn't touch the soup though the black bread was delicious. She drank her water. Prayed it was bottled or boiled. What else would they be drinking on an island? She banged on the cell door. Demanded more water. That was the most shocking revelation of her thirty-six hour ordeal in prison. The measure of true fear was how quickly your throat went dry. And stayed dry.

"You cannot possibly expect me to believe your fantastic story," Krylov said. "You are a journalist. You come to Gvozdev—you call it Big Diomede—to do research on polar bear hunting and after some drinking the local men play a trick on you, and send you on a snowmobile trip to Russia."

"And you can't possibly believe I'm a spy," Lauren said. "What is there to spy on here? And what idiot would go about it like this?"

"I didn't suggest you were a spy."

"Then what are you suggesting?"

"That you are not telling me the truth. I was stationed in East Berlin from 1984 to 1989. I met many accidental tourists. People who needed to cross the border for one reason or another. I can always tell when someone is lying to me. And you, madam, are lying to me."

"Did you check the snowmobile?"

"We did."

"And?"

"It is as you say. The brakes and the steering were disabled. The throttle was locked in place."

"There you go. That proves it, doesn't it?"

"That proves you arrived by the means you say. It says nothing about your motive for coming here. Which is the essence of your lie. Rest assured, madam. You will tell me the truth before all is done. One way, or another."

"Did you go on a computer and check the Sports Network like I told you? My picture is on their website. Google me. You must have Google in Russia. You'll get a million hits. A million. Why would any journalist come to this Godforsaken place to spy? Why? Answer me that one question."

"We are checking your credentials—"

A prim woman in uniform knocked on the door. She held a laptop computer in her hand. She said something in Russian. Krylov waved her in. As she approached, she glanced at Lauren. Lauren knew that look. It was the look sports fanatics gave her when they recognized her on the street. She wasn't a household name. It was always a thrill when someone was wowed by her presence.

The female soldier hit a few keys. The speakers came alive. Krylov and the soldier peered at the monitor. Lauren heard her own voice, reporting at a World Cup skiing event. Krylov alternated glances at her and the monitor. He asked a question. The woman hit a few more keys. They studied the monitor some more. Probably the Sports Network's website. The clatter of her teeth subsided. They knew who she was.

Krylov dismissed the soldier. After she left, he spoke with someone on the phone. Ten seconds later, the guards reappeared.

"You will be taken back to your cell now. Your clothes will be returned to you with my apologies. You will be given all the food and water you desire. I will make some phone calls. I'm sure you'll be departing the island as soon as proper arrangements can be made."

"I'd like to repeat my request to be taken to the nearest American consulate."

"Your request is noted. It's just a matter of time until it is granted. Now that it's clear you're Glienicke Bridge material."

"Excuse me?"

"It's a Cold War term. The Glienicke Bridge connects Potsdam and Berlin. Potsdam was part of East Berlin. The bridge is the place where prisoner exchanges took place."

"Prisoner exchanges?"

"Don't worry. I'm not suggesting you're going to Glienicke, or that you'll be exchanged for another human being. But all good business depends on *quid pro quo*, doesn't it? I'm sure your embassy in Moscow will be pleased to strike a deal on your behalf."

The Russians would tell the American government a drunken journalist had taken a snowmobile ride to Big Diomede. The American government would tell the Sports Network one of their reporters had created an international incident. They would have to engage in *quid pro quo* to secure her release.

Bile rose up Lauren's throat.

"I'm sorry to have doubted your journalistic credentials, Ms. Ross," Krylov said, as the guards took her away. "You see, there was a situation with another American woman last year. A woman and a boy. I thought perhaps . . . But no. It was my mistake."

CHAPTER 19

NADIA TOOK A TAXI TO NATASHA VALENTIN'S WHITE STUCCO mansion in Lowndes Square, a residential section in a part of London called Belgravia. The mansion had been broken up into condominiums. A stocky butler let Nadia in and guided her to a modern living room. Dark paneling covered the walls. Nadia took a seat on a rich burgundy sofa flanked by glass tables with gilded frames.

Natasha, boobs overflowing in a leopard skin jumpsuit, bounced down a leather-clad staircase.

"There she is," Natasha said. "The girl who whispered the magic words."

"Simeon Simeonovich."

"How did you know I'd care?"

"I didn't. But he owns a soccer team and I figured you might be a fan."

Natasha cracked a smile.

"And he's one of the world's most eligible bachelors," Nadia said.

Natasha chuckled. "You work for him?"

"He's my client."

"And this is a matter of life and death?"

"Yes."

"And I can help?"

"Yes."

"And if I help you I'd be helping Simmy?"

"Indirectly."

"What does that mean?"

"That means you'd be helping me tremendously, which means I'll be better emotionally prepared to do a good job for him. Which means your help will be beneficial to him."

Natasha frowned. "So this isn't about Simmy?"

"Not directly."

"Big mistake. Let me give you some advice. Never underestimate the pretty girl. Now, should I call Otto in here, or do you want to tell me who you are and why you're here?"

"That depends."

"On what?"

"How close were you to your deceased stepson?"

Natasha studied Nadia. Shock registered on her face.

"Oh my God," Natasha said. "You knew him. In the Biblical sense. You're his type, aren't you? A little older, but still attractive. Smart—and more importantly—you weren't interested. Nothing turned that boy on more than a challenge—"

Nadia decided to speak the truth. Natasha struck her as a plain-speaking woman who would not respond well to a lie. It was a gamble, she knew, but at least she'd be speaking from the heart.

"No, Natasha. That's not it."

"It's not?"

"No. I could make up a story and pretend what you said is true. But I won't do that. I'm going to tell you the truth, and then if you want me to leave, I'll do so immediately."

"This is getting interesting."

"I'm the legal guardian of the boy who's accused of killing Jonathan."

Natasha's eyes widened.

"It's true. He's a great kid, but he refuses to tell me what happened. I came here because I know Jonathan was here for his father's funeral two to three weeks ago. That's exactly the time when my boy got a call on his cell phone from London. A week later they met on a street and somehow Jonathan was killed."

Natasha remained speechless.

"Do you want me to leave?"

Natasha considered the question. "Do you have a picture of the boy?"

"Do I have a picture? Yes. I have a picture of Bobby. Why are you asking?"

"Let me see it."

Nadia opened her wallet and pulled out two photos of Bobby. One was his Fordham Prep hockey team picture. The other one was of the two of them at the Statue of Liberty. She showed them to Natasha.

"Same picture I saw on his sports team's website," Natasha said.

"You saw Bobby's picture online?"

"The story made the papers here. I was told about the arrest. I looked him up."

"I'm confused. Why did you ask to see a picture of Bobby if you already saw one?"

"To make sure you are who you say you are. Forget the tea. Let's have a spot of champagne. Johnny boy is dead. That's a cause for celebration if there ever was one."

Otto brought a bottle of chilled Bollinger. He poured two glasses and left.

"To freedom," Natasha said.

Nadia thought of Bobby. "To freedom."

They clinked their glasses and drank.

"How do you like the décor?" Natasha said.

"It's gorgeous."

"It's Candy & Candy, the top interior designers in London."

"In a masculine way."

"I'm a devout heterosexual. Masculine is gorgeous to me. My husband. One thing I can say about the bastard—may he rest in peace. He only wanted the best."

"I'm sorry about your loss. I mean, where your husband is concerned."

"Don't be. You know what they say in London? You want a romance, date a Russian. But if you want a good marriage, marry an Englishman."

"How did you meet?"

"Through a dating service. He was older, you know? He knew how to treat a woman. He bought me gifts. Flowers, jewelry. We didn't have sex until our fourth date. Next day, he bought me a Mini Cooper. Who does that?"

"A gentleman."

"That's what I thought."

"No?"

"The night of our wedding, when he was finished with me, he sent his son in for sloppy seconds."

Nadia wondered if she'd heard correctly.

"He said it was an old tribal custom from the village where his ancestors came from in Russia."

"Oh my God."

"By then I was so drunk, I couldn't fight him off. He wouldn't stop. It went on for hours. And became a regular thing."

"Why didn't you leave? Or call the police?"

"Because Ivan would have killed me. So I stayed. And now I'm single and rich. I earned my money."

"Yes. I should say so."

"And today I buried the father of my child. May he rot in hell."

"I'm sorry for your suffering," Nadia said.

"Honestly, I'm glad I have someone to talk to. Sometimes it's easier to pour it all out to a complete stranger. Once you get to know someone, you care too much what they think of you."

"I was thinking the same thing recently."

"You know what my husband said to me on his deathbed?" Nadia shook her head.

"Bury me at Harrods. That way I know you'll visit me at least once a week." Natasha tightened her jaw. "I didn't bury him at Harrods."

They drank more champagne. A petite young nanny came downstairs with a baby girl. Natasha held her baby and fell into a trance. She carried her around the living room for ten minutes. She sang a lullaby. Afterward, she told the nanny to give her a bath.

"What do you know about your late husband's life in Russia?" Nadia said.

"Not much. I know he owned a lumber company in Siberia."

"Siberia?"

"That's what he told me. That's where his money came from. He got dividends every year. Supposedly I'm going to inherit the company. But it's Russia, right? We'll see if I'm so lucky. No matter, Ivan accumulated a big bank account for me here."

"Do you know how he came to own the company? Russia was part of the Soviet Union during most of his life. It was a communist country. He couldn't have owned the company back then."

"Yeah. He told me a story about those days. He said he put in an order for a new car once. A month later the salesman called and said, 'Good news. Your car will be delivered exactly six years from today.' Ivan said, 'That is great news. Do you know if it's going to be delivered in the morning or the afternoon?' The salesman said, 'Why?' Ivan said, 'Because I already have an appointment with the plumber in the afternoon.'"

"My father told me the same story about life in Ukraine."

"He did? Damn. I should have known. Ivan wasn't the creative type. He was a general manager before he owned the lumber company."

"A general manager? Of the lumber company?"

"No, for some government office. He said he was an administrator for the government."

A government official, Nadia thought. A Soviet bureaucrat. An *apparatchik*. *Apparatchiks* controlled the former Soviet Union, including Ukraine. Was there, perhaps, a connection between the old man and Bobby's father? They were of the same generation, probably similar in age. If only his father were alive to answer that question.

"Let me show you a picture," Natasha said.

She retrieved a photo album from a cabinet. She flipped to a family portrait of her, a vigorous-looking man twice her age, and his handsome son, Jonathan Valentine. The older man looked imperial, the younger one entitled. The older one sported a huge gold ring with a black gemstone carved into the number three.

"There we are," Natasha said. "The threesome. Together. And that wasn't the only time and place we were a threesome."

"Would you mind if I borrowed this picture?"

"What for?"

"I want to show it to Bobby. You never know. Maybe it'll get him to talk to me."

Natasha shrugged. "Suit yourself."

"I'll make a copy as soon as I get home. I'll send you the original back in the mail."

"Don't. It reminds me of the night before that picture was taken. That's one I'd rather forget. Like some others."

Natasha took the photo out of the album and handed it to Nadia.

"Did you ever hear either of them talk about a boy in America?" Nadia said.

"No."

"By the name of Bobby?"

"Never. But you have to understand. Ivan only spoke Russian to Jonathan. He changed his son's name because he didn't want him to be discriminated against in London. But he taught him Russian. When they got together, I didn't understand much. That's how they wanted it. And I didn't mind."

"Did Ivan have any business in America?"

"Not as far as I know. It was all in Siberia."

"Why did Jonathan move to New York?"

"Because London wasn't big enough for him. He said New York was the center of the world. And that's where he was going to make his fortune. I did everything I could to encourage it, believe me."

"I'm sure you did. I suspect his father wasn't happy."

"No, but he could never say no to his son. Jonathan wanted to be Donald Trump. Actually, he wanted to be one of Donald Trump's sons. He worshipped them. He wanted to make his mark on the world in New York real estate. So he moved to New York and got a degree. And his father got him a job at some big real estate company through his contacts here. And bought him an apartment. Should I keep it or sell it?"

"Do you see yourself visiting New York often?"

"Are you going to tell Simmy about me?"

"If the opportunity arises, yes."

"Then I'll keep it. For now. And Bobby? How old is he?"

"Seventeen."

"And they're keeping him in prison?"

"Yes."

"He must be scared."

"Yes. But he never shows it."

"And you believe he's innocent?"

"He's innocent, yes."

"Then I hope he's set free soon."

"Me too."

"As you go about trying to prove he's innocent, if you run into Jonathan's real killer, would you give him a message from me?"

"What's that?"

Natasha took a deep breath and exhaled. "Tell him I said thanks."

CHAPTER 20

LIGHTS SHONE ON THE TOWER OF LONDON. STARS GLITTERED. A ship with a mast passed under Tower Bridge.

A model in an embroidered Russian dress greeted Nadia on the slip at St. Katherine Docks. Two beefy men dressed as Cossacks flanked her. Laughter and Russian folk music flowed from Simeon Simeonovich's gigayacht behind her.

The model cast a disapproving look at Nadia's business suit. "Name?" She spoke with a Russian accent.

"Nadia Tesla."

She checked her computer and frowned. "I'm sorry. I don't see it here."

Nadia switched to Russian. "I was a last-second addition."

The model's eyebrows shot up in surprise. She glanced at Nadia's pants. "Yes. I guess so," she said in Russian. "May I see your invitation?"

"I don't have one." Nadia handed her a business card. "But I do have an appointment." She checked her watch. "Mr. Simeonovich is expecting me in his office in seven minutes."

The model gawked. "You're the one?" She tossed her head back and laughed.

"If you're talking about his meeting with the forensic investment analyst he hired, yes, I'm the one. Why is that so funny?"

"It's funny because he wouldn't give me your name. All he did was describe you. And you're not what I expected. In fact, I have to be honest with you. I was looking forward to meeting you all night, and now I'm so disappointed."

"I'm going to make a wild guess it's not the first time."

"What, that he was mischievous with me?"

"No. That you were disappointed. How did he describe me?"

"As having the biggest set of balls he's ever seen."

Nadia climbed aboard the yacht. She'd read about the eight hundred million dollar boat in an online financial magazine. It featured a military-grade missile defense system, armor plating, and bulletproof windows. It also boasted two helipads, two pools, and a paparazzi-proof electronic anti-photo shield with a laser beam. There was some doubt in the press whether the latter worked, but no one had the pictures to prove it didn't.

Crew outnumbered guests two to one. They poured vintage 1999 Bollinger champagne, Legend of Kremlin vodka, and 1989 Château Petrus. The women varied in ages but the men were all older. Everyone wore traditional Russian clothes except Nadia.

A crewmember escorted Nadia to a teak office. The only personal touches were the family photos aligned on a console behind the desk. Two children, a boy and a girl, pre-teens, and the girlfriend. The first wife had been a chemist. The girlfriend was a former violinist for the Vienna Philharmonic turned fashion designer.

Simeonovich was on the phone when Nadia walked in. He stood up as soon as he saw her. Cut the call short. When he greeted her, he extended his hand and bowed a bit. After they shook hands, he joined her in the seating area.

Nadia had decided ahead of time to speak English unless he did otherwise. If she started speaking Russian to him it might imply she thought his English was inferior.

"I didn't realize it was a costume party," Nadia said. "If I had known . . ."

"Yes? If you had known?"

"I'd be wearing the exact same suit."

He chuckled.

Something stirred inside Nadia. The way he bowed and stood up when she came into the room reminded her of old school chivalry. And he was the thirty-seventh richest man in the world. Nadia wanted him to like her, and the realization surprised her. She had no time or energy to think about romance let alone engage in it.

"Why the Cossack theme?" Nadia said.

"My ancestors were Cossacks in southern Russia during the seventeenth century."

"Mine were with the Ukrainian Cossacks that rebelled against Poland in the seventeenth century."

"How did that turn out?"

"The leader of the Cossacks made a treaty with the tsar. After he died, Russia took over the country. Ukraine ended up under Russian control for the next three hundred years."

"You're an American but this matters to you," he said. "Your Ukrainian heritage is important to you."

"You're right, Mr. Simeonovich. I'm an American."

"Call me Simmy, please. I'm not a fan of physical warfare. It's a waste of life and energy. I served two years in the Russian army on the Chinese border. We had a few incidents that never made it to the press. And at those moments I used to think, I hope I do not die this way, over a petty border dispute. War is inevitable but it should be fought on the economic front. What do you think?"

"I agree. War is inevitable."

"You are a warrior, aren't you?"

"I'm just a woman trying to pay her rent."

"I disagree. The test Ehren put you through to get this job. That was war, wasn't it?"

"It was a battle."

"What was your strategy?"

Nadia explained how she decided to focus on the owner of the companies instead of the financial statements. "I had to step out of my comfort zone to win."

"You were the only candidate to name all three companies."

"I got lucky."

"And the only one to tell my driver to tell me she was looking forward to working with me."

"I have your investment banker, Ehren, to thank for that."

"Why Ehren?"

"He's such a sweet and humble guy. He was desperate for me to win. I didn't want to disappoint him."

Simeonovich's lip curled upward. "You didn't disappoint, period."

Nadia felt herself blushing. "So what's the job?"

"Forget the industrial company for now. There's a new development. I'm circling an energy company in Ukraine. It's public, listed on the Ukrainian Stock Exchange, but so what? I have no confidence in the integrity of the financials. I need someone to turn them inside out. Also study the reserve analysis. Verify all outstanding indebtedness, triple-check the ownership structure, basically vet the entire enterprise top to bottom."

"What's your timetable?"

"Yesterday."

"I understand. What's your real timetable?"

"Seven days. Preferably less. You can get started on the financials in New York but you're going to have to go to Kyiv at some point. I want you to meet their CFO in person. The sooner the better."

Nadia had no idea how she would juggle the job and get Bobby out of jail but she had no choice. "I'll have my initial scrubbing done within forty-eight hours. I'll be in Kyiv within three days. I'll be done with the entire project in one week's time, assuming management is cooperative. Is that a fair assumption?"

"Sure. Management loves me."

"They do?"

"Take a corporate raider, mix in ethnic tension, what's not to love?"

"But they will talk to me, right?"

"They better if they value their jobs. As of today I'm the largest single shareholder."

A knock on the door. A young woman entered. Nadia recognized her from the picture on his desk. The girlfriend.

"Young Rothschild might make a big donation if you come out and talk football with him," she said in Russian.

Simeonovich cringed. He'd just bought one of England's top professional soccer teams, the second oligarch to do so after Roman Abramovich. "Is this absolutely necessary?"

"Only if you don't want to sleep alone tonight. I already put myself out there and told him you'd come out. Be a big boy now, would you please?" The girlfriend glanced at Nadia, dismissed her with a sour look, and closed the door behind.

"Donation?" Nadia said.

"I'm raising money for a hospital in Chukotka," Simeonovich said. "You know Chukotka?"

"I've heard of it," Nadia said. In fact, she knew it intimately. It was the northeastern-most part of Siberia. But that wasn't the reason her blood pressure spiked. "It's in Siberia, isn't it?" Valentine had earned his fortune in Siberia.

"It is. My foundation is putting money into the region to modernize it. Raise the living standards. And the answer to your question is no. I didn't know Ivan Valentin or his son. We were part of the same community, but we travelled in different circles."

Nadia was speechless.

"You seem surprised. You didn't expect me to do a background check on you? I know you're guardian to a boy accused of Jonathan Valentin's murder. I know you went to his funeral yesterday. I know you had coffee at the widow Valentin's house."

Nadia expected him to do a background check, and possibly be informed about her presence at Valentin's funeral. But she didn't expect him to deduce the reason she'd asked him if Chukotka was in Siberia. Nadia swallowed her shock and seized the opportunity to match wits with him.

"Her name's Natasha. She's actually very nice. She's a big fan. She'd like to meet you."

"That's sweet, but she's not my type."

"Why? Too tough?"

"No. Too obvious."

"Is my situation in New York with Bobby—the boy who was arrested—going to be a problem for you?"

"Look. I created a competition among the best analysts in the world with the language skills I need. You won. You're the best. I don't care what else is going on in your life as long as you get the job done. Are you going to get the job done?"

"Yes."

"That's all I need to know. In a minute, my chief financial officer is going to come in here. He's going to give you access to a secured website that will have all the financials you need to get started on your analysis. He'll also give you his contact information in case you have questions."

"I'll start work immediately."

Simeonovich grabbed a business card from a holder and scribbled something on the back. "This is my cell phone number. I want you to call me every day at four p.m. with an update on your progress. Not 3:59. Not 4:01. Four p.m. London time."

"Done."

"Also, you should know that we stress family values at the Orel Group. That's very important to me because I'm trying to build a company that lasts, not make a quick buck. So while you're my employee for the next few weeks, please consider yourself part of that family. Consider me at your disposal if there's anything I can do to help you."

"Help me?"

"Yes."

"With what?"

"Anything." Simeonovich glanced at the photos of his children. Turned back to Nadia. "Anything at all."

CHAPTER 21

Victor Bodnar smiled as the Sunday morning sun warmed his face in Tompkins Square Park in the Lower East Village. The Timkiv twins sat across from him eyeing separate chess boards. Victor was playing both of them at the same time.

They'd proven themselves to be invaluable in Ukraine last year and he'd arranged for them to join him in New York. The Gun wore a tattoo on his right arm. It featured a gun beside the ace of spades, a bottle of vodka, a ten-ruble note, and the profile of a girl with serpents for hair. The Ammunition wore the same tattoo on the same arm but his featured three bullets instead of a gun.

The tattoos were reminders the boys had spent time in Corrective Labor Colony Four. In Kyiv, the tattoos were a sign of strength. They generated fear and commanded respect. In New York City, they were liabilities. They drew attention to their owners and spoke of vanity, violence, and a life of crime. That is why Victor had instructed them to wear long sleeve shirts with collars the moment they arrived in the United States, six months ago. And now Victor's prudence was the source of his problem. He couldn't tell them apart.

At least not on the street. In the park, it was an entirely different matter. He'd been teaching them chess since the grass had thawed. They were both quick learners. This was not entirely surprising since they were expert computer hackers. In personal style, they were quite different. The Ammunition loved the Queen's Gambit. He sacrificed pawns for a stronger center and routinely exposed his king. He was bold and decisive. The Gun, on the other hand, preferred the Pirc Defense. He allowed his opponent to build an imposing center and turned it into a target for attack. He was patient and clever.

In Victor's experience as a thief and a con man, chess was a manifestation of a man's likely behavior on the streets. Individually, the twins could be beat. Together, however, they were invulnerable. As long as their coach optimized their collective skills.

Victor moved his knight and completed the Berlin Defense.

"Checkmate," he said.

The Ammunition stared at the table and swore.

Victor changed seats to face his brother. Twelve moves later he beat the Gun. The brothers had now lost a combined seventy-two consecutive matches.

"Eventually, one of us is going to beat you," the Ammunition said in Russian.

"It's only a matter of time," the Gun said.

"The day either of you beat me is the day you should leave me," Victor said.

"We'd like to make some money first," the Gun said. "I know a guy in Brighton Beach who knows about a shipment of marijuana coming in through New Jersey. The protection's weak. It would be an easy score."

"No it wouldn't," Victor said.

"How do you know?" the Gun said.

"If it was easy, the guy from Brighton Beach wouldn't be asking for your help."

"I met a girl who works as the accountant in the home office of a big department store," the Ammunition said. "She's a user. She needs money. She has access to a database of credit cards. We could keep the upfront payment low. Pay her a back-end once we turn them over."

"Your final reward may not be to your liking," Victor said.

"Why do you say that?" the Ammunition said.

"Because users inform on others when their habit lands them in jail."

The Timkiv twins rolled their eyes at each other.

"You've got to let us work, Victor," the Ammunition said.

"Yeah, Victor," the Gun said.

Victor spread his palms over the chess tables. "You are working."

"Not chess," the Gun said. "You've got to let us do something that's going to put money in our pockets."

"Exactly," Victor said. "I'm glad we're on the same page."

The twins frowned.

Victor's cell phone vibrated. He stepped away for some privacy and answered it. When he heard his daughter's voice, his heart soared, as always.

"Anything new from Iryna?" Victor said in Ukrainian.

"No," Tara said. "Father, why did you ask Iryna to get involved with that boy? What's so important about this locket you want her to find for you? It's just a piece of jewelry his father handed down to him before he died, isn't it?"

"Maybe," Victor said. "Maybe not. It's best not to get into details right now."

An old friend had bought a watch on the street from a desperate-looking man for twenty dollars, thinking it was gold. When he scratched the back of the face, however, it turned out to be gold plated. Beneath the gold were a man's initials. When Victor saw this, he wondered. What if the priceless formula for a radiation countermeasure was etched on Adam Tesla's locket beneath the gold plating?

"The fact the boy never let Iryna touch the locket after a month of dating tells me something," Victor added. "Especially given she asked to take a look at it while it was hanging around his neck. And he refused."

"What does it tell you?"

"That I'd like to have a look at it myself."

"But how could a piece of old jewelry be so valuable you'd want to steal it?"

"Your father is a thief, sweetheart. Always was. Always will be. Beyond that you don't need to worry yourself about anything. Know that I'm doing my best to leave you and my grandson as big a fortune as humanly possible."

"Yes. I know that."

Victor could hear the excitement in her voice. Money had that effect on even the purest conscience. "That locket must be in prison with the boy's other possessions. Tell Iryna not to bring it up anymore but to stay vigilant. Tell her to keep listening. And remind her how much she enjoys America compared to her prior life milking cows in the breadbasket of Europe."

Victor said good-bye and hung up.

Thieves-in-law, members of *Voroskoi Mir* such as Victor, were not allowed to have families or children. But this was America, not Ukraine or Russia, and most of the old thieves were dead. Who cared if his casual affair with a baker in New York produced a child twenty-eight years ago? He cared. That's who cared. His discovery that he was a father—and now a grandfather—thirteen months ago was nothing less than a rebirth. He had passion again. He had a purpose again.

And it was a more powerful motivator than anything he'd ever known.

CHAPTER 22

NADIA RETURNED TO NEW YORK ON SUNDAY NIGHT. ON Monday morning, she visited her elderly friend, Paul Obon. His Duma bookstore in New York's Lower East Side catered to English-speaking people of Ukrainian descent from all over the world.

Obon had immigrated to America with Nadia's father. She'd known him her entire life. Nadia had called ahead and asked him to see what he could dig up on Ivan Valentin. She also wanted to learn more about Russian oligarchs in general. To better understand Ivan Valentin and discover his son's connection to Bobby, she thought it would be beneficial to know his world. And she'd be learning more about Simeon Simeonovich as well.

They stood at the front desk drinking tea.

"The oligarchs gained their wealth in two stages," Obon said. "First, when Yeltsin succeeded Gorbachev in 1991. The Soviet Union had collapsed. The Russians couldn't feed their people. There was a global recession. They couldn't trade their resources, couldn't generate cash. So Yeltsin's cabinet came up with a voucher scheme. The government offered the population vouchers to buy shares in privatized companies in exchange for cash. Mostly agricultural and service companies."

"Free enterprise," Nadia said.

"The average Russian spent a month's wages to buy a future stake in a private company. But most didn't understand what they owned. A few did. Hustlers set up kiosks that traded vodka and cigarettes for vouchers. Stalls popped up outside farms and factories. Former KGB agents encouraged people to part with their stakes."

"If you're a first generation American and your parents lived behind the Iron Curtain, hearing that is no surprise."

"It was the same in Ukraine and the other Soviet countries. Yeltsin sold one hundred forty-four million vouchers. That represented half of the entire Russian economy."

"For how much?"

"Twelve billion dollars."

"Most large American companies are worth more than that."

"And that was Yeltsin when he was sober. By 1995 he was drunk and barely in control of the country. There was money laundering, corruption. A group of businessmen made a backroom deal with Yeltsin. They offered to lend him cash if he put up shares in the other half of the economy as collateral."

"The other half of the economy being natural resources."

"The loan for shares program gave the businessmen the right to acquire those companies if the government defaulted on the repayment of the loans."

"Which was inevitable."

"An auction was held. Only select businessmen were allowed to participate. The *apparatchiks* controlled the bidding process. It was a complete sham."

"How much did the loan for shares scheme raise?"

"In the range of fifty billion dollars."

"For all of Russia's natural resources."

"No. For all of Russian's natural resources, metal industries, and telecommunications businesses."

"That's less than one third the value of General Electric."

"A man should never sell state assets and drink vodka at the same time. Loan for shares gave birth to the oligarchs. When the world economy and commodity prices recovered, they joined the ranks of the richest men in the world."

Nadia handed Obon another book. "Was Simeon Simeonovich one of them?"

"No. He bought his businesses one at a time from the others."

"I'm surprised. If they were good businesses, why did they sell?"

"Because Putin told them to."

"You're kidding me."

"No. There was an epic meeting among the oligarchs and Putin on July 28, 2000. By all accounts it was like something out of *The Godfather.* The oligarchs had gotten out of control. The conspicuous consumption, the arrogance. The population was sick of them. They were sheltering their income, avoiding taxes. They were complaining about corruption and inside dealing. Demanding social change."

"To protect their money."

"From the same lawlessness they used to earn their fortunes. Putin ordered the oligarchs to report to him regularly. As penalties for inappropriate behavior, he would demand certain businesses be sold from time to time. Otherwise he told them they could keep their gains if they paid their taxes, gave back to the community, and stayed out of politics."

"And what if they didn't?"

Obon grunted. "Let me put it this way. There's an old Russian joke. Stalin's ghost appears in a dream to Putin. He asks advice on how to lead the country. Stalin says, 'Round up and shoot all the democrats, then paint the interior of the Kremlin blue.' Putin frowns and says, 'Why blue?' Stalin smiles. 'Ah,' he says. 'I knew you wouldn't have a problem with the first part.'"

"I read that Simeonovich is close to Putin. Like Abramovich."

"That's why he's been a beneficiary of some of the forced sales. He's a Cossack. He loves Russia. He invested hundreds of millions to improve living standards in Siberia. And Putin has a soft spot for him for this reason. "

"If you were me, would you trust him?"

"You're doing a job for him. It's he that must trust you. Still, he's not the worst of the lot. I'd put more faith in his word than Ivan Valentin's, that's for sure."

"What did you find out?"

"An *apparatchik*. An agent of the Soviet apparatus. A lifetime communist bureaucrat. Born in 1940 in Kotelniki outside Moscow. Went to college at the Branch Kotelniki University of Nature. Got his start coordinating schedules for sanitation runs in Kootenai in 1967. Graduated to running the entire sanitation department in 1974. Promoted to second-in-command in Moscow in 1979. Credited with introducing the garbage compactor to the Soviet Union. Became head of sanitation in Moscow in 1981 and guest lecturer at Moscow University on the same topic. Moved to the Ministry of Atomic Energy in 1985 and became a member of the Ecology Committee. That was his post when the Soviet Union dissolved."

"Atomic Energy? A sanitation worker?"

"He was in charge of nuclear waste disposal at Krasnoyarsk. A plutonium production site. Still a repository today for over a million and a half liquid curies of nuclear waste buried several hundred meters deep. They supply the local population with water out of storage tanks buried right next to the nuclear waste."

"Nuclear waste?" Nadia's ears perked up. No place had more nuclear waste than Chornobyl, Ukraine, where her uncle lived and Bobby visited. "Where is Krasnoyarsk?"

"Siberia."

"Siberia." Chornobyl, however, was a long way from Siberia. "His timber company is in Siberia."

"A classic case of an old red director getting an inside deal in the loan for shares scheme."

"But where would he have gotten the cash for the loan?"

"From his friends. Other *apparatchiks*. They're all part of one cabal or another. He married twice. Divorced the first wife. One child. Ivan, born 1981. Moved to London in 1999 but kept homes near Krasnoyarsk and in Moscow. First wife died a few years ago during a trip back to Russia. No record of the cause of death."

"But he was never posted in Ukraine."

"No. But as a member of the Ecology Committee he was in charge of the clean-up of the Chornobyl nuclear plant disaster."

Chills shimmied down Nadia's spine. "Do you know if he travelled to Chornobyl?"

"That level of detail wouldn't be found in the Politburo archives. You'd have to go to Kyiv and search the Central State Historical Archives yourself."

Memories of her week in Kyiv flitted in and out of her mind. "I may do just that."

CHAPTER 23

Lauren sat across from her boss, Richie Glass, in the Italian restaurant's rustic dining room. The spices from the Tuscan steak exploded on Lauren's tongue. The red wine tasted like the nectar of the gods. The kind and merciful gods. The ones who watched over her in jail cells in Big Diomede, Magadan, and Moscow. The ones who delivered her alive and in good health back home to Connecticut.

"When you said you were taking me to Toscana on a Monday night for early dinner I was touched," she said. "I thought you'd be furious. I was afraid you'd fire me as soon as I walked in today."

Richie lowered the glass from his lips. "Don't be ridiculous. You know I respect you too much to do that."

"I'm halfway there, Richie. He didn't grow up in Alaska. He's not from Kotzebue."

"Who?"

"Bobby Kungenook. Who else?"

"Oh, right. Then where's he from?"

"He entered the U.S. via Little Diomede Island and he crossed Big Diomede to get there."

"I thought you said he's not from Alaska."

"He's not. I didn't say he was from Diomede. I said he entered the country via Diomede. Because he was coming in from Russia."

"Russia?"

"Yes. He's fluent in Russian and Ukrainian. And he entered the country via Little Diomede. What's close to Little Diomede? Big Diomede. That's Russian soil. Beyond that? Siberia. I think he might be Russian."

"Russian? How did a kid named Bobby Kungenook end up in Russia?"

"I don't think Bobby Kungenook is his real name."

"Why not?"

"The real Bobby Kungenook vanished as a child. No one wants to talk about him. He doesn't feel real."

"What about his parents?"

"Supposed parents. They died eight years ago."

"Maybe that explains it. There's a big Russian influence in the Arctic Circle. Maybe he went to live with family in Russia. Or Ukraine. Or wherever."

"No. If that was the case there'd be nothing to hide. There'd be no reason for a cop to threaten my life in Kotzebue, or show up on Little Diomede and send me on a one-way trip to Russia."

"Right." A shadow of doubt passed over Richie's face. "Tell me how that supposedly went down again?"

Lauren told him about her experience on the snowmobile and how she ended up a Russian prisoner. She'd told it to the FBI agents so many times it didn't sound ridiculous to her anymore. She hadn't done anything wrong. She was the victim.

"And why was there alcohol on your breath?" he said.

"A woman forced me to have a drink with her."

"That's funny."

"Why is that funny?"

"You're not exactly the type who gets forced into doing anything she doesn't want to."

"She tricked me into thinking I was bonding with her," Lauren said. "It would have been rude to say no once she poured the shots."

"And your wallet? Your passport? Why would you leave those behind if you were going on a joyride on the Bering Strait?"

"It was not a joyride."

"So, you admit it. It was a calculated move. You did it on purpose."

"What?"

"I know you. You have poor self-control when you're obsessed with a story. You wanted to see what you'd find out on the Russian island so you decided to just show up, thinking you could convince them you were there by mistake, and that they'd let you go."

"That's bull. I did no such thing."

"Was the trip worth it?"

"Excuse me?"

"Did you learn anything from the Russians?"

Lauren leaned forward. "The officer that interrogated me on Big Diomede. His name was Krylov. He was an FBI type. He said there was a similar incident last year. Richie, he said it was a woman and a boy. A woman and a boy, Richie."

"My God. You did do it all on purpose."

"No. Richie . . ."

"And caused an international incident."

Lauren sat back. "No one said anything. There was nothing in any papers. There was nothing online. In America, or in Russia, last I heard."

"Just because it's not in the papers, doesn't mean it wasn't a disaster. For you, the Sports Network, the country."

"What do you mean, the country? I mean, I know some people had to waste a little time on me, but it didn't cost anything to get me back. It's not like there was a prisoner exchange or anything like that."

"Lauren, the Russians accused you of being a spy. Of using your journalistic credentials as a cover to get a look at Diomede. Did you know they relocated all their natives off the island to Siberia? Did you know Big Diomede is a military installation two miles from the border of its arch-enemy, the United States?"

"What do you mean it was a disaster for the country?"

"Remember the Russian spy they found in Manhattan? She went by the name Lana Channing."

"The hottie. She was on the cover of all the papers."

"Her real name was Lana Alexandrova Blin. She had a bunch of affairs, including one with the CEO of a conglomerate that controls a major defense contractor. There were concerns she had access to plans for advanced weapon development. Word is she's back in Russia. As part of a prisoner exchange."

"Oh shit."

"The Sports Network is in hoc to Washington for getting you out, baby. So you see, I'm afraid you crossed the line on this one. And I don't mean the International Date Line. By the way, what was that like, did you feel older when it happened? I sure hope so. Because you've given all of us a lot of gray hairs in the last few days."

"Richie, I'm sorry. I didn't do anything on purpose. I swear to you. But this is the story of a lifetime. I'm telling you. In the end it's going to be worth it."

"Are you kidding me? Some might-be hockey player is actually Ukrainian? Who cares?"

"No. It's more than that. It has something to do with this locket."

"Locket? What locket?"

"A locket that he kept around his neck. It fell off during a game and he stopped playing. He stopped playing. Who does that? I have the video on my computer. On my computer."

Richie looked disgusted. He turned and nodded at two heavyset guys at a table across the dining room. They stood up and approached.

Lauren had spotted them early on. They had looked familiar, like former football players, but she couldn't put names to their faces. Now she realized they weren't former football players. They were former cops turned private security guards. She'd seen them at the Network's headquarters before. To escort a volatile anchorman out of the building when he was fired.

"You didn't invite me to dinner for old time's sake," Lauren said. "You invited me here so I wouldn't make a scene in front of the others." A nail dug into her palm. Lauren realized she was gripping the steak knife with all her might.

Richie removed a folder from his briefcase. He placed it on the table beside her half-eaten tiramisu. "This is your termination agreement."

"You prick."

"It provides you with medical benefits and severance for twelve months. That's generous."

"I shouldn't be surprised you didn't fight for me. They say once you sleep with your boss, it's only a matter of time until you're fired. Especially if he's married."

"Fight for you? You still don't understand the magnitude of what you've done. The benefits and severance are contingent on your signing a confidentiality agreement. If you breach it, we will pursue any and all legal remedies." Richie leaned closer. His tongue darted between his lips. "Which means if you try to tarnish my reputation in any way, I'll make you wish you were still in a Russian prison cell."

Lauren remembered when she first met Richie. He dazzled her with charisma, romantic dinners, and five-star hotel rooms. Until he hired the next girl. "You mean your reputation for screwing the new girls?"

"You'd just finished law school and realized you didn't want to be a lawyer. I gave you your shot. I made you. And this is how you repay me? Go ahead. Call a presser. Say what you want. No one's going to listen. Your integrity is shot. Your career is over."

Richie stood up. "The boys will drive you home. Your personal possessions are in boxes in the trunk of their car. Have a nice life, sweetheart."

"You, too, Richie. Drive fast. And when you see those red lights at intersections, ignore them. They don't mean anything."

CHAPTER 24

JOHNNY WAITED FOR NADIA ON THE BENCH NEAR THE carousel in Central Park. His stomach turned with giddy anticipation as it always did when he was about to see her. This morning the sensation was even more intense. He'd arranged for a surprise visitor. He was due to arrive in fifteen minutes. If the visitor upset Nadia, Johnny would bear the blame. No matter, he told himself. Her safety mattered to him the most, and this visitor could help ensure it.

Nadia appeared on the hilltop first. Her eyes looked a bit worn but her expression was calm, her stride purposeful. When she got to the carousel, they hugged. He held her gently, like a lawyer and friend, and sat down. It was the exact same spot where they'd sat a year ago. Nadia had left for Kyiv the same day. She returned home with Bobby a month later. Johnny survived a mob interrogation on her behalf.

"Same bench," Nadia said.

"You noticed."

"I didn't know you were the superstitious type."

"Well . . ."

"Or sentimental."

"You don't know me at all."

"Really. For example."

"I have a surprise for you today."

"I don't like surprises."

"You're going to love this one. It's going to make your trip to Ukraine ten times more enjoyable. Did you try to see Bobby today?"

"Yes."

"And?"

"He refused."

Johnny shook his head. "Don't worry. I'm going to break through to him."

"But you haven't broken through yet. What makes you think he's going to start talking all of a sudden?"

"We have a lot in common. We both came from nothing. I'm establishing a rapport. Telling him stories about growing up on the docks. And then there's the trump card."

"What trump card?"

"Iryna. He's worried about her. When his worry turns to fear, he'll tell me everything that happened that night."

"How can you be so sure?"

"He's in love with her."

"No. I see that. How do you know his worry is going to turn into fear?"

"It's impossible to be in love and not be scared for the one you love."

Nadia opened a large envelope and removed a photograph. "This is a picture of Valentine's father. I don't have any reason to believe Bobby ever met him in Ukraine but I'd be curious about his reaction if you showed him the photo."

Johnny nodded. "He looks like a serious man." In the picture, Valentine's father wore a fancy gold ring with the number three carved from onyx. "Funny."

"What?"

"I've seen that ring before." Johnny opened his briefcase. "I got a large envelope from the district attorney this morning. Discovery. Not sure it's everything but it's a start. Take a look at this."

He pulled out a stack of pictures of the victim at the crime scene. In the top photo, the gash in Valentine's neck was so wide he was almost decapitated. Johnny leafed through the pictures until he found the one he was looking for. It was a close-up of Valentine's right hand. It was curled into a half-fist. A band of gold and onyx shone around his ring finger.

"It's the same ring," Nadia said.

"Either they both had one—"

"Or the father gave it to the son on his deathbed."

"I wonder what the number three stands for."

Nadia shrugged. "There was Natasha, the father, and the son. Not to be confused with the Holy Trinity."

"Who's Natasha?"

"Valentine's second wife."

"Was she wearing a ring?"

"Yeah, but it was a bit different. It had a diamond. The size of a golf ball. So what's this surprise?"

"I thought you hate surprises."

"I do. But it's a long flight and there aren't going to be any fun and games when I get there. Unless my billionaire oligarch client insists on taking me to dinner."

"Oh, yeah? What's he like? Does he expect people to bow before him?"

"No. Actually, he does the bowing. He's different. He seems nice, even caring. I like him. He has a presence about him. And twenty-five billion dollars doesn't hurt."

"Glad to hear it." Johnny hid his disappointment. "Your surprise just got here."

Nadia frowned.

Johnny nodded at the man standing over her shoulder. "You're going to have company on your trip."

"I am?"

Nadia's brother, Marko, gave her a bear hug from behind.

"Yes, you are, Nancy Drew," Marko said. "No way am I letting you go back there alone."

CHAPTER 25

After Nadia and Marko left for the airport, Johnny drove to Rikers Island. His meetings with Bobby reminded him of when he first became a criminal trial lawyer. The man who hired him, a gritty litigator renowned for his ability to sway a jury, made him practice his opening and closing arguments pertaining to his first case for hours. Johnny remembered delivering his arguments to an audience of one in similar confines but feeling as though he was talking to himself. His boss rarely interrupted him. But when he did, his words left a mark.

It was only a matter of time before Bobby talked, too, Johnny thought. And left his own mark.

"The preliminary hearing is in seven days," Johnny said. "The DA will probably offer a deal. The judge will encourage it. The system's overloaded. He'll try to save the State of New York the cost of a trial. Problem is, they have a confession and an eyewitness."

Johnny waited for some reaction but Bobby just sat there in his chair with his usual expression. Glum, bored, and arrogant, not giving a damn about anything Johnny had to say.

"Did you hear what I said? They have an eyewitness. Does that make sense to you? Did you see someone watching you?"

No reaction. None at all.

"You've got to help me, son. If you don't, they're going to lock you up and throw away the key. And I don't care how much you think she loves you now, Iryna is not going to sit around waiting for you to be released in the afterlife. She may be young, and she may be in love, but she isn't going to be stupid in love for the rest of her life."

Johnny thought that might get a rise out of the kid. It didn't. He kept his eyes on the floor.

"You seen her recently?" Johnny said. "How's she doing? I wonder what she's doing right now. I wonder if she's safe. Or if whoever caused you to stab Valentine is more of a threat to her than you realize. If you love someone, don't you want that person to know the risks she's facing every day?"

Bobby shifted his gaze to the wall. As his eyes passed Johnny, he looked through him, as though he wasn't even there. That type of detachment wasn't easy. Johnny knew from years of experience in the courtroom cross-examining witnesses and connecting with juries. The kid was creepy, the way he could disengage, but given what he'd endured as a child of Chornobyl, that probably shouldn't have been a surprise. People avoided him. Viewed him as a pariah. Adults and kids alike. Folks around Kyiv had an irrational fear of being contaminated with radiation poisoning, Nadia had said.

"Okay. I get it. You're not going to talk to me. Fine. Continue to be selfish. You know what's best. Your lawyer, the woman who brought you to America, your girlfriend—none of us matter. I still need you to do something for me, though."

Bobby didn't move.

"I need you to take a look at two pictures for me. You don't have to say anything if you don't want to. Obviously. But Nadia made me promise to have you look at them, and I don't want to catch shit from her for not doing what she asked. You know what I'm talking about where that's concerned, right?"

Bobby's lip curled upward.

"Cool." Johnny pulled out the picture of Valentine. "This is the victim after you finished stabbing him with your homemade screwdriver. Per your confession, that is."

At first Bobby didn't move. A few seconds later, he glanced at the photo through the corners of his eyes. No reaction.

"See how the right fist is half-closed? It looks as though he had his fingers curled against something. Like a knife. The knife you said he was carrying. But there was no knife at the crime scene. When you left Valentine, was he still holding the knife in his right hand?"

Bobby looked away. Johnny counted to ten to make sure he wasn't about to talk.

Johnny revealed the second photo, the one of Valentine's father. "What about this guy? He look familiar?"

Bobby glanced at the photo. A look of fear washed over his face. It came and went in a flash but it was unmistakable.

"Valentine's father," Johnny said. "Did you know him?"

Bobby's complexion darkened.

"Did your paths cross in Chornobyl? In Kyiv?"

Bobby turned away from Johnny.

Johnny repeated his questions. Bobby didn't respond.

Johnny put the photos away. He locked his briefcase and stood up to leave.

"We'll see what Nadia digs up. She's flying to Kyiv on business. While she's there, she's going to look into the old man's past."

Bobby sat up in his chair. "No. She can't do that."

Johnny stepped toward him. "Why, Bobby? Why can't she do that?"

"She just can't. She must not. She must not do that."

"Why?"

Bobby sprang to his feet. His cheeks swelled. "Because they'll kill her. You've got to stop her. Are you listening to me? You've got to stop her now."

"It's too late. She got on the plane after she called me."

Bobby collapsed into his chair. He didn't say anything more.

Outside the prison, Johnny called Nadia and left her a voice mail about what Bobby had said. She would hear it when she landed in Kyiv. Then he left Rikers Island, two of his predictions fulfilled. First, the kid had spoken and left his mark. Second, concern had turned to dread. A boy's past threatened a woman's life. Her predicament struck fear in a man's heart.

But it was Nadia, not Iryna, who was in danger. And it was Johnny who felt helpless.

CHAPTER 26

THE SCENE AT PASSPORT CONTROL AT TERMINAL F AT Boryspil Airport resembled a rugby scrum. Arriving passengers jockeyed for position among six lines. People argued in Russian and Ukrainian. Nadia had negotiated the scrum last year during her first visit to Kyiv. It took her two and a half hours to pass through immigration and find her baggage at another terminal.

She sliced her way between two lines to a desk surrounded by two columns. Grabbed two customs forms and turned to Marko. She had Johnny to thank or blame for Marko's company. She wasn't sure which word applied yet. He'd been her big brother when they were kids but as adults they'd grown apart. She worked as a financial analyst, he owned a strip club. More importantly in this situation, she prided herself on proper conduct while traveling in a professional capacity. She was concerned her brother wouldn't share that philosophy. Still, having him with her made her feel more secure. And two people could investigate faster than one.

She caught his eye and motioned toward an empty line without a border official. "That's us," she said.

Marko stood staring at the scrum. "This is a joke, man."

"Marko." She nodded toward the vacant line. "Move. Before someone else gets there first."

"That line's closed."

"It's VIP. It was recently added for government officials, dignitaries, and other important visitors."

Marko raised his eyebrows. "And?"

"You're underestimating your sister. Let's go."

He followed her toward the vacant line.

Nadia and Marko had spoken Ukrainian since childhood. In Nadia's experience, the choice of language defined a relationship. Switching to English would have felt awkward. Yet that's exactly what they'd agreed to do once they landed in Kyiv. It reduced the risk of eavesdropping. Now that they'd exchanged words in English for the first time in their lives, Nadia realized the experience wasn't as strange as she thought it would be. It was far worse. Changing languages removed intimacy. It was as though they'd have to get to know each other all over again.

The border officials wore pale green uniforms. They looked like relics from the Soviet era. Nadia had heard stories ad nauseam from her father about the KGB. For her, the uniforms echoed with the sounds of persecution, detention, and torture.

Nadia caught the attention of one of the officers. She gave him a set of VIP credentials, faxed to her by someone from the Orel Group. He studied them and called a supervisor over. The supervisor reviewed the documents. Meanwhile, Nadia and Marko filled out the forms she'd picked up from the desk.

The last time she'd entered the country she was asked a variety of intrusive questions, including her parents' birthplaces and her political affiliation. This time the border officials didn't ask any questions. Instead, the supervisor took the forms, stamped Nadia's and Marko's passports, and welcomed them to Ukraine.

Nadia and Marko collected their luggage and exited the baggage claim area. Nadia powered on her cell phone to see if she had voice mail. On the other side of the window, the taxi area looked like a bumper car racetrack.

"The taxis are ugly, too," Marko said. "I read they try to rip you off. Charge you three hundred *hryvnia* for a trip to Kyiv when you should be paying one-sixty. I may have to kick some ass."

"No. There will be no ass kicking in Kyiv. I'm here on business. Working for an important man. Your behavior will reflect on me, Marko. Please remember that."

"You always did take yourself too seriously. But don't worry. I won't embarrass you. At least not too much."

Nadia rolled her eyes. She'd feared having him along was a bad idea and now she was certain it was a mistake. She scanned the crowd of drivers holding signs. A meticulous woman in a corporate suit barged forward. She held a piece of white cardboard with Nadia's name printed on it in perfect font. Nadia walked over and introduced herself.

"On behalf of the Orel Group," she said in Russian, "Welcome to Ukraine. Your car is waiting outside."

Nadia glanced at Marko. Waited for gratitude or a compliment.

"Lucky for you they know who I am over here," he said.

Nadia rolled her eyes. On the way to the car, Nadia noticed she had a voice mail. She pressed the phone to her ear, turned the volume low, and listened to a message from Johnny.

"Bobby went ape-shit when I showed him old Valentine's picture," Johnny said. "Ape-shit. Said you should turn around and come back home immediately. Said your life is in danger. Call me as soon as you get there. I don't care what time it is."

She hung up. Marko looked at her, his eyes asking her what the call was about. She had updated him on the basics concerning Bobby's situation on the plane.

"Johnny," she said. "According to him, we're back on the Appalachian Trail."

Marko nodded. He understood immediately what she meant. Their lives had been in danger on the Appalachian Trail when she'd taken her Ukrainian Girl Scout survival test.

They sat in the back of a stretch limousine. The woman who greeted them slid beside the driver, a fresh-faced male equivalent.

"Evgeny was the finest driver on the Kyiv police force," the woman said. "Until the Orel Group hired him away. He is very fast, but very safe. We will have you at the Intercontinental in no time."

The driver guided the car out of the airport. The woman pointed out the bottles of spring water, vodka, and Scotch.

"First time in Ukraine?" she said.

"Not for me," Nadia said in Russian. She motioned toward Marko. "Yes for him."

"We were born in America but this is our parents' homeland," Marko said in Ukrainian. Unlike Nadia, he didn't speak Russian. Although some basic words sounded the same, it was impossible to have a deep conversation using both languages. "We were raised in a Ukrainian community. We went to kindergarten speaking only Ukrainian."

"Your language is amazing," the woman said, with a crude Ukrainian accent. To a Ukrainian-American, it sounded like ghetto. "Textbook Ukrainian. Like they speak in Lviv. In Western Ukraine."

"So let me ask you a question," Marko said.

The woman lifted her eyebrows. "Yes?"

"Why are you speaking Russian to me as though I'm in Moscow?"

Nadia kicked Marko in the shin. He'd always been a rabid Ukrainian nationalist within the American community. She understood he hated any sign of Russification but this was not the place to be demonstrative. He glared at her as though he had no choice but to make the comment.

The limo was so long the woman saw Nadia's kick. "No, Ms. Tesla," she said in Ukrainian. "It's a good question." Nadia had to give her credit. Russian was the woman's primary language but she was speaking the language common to everyone in the car. "It's a matter of history."

"History didn't make you speak Russian instead of Uke when you met us at the airport," Marko said. "What are you talking about?"

Nadia kicked him again.

"In the 1970s, the leaders of the Soviet Union implemented a program called 'Russification'," the woman said.

"By 'leaders of the Soviet Union' you mean the Russians," Marko said. "You mean that bastard Brezhnev."

"Marko," Nadia said.

"Yes," the woman said. "The Politburo and Leonid Brezhnev. The Ukrainian language was forbidden in universities. Pro-Ukrainians were called nationalists. They were persecuted, arrested, put in jail. It got to the point where Kyivans had two choices: send their kids to Russian-speaking schools and tow the line, or move out."

"Move where?" Marko said.

"Moscow."

"No way."

"There was more opportunity in Moscow for Ukrainians to speak Ukrainian than in Kyiv. By 1980, Russian was the only language spoken in Kyiv. Only since independence in 1991 has the Ukrainian language started making a comeback here."

"Thank God I waited until now to come here," Marko said.

"Yes," the woman said. "For your sake, I am also glad you waited." She turned forward, grabbed a clipboard, and started confirming tomorrow's itinerary with the driver.

Nadia glared at Marko. "You cannot be this way."

Marko appeared confused. "What way?"

"Sarcastic, argumentative, confrontational. In short, an asshole. You cannot be an asshole when you're a guest in someone else's country."

"Oh, come on. You know me."

"I'm here on business, Marko. I'm getting paid."

He sealed his lips and looked out the window.

The driver turned on the radio. Modern interpretations of traditional Ukrainian folk music started up. A crescent moon hung in the sky. The limousine glided along the tarmac. Green pastures and clusters of forest rolled by.

Memories from last year's trip flitted in and out of Nadia's mind. The search for Clementine Seelick, Bobby's aunt. Nadia's escape from her pursuers in the tunnels of the Caves Monastery on her hands and knees. And then, Chornobyl, the locket, and the escape with Bobby back to New York.

They crossed the bridge over the river Dnipro. Lights from Kyiv's skyscrapers illuminated the golden domes of its eleventh century churches and cathedrals.

When they got to the hotel, Nadia and Marko stepped out of the limo. The driver removed their luggage from the trunk. Two well-dressed young men were arguing about something.

"Evgeny will pick you up at nine a.m. to bring you to Orel Group offices," the woman said. "If that is convenient."

"Thank you," Nadia said, "but I need to get started earlier. I need to be there by seven a.m."

"Then he will pick you up at six forty-five a.m." She glanced at the driver to make sure he understood. He nodded politely.

One of the young men struck the other in the face. The injured one screamed. Brought his hands to his nose.

A bell captain and two hotel doormen came running.

"What happened here?" one of the doormen said.

The injured man removed his hands from his nose. They were covered with blood. It streamed down his face from his nose.

"This man punched me for no reason," the injured man said.

He pointed at Marko.

"What are you talking about?" Marko said.

"That's a lie," Nadia said.

She remembered her experience last year in Kyiv. Thugs pretended to be cops, planted dope on her, and tried to extort a bribe. This was a scam, too, she realized, but what was the angle?

Marko was going toe-to-toe with the assailant, threatening to stick his head in a blender for being a lying bitch. The driver and the woman were trying to back him up but there was too much screaming. It was chaos.

It was a diversion.

Nadia turned. Their luggage was gone.

"Our luggage," she said. "Our luggage is gone. It's a scam to get our luggage."

She looked left. Nothing. Glanced to the right. Nothing. She swore. Looked around again. Further out this time. She was vaguely aware the two miscreants were running away. Who cared. She needed her luggage.

There. Across the street. A third young man wheeled their luggage toward a taxi. One bag in each hand.

"Thief," Nadia said. "Stop him."

She sprinted toward him.

A rawboned man in a tan suit appeared from nowhere and blocked the thief's path. He didn't touch the kid. He simply spoke to him. Three sentences. Maybe four. Nadia couldn't hear what he said but the younger guy dropped the bags and ran away.

The rawboned man helped her retrieve their bags. Up close he appeared to be in his early fifties, with a military crew cut.

"Thank you," Nadia said in Ukrainian. When he frowned she repeated herself in Russian.

His peppercorn eyes twinkled. "You're welcome. I was in my car waiting for my wife." He pointed to a white BMW with black rims. "I saw the whole thing happen." He sounded quite pleased with himself. "You are a tourist?"

"Yes."

"Where are you from?"

"America."

"I love America." He turned serious and wagged his finger. "Just remember when you go back to America to spread the word. Not everyone in Ukraine is corrupt and criminal."

He returned to his car as Marko arrived, out of breath.

"He speak Russian or Uke?" Marko said. He waved to the good Samaritan, who smiled and waved back.

"Guess," Nadia said.

"Damn. I wanted to like him so bad."

CHAPTER 27

THE GENERAL WOKE UP EXCITED AND ENTHUSED. HE WAS expecting news about the Tesla woman this morning. What started out as a matter of honor was becoming an even more intriguing proposition.

After washing and dressing he took his breakfast in the study. He never ate breakfast with his wife. He had his butler deliver it to his study instead. If he were to eat breakfast with Asya, the layers of fat in her chin might hypnotize him. He might start counting them. By the time he was done it would be time for lunch. That was unacceptable, eating two meals back-to-back with no productive activity in between, even for a retired military hero.

What a cow she'd become, he thought. Once she turned fifty, her metabolism slowed and she shed all inhibitions about portion control. Divorce was allowed in the Orthodox Church and he owned a few judges. He could have dumped her for a nominal settlement years ago and married the ballet instructor. She was always making eyes at him and his Mercedes AMG, the one with the hand-built engine. But if he divorced, the other four remaining members of his hunting club, the Zaroff Seven, would have never looked at him the same. They were old-school Soviet boys. Appearances mattered. Screw the farmer's daughter—or son—if you had to, but for God's sake do it in private, and don't dissolve the marriage.

The General was realizing the truth more and more each day. He had no choice. There was only one way out, one course of action that would allow him to save face. He was going to have to kill her. But this would cause his grandchildren to cry at her funeral. He couldn't stomach the thought of seeing his grandchildren cry for any reason. And so he went on with the status quo, eating his buckwheat cereal with blueberries in his study every morning, surrounded by the trophies that hung on his wall. Bear, wolf, lynx, argali sheep, red stag, Caucasian tur, snow sheep, wild boar, Siberian tiger. The heads of every animal worth hunting within the boundaries of the former Soviet Union.

He finished his breakfast and tried to motivate himself to deal with the horror that awaited him in the other room. First however, the phone call that would deliver him good news.

It came at 9:05 a.m. Sevastopol time.

"You're five minutes late," the General said. "I hate tardiness." Saint Barbara knew that, and still he hadn't called on time.

The General's former protégé had been a colonel in the Russian army. The colonel had earned his nickname in the Chechen republic of Ichkeriya in 1999. Article 148 of the local criminal code forbid anal sex between people of any sexual persuasion. First and second time offenders were caned. Third-time offenders were beheaded or stoned to death. These local laws were against Russian law. When the colonel personally intervened to prevent a mute prostitute's murder, the General began to call him Saint Barbara, the patron saint of delivery from sudden death.

"Don't blame me," Saint Barbara said. "Blame the woman in front of me that ordered five lattes to go."

"You should have allowed yourself a larger margin for error. A great hunter allows for error."

Saint Barbara didn't answer but the General could picture him rolling his eyes on the other end of the line. Insolent child. But what was he expecting? Saint Barbara was only forty-nine. This younger generation was for shit. No wonder Russia was falling apart.

"Some punks tried to steal her luggage," Saint Barbara said. "I made an executive decision and stepped in. Otherwise she'd be wasting time replacing her things instead of getting on with her search."

The General paused to think. "I agree. And even worse, it would ruin her disposition. We can't have that. We need her to be happy. Optimistic. Until it's time for her to be realistic. Good decision."

"Thank you."

"She saw your face?"

"They both did."

"Both?"

"She's traveling with her brother."

The General thought about this development. "I'm not sure that's such a bad thing. That there are two of them now."

"I thought you might say that."

"And as for seeing your face, that doesn't matter. As long as you don't let her see it again. Until the time comes when it's the last face she sees."

"The brother's at the Central State Historical Archives this morning. And she's at Simeonovich's offices."

"Keep me informed."

The General hung up and rubbed his hands together. It was going to be a good day after all. Then he remembered his appointment. His semi-annual horror awaited him. And now he was ten minutes late. He cringed. They would make him suffer for being tardy, especially since he'd reamed them new assholes for keeping him waiting five minutes one time.

The General reached into his desk drawer and grabbed the only weapon that would work against the enemy he was about to face. Stormed out of his office determined to dispose of it within five minutes.

He walked down the hallways and burst into the grand living room. There they were. The liberals. Three of them, all women, none over the age of thirty-nine. Or so they said. Pride, Prejudice, and Prada.

"There you are, General," Pride said. She glanced at her watch. "We were beginning to worry your clock might have stopped."

The General bowed. "My apologies, lovely ladies of the Siberian Environmental Protection Committee. Some issues at one of my aluminum plants. Let's see if I can make it up to you. Look." He brandished his weapon and held it like a hatchet. "I've brought my checkbook."

CHAPTER 28

NADIA SCRUBBED BOOKS ALL MORNING. THE OREL GROUP'S acquisition target had some problems. Serious problems. Normally, this was good news. A forensic security analysis was similar to an IRS audit. The analyst needed to prove his worth, and this was best accomplished by finding something was wrong. The discovery of some minor accounting irregularities that didn't threaten the client's agenda secured victory for everyone. The analyst proved his worth and justified his fee.

Except in this case the irregularities weren't minor. Nadia's findings might deal a blow to Simeon Simeonovich's ambitions. Clients didn't react rationally to such news. Especially the rich and mercurial. Sometimes they blamed the person delivering it. They might not admit it to the analyst's face, but they might withhold a recommendation. A positive referral from one of the world's richest men could make her career. A negative one could kill it. Prospective clients would question the absence of one.

When she arrived in the morning, Simeonovich invited her to lunch at his favorite Kyiv restaurant, Spotykach. Nadia quickly looked it up online and found it was the top-rated Eastern European restaurant in town. An old-school Soviet brasserie serving gourmet Ukrainian food. Nadia had been eating Ukrainian food from the womb. The thought of a top chef producing a twist on *varenyky* whet her appetite. Once they got in his Bentley, however, he told the driver to take them to his private club in Podil. Nadia hid her disappointment. He offered no explanation. Instead he served as her tour guide.

Podil was the oldest section of Kyiv. A winding thoroughfare revealed monuments, castles, and cobblestone streets. He pointed out a section called *Zamkova Hora*, or Castle Hill. It was one of several parts of Ukraine known as *lysi hory*, or bald mountains, inexplicably bare peaks surrounded by dense forest. According to Ukrainian folk mythology, ravens, black eagles, and other paranormal creatures gathered at *Zamkova Hora* for their "Sabbath." Local satanic groups also gathered there to conduct their rituals since Ukraine proclaimed its independence in 1991. A special place for ritual sacrifice still stood.

Simeonovich also pointed out the funicular train that connected Podil to central Kyiv along a steep descent. Nadia didn't tell him she'd jumped onto the funicular to evade one of her pursuers last year. The porker beside her had reeked of garlic and the experience had increased her sympathy for sardines. But the chase electrified her. The funicular had given her a twenty minute lead on her pursuers.

Simeonovich escorted her to an art deco salon at the River Palace, a members-only casino. Geometric abstract art hung on the walls. A team of attractive waiters and waitresses provided impeccable service. Nadia had her heart set on Ukrainian food but none was available. She ordered the lake trout from the Carpathian Mountains instead. He ordered the lamb chops and a bottle of 2000 Château Lafit Rothschild from his personal wine cellar. He offered Nadia a selection of white wines but she passed. He tried the wine, deemed it satisfactory, and waited for the sommelier to decant it before asking about her analysis.

"I'm afraid it's not good," Nadia said.

"Why?"

"If you deconstruct the changes in cash, working capital, and receivables over the last five years, they don't jive with the changes in actual cash in the bank statements. There's slippage."

"Meaning?"

"Someone's tapping the bank account."

"Embezzlement?"

"Yes."

"Have you spoken to the chief financial officer about this?"

"His signature is at the bottom of the financial statements."

"It is, isn't it."

"You're not surprised."

Simeonovich didn't answer.

"Of course not," Nadia said. "Why would you be surprised if you knew it all along?"

He maintained his poker face.

"You wanted me to confirm what you already knew."

"Perhaps," he said.

"There's embezzlement. And yet you still paid an analyst to look at it. That means you want this company."

"Why do I want it?"

"The oil reserves have peaked. The natural gas reserves are unremarkable. But their shale gas reserves are huge. With current advances in horizontal drilling, if you can keep the environmentalists at bay about leakage rates and methane release, there could be massive upside."

"If the company was purchased at the right price."

"And if an independent securities analyst with a decent reputation—was that too pompous?" Nadia said.

"It was an understatement."

"Thank you. If an independent securities analyst with a good reputation confirms there are accounting issues, the stock price is going down. The price will be right."

"I hope so."

"All perfectly legal."

"To say the least. The existing shareholders should know what they own. But I didn't hire you to confirm what I already knew. I need you to go deeper to make sure there isn't anything else I'm missing."

"If the independent appraisals on the shale reserves were overstated—"

"The appraisals are fine. The shale is there. My team knows the fields inside out. I just need you to continue what you're doing."

"Okay. That's no problem. I have about a day's work left and I'm done. I was thinking about doing some sightseeing for a couple of days with my brother before going back to New York. I can work on the report on the train and at night. I can have it to you within three days."

"That will be fine. Where do you plan on going?"

The truth was they had no agenda yet. It depended on what Marko discovered at the archives. For all she knew they'd never have to leave Kyiv.

"We're not sure. I've always wanted to go to Odesa."

"Smells like petrol but has a wonderful sense of humor. Perhaps you'd like to borrow my plane. One of my men could fly you over. Another could act as your escort. It never hurts to have a local at your side in Ukraine. Especially a reliable one."

It was tempting, Nadia thought. A private plane and a guide would eliminate logistical concerns. But they would also compromise her privacy. She knew from last year's experience she couldn't afford to trust anyone.

"That's kind of you Mr. Simeonovich, but my brother and I can take care of ourselves. We like to rough it."

"Call me Simmy, please."

"How did you get your start in business, Simmy?"

"I bought my first factory in Siberia in 1994. It was a copper smelter. Russia was still wild back then. Capitalism was just taking hold. Many of the people who ran the old country felt they were entitled to own part of the new one. The laws were weak, and they didn't think those applied to them. They used intimidation to take over small businesses. This may be hard for an American to understand."

"Not an American with Ukrainian parents. If you told me the KGB and *apparatchiks* didn't intimidate to fill their pockets, that would surprise me."

"When I bought my smelter there were two other people in my company. A professor and another metals trader. We'd gone to university together. And we'd served in the army. So we knew how to protect ourselves. A man came by during the first month and made me an offer. I refused. From that day on we started sleeping at the smelter. One day I had to go overnight to Kharkiv to meet with a customer. When I came back the next day, both my friends were hanging by a rope from a chute."

"That is awful. Did you ever find the people responsible?"

"Finding is not the issue. I can find anyone I want. Patience and prudence are the issues. A man in my position has to be careful. An impulsive action can create a reaction from powerful people. Like I said, I prefer to fight war on economic terms. The guilty parties are known to me. When the time is right, I will see to it they pay with their fortunes."

"I'm sure you will."

A team of waiters arrived with their entrees.

"Are you sure I can't convince you to take my plane? I'd be more comfortable knowing one of my men was with you. American tourists tend to stand out, especially the ones who go around speaking fluent Ukrainian."

"We don't mind standing out. We *are* tourists."

Simmy smiled. "Then please keep my phone number handy. Just in case."

CHAPTER 29

L AUREN PLAYED MONOPOLY WITH HER MOTHER AND SISTER growing up. She had mixed feelings about the Monopoly man himself. She hated him when she won ten dollars for second place in a beauty contest. Who was supposed to be happy with second place? She loathed him when she had to pay for repairs on hotel-laded streets, and despised him when she had to pay each player fifty dollars because she'd been elected Chairman of the Board. What kind of nonsense was that? She was made CEO and she paid others? Clearly the folks at Hasbro had an ass-backward view of corporate America.

And yet when she got a Get Out of Jail Free card, the sight of the Monopoly man elated her. She loved that card. Tucking it under her side of the board, knowing it gave her flexibility. Under certain circumstances she might want to hide in jail. Let others land on houses and hotels and pay the rent. In other circumstances, she might want to get out quickly and attack.

Like now.

The man behind the front desk at the Duma bookstore on Seventh Street didn't resemble the Monopoly Man. He *was* the Monopoly Man. When Lauren crossed the street from St. George's Ukrainian Catholic Church and walked into his place of business on Wednesday morning, his glasses fogged up. Of course they did. She was wearing her Emma Peel outfit. A black cashmere turtleneck and black jeans that clung to her curves. Add a flip hairstyle and a perfect make-up job and she was a weather-controlling machine that no man could refuse.

"Are you Mr. Obon?" Lauren said.

Still staring at her torso, looking dazed. An affirmative noise escaped his lips.

"My name is Lauren Ross. I'm a reporter. I just met with Father Bernie across the street."

She was following up every possible lead on Bobby Kungenook. The story consumed her mornings, afternoons, and nights. Someone else in Nadia's circle of friends might know something about Bobby. A phone call to the priest had confirmed she was a member of his parish. A visit had produced a reference to her lifelong friend, the bookman.

Her words jolted him. "Reverend Bernard," he said. He followed up with a nod and a smile, as though he wanted her to know he wasn't trying to be a jerk.

"Yes. I'm sorry. Reverend Bernard. I was asking about a woman by the name of Nadia Tesla. He didn't know her well but said you might. He said you were the man to go to about all things Ukrainian in New York City."

Obon beamed. "I don't know about that. The reverend is too kind. I'm just a bookman."

He spoke with a heavy Eastern European accent but Lauren had no problems understanding him.

"Do you know a woman by the name of Nadia Tesla?" she said.

He brought a finger to his lips. "Hmm. Nadia Tesla. No. I don't think I know anyone by that name but let me think about it for a moment. A man reaches a certain age, there's so much information stored in his brain, it becomes confusing at times. And sometimes people use nicknames and we know them by another name. I have some rare books that need binding. Would you mind?"

They moved to a small table in the center of the store. A tall stack of old books without dust jackets rested atop it. Obon took a plastic cover from an open box and folded it around the binding of the first book.

"You're a reporter?" he said. "For what newspaper?"

"Not newspaper." This was the first time she was being asked about her credentials since she'd been fired. "I did work for a newspaper in college. No, television. I'm a reporter for a television network," she said.

"Oh," he said, disappointed. "I don't watch television. I have one. I used to watch it when the president talked to the country, but it doesn't get any channels anymore."

"You don't have cable?"

"Too expensive."

"You're right. It is."

"If you work for a television network, you must be a famous person. Perhaps I should have recognized you when you walked in."

"No, no—"

"If that is so I apologize. What television network do you work for?"

"The Sports Network."

Obon finished attaching the binding to the book and started a second pile. "Sports? Is this Nadia Tesla a sportsman?"

"A sportsman?"

Obon smiled and nodded. "Yes. A gymnast or an archer, perhaps."

"No, she's not that kind of sportsman."

"Then why are you looking for her?"

"I'm looking for her because I'm doing a story on a young hockey player from Fordham Prep School. His name is Bobby Kungenook. She's his guardian."

Obon stopped working. "Bobby Kungenook? Now that name I've heard before."

Lauren couldn't believe it. "You have?" She touched his shoulder. He deserved some Emma Peel for the mere suggestion he knew the kid. "How? Where? And why?"

He laughed. "That's too many questions at once for an old man." He turned pensive. "I'm not sure where I heard the name." He snapped his fingers. "No. I am sure. Yes I am. I was playing chess with an old friend in the park the other day when the name came up. But I can't remember how it came up."

"Think about it for a moment, please."

He immersed himself in thought. His breathing turned heavy, his face darkened, and he looked as though he was going to be sick. "I wish I could remember the particulars of the conversation," he said. "But I can't."

Lauren put her hand on his shoulder again. "It's okay, Mr. Obon. Thank you for trying. Who's your friend?"

He frowned. "Excuse me?"

"Your friend. The one you played chess with when Bobby Kungenook's name came up. I'd like to talk to him."

His face lit up. "Of course. That's a brilliant idea." He retrieved a pencil and some paper. "He's a wise old man. Made his money in the food business. People come to see him for advice on Sunday afternoon. I'm sure he'd love to meet you. He lives a few blocks away. This is his address."

Obon slid a piece of paper to Lauren.

"What's his name?" she said.

"Bodnar. His name is Victor Bodnar."

CHAPTER 30

O N WEDNESDAY MORNING, NADIA HIRED A HOTEL CAR TO
drive her to the city of Korosten, Bobby's hometown,
ninety-eight miles northwest of Kyiv. Nadia mentioned that she
was working on a sensitive business matter, feared being spotted
by a member of the financial press, and didn't want to exit via
the front door. Instead, she preferred the driver pick her up in
the hotel garage at 7:30 a.m.

She took an otherwise empty elevator directly to the garage.
An attendant was driving a car out as she walked in. No other
people in sight. There were only fifty-five parking spots. Forty-
eight of them were taken. She weaved through the lot and glanced
inside each vehicle. They were empty.

After the driver picked her up, Nadia dropped some papers
in the foot well of the adjacent rear seat. She ducked beneath the
front seats and hid from view as the car pulled onto the street.
Didn't rise for air until he'd made two turns. To her knowledge,
no one had seen her in the hotel or the garage. She had no tan-
gible reason to suspect someone was watching her but she assumed the worst. Last year her pursuers had planted a GPS
device in her bag at the airport. From then on, paranoia served
her well. If someone was watching the vehicles exiting the garage
an empty car had pulled out.

Bobby's hometown was an industrial city with a population of 66,000. It was famous for its potato pancake festival and its close proximity to Chornobyl. After the nuclear disaster on April 26, 1986, Korosten was declared a zone of voluntary evacuation.

Nadia had debated the prudence of going there. On the one hand, she knew little about Bobby's background. Perhaps an inquiry would reveal some clue pertinent to his relationship with the Valentins. On the other hand, she didn't want to encourage anyone else to start asking questions. She didn't want to reveal herself.

Nadia decided to compromise. She would limit her inquiries to his school and the hockey coach who'd raised him. She would approach no one else. Furthermore, where the school was concerned, she would not reveal her true identity.

The driver dropped her off in front of Secondary School Number Four. Bobby had told her which school he'd attended, and Nadia had made an appointment with the administrator yesterday. She was a soft-spoken middle-aged woman named Hanna Figura. She sat behind a bare metal desk with a bouquet of wilting sunflowers. Nadia reminded herself they knew Bobby by his real name here. They knew him as Adam Tesla.

"What is your relation to Adam?" the administrator said.

"I'm his aunt." She was actually his cousin but they shared a long-running joke that she was his aunt. She liked the idea of being an aunt, she'd told him. Aunts possessed authority with minimum responsibility.

"From?"

"Canada."

Her eyes widened with surprise. She nodded. "I was going to guess western Ukraine. Or Poland. Not North America. Who taught you to speak?"

"My parents. The community in Toronto."

"You're an aunt on the mother's or father's side?"

"Father's side," Nadia said, sticking to the truth as much as possible. "Not that I ever met him. Or any other relatives in

Ukraine. That's why I'm here. I was researching my family tree. And it seems everyone's gone. Except perhaps Adam. That's why I was so disappointed when I called yesterday and you said he disappeared one day."

Hannah's smile vanished. "I called his guardian several times. He said the boy ran away. Vanished. I shouldn't be surprised, I guess."

"Why do you say that?"

"He's a child of Chornobyl. You know that, right?"

"No," Nadia said, feigning ignorance. "I don't know anything about him."

"Where to begin." Hanna took a deep breath and exhaled. "I only met his guardian once. A surly old brute who played on the Russian Olympic hockey team. He told me some things about Adam's parents." Hanna softened her voice. "Did you know Adam's father?"

"No," Nadia said. In fact, she'd met him last year a week before he died. "I heard stories, though."

"That he was . . ."

"A criminal. A thief. A con man."

Hanna appeared relieved she wasn't the one who'd had to use the words. "Adam never mentioned him. And the teachers knew not to ask about him. Some said he'd died. Others said he was in jail. But he must have ended up living off the grid in Chornobyl because that's where he met Adam's mother."

"Who was his mother?" Nadia said. She knew the answer.

Hanna shrugged. "Again, what I'm giving you came from his guardian and I only spoke to him once. According to him Adam's mother was an American woman who came to Russia to be a—how shall we say it—a professional hostess. The riches she was promised didn't come to fruition. Instead she became addicted to drugs, moved to Kyiv, and ended up servicing the men who worked on building the shelter in the Zone. The shelter is what they call the sarcophagus built around the reactor that exploded. I'm told the pay was high because one never knew if a man had been exposed to too much radiation."

"And my uncle was supposedly there at the time."

"That's what Adam's guardian told me. Of course gossip spreads in school. It always does. Adam was born in a hospital, here, in Korosten. But the children spread rumors that he was actually born in Chornobyl. That his mother is the only person to give birth to a child within the Zone of Exclusion. Even worse, they said he was born inside the sarcophagus. Behind his back they called him 'the boy from reactor four'."

"That doesn't surprise me." Nadia remembered being bullied during grade school for having a Russian-sounding name. Kids didn't care that she wasn't Russian, and that her parents had escaped the Iron Curtain. "Where is his mother now?"

"She died during childbirth."

That was consistent with what Nadia's uncle had told her last year.

"Once, in seventh grade," Hanna said, "a new student moved here from Zhytomyr. I was parking my car when I heard three boys telling him about Adam. They warned him not to get close to Adam, that he could get infected if he touched him, or even breathed the air surrounding him. They said no girl would come within three meters of him, and that he was destined to live and die alone. Right at that moment, Adam walked by with his military knapsack filled with rocks, as he always did. And the kids started chanting 'Freak, freak, freak.' When I ran out from behind the partition blocking the cars from stray footballs and made myself visible, the new boy was already chanting with them."

"Wait. Why was his knapsack filled with rocks?"

"Training. To make his legs stronger. For hockey. The boy lived for hockey. It was his therapy. And his guardian—the brute. He had sadistic training methods."

Which worked, Nadia thought to herself. "Did Adam have any friends?"

"Just Eva."

"Eva?"

"His guardian's niece. They lived under the same roof. Eva was two years older. She suffered from a thyroid affliction. It's a common genetic disease among children whose mothers had radiation syndrome. He followed her like a puppy dog. She never seemed to mind. Another loner. Black hair and purple lipstick. She dressed like a witch every day. They were kindred spirits. They had only each other."

This was the first Nadia had heard of a girl. "May I speak with her? Or did she graduate?"

"I'm afraid she passed away two years ago."

"That's awful."

"It broke her uncle's heart, too. Even brutes have feelings. He held on while Adam was still there, but once the boy disappeared loneliness got the better of him. He also died. About six months ago. Alcohol poisoning."

Nadia's spirits sank.

"I'm sorry to be the bearer of bad news," Hanna said.

"I was planning to pay him a visit next."

"At least I've saved you the trip."

"Is there anyone else I can speak to? Was Adam close to one of the teachers?"

"Adam wasn't close to anyone. He rarely said a word if he wasn't asked a direct question in class. The teachers developed a phobia for him, too. It's sad, but true. No one was confident there was no risk of contamination from touching him, breathing the same air as him, being in his vicinity. People understood it was nonsense intellectually but they had trouble accepting it psychologically. The truth is some of the teachers weren't keen on having him in their classes."

"Is there anything else you can tell me about him? Anything at all?"

Hanna wet her lips and glanced at the door to her office, as though making sure it was closed. "Well there was that rumor about Eva and him."

"What rumor?"

"That their guardian gambled and drank his pension away, and forced them to do something to supplement the family income."

Nadia cringed. Prepared to hear something hideous. "What did he force them to do?"

"Steal from the dead."

Nadia frowned. "What does that mean, steal from the dead? Rob graves?"

"That is what a teacher told me. She heard Eva utter the phrase to Adam in the hallway. Once. Only once. I demanded an explanation from Adam but he denied Eva ever said it."

A wave of relief washed over Nadia. She'd feared the hockey coach—as Adam called him—had forced the kids to do something even more unsavory for money. Digging up a grave sounded illegal and immoral, but there were worse things.

"They must have been desperate," Nadia said.

Hanna nodded. "People go to their graves with the craziest things. Rings, watches—I had an aunt who asked to be buried with her money in case the houses on the beach are cheaper on the other side."

"Problem is," Nadia said, "I'm not sure it's a capitalist system on the other side. And even if it is there are no guarantees for anyone but the rich."

Hanna smiled wearily. "Tell me about it."

Nadia thanked her and left. She climbed into the car and asked the driver to take her back to Kyiv. Along the way she pictured Adam and a young witch with purple lipstick breaking into a casket in search of gold.

To open the casket, they used a screwdriver. To see inside it, they shined a flashlight.

CHAPTER 31

A FTER SHE RETURNED TO THE HOTEL, NADIA WALKED TO the Saint Sophia Cathedral and waited for Marko at an outdoor café. She'd convinced Marko to come straight to the café after he was done with his work at the Central State Historical Archives. No sightseeing. No pops at a bar that struck his fancy. No attempts to pick up the first Ukrainian temptress willing to talk to him.

In Kyiv, Nadia's father was never far from her mind. He died when she was thirteen, when the thought of a free Ukraine was preposterous. If he could see her sitting outside Saint Sophia in his homeland, the country liberated, he would have died and gone right back to heaven. He'd taken an active role among Ukrainian-Americans, a community of immigrants that believed it was their responsibility to keep Ukrainian culture alive in the free world during Soviet oppression.

It was her father who took her on the Appalachian Trail at age twelve, to the precise spot where Connecticut, Massachusetts, and New York met. There, compass in hand, he pruned two branches to create a circle of light on a bed of pine needles. Told her to sit down in the light. Asked her if she understood she was the luckiest girl in the world to be living in the best place on Earth.

He explained what she already knew. That the Soviet Union was in the process of destroying all traces of Ukrainian culture. Its only sanctuary was the free world. Its only hope was the next generation. She was the future of Ukraine. To survive in America as an immigrant's daughter, she would have to be strong. She would have to be resilient.

And so he handed her a sleeping bag and a knapsack with three matches, food and water for one day, a mess kit, some rope, a compass, a poncho, and her twelve inch Bowie knife. He told her he was proud of her and certain she wouldn't disappoint him. He said he would return to pick her up in three days at that precise spot. Then he left.

Nadia had been a member of a Ukrainian youth group called PLAST. Summer camps occupied the middle ground between American scouting and ROTC training. Nadia had trained for the three-day survival test since age eight. She knew to find high ground. She knew how to build a lean-to. She knew how to start a fire, and she could boil water and set traps to catch small game. She knew how to defend herself even though she was only twelve. Three days and two nights alone on the Appalachian Trail should have been a routine exercise.

But, of course, it wasn't.

After a half hour wait, Marko cast a shadow in front of the cathedral. He was breathing heavily.

"Valentine visited the nuclear power plants at Chornobyl every year between 1985 and 1990," he said.

Valentine. Power plants. Chornobyl. 1985 to 1990.

The words sounded too good to be true. They provided a possible link between Valentine and Bobby.

"That's incredible," Nadia said. Then she remembered Marko was not a forensic securities analyst. "Are you sure?"

Marko sat down, took the napkin from under her coffee, and wiped his forehead. "The Ecology Committee had a bunch of sub-committees. One of them was the Chornobyl Nuclear Power

Plant Monitoring Committee. It was created in September, 1986 after reactor four exploded. The three guys on the Chornobyl Committee were the three youngest guys on the Ecology Committee."

"Because the old guys didn't want to get exposed."

"Who would? They put Valentine on the Chornobyl Committee as soon as he showed up. So we've established a connection between him and Chornobyl. We know he visited the area regularly. The only problem is that was 1985 through 1990. And Bobby wasn't born until 1996. So we're back at square one."

"Not necessarily," Nadia said. "The Ukrainian government took over sole management of the plants when it proclaimed independence. If you were assuming responsibility for a mess like that, and there were people with previous knowledge of the disaster, wouldn't you hire them as consultants? At a minimum they're a low cost insurance policy against missing valuable information."

"And if that's the case, Valentine might have kept making trips to Chornobyl for years."

"He might have done just that."

"How do we find out if he did?"

"We ask someone who's intimate with the Zone."

"The Zone?" Marko said.

"The Zone of Exclusion. No one's allowed within a nineteen mile radius of the reactors without permission."

"You know someone like that?"

Nadia remembered Karel, the botanist with Einstein hair who hit on her as soon as he saw her in the café near the nuclear power plant, only to reveal he knew exactly who she was and what she was doing in Chornobyl.

"I do," she said.

CHAPTER 32

L AUREN CLIMBED THE STAIRS ABOVE A CLOTHING BOUTIQUE named Cry Wolf and rang the doorbell. The door opened within five seconds, as though Victor Bodnar was expecting her. A strikingly handsome young guy with short blond hair let her in. He said hello with a thick Russian accent. As he closed the door behind her, his short sleeve inched up to reveal part of a tattoo. A girl with snakes for hair. Poor guy, Lauren thought. Still in his early twenties but he already held the opposite sex in low regard.

"Please allow me to escort you to the kitchen," he said. "Mr. Bodnar will visit guests in his kitchen."

He bowed, turned, and led the way. As though that wasn't weird enough, when they walked past the living room on the right, she spotted his clone reading one of those soft-core men's magazines with some actress on the cover. They were identical twins. Had to be. And to top things off, the twin stood when he saw Lauren and gave her his own little bow.

"Good morning, madam," he said.

Not gay, she thought. Just super polite. A little odd, but there was nothing wrong with that. Lauren had a healthy respect for eccentricity.

The kitchen looked like an insane asylum for a chef. It was entirely white, with linoleum and appliances from the 1980s. Not a speck of dust or dirt. Toaster, microwave, and cookies jars perfectly centered and standing at attention.

The kid pulled the chair out for her at a small circular table. Lauren thanked him and sat down, put her bag on the adjacent chair. Who would have thought? One Russian kid had more manners than all the men at the Sports Network combined.

She heard footsteps. Coming rapidly down some stairs. Too fast and too many to belong to one person.

A tuxedo cat appeared in the kitchen. Tail up. It studied Lauren. Her mother had been a cat rescuer. Never fewer than two in the house. Lauren slid her chair out and patted her legs. The cat trotted forward and jumped onto her lap. It arched its back to accept Lauren's pets.

"Damian, leave the young lady alone."

Lauren twitched. The cat flew off her lap.

A short old man stood in the doorway. He was dressed in vintage immigrant tweed. He was unremarkable in every way. And in that way, he was remarkable. He seemed as though he could blend with air. There was something relaxing about him. Lauren felt immediately at ease.

He introduced himself as Victor Bodnar.

"Vodka?" he said. He reached into a pantry and pulled out a bottle and two glasses.

"No," Lauren said. "The last time I had a shot things didn't turn out so well for me."

The creases in his face deepened. Lauren feared she was insulting him, but too bad. She'd learned her lesson on Little Diomede Island.

His disappointment vanished as though he could read her thoughts. "A wise move," he said. "Drinking in the morning is never a good thing. But sometimes an old man needs a little encouragement to get through the day."

He poured himself a shot and raised the glass in her direction. "*Na Zdorovya.*" He knocked it back, and sat down across the table from Lauren.

"Mr. Obon said you once mentioned a boy named Bobby Kungenook to him," Lauren said. "I'm a reporter—"

"Obon says nice things about you. I love young people. So nice to meet a new one. Tell me some things about yourself first. Indulge an old man, please."

Lauren took a breath. She sensed if she refused she wouldn't get anywhere. "What would you like to know?"

"Where were you born?"

"Hawaii."

"What is your father's given name?"

"Remy."

"Where was he born?"

"Mississippi."

"Do you have any brothers or sisters?"

"I have a sister."

"When you were a child, did you play with dolls or other girls?"

"Neither. I didn't have any friends. Or dolls."

His eyes narrowed to slits. "Whose voice from childhood do you miss the most?"

Lauren didn't know why she was answering him honestly except that there was something compelling about him. And therapeutic about the moment. "My mother," she said, her voice cracking.

"And where is your mother now?"

"She's gone."

Victor nodded sympathetically. "And if I offered you a clear conscience or ten million dollars, which would you choose?"

Lauren remembered getting the phone call from her father on her mother's last day. He hadn't been home the night before. Another starlet, no doubt. He told Lauren her mother wasn't answering her phone. When Lauren called her mother a minute later, there was still no answer. She should have left the house immediately.

"That depends," she said.

"On what?"

"If a clear conscience means I get my mother back."

Victor held her eyes with his for a moment. Then he reached out and patted her on the arm.

The buzzer to the door sounded. Victor turned his head to listen. Footsteps from the living room to the front door. A deadbolt slid open. More footsteps. People walking into the apartment. More than one person. One of the twins said something in Russian or Ukrainian, but no one answered.

Victor fixed his collar. He stood up and took a deep breath, as though preparing for something that might tax his constitution.

"Forgive me, please," he said. "I forgot I had an appointment. Stay right there. This won't take long." He started out of the kitchen and stopped. "Sometimes I'm asked to help resolve disagreements in the community. Two guests have arrived. Enterprising types. They've asked for my help to resolve a business dispute. Why don't you come to my courtroom as an observer?"

"Courtroom?"

"Yes," Victor said, as though there were nothing peculiar about his calling a room a courtroom. "You might find it interesting."

The reporter in Lauren asserted herself. She was up even before she said yes. A voice inside her told her to be cautious, but the reporter within her silenced it. If Victor Bodnar resolved disputes in the community, he might be the type of man who knew everything about everyone. Including Bobby Kungenook. If that was the case, her best course of action was to flatter and play along with him. She grabbed her oversized bag from the floor.

"I don't allow bags in the courtroom," Victor said. "Everyone must follow that rule, I'm afraid."

"Why?"

"Because I don't have an X-ray scanner or a metal detector."

Lauren waited for him to laugh, chuckle or grin to show he was kidding. He didn't do any of those things. Instead he stared at her bag and waited. Lauren lifted her wallet and computer out of her bag.

"The wallet, yes," Victor said. "The computer, I'm afraid not. No cell phones, no electronic devices of any kind. I can assure you your computer will be safe inside this kitchen. There are only my nephews here. I trust them with my life."

No phones or electronic devices, Lauren thought. The parties to this dispute were starting to pique her interest. Lauren slipped the computer back in the bag.

Victor eyed the purse. "If you give me your word there is no weapon or tape recorder, I won't insult you by asking to look inside."

She was the one who chuckled. Popped the purse open and unzipped the change compartment. Tilted it toward Victor so he could see inside.

He grimaced, as though mortified she was being subjected to such scrutiny, and threw his right hand up in disgust for good measure. But he still snuck a look inside.

"This way to the courtroom," he said.

He turned and headed up a narrow flight of L-shaped stairs. Lauren followed. Victor's earlier words resonated. He called the two parties to the dispute "enterprising types." His obsession about recording devices suggested something sensitive was going to be discussed. His concern about security meant the visitors to his courtroom could get violent. Probably had been violent in the past.

What if by "enterprising types" he meant criminals? What if she was walking into a mock courtroom where mob disputes were resolved? Obon said that Victor Bodnar made his fortune in the food business. He didn't look like any baker, farmer, or grocery store operator she'd ever seen. What was she walking into?

Not a nice little story. A great story, Lauren thought. One that could catapult her out of the sports section and onto the front page.

The stairs opened up to a second floor with a narrow corridor and three doors. She followed Victor into what she guessed was originally a bedroom. It contained a rectangular wooden table with two empty chairs on one side, and three chairs on the other. The parties to the dispute sat on the latter side with an empty chair between them. It looked like an imaginary boundary, a buffer to prevent an accidental elbow that might lead to fisticuffs.

Except the parties to the dispute were grandmothers in Sunday dresses. One wore white gloves, the other a black hat to match her dress. The one with the white gloves held a cane. The other wore a hearing aide. At first Lauren wondered if it was a joke. But then she studied the expressions on the women's faces and she knew that for them, it was no joke at all.

One of the nephews marched into the room. He stood beside Victor, who turned to Lauren.

"We must speak Ukrainian. But my nephew will translate for you."

Victor gave a speech. His nephew bent down on one knee and translated into Lauren's ear.

"We're here to settle an argument. One person has been harmed. The other person is accused. The wronged party is demanding compensation from the other for lost income. This is a courtroom. Verdicts are final. There is no appeal. Punishment if you don't follow the court's verdict will be quick and severe. Do both of you agree to be bound by this courtroom? The verdict and the sentencing?"

Both women nodded.

"Very well," Victor said. He stood up, moved to the other side of the table, and sat down in the empty chair between the two women facing Lauren. He grasped one woman's hand with his left, the other's with his right. "You both grew up in the same village in Ukraine. Together you've served the best hunter's stew in town in your little restaurant for over twenty years. How did it come this far?"

"She's a philistine," one said. "She wants to use cabbage instead of beetroot and add lemon to the borscht."

The other one bristled. "We get a customer asking for this every week."

"Who cares what the customer asks for? If he asked for turpentine in a glass, would you serve it? Only Russians use nothing but cabbage. Only Russians add lemon to their borscht. I will not serve Russian dishes in my restaurant."

And so it went on for ten minutes. Eventually Victor persuaded them to compromise on adding the Russian version of borscht to their specials.

"A good host is a humble host," Victor said. "He puts his guests' desires above his own. And a Ukrainian restaurant should maintain its purity. There's enough confusion about Ukraine and Russia."

Victor's nephew escorted the women out.

Lauren followed Victor back to the kitchen. She returned her wallet to her bag, which was exactly where she left it.

"That wasn't what I expected," she said. "Why the concern about security and electronic devices to resolve a dispute between two cooks?"

"Disputes in my courtroom involve all sorts of people. I found it best to keep a consistent set of rules and apply them to everyone. That way there's no risk of an unpleasant surprise. People aren't always who they seem to be. Now, what was this boy's name again? The one you asked Obon about?"

"Bobby Kungenook."

A light came on in his eyes. "Ah, yes. Bobby Kungenook. I remember that name."

"You know him?"

"No. My daughter does. She runs a bakery in Brighton Beach. Her protégé, a girl named Iryna, is dating him. Or was, at least. You know how kids are. And now that the boy's in jail—I must have mentioned it to Obon the next day."

"What is your daughter's name? Where exactly is her bakery?"

Lauren got the address for Tara's bakery.

"Have you seen his guardian, Nadia Tesla, recently?" Lauren said.

Victor frowned. "Who?"

Lauren studied him. He appeared genuinely confused. "Nadia Tesla."

"I'm sorry. I've never met anyone by that name."

Lauren grabbed her bag and thanked Victor for his hospitality and help.

Victor bowed. "Good luck."

"Don't worry. I'll find him."

"No. I meant with your conscience."

Lauren smiled and tried to ignore the comment. She didn't have time to wrestle with the past.

As she climbed down the steps to the street, the contents of her bag shifted to one side. She paused at the base of the stairs to adjust the position of her computer. When she reached in and grabbed it, the metal felt hot to her touch.

That made no sense, she thought. It hadn't been sitting in the sun and she hadn't used it for two hours. But it was hot.

Someone else must have turned it on.

Victor's other nephew. The one who'd been reading the men's magazine. He must have snuck in and turned it on.

Lauren raced to the Starbucks on Second Avenue. She bolted inside and booted up her computer. There was a way to check if someone had logged on recently. There had to be. But she had no idea how to do it.

Lauren logged in. She asked herself why anyone would want to hack into her computer. Her address book, she thought. It contained passwords for certain websites but they were coded in a manner only she would understand. Is that what Victor Bodnar was after? Were the nephews identity thieves? She had nothing else valuable on her computer. Nothing of any great personal meaning. Nothing of any professional interest to anyone—

Except for the video.

She searched for the video clip of the first time she saw Bobby Kungenook play hockey. It started when an opponent checked him hard into the boards. Bobby fell. But instead of getting up and rushing back to prevent a goal, he paused to pick something up off the ice. A locket tied to a necklace that had come loose from around his neck. Right away Lauren was certain there was something special about that locket.

She didn't know how to figure out if someone had accessed her computer, but she knew how to tell if someone had opened a file. She let the cursor hover over the file containing the video clip and right-clicked the mouse. Scrolled down to "get info" and clicked again.

The file had been opened eleven minutes ago.

Lauren slammed the laptop shut. Didn't bother to log out. Didn't bother to power down. Just sat there stunned. How did Victor Bodnar know to look for the video? Obviously he didn't. But the minute she showed up asking questions about Bobby Kungenook, Victor made sure one of his nephews got a look at her computer. The video was easy to find. Lauren had labeled it "B.K. Hockey."

She took three deep breaths. A simple exercise her mother had taught her. Her mother had used it to fight stage fright. And camera fright. And husband fright. Her mother. How she wished she was here with her now.

The conclusion was simple. Victor Bodnar was connected to Bobby Kungenook.

Lauren stored her computer back in the bag. She hurried back to First Avenue along St. Mark's Place. Tucked her body behind the corner of the block. If Victor came out of his apartment halfway down the block, she'd see him. And she'd be able to pull back before he saw her.

She checked her watch. Seventeen minutes had elapsed since she'd left Victor's apartment. Barely enough time to watch the video clip, discuss it with his nephews, go to the john—old men were always going, weren't they?—and make his next move. The odds were in her favor he was still in the house. What if one of the nephews came out? She'd let him go, Lauren decided. Victor Bodnar was a man who got other people to do what he wanted them to do. If the video clip spurred him into action, he'd be making the move himself.

Lauren decided she would wait for him.

And see where he led.

CHAPTER 33

A CURTAIN SHIELDED THE LIGHT FROM THE KITCHEN WINDOW. Victor finished watching the video of the boy everyone called Bobby Kungenook for the third time.

"That's enough," he said. "I've seen all I need to see."

The Gun's fingers flew over the keyboard. A few seconds later he closed the electronic notebook.

It was amazing, Victor thought. The communists would have never had a chance if these gizmos existed in the days of the Soviet Union. They couldn't have deceived the population the way they did. Information would have travelled too easily.

"You were right all along," the Ammunition said.

"The locket must be money," the Gun said.

"Any idea what's in the locket that makes it so valuable?" the Ammunition said.

"What's inside the locket isn't what makes it valuable," Victor said. "There's nothing but a dream inside the locket."

"A dream?" the Ammunition said.

"Yes. A dream you are both living, though you probably don't even realize it. Forget about the contents of the locket. I have seen the contents of the locket. The money is not inside the locket. The money *may be* the locket."

"How can that be?" the Gun said. "Gold, platinum. It's not big enough for the metal to be worth that much."

"It doesn't look like a queen's treasure or an antique," the Ammunition said.

"The locket was supposed to contain a priceless formula," Victor said. "That I know because I was one of the men who chased it halfway around the world. That's what the boy's father told Nadia Tesla. It didn't. But I saw a piece of jewelry recently that made me think. What if it was somehow inscribed under the gold? What if the boy's father was actually telling the truth? What if there really is a formula? Two things we know for certain. First, his father was the greatest thief I ever knew. If there were a man capable of stealing such a treasure, he was the one. If there were a man devious enough to hide it in such a way, he was the one. Second, we need to acquire the locket."

"But where is it?" the Gun said.

"We know it's not in his apartment," the Ammunition said.

"Indeed," Victor said. "If it were yours, where would you keep it?"

The boys answered in unison and without hesitation. "Around my neck."

"Which means what?"

"It's in storage in prison," the Ammunition said.

Silence fell over the table for a moment. Victor allowed the boys to digest the implications of what had been said.

"We have to get it out of there," the Gun said.

The Ammunition said, "Which means we have to get him out of there."

Victor smiled. "And how are we going to do that?"

"We buy a few more cops," the Gun said.

The Ammunition frowned at him. "This is America. You may be able to buy your way out of some things but not a murder charge. Be serious." He turned to Victor. "No. We have to get him out the hard way."

"And what way is that?" Victor said.

A light flickered in the Gun's eyes. "The legal way," he said.

"We have to play chess," the Ammunition said.

Victor put his hands together slowly and clapped three times. "Bravo." He stood up and headed toward the closet.

"Why did you tell the reporter that Iryna is dating Bobby? Why would you risk letting her get close to Iryna?"

"It's public information. Iryna and Bobby are on this Facebook abomination together. I told Lauren Ross what she already knew, or was going to find out. By doing so, I won her trust. And his name is not Bobby Kungenook. He is Damian Tesla's son from Korosten. Born in Chornobyl to a prostitute from Alaska. His real name is Adam Tesla. He is Nadia Tesla's younger cousin."

Victor slipped into his light overcoat. It was made from virgin wool. He stole it from an American oil tycoon named Hammer in a hotel lobby in Kyiv forty-two years ago.

"Where are you going?" the Ammunition said.

Victor frowned. Just as they showed evidence of progressing, one of them asked a moronic question.

"Not me," Victor said. "We. We are going to offer the boy's lawyer our services, of course. How else are we going to get him out?"

CHAPTER 34

NADIA CALLED THE NATIONAL COMMISSION FOR RADIATION
Protection of Ukraine, identified herself as an American
journalist, and told them she'd met a scientist during a tour of
Chornobyl last year. All of that was true, except for the journalist
part. After being transferred to the right party, she was told Karel
Mak had been declared a prospective invalid by the Division of
Nervous Pathologies in Kyiv. It was responsible for monitoring
the health of people with injuries related to the nuclear fallout in
Chornobyl.

Another phone call revealed that his disability checks were
being sent to his last known address. An apartment in Lviv.
Nadia called the phone number on record but it had been dis-
connected. He wasn't listed in the Lviv phone book, either. Neither of these developments surprised Nadia, as many people in
Ukraine were disconnecting their landlines to save money and
relying on their cell phones for primary communication. Karel
had probably failed to update his telephone number with state
agencies. That wasn't a surprise either. He wanted to get checks,
not phone calls. Nadia decided that if monthly checks were
being sent to the address on record, odds were high he'd be
there. If corporate America had taught her anything it was to
follow the money.

Nadia and Marko left on the overnight train for Lviv at 10:15 p.m. The trip would take six hours. While Marko slept, Nadia thought about her father. He'd hailed from the western strip of Ukraine bordering Poland known as Galicia or *Halychyna*, derived from the name of the medieval city of *Halych*. Lviv was the unofficial capital of *Halychyna*, historically the epicenter of the nation's quest for independence. To listen to her father, this was the real Ukraine. People spoke Ukrainian, not Russian. Nationalist sentiment ran hot.

Now, on the train headed to Lviv, Nadia felt as though she was going home for the first time. A different home. Not her primary home. She was an American. This was her parents' home. It was the place that had shaped their souls.

Nadia ate a protein bar during the last half hour of the trip. They arrived in Lviv at 6:35 a.m., fought off the gypsy drivers, and took a licensed taxi from the train station to the Leopolis Hotel. Their rooms weren't ready but they checked in and stored their luggage, except for a small canvas bag Nadia had packed earlier. She tucked her purse beneath the clothes in the bag, too. A concierge recommended a breakfast place in the center of town. Nadia made sure it had outdoor seating. Afterward, Nadia and Marko sat in the lobby and studied a map like tourists.

She'd first noticed the bald man with the pointed chin on the train reading a woodworking magazine. He was sitting alone in the same car. The car was only half-full but he'd taken the seat adjacent to the lavatory so the entire cabin was in front of him. Who wanted to listen to the door opening and closing during the entire trip, and absorb the occasional smell that emanated from within? A spy, she thought. That's who.

And then when the taxi driver lifted their luggage out of their trunk, she caught his profile in a black Renault cruising past the Leopolis. He didn't have time to rent a car. That meant there were at least two of them. Each time she saw him Johnny's words rang in her ear.

Your life is in danger.

Nadia and Marko left the hotel and walked along a cobblestone street to Rynok Square in the center of town. Forty-four architectural masterpieces from various eras formed the square's perimeter. They'd survived centuries of wars and invasions. Their front doors looked like entrances to castles. Some of the mansions boasted elaborate carvings. One featured a row of intricately sculptured knights along its rooftop.

The air smelled of freshly ground beans. They found their restaurant, Kentavir, at 34 Rynok Square. It was a few minutes after 8:00 a.m., and the outdoor seating area was already half-full. The patrons spoke authentic Ukrainian.

Nadia and Marko chose a visible yet private table where no one could hear their conversation even though they were speaking English. They ordered omelets with buckwheat bread and homemade cherry preserves. Nadia asked for tea. Marko chose coffee. After they placed their orders, Nadia panned the crowd.

There he was. Alone. Wearing sunglasses now. And reading a newspaper. A server arrived at his table.

"Look at that waitress with the legs and the braided hair," Marko said. "You see a ring? You think she's single? I think she looked at me when she walked by."

"Focus, Marko. Please?"

Marko glared at her and took a deep breath. "Feels like home. *U-kra-yi-na.*"

"Yeah. Except at home I feel safe."

"I got your back, baby."

"And I've got yours. The problem is we both have to turn our backs to get anywhere."

"You think we're being followed?"

"Bobby told Johnny our lives are in danger. When a kid not talking decides to talk, you have to consider his words. And I don't think we're being followed. I know we are."

"No way. I've been keeping an eye out. I don't see anyone."
He started to turn.

"Don't look. Don't look."

Marko looked back at Nadia.

"I don't want him to know we've spotted him."

"You sure it's not your imagination?"

Nadia described the two times she'd seen him before and her plan.

"Even if you lose them," he said, "we'll have to go back to the hotel. Eventually they'll catch up with us."

"I don't care about that. I don't want them to follow me to Karel's apartment. I don't want them to know who or what we're looking for. And I don't want Karel put at risk."

"You're going to eat first, right?"

"No," Nadia said. "I ate on the train. He saw us order breakfast. It's only natural for him to let his guard down. He'll be more focused after we finish eating. Don't forget to get my bag. If no one else takes it first."

"You got it."

"We should put him even more at ease before I leave, though."

"What are you thinking?"

"Laughter."

"That might be tough. Neither of us has a sense of humor."

"Did you know Sherlock Holmes is the butt of many Russian jokes?"

Marko started to grin, then narrowed his eyes. "You serious?"

Nadia nodded. "Holmes and Watson pitch a tent and go camping. Holmes wakes Watson up in the middle of the night and says, 'Watson, what do you deduce from all the stars in the sky?' Watson says, 'It tells me there may be life beyond Earth.' Holmes says, 'Watson, you're an idiot. Someone stole our tent.'"

Marko shook his head and chuckled. Actually showed his teeth.

Nadia couldn't tell if she'd really made him laugh or not but she smiled nonetheless. She liked that one. "Ladies' room. Be right back."

She took her canvas bag and walked toward the front door to the restaurant. Not too slowly, not too quickly. Like any woman going to freshen up.

She swung the door open. A hostess greeted her without a smile.

"I'm sitting outside," Nadia said. "Which way to the bathroom?"

The hostess pointed to a corridor beyond the dining room.

Nadia marched into the ladies' room. It was empty. She locked herself in a stall. Slipped out of her blazer, skirt, and blouse. Took new clothes out of her canvas bag. Put on a sweater, jeans, and a light jacket. Wrapped a black scarf around her hair and put on her sunglasses. It was the same scarf she'd used to escape the Caves Monastery in Kyiv last year. She'd packed it as a precaution and for good luck. She grabbed her purse and stuffed the rest of the clothes in the canvas bag. Left the bag in the stall.

She walked out of the restroom and turned right, away from the front door. A tray clattered outside. A woman shrieked. Something crashed to the ground. Men shouted.

Marko had taken down the man with the pointed chin, she thought. Just as they'd planned.

Nadia burst through a door marked "Employees Only."

One cook stood poised over five omelets. Another hovered over ten pancakes. A server turned to Nadia. It was the same woman who'd taken their order. She showed no signs of recognizing Nadia.

"I can't go back out there," Nadia said. "My boyfriend said he's going to kill me. Is there a back door?"

Stunned faces. The server pointed to a door behind a stack of potato sacks.

Nadia hurried out of the restaurant. She emerged in an alley beside empty vegetable crates and a dumpster. A pile of ashes and a zillion cigarette butts. Even though she'd changed clothes, Nadia preferred not to be seen exiting the rear of the eatery. At least one man would be watching the back street. She was sure of it.

She cut right across an alley joining the adjacent buildings. The last building had a sign on the rear entrance. Central Square Hostel. A man was wheeling boxes from a laundry company inside. He paid no attention to Nadia.

She turned left down an access road for deliveries and emerged one block north and half a block east of where she'd been sitting. A quick glance left. A delivery van blocked her view. She craned her neck. Quickly snapped it back. The Renault was parked near the back of the restaurant, a block away.

Nadia marched in the opposite direction, north by northwest, block by block, without consulting her map. She only had to travel a mile to get to her destination. She knew from memory she was heading in the right direction. It didn't matter if she was off a block or two from the optimal course.

After ten minutes of walking, the neighborhood turned residential. Neoclassical apartment buildings lined one-way streets. Cars parked diagonally on one side of the road, bumpers pointed toward the curb. A smattering of pedestrians hurried to work. Nadia stopped near two mothers chatting beside a day care center to consult a map. There were no cars or pedestrians behind her. She was certain she'd lost both tails. She oriented herself and moved on.

She arrived on Yakova Rappaporta Street ten minutes later. A red-and-yellow brick castle with a silver dome towered over the other buildings. It looked like a mosque but contained etchings of the Star of David above some of its windows.

Yakova Rappaporta became Vilna Street. *Vilna* was the Ukrainian word for "free," as in freedom. Karel's apartment was located in a three-story stone building with a wrought iron balcony overlooking a grove of trees planted along the sidewalk. Blue and black graffiti marred the walls.

Nadia entered a foyer through a red wooden door. She found the name Karel Mak next to a buzzer for apartment #3B. She rang the buzzer several times. No one answered. She'd prepared for the possibility he wouldn't be home, or answer his doorbell if the visitor didn't have an appointment. Nadia rang the buzzer marked "office."

A cranky woman answered. "Who's there?"

"I'm looking for Karel Mak. I'm a friend of his."

"Impossible. Karel has no friends. Go away." The static died.

Nadia counted to ten. Pressed the buzzer again.

"Who's there?"

"I really am a friend of Karel's. I'm from America. I met him last year—"

"Impossible. Karel's never been to America. Go away." The static died again.

If the woman knew he'd never been to America, that meant they were friends. Nadia didn't wait this time. She pressed the buzzer three times in rapid succession.

"I'm calling the police," the woman said. Furious now.

"I didn't meet him in America. I met him in Chornobyl village."

A pause. Three seconds later a louder buzzer sounded. The door unlocked. Nadia walked into a foyer. A hallway led to apartments. A staircase led upstairs. There was no elevator.

A door opened down the hallway. A svelte old woman stepped out. She had sunken cheekbones and wary eyes. From a distance she looked middle-aged but up close she looked ancient. The lines in her face contrasted with her brown hair color.

She wiped her hands on an apron. "I'm making breakfast. Come, *kotyku*. Come."

Kotyku was the endearment Nadia's mother had used growing up. It meant "kitten." The sound of the word slowed Nadia's pulse.

She followed the woman to her apartment. A mezuzah was attached to the doorframe. Nadia had learned about it from her Jewish neighbors in New York City. It was a small case that contained a piece of parchment with a passage from the Torah. The mezuzah fulfilled the Biblical requirement to post the specified passage at the entry to one's home.

Nadia stepped inside. The woman closed the door. She turned and pointed a pistol at Nadia with both hands. They shook lightly.

"I survived the Lviv ghetto. I'll survive you. Now who are you and what do you want with my son?"

CHAPTER 35

THE GENERAL COULD BARELY CONTAIN HIS EUPHORIA. HE'D been waiting for this morning for a month since making arrangements for her arrival. He could tell from the website she was a temptress. A seductress. The man who had the privilege to hold her, use her, and possess her would realize new heights of pleasure. Of that he was certain.

His wife understood he had passions even age couldn't extinguish. He had to give her credit for that. At first she balked when he told her he was building an enormous studio behind their mansion. It would look hideous beside the English garden, she said. But then he explained the benefits of its creation. He would travel less often. He'd get satisfaction in his home as opposed to seeking recreation outside it. This was the type of compromise that prolonged marriages, he explained. He told her he was going to sound-proof the studio. That he would host visitors, on occasion. And that she should never step foot into that building if she valued her life.

When he told her precisely what he'd be doing in the studio she finally understood. Marriage was not his primary fulfillment. He could see the look of resignation in her eyes. The realization that his trips abroad had not been merely business, but the source of the joy that kept him alive. Alive, by God, like a man was supposed to feel.

The General sipped his coffee at the desk beside the king-sized bed in the studio. The bedroom flanked the living room which opened up into a small kitchen. A wall separated the living quarters from the rest of the studio which was comprised of a single ballroom.

He stepped into the ballroom, cup in hand. Two partitions formed a triangle against a side wall. She was there, waiting quietly for him, the way a good mistress should. He loved this moment. The sense of anticipation. Prolonging that moment of rapture when he first put his hands on her—

His cell phone rang.

He cursed it. Walked to the kitchen, put his cup down, and answered it.

"We lost her," Saint Barbara said.

The General heard the words but couldn't believe the message. "Sorry. Say again? I thought I heard you say you lost her. We must have a bad connection."

"You heard right," Saint Barbara said. "We lost her."

"Explain."

"They checked in to the Leopolis. Then they went to breakfast at Rynok Square. They ordered food. Shared a laugh. Then she went into the bathroom and never came out."

"What do you mean she never came out? Did your man check inside the bathroom?"

"He tried. But her brother collided with him. Made it look like an accident. By the time he checked the bathroom, she was gone."

The General ground his teeth. "Then if she was gone, obviously she came out the bathroom. Come on, man. You're smarter than this. Are you ill?"

"I didn't mean she never came out. I meant they never saw her come out. Not the man in the front. Or the man in the back."

"How can that be?"

"The man in the front found a bag in the bathroom. It had her clothes in it."

The General chuckled. "Smart girl. She keeps this up I may fall in love with her."

"What do you want me to do?"

"Don't panic. She was in Ukraine and Russia last year, yes?"

"That's what Border Control said."

"And there was a watch list on her passport when she was in Russia. Who put it on and then took it off?"

"The deputy minister of the interior."

"Call him. Tell him I said hello. See if you can trace her steps from the moment she landed in Kyiv last year. This time she didn't go anywhere except Simeonovich's office. Who else does she know in Ukraine? Whom did she meet with last year? Remember the urgency. She is the boy's guardian. The boy killed Valentin's son. She will pay. It is a matter of honor. Call me back in an hour." The General glanced at the partitioned area. "Make it two hours."

He hung up.

As a rule, the General shut his cell phone off whenever he was busy with the fulfillment of his dreams. This time, however, he kept it on. News of this Tesla woman was starting to qualify as such.

He marched to the side wall. Took a deep breath, pulled the partitions apart, and stepped back to eye his prize. He lost his breath.

She lay fully assembled on a table next to the carrying case in all her glory. The Nosler Model 48 Professional. Satin black composite stock. Match-grade stainless steel barrel. One piece steel-hinged floor plate. Magazine release in the trigger bow for fast reloading. In the trigger bow, he thought. How ingenious. How intoxicating.

The General lifted the rifle off the table and held it for the first time. 3.4 kilograms of pure ecstasy. Expensive, though. Three thousand American. But that was a good thing. Quality never came cheap except with tramps and traitors. The rifle was sub-moa, which meant he would be able to shoot a grouping of bullets approximately one inch apart at one hundred yards. To help him achieve that goal, the General had purchased some high end glass, a Schmidt and Bender scope. He caressed the barrel. He named all his rifles after women. He would call this one Nadia.

The ballroom featured curtains and a stage but it was actually a shooting range with proper ventilation and reinforced walls and roof. Seven stations faced seven targets. The General brought the rifle and carrying case to the center station. He doubled up on ear protection. First the plugs followed by the earmuffs.

He loaded the rifle, assumed a balanced shooting stance, and acquired the target. It was a hundred meters away.

The General fired. Afterward, he retrieved the paper target.

There was a hole in the woman's head.

CHAPTER 36

N ADIA STARED INTO THE BARREL OF THE GUN. THE WOMAN
was serious. The mere mention of a World War II ghetto gave
her instant credibility. She had witnessed horrors beyond Nadia's
comprehension. Who knew what she'd done to survive? Shooting
a stranger dead in broad daylight was unthinkable to most people. But to a mother with such a background who thought she
was protecting her son, not so much.

"My name is Nadia Tesla. I met Karel at the café outside the
power plant in Chornobyl last year. I told him I was a journalist
but he knew better. He knew I was there to see my uncle who'd
sent me a message to America that he had something valuable.
Something very valuable. Karel took me to see my uncle, and
then he showed me wolves."

"You say your name is Nadia Tesla? What did my son call
you? Did he call you Nadia? Or did he call you *Panna* Tesla?"
Panna, with a pause on the 'n,' was the Ukrainian word for Miss.
"I raised my Karel to be a gentleman. I'd like to know if I succeeded."

Nadia sensed it was a test. "He didn't call me by either of
those names. He called me Nadia-*Panya*."

She raised her chin and studied Nadia, as though for the first
time. "Oh. So you're that Nadia Tesla."

Nadia's father had used that line all the time. Nadia could see his lip curling up as he said it. She knew she was out of harm's way. It was a classic, old-school Ukrainian line that implied the given person was one of the good guys.

"Who are your parents? Where are they from?" Karel's mother said.

"My father was born in Bila Tserkva. My mother was born in Kyiv. They moved to Lviv when they were teenagers. Then they immigrated to America. My mother's retired. My father passed away when I was thirteen."

She waved the gun at Nadia. "What are their names, *kotyku*? Their names?"

"Maxim and Katerina."

She studied Nadia again. "Oh. Those Teslas." She turned and put the gun in a drawer.

Nadia didn't bother asking if Karel's mother knew her parents. She knew the answer was no. She'd asked their names to make sure they didn't stir a memory. A bad one, Nadia suspected.

"Is Karel here?" Nadia said.

"No. Karel is gone."

"Where did he go?"

"Have you had breakfast yet? When did you get into town?"

She insisted Nadia sit down at the kitchen table. For the second time since Bobby had been arrested, a woman with a gun served her tea. If there were a third time, Nadia was certain it wouldn't go so well.

Nadia explained that she'd flown to Kyiv on business, and come to Lviv to see her parents' adopted hometown.

Karel's mother poured water into cups. "What religion are you? Orthodox or Catholic?"

"Catholic." Nadia remembered the Mezuzah. "Why do you ask?"

"Because if you had said neither, that you are an atheist, that would have told me something about you."

"What would it have told you?"

"That you are like my son." She smiled. "He was born a Jew but became a scientist. He only believes in that which he can prove. Though he's searching. He's questing. He's trying to find a being higher than the equation."

She served tea with rugelach and poppy seed cake. Nadia started with the poppy seed cake. She could never resist it. This one had raisins and nuts and melted in her mouth. Nadia sensed that Karel's mother was as lonely as she was wary. Her best approach to find Karel was to continue the conversation and be sociable.

"I noticed the castle up the street with the star of David on it," Nadia said. "What is that building?"

"That was the Jewish hospital," she said. "It was dismantled in 1965. Now it's a tourist destination."

"Why was it dismantled?"

"Because it had fallen apart. It was no longer necessary after the war because the Jewish quarter ceased to exist."

"What do you mean, ceased to exist? You're still here, right?"

"Yes. I'm still here. In 1939 before the war, there were one hundred and twenty thousand Jews living in Lviv. In 1941 that number grew to two hundred and twenty thousand. Refugees from Western Poland. That was half the city's population. Today there are only two thousand of us left."

Nadia didn't know what to say. She knew what the Nazis had done. Everyone knew. But the Nazis had been gone for more than half a century.

"The first daily Yiddish newspaper in the world, the *Lemberger Toblat*, was published in Lviv in the nineteenth century, when it was under Austrian rule. Lviv was a center of Yiddish literature. Ukrainians and Jews who lived in Lviv got along very well. Until the cooperatives came."

"The cooperatives?"

"Ukrainian communities consisted mostly of farmers. Jewish communities consisted mostly of shopkeepers and moneylenders. When the farmers pooled their resources to buy and sell products without a middleman, it created tension. Many Jewish people lost their jobs."

"Did any of your family survive the war?" Nadia said.

"No. My parents were shipped to Belzec in May, 1942. That was four months after my only brother was hanged to death from the gallows the Nazis set up in the town square. He was part of the armed Jewish resistance. His last words were 'the sun still shines.' He was captured by the SS paramilitary death squad, who were assisted by the Ukrainian auxiliary police. Most Ukrainian kept to themselves during the war. But some didn't. That was the second of two major pogroms in Lviv. You know what a pogrom was?"

Nadia shook her head.

"A legal riot against Jews with the full support of the law."

"Horrible. How did you survive?"

"The resistance hid me. I was passed on from sanctuary to sanctuary until the war ended. The Nazis never found me. I was one of the lucky ones."

Nadia took a bite of rugelach and sipped her tea. "I need to find Karel. I need to ask him some questions about things that went on in a place I cannot talk about. It's a matter of life and death for someone I love."

"He went on a pilgrimage to Zarvanytsia."

Nadia had never heard of the place. She shook her head.

"It's a small village in Ternopil. It's known for its miracle-working icon of the Mother of God."

Nadia frowned. "But I thought he was—"

Karel's mother raised her eyebrows. "Jewish?"

"No. A scientist."

"He is. But as I said, he's searching for something more."

Nadia stood up and thanked her for her hospitality. She started toward the door.

"He said you might show up here some day, you know."

Nadia wheeled. "He did? When did he say that?"

"When he retired and moved here. About seven months ago. He'd bought the building years before in preparation for retirement."

"Why would he have thought that back then?" Nadia asked the question aloud, even though she was asking herself.

"Because he is Karel. His father was one of the scientists that worked on the Manhattan Project. He is a special boy. He sees the future."

CHAPTER 37

JOHNNY TANNER CLIMBED INTO THE ELEVATOR WITH HIS clients on the fourth floor of the Superior Court building in Elizabeth, New Jersey. It was only 9:15 a.m. but Wednesday was already turning out to be a good day.

He'd gotten the charges dismissed against the James brothers. Both in their forties, lifelong criminals. After a five-year stint in Mid-State, they'd given up crime and opened a car wash in Newark. But their probation officer demanded ten percent of their monthly gross. When they refused, she planted a kilo of heroin in their bedroom during a monthly home inspection. They were arrested. Johnny called the cops and shared his suspicions. They arranged for another client of his to wear a wire. When the probation officer demanded ten percent from that client, too, the cops arrested her. A judge released the James brothers this morning.

"That was the shit, Johnny," one of the brothers said.

"Free car wash for life," the other brother said. "Towel dry and tire shine still cost you á la carte, though. You know what I'm saying."

"No problem," Johnny said. "My tires always shine. No matter what the weather."

Outside, afternoon clouds hung low. The air smelled of exhaust. Pedestrians lollygagged past the Furniture King and the Bargain Man. They would scatter before night fell. This was a town where the police secured their cruisers' steering wheels with the Club. Anything could be stolen, anyone could be robbed at any time. That's why Johnny loved Elizabeth. The streets pulsated with their own heartbeat. They teemed with real people who had real problems. It was the place he loved to call home.

His next appointment was at Rikers Island with Bobby. If the day's momentum continued, the kid would explain why he thought Nadia's life was in trouble. He looked close to cracking. He hadn't said anything yesterday when Johnny visited, but he wasn't his cool self anymore. He'd fidgeted in his seat, taken deep breaths, and looked like a stick of Ukrainian dynamite ready to blow. All Johnny needed to do was figure out how to light the fuse.

Johnny walked two blocks to the lot where he parked his car. A vintage Monte Carlo SS. It was rude, crude, and could not be subdued. He passed an old Lincoln Town Car parked on the side of the street. The only reason he noticed it was because of the two blond twins sitting in the front seats. They eyeballed him the whole way. Didn't bother to hide their interest.

Johnny's guard shot up. Something was wrong. And then he saw him. Leaning against Johnny's Monte Carlo, sucking the last bit of nicotine out a cigarette, looking like the most harmless man in the Tri-State area.

Victor Bodnar.

Elder statesman. Thief. Murderer.

Johnny had met Victor when Nadia returned to New York with Bobby last year. So much for the good day, Johnny thought. Now he was the one with the real problem.

"Get off my car," Johnny said.

Victor stood up. The speed with which he followed the command shocked Johnny. It told him the old man wanted something from him. It told Johnny he had an edge in the conversation that would follow.

"I thought we had a deal," Johnny said. "I thought we were never going to see each other again. On this Earth, that is."

"You're mistaken," Victor said. "We never agreed to anything like that."

He spoke with a thick Russian accent. No, not Russian. Ukrainian. If Nadia had read his mind she would have smacked him for mixing up the two. Fortunately, she couldn't read his mind.

If only she could.

"No," Victor said. "Last we saw each other in the basement of the butcher's shop, you threatened me. And then you left."

Victor had killed his cousin from Ukraine and two of his bodyguards. Johnny hadn't witnessed the murders because he was tied up in the meat locker next door. But he'd heard the gunshots. Victor had freed Johnny on the condition of silence. Nadia had become involved with Victor because she'd inadvertently caused his art smuggling operation to be closed down by the FBI. That's how everything had started. Johnny remembered his last words to Victor. If any harm came to Nadia, he promised to find Victor and square it. Johnny had meant it. But now his words seemed inadequate, his vow of revenge meaningless.

He had to prevent any harm from coming to Nadia. He had to deal with any risk to her beforehand.

"I didn't threaten you," Johnny said. "I made you a promise."

"If a promise ends badly for the other person it's a threat."

"Really? Who cares? What do you want?"

"For things to end well for everyone."

"Come again?"

"For things to end well for everyone."

"We're having a bit of a language issue here. You're a philosopher. I'm a lawyer. I don't speak philosophical. You want to translate that into English?"

"I want to help you."

The twins appeared behind Johnny. He hadn't even heard the doors to the Town Car open, let alone close. Up close they looked a bit more mature than through the windshield. And tougher. Johnny could see it in their eyes. They looked unconcerned they might have to harm another human being to get what they wanted. Johnny knew that look. The James brothers wore it. It defined the most dangerous people in society. People that had a different set of morals, or none whatsoever.

"You want to help me." Johnny smiled. "*You* want to help *me*."

"Yes. Very much."

"With what?"

"Not what. Who. The boy in prison. The boy that calls himself Bobby Kungenook. I want to help him. And his surrogate mother."

The idea was so preposterous Johnny didn't know what to say. Except Victor wasn't laughing.

"Sure you do," Johnny said. "That's what thieves and killers do. Help widows and orphans."

Victor tossed his cigarette butt. The ember burned orange-red. He placed his toe over it and ground it into the asphalt. The flame died. "I'm not the same man you knew last year. I found out I have a daughter. And now a grandchild."

"Congratulations."

"I want to help the people who helped me."

"I remember you chasing Nadia and Bobby around the world. How exactly are they supposed to have helped you?"

"My cousin, Kirilo, chased them as well. Even before that he'd sent an assassin to kill me. The woman and the boy put me on an even playing field with him. The chase created the opportunity for me to tilt the field in my favor. I was able to eliminate him before he eliminated me."

"So you want to thank Nadia and Bobby by helping him? How?"

"By helping you get him out of prison."

Johnny laughed. "This keeps getting better. How exactly are you going to do that?"

"I have a contact inside the police department. He tells me there's an eyewitness. You will give me the name of this eyewitness and I will have a conversation with him. I will convince him to stop lying and tell the truth."

"You're out of your mind. I'm an officer of the court. I'm sworn to uphold the law. Are you even capable of understanding what that means?"

"I'm not going to convince a witness to lie. I'm going to make him understand he must tell the truth." Victor lowered his voice. "You and I both know this boy. We know his real name is not Bobby. We know how he got here. We know why he came here. There is no chance—I repeat, no chance—that he killed that man unless it was self-defense. Can we at least agree on that?"

Johnny didn't want to agree with him about anything. Anything. But on this question, he had no choice. "Yeah. We can agree on that."

"Good. And can we also agree that given Adam confessed to the crime, and he hasn't taken back the confession, there's no guarantee he's going to help himself? He's prepared to spend the rest of his life in prison."

Johnny thought it over. As much as he thought Bobby might crack any day there was no guarantee he would ever tell the truth. Johnny had no choice but to agree with the old bastard on that one, too. "Yeah. We can agree on that, too."

"Good. Now, how important is this boy to Nadia?"

Johnny remembered Nadia sitting on the edge of her seat during Bobby's hockey games, fists clenched.

Victor nodded before Johnny said anything. "Of course he is. And who is Nadia counting on to keep the boy out of prison for the rest of his life?"

Johnny imagined a guilty verdict. Bobby remanded into custody. The sentencing. Bobby being taken away in cuffs for good. He pictured Nadia crying. No, he thought. It would be worse. She wouldn't cry. Her eyes would water but no tears would flow. She'd keep her sorrow bottled up inside where it would gradually eat her up. Prevent her from experiencing joy. Reduce her life expectancy.

"The idea of me handing over a witness's name to you is a joke. It's a non-starter. So don't even go there again. But if your fair-haired protégés behind you here somehow acquired it, tell me again, what exactly would you do?"

Victor answered the question.

Afterward, Johnny drove to a diner three blocks away behind the Elizabeth train station. He ordered an iced tea and reviewed Bobby's case file. The twins came in a few minutes later. They ordered coffees and sat at the table beside him. Johnny went to use the men's room. He left the file open.

When Johnny came out of the men's room, the twins were gone.

Johnny drove to Rikers Island. He dwelled on the ethical implications of what he'd done. Once he arrived and started walking toward the prison, however, his thoughts turned to the true motive behind Victor Bodnar's actions. Johnny didn't believe the old man gave a damn about Nadia or Bobby. Sure. Maybe he'd mellowed. A child and a grandchild could change a man. But he had ulterior motives. He was a born thief. He had stolen all his life. That's who he was, and that's what he did.

If the ulterior motive required Bobby's safe release from prison, that meant the kid had something worth stealing. Something Victor couldn't locate without Bobby's help. That could be only one thing.

The locket.

Everyone thought it was worthless, but what if it wasn't?

CHAPTER 38

L AUREN FOLLOWED VICTOR BODNAR AND THE TWINS TO A
parking garage two blocks away from his apartment. As soon
as she saw them walk into the garage, she hailed a cab and waited
by the curb. Five minutes later the garage attendant pulled out
in a Lincoln Town Car. Victor handed him a tip. One of the
twins opened the back door for him, and they took off toward
the West Side.

Lauren told the driver to follow them. They took the Holland
Tunnel to Route 9 in New Jersey to Elizabeth. Not the portrait of
American urban serenity. Even the McDonalds had iron bars on
the windows. One of the twins jumped out at the entrance to one
of the courthouses. He came back out fifteen minutes later. They
circled around the guest parking lot and pulled up by the side of
the road across the street. When a formidable-looking guy in a
ponytail rounded the corner, Victor walked over to the Monte
Carlo.

At first she thought the twin was there to attend a hearing.
After all, one of them had hacked her computer. But when he
came back out she realized it was something else. The man with
the ponytail looked like an MMA fighter turned lawyer. He had
to be Victor's attorney. He walked a hundred yards before he

saw Victor. Lauren was seated in the cab the same distance in the opposite direction, wedged between two economy cars.

From her vantage point, Lauren couldn't deduce anything about the meeting. There was a moment when Victor made a big show of stomping out his cigarette, and another one when the twins came over, but other than that nothing noteworthy happened. Lauren wondered if the old man was the head of a criminal enterprise built around identity theft. Maybe there were criminal charges outstanding in his name, she thought.

Her gut told her to follow the lawyer. At a minimum he knew Victor Bodnar. He was another potential source of information. She knew where Victor lived. Her journalistic instincts told her it would be helpful to know more about the lawyer.

Her taxi followed his Monte Carlo out of New Jersey and into the Lincoln Tunnel. He drove aggressively. When he darted into the left lane, an SUV snuck behind him. It obscured the Monte Carlo.

"You're going to lose him," Lauren said.

The taxi driver didn't respond. He continued rolling along at the same pace in the right lane, speaking Arabic under his breath. He'd been having a phone conversation from the moment she'd gotten in the car.

"Hey." She tapped his seat back. "Are you listening to me?"

He twisted his neck toward her and gave her the thumbs up. Kept jabbering away the entire time. Meanwhile, the Monte Carlo was nowhere in sight.

Lauren slapped the seat back. "I'm paying to follow that Monte Carlo. If you lose him, you're not going to get paid. Do you understand English?"

The road twisted. Traffic slowed.

Half the taxi emerged into daylight. Traffic stopped. The Monte Carlo sat idling five cars ahead, three vehicles back from the red light.

"Yes, I speak English," the driver said, with a refined English accent. "I'm a graduate of the Massachusetts Institute of Technology."

Lauren slid back in her seat. Her hands left sweaty imprints on the driver's seat back.

The driver resumed his phone conversation in Arabic. The Monte Carlo turned onto a bridge headed for Rikers Island. Bobby Kungenook was being held at Rikers. The lawyer in the Monte Carlo could be *his* attorney.

"Don't go on that bridge," Lauren said. "Turn around. Turn around. Take me back to Manhattan."

The fare was up to sixty-three dollars.

Lauren booted her computer and used her USB modem to jump on the Internet. She dug up an old story on the *New York Post* from the day after Bobby was arrested. His attorney, Johnny Tanner, was quoted as having no comment for the press. Lauren searched for an attorney by that name, and found the law offices of Brian Nagle in Union. She opened the web page for attorney profiles. There was the handsome man with the ponytail.

Now she had two leads.

The boy's girlfriend and his lawyer.

CHAPTER 39

NADIA RENTED A SKODA SUPERB IN LVIV. NO CURRENCY arbitrage at the car rental. Costs were denominated in Euros, not *hryvnia*. The fee was the equivalent of $110 for the day. For $90 more, it came with a driver. But before she could close the deal, Marko pulled her aside.

"Waste of money," he said. "If there's one thing I can do, Nancy Drew, it's drive. You know that."

"I do know that," Nadia said. "But driving is not the only objective here."

"It's not?"

"No. Driving and not getting us arrested for speeding and then instigating a fight with the cops is."

She tried to push past him but he held her back. Glanced at the pale, fifty-something man who would be the driver.

"How can we trust this guy?"

"For all the people following us know, we're taking the train back to Kyiv or somewhere else. Even I didn't know which car rental place I was going to use until the last minute. They'll be following us. For sure. And we probably won't even know it. But the car's okay. Trust me."

"The supply is short."

Nadia glanced out the window. "I see plenty of cars."

"Not cars. Trust."

The Skoda reminded Nadia of a Volkswagen Passat but with more legroom. They drove two and a half hours south past fields and farmland. Wheat undulated in the afternoon breeze. Cows grazed. Farmers worked rusty tractors from the Soviet era. Nadia and Marko kept their eyes on the side view mirrors. Traffic thinned as they moved farther away from Lviv. They drove a two-mile stretch without seeing another vehicle. But Nadia was certain someone was back there.

A hundred miles later they arrived in Zarvanytsia. Population three hundred. Clusters of small homes perched on a hill. A village carved out of the forest sat below. Churches, shrines, and monuments comprised the village. A group of fifty tourists surrounded a shrine for the Blessed Virgin. Others wandered in and out of the churches.

The driver dropped them off near the entrance to the pilgrimage complex. Nadia and Marko marched toward the visitor's center across a stone promenade.

"His mother said he's staying here?" Marko said.

"Yeah. She said he was meeting a friend."

"She didn't give you a name?"

"Nope. She said she doesn't know the person's name. Or if it's a man or a woman. I got the sense she thought it was a woman he was keeping from her."

"A man keeping his girlfriend a secret from his mother? How old is he?"

"Late fifties, early sixties, my guess."

"Poor guy."

"The funny thing is, Karel's mother said this was typical of him. That he'd always been secretive."

Marko frowned. "Why is that funny?"

"Because as soon as I met him in the Chornobyl café he started confiding in me. He pulled me right in."

They walked through the central gates to the main building. A short woman with spiked hair greeted them with a scowl. Nadia asked her if she'd seen Karel today.

"I saw Karel yesterday," she said. "But not today." A fresh-faced nun sauntered by. "Sister. Have you seen Karel Mak today?"

The nun walked over to them. "I saw him yesterday at the early morning liturgy." She greeted Marko and Nadia and asked where they were from.

"New England," Marko answered.

"Karel likes to spend time in the churches," the nun said. "I'm on my way to the main church. Why don't you walk with me? I can orient you."

They followed the nun across the promenade toward a gleaming white church. Four copper cupolas surrounded one golden one. The church stood elevated above a courtyard that led to the promenade. It looked as much a castle as the churches in Kyiv. Nadia and Marko peeked inside. Nadia looked around for Karel. She didn't find him.

The nun insisted on showing them the shrine of the Virgin Mary. A black dome with gilded edges contrasted with a white sculpture. Water poured from the walls along the structure's base.

"The history of the village dates to the thirteenth century," the nun said. "In 1240 a monk was fleeing the Mongol invasion in Kyiv. He stopped to drink from this spring and pray to the Blessed Virgin. Then he fell asleep from exhaustion and saw the Mother of God. When he woke up he found the miracle-working icon in the village. He stayed and built a chapel. A duke later ordered the icon to be delivered to him. He was very sick. The monk refused. The duke came to the chapel instead. He prayed in front of the icon and was cured. In tribute, he built a church and a monastery here.

"The churches were destroyed and rebuilt through the centuries. When Stalin took over, he burned everything to the ground. He saved one church and turned it into a warehouse. Otherwise it was scorched earth. Ukrainian Catholic services were banned at the risk of death. But the villages hid the icon and spoke the liturgy on Sundays in their homes until 1991 when Ukraine was free again."

The nun crossed herself. Nadia followed suit though unsure why.

"Praise Jesus," the nun said. "And may God help you in all your endeavors."

She pointed out two other churches. One was the Church of the Annunciation and the other was the Holy Trinity. Then she bid them good-bye.

"What she doesn't tell you about is the thousands of people who've come here over the years and *not* been cured," Marko said.

He stepped forward to one of the holes in the shrine's foundation. Spring water streamed out. He rinsed his hands, cupped them together, and drank.

Nadia gave him an incredulous look. "Look at the nonbeliever."

"It's the smart move," he said. "I mean, what if I'm wrong and I'm missing out on a real magic potion of some kind?"

She shook her head. "Magic potion. Nice."

"You're next," Marko said. "Come on. This is the Uke version of Our Lady of Lourdes. It's a once in a lifetime chance. Hell, you must drink the water."

A tourist glared at Marko. You never knew who spoke English, she thought.

"Language," Nadia said, in a scolding tone. "Let's go. Forget the water. Let's check the other churches."

"'Forget the water,' she says. Nice. This from the former altar girl."

Church had been a sanctuary growing up. She'd been a believer. She'd loved kneeling in the pews. Prayer dissolved her angst. But through the years she'd lost her faith. It would have been a lie to say she didn't believe in God at all. No. She assigned a probability curve to it, like any good mathematician. As she matured, she subconsciously decided the odds God existed were low. Still, standing here in this holy place, she couldn't help but feel a stirring. She wasn't sure if it had something to do with faith itself, or the emotional sanctuary it had provided her in her youth.

When Marko gave up and started past her, Nadia stepped toward the spring. She let the water wash her fingers. Made sure Marko wasn't looking so he didn't get any satisfaction. Scooped some up to her lips.

The monk in the black robe came into her peripheral vision as soon as she went for the water. She wouldn't have thought twice about him except he darted out of sight. As though he regretted revealing himself.

Nadia caught up to Marko.

"We've got company," she said. "Shaved head. Blue eyes. Big guy. He's wearing a brown robe with a white braided belt. Can't possibly be a real monk."

"You sure?"

"What, that he's not really a monk?"

"No, that he's tailing us."

"Let's find out."

They checked the other two churches. Nadia didn't see Karel in any of them. When they got to the last church, the smallest of the three, six tourists were studying the spare interior.

"Your turn to go out the back," she said to Marko.

Marko glanced toward the altar and the entrance to the sacristy, the room where priests kept vestments and vessels. Marched right down the center aisle, crossed himself three times Ukrainian Catholic style, and disappeared inside it. As though he were a priest going to get dressed. He moved with such confidence anyone who was watching would assume he belonged. Nadia kneeled in a pew and repeated three Our Fathers and Hail Mary's in Ukrainian to herself. It was her old ritual. The words rolled off her tongue effortlessly. Words she could never forget. Then she left the church.

She didn't see the monk outside. Nadia walked back toward the pilgrimage center. She passed a group of thirty tourists snapping pictures of the main church. One of the tourists held a camera at the ready. It boasted a massive telephoto lens.

Nadia stopped and burst into a smile. "Hi," she said.

The man with the camera turned. Nadia stared into the lens. It provided a wide angle reflection. Nadia spied the monk thirty paces behind her.

"Oh, excuse me," Nadia said. "You look like someone I know."

She ambled toward the Pilgrimage Center. Climbed some steps, made her way around a balcony that faced the Strypa River.

Trees hugged the creek. Clusters of people admired the view. The sound of rushing water drowned out their voices. Nadia moved to the far end of the balcony. She stood, took a look at her watch, and waited.

The monk wandered in seventeen minutes later, hands folded over his chest as though he was reflecting. Nadia looked away. She could still see his eyes in her peripheral vision. He scanned the balcony, found her, and focused on the river. He didn't seem surprised when a monsignor in a black cassock with red trim walked up and put his arm around him. Once he saw it was Marko, however, his expression morphed into one of shock and fear.

By the time Nadia walked over, they'd already exchanged quiet words.

"He says he really is a monk," Marko said. "And if you listen to him, I think you'll agree."

"I'm with the Basilian Fathers in Krekhiv," the monk said. "I'm a friend of Karel's. I heard you ask for him in the Pilgrimage Center."

His effeminate delivery stunned Nadia. It was a complete contrast to his rugged appearance. Up close, Nadia realized he wasn't rugged. His build was deceptive. He was tall and wide but his face was soft.

"Where is Karel?" Nadia said.

"Gone. On another pilgrimage. He left yesterday afternoon."

Marko, arm still around the monk's shoulder. "Where to?"

"The Priest's Grotto."

"The Priest's Grotto?" Nadia said. "Where's that?"

"It's near the village of Strilkivtsi. About a hundred kilometers south of here."

"What's so special about it?" Marko said.

"It's one of the longest gypsum caves in the world. It's a special place with a special history. He wanted to experience it. The fear. The suffering. The courage."

"How long is he going to stay in these caves?"

"Three days."

"How can someone find him if he's needed?"

"There are several main rooms in the caves. Any experienced guide will know them. He's staying there."

Marko and Nadia exchanged a knowing glance. She nodded. He patted the monk's shoulder and removed his arm.

"Who are you?" the monk said.

Nadia introduced Marko and herself.

The monk's eyes shone with recognition. "I know all about you."

"You do?" Nadia said.

"Yes. You're a journalist. You met him in Chornobyl village when you were doing research for an American newspaper."

"That's right," she said. That was the cover she'd used. Either Karel didn't tell him the truth or the monk didn't want to admit he knew who she was. "And what's your name?"

"My name is Yuri Salak."

Marko and Nadia asked him more about the Priest's Grotto. Nadia got the phone number for the Basilican Monastery in Krekhiv in case she needed to speak with him again. Afterward, Nadia and Marko started back toward the rental car where the driver was waiting.

"We have to get back to the hotel and find a guide," she said.

"Hey," Marko said.

Nadia turned. Marko hadn't moved.

"Aren't you forgetting something?" He pinched the cassock.

"Oh. Right." She'd forgotten he was wearing it. The disguise gave him anonymity, credibility and access, especially in a religious country such as Ukraine.

"I can tell what you're thinking," he said. "Tempting, isn't it?"

"What's that?"

"Monsignor Tesla. No one messes with a priest."

Nadia cringed. "Have some respect for a holy site, would you? Let's put that back where you found it."

"You sure?"

Nadia headed back toward the church. "Yes, Monsignor. We have sinned enough already."

CHAPTER 40

THE TWINS INSISTED ON RENTING A FANCY CAR TO SEDUCE the witness to the murder. Something called a Porsche Panamera. At first Victor refused. They owned a Lincoln Town Car. The ultimate American limousine. They didn't need some German monstrosity, he told them. But the boys insisted. The Town Car was too old. It looked used. And it wasn't edgy enough. Edgy? Victor said. Edgy? He dreamed of introducing their necks to the knife-edge of his hand. The rental cost $799 for one day, plus tax. Almost $900. When Victor arrived at Ellis Island, he didn't have nine cents in his pocket. The world had gone mad.

Two years ago he wouldn't have cared about the money. But everything had changed. In Victor's mind, every penny belonged to Tara and his grandson. Every penny spent had to be justified. It had to pay for a necessary expense or produce a reasonable rate of return. The twins argued the locket offered the prospect of an exceedingly reasonable return. Victor agreed.

The Gun wore a black suit and tie and aviator sunglasses that made it less obvious his twin was in the back seat. He drove. The Ammunition had bought a new blue suit. He wore a white shirt open at the collar underneath it. Flashed a knock-off gold Rolex around his wrist. He sat in the back beside Victor, adjusting his collar.

"Hugo Boss," he said with a grin.

Victor grimaced. "Don't do that. Don't ever do that."

"Do what?"

"Refer to yourself as the boss."

"I wasn't. That's the designer's name. The one who made the suit."

"And why do you think he chose that name?"

"Because his mother gave it to him?"

"I sincerely doubt it. Even if she did he could have changed it."

"Then why did he choose it?"

"So the word 'boss' rolls off your tongue and you buy more of his suits."

"What's wrong with that?"

"You keep saying it, next thing you know people will believe it. Only two things can happen to a boss. He can be fired or he can be assassinated."

"That's a bit extreme, Victor. Isn't it?"

"No one ever plotted to kill the peasant."

"What about Stalin?"

Victor tried to find flaw in the remark. "Have I told you I don't like to be in the car with anyone smarter than me?"

"Besides, I don't think there's a designer named Hugo Peasant."

Victor grunted. "Insolent child." He could see the Gun smiling in the rear view mirror. He turned back to the Ammunition. "I can see the modest improvements in your chess game are going to your head. I'm going to have to start trying now."

The twins laughed, hurled polite insults, and challenged him to matches as soon as they took care of business. They were good kids, Victor thought. Supremely talented with the computer, physically capable, and more clever than he originally thought. He hoped circumstances didn't arise where they both had to meet a boss's inevitable fate.

They drove to the Bronx to pick up the part-time security guard, part-time actor. When they exited off the highway onto a street called Fordham Road, the name struck a chord. Victor noticed the campus of buildings. He realized how he knew the name. It was the boy. Adam Tesla. He went to a private school called Fordham. In the Bronx, no less. Victor saw the sign for Fordham University. The boy's prep school had to be nearby. Then he thought of his grandson, and wondered if Tara's boy would turn out to be a good student. Remembering his grandson made him think of Adam as a human being. For the first time ever Victor actually felt bad for the boy. He was not used to sentiment and the sensation unnerved him. Yet at the same time, it energized him. Yes, he wanted the locket, but murder? Someone was framing the boy. A good Ukrainian boy. That was just plain wrong.

They picked up the actor in front of a small, red-brick house on a street filled with similar homes. All the buildings looked the same in the Bronx. Like the former Soviet Union only the houses were pretty. The Ammunition stepped out of the car and left the rear door open. The actor was in his fifties. Beer, steak, and potato chips, Victor thought. He watched and listened as the Ammunition smiled and stuck out his hand.

"Peter Slava," the Ammunition said. "CEO, Carpathian Film Productions."

The actor said his name but a passing bus drowned it out. He made a big sweep with his right hand and then drove it into the Ammunition's. "Good to meet you, Pete."

They shook hands and got in the car. The Ammunition sat next to his brother. The actor climbed in the back beside Victor. His head grazed the car's ceiling and his body filled the seat.

The Ammunition turned. He glanced at the actor and opened his palm toward Victor. "I'd like you to meet the legendary Ukrainian film director, Andriy Shevchenko."

Shevchenko was the best Ukrainian soccer player in the world. The twins idolized him because he'd married a Milanese model and was best friends with Giorgio Armani. They'd begged Victor to use the name. Given Americans didn't know anything about soccer, and the actor didn't know the name ahead of time, he didn't see the harm.

Victor flashed his decaying yellow teeth, thinking they'd add gravitas to his vintage tweed suit. He stuck his hand out and nodded as though he didn't speak English.

The actor's eyes shone with desperation. He wanted the supposed role so badly, Victor thought. He had to hand it to the twins. They'd understood the man's ambition from his website. The twins had been able to become intimate with the man without meeting him.

The actor shook his hand. "It's a privilege, sir. A real privilege."

Victor spoke to the Ammunition in Ukrainian. He vowed to beat him in four moves this afternoon. Not five. Four.

The Ammunition kept a straight face. Nodded with understanding. "The director says you look familiar. He would like to know if maybe you met at Cannes last year? He was there with his old friend, Terrence Malick."

The actor's eyes widened, then he lowered his head and chuckled. "No. Only in my dreams. He must have mistook me for someone else. Please tell him I appreciate the audition. And for picking me up like this."

The Ammunition told Victor the actor was bigger than he appeared on the website. He reminded Victor he'd been a cop for a few years and that they'd have to be careful. Victor agreed, and randomly mentioned *Law and Order SVU* and *Blue Bloods* in English during their brief discussion.

The Ammunition turned back to the actor. "The Director says to tell you he's seen your work on *Law and Order SVU* and *Blue Bloods*. Even though you only had a few lines of dialogue, he says you had presence. He has discovered several Ukrainian film stars in the prime of their careers this way. And no problem on the ride. He likes to get to know the stars of his films in a casual way. Like this. Off the set, you know?"

The Ammunition had called the actor two hours ago and e-mailed him pages from a make-believe script. Given him no time to check on anyone's background, not that it would have mattered. There was nothing on the computer about the Ukrainian film industry. The only thing he'd done to whet the actor's appetite was to plant a fictitious newspaper article online about Carpathian Film Productions's plans to produce a Ukrainian-American gangster film. The article mentioned co-producing partner Peter Slava had arrived in New York last week to begin casting. The Ukrainian actress Mila Kunis was rumored to be auditioning for the role of the loving daughter.

They drove to the Ukrainian butcher's shop on Second Avenue in the East Village.

When they got out of the car, the actor saw the store, smiled, and nodded.

"The director prefers to audition on the real set," the Ammunition said. "It leaves nothing to chance."

"Authenticity," the actor said. "I love it."

A butcher in a blood-stained apron came out and unlocked a pair of steel doors in the sidewalk. He opened them to reveal a narrow staircase leading to the basement. Victor led the way. The actor followed. After the twins descended, they guided the actor to the meat locker. Victor waited to make sure the butcher locked them in before joining the others.

Slabs of beef hung from hooks. Kielbasa dangled from the ceiling. The chill cleared Victor's sinuses. Puffs of steam formed at mouths and noses. The biggest one hovered near the actor. Of course it did, Victor thought. He was the most nervous.

A chair occupied a vacant space front and center. It was a special chair Victor had designed to his personal specifications twenty-five years ago. It was an exact replica of the one he'd experienced in the forced labor camp in Siberia, the *gulag*, whenever some of the grain in the kitchen went missing.

"The director will begin the audition immediately," the Ammunition said. "Time is of the essence. He has an appointment in an hour with the Ukrainian-American actress Vera Farmiga. She's reading for the part of the psychotic daughter."

The actor closed his eyes and took three deep breaths. "Ready," he said.

"We will save the script for later," the Ammunition said. He snatched the sheet of paper from the surprised actor's hands. "The director likes to start with a little improvisation."

"Improv?"

"Yes. There's no substitute for it. Instead of the part of the mobster interrogating the liar, you will play the liar. The director calls it role reversal."

The actor blinked as though trying to catch up. "I get it. To help me associate myself with the other side." He smiled. "So I can understand the liar's mentality."

"Exactly. It's important you understand what it means to be a liar."

"I get it. I can do that."

The Ammunition motioned toward the chair with an open palm. "To sit here, please," he said.

The actor sat down. Fidgeted until he was comfortable. Rotated his neck in a circle to loosen up. "Bring it on," he said.

The Gun approached the chair from the left.

"To make the scene authentic," the Ammunition said, "the director prefers to use the same props he uses during the shoot."

"What props?" the actor said.

"Please put your hands on the armrests and your feet against the legs."

The actor appeared confused but obeyed. Of course he obeyed. A man who dreamed of seeing his name in lights would do anything.

The Gun slammed the left armrest. A steel cuff sprang from beneath. It wrapped around the actor's wrist and secured it to the chair. The Gun kicked the chair's leg. A leg iron snapped around his ankle. The Ammunition did the same on the right side.

Shock flashed in the actor's eyes.

The Ammunition touched his shoulder. "Not too tight, are they? We can loosen them if you want."

The actor started to answer.

"Action," Victor said in Ukrainian.

The Ammunition repeated the word in English.

The actor closed his mouth.

The Ammunition circled to the back of the chair. Leaned into the actor's ear. "Did you really think you would get away with it?"

The actor frowned. "Get away with what?"

"The murder."

"What murder?"

"The murder of the businessman."

Confusion washed over the actor's face. He wasn't half bad, Victor thought.

"What businessman?" the actor said.

Victor stepped forward. "The British businessman," he said. "The man who went by the name of Jonathan Valentine."

"You speak English—" The actor grimaced. "Damn. Sorry. I didn't know you spoke English. That caught me off guard. Can we take it from the top?"

"No need to," Victor said. "We can pick up where we left off."

The actor nodded. "Where was that again?"

"The British businessman in the Meatpacking District," Victor said. "Jonathan Valentine. Why did you kill him?"

The actor blanched. Recognition shone in his eyes. "Who . . . who are you?" he said.

Victor remained mute. The actor was the witness to the killing. The twins had gotten his name from Johnny Tanner's file. Victor had no reason to suspect the witness was the murderer. But the suggestion flowed with the script. It elevated the stakes and served notice to the man he was in trouble.

The actor glanced from Victor to the twins and back to Victor. He tried to stand. The shackles clattered. He snapped his wrists. The cuffs restrained him.

"You're no director," he said.

"But you really are an actor," Victor said. "You seemed like a good man a minute ago. But now you will tell us the truth, won't you?"

"Screw you, asshole. Who are you?"

"It doesn't matter who I am. What matters is what your motive was for killing Valentine. And why you accused an innocent boy of something you did."

"Innocent boy. Right." Fury mixed with laughter. "Do you have any idea who you're messing with, Trotsky? I'm an ex-cop. Did you know that? Do you know how much trouble you're in?"

"You should look at your wrists and ankles again."

"Listen, asshole. If you hurt me in any way, that's witness tampering. Any judge is going to see that."

"I'm not going to hurt you in any way. Why would I want to hurt you? I need you in perfect condition when you walk into the police station in one hour and tell them the truth about how and why you killed Valentine."

"I killed him?" The actor sounded and looked sincerely appalled. "That's a joke, right?" He raised his chin. "I'll make you a deal. Stop this now and I'll let this slide. I don't know who you are, maybe you're the boy's grandfather. Or godfather. I can respect that. Uncuff me and we'll call it a day."

Victor smiled. "You don't play chess, do you?"

The actor frowned. "What?"

"Chess," Victor said. "You don't play, do you?"

"You're kidding me, right?"

"Chess is to life as integrity is to a policeman. It helps you make the right decisions before you need to make them."

The actor stared at Victor. "You made more sense when you were speaking Russian. And I couldn't understand a word you were saying then."

"Why did you kill Valentine? Why did you accuse the boy? Tell me now and I will spare you the worst possible agony a man can know."

The actor laughed. "That's funny. You agreed you can't hurt me or it'll be obvious someone tampered with me. And then you told me yourself you'd never do me no harm. So you see, that threat doesn't carry much weight. You got no play here."

"My play is in your wallet," Victor said.

"Excuse me?"

"You will speak the truth in exchange for the safe return of the contents of your wallet."

"I hate to break it to you, but in case you didn't notice, I'm no Rockefeller. I got two credit cards, one's maxed out, and about forty-three bucks in my pocket."

"It's not a matter of money."

"Oh no? What then? The ten dollar cowhide?"

"No. The picture I am certain I'll find inside it."

The Gun reached into the actor's front pant pocket for his wallet. He struggled to pull it out. The actor appeared stunned, as though processing the implications of Victor's statement and realizing he couldn't contemplate it. The Gun handed Victor the wallet.

Victor searched the compartments until he found what he was looking for. A picture of two teenagers. A boy and a girl. The girl had her arm around a third person who'd been cut out of the picture. The mother. Another American divorce.

"Keri and Tommy," Victor said. "Did I get the names right?"

The actor strained to free himself. "Don't even think of touching my family."

"I'm not going to touch your family," Victor said.

The Gun showed the actor a computer that looked like a child's sketching toy. He played videos of the actor's two children leaving school an hour ago.

"The men who took those videos will," Victor said. "And there will be nothing you can do about it. Because it's going to happen before you get home unless you go to the police immediately and tell them exactly what happened. If you place a phone call, try to alert a friend, do not comply with my demands in any way, you will never see your children alive again."

The actor exercised his ego. He spat, swore, and threatened. Victor let the words float by. The outburst was to be expected. When the actor exhausted himself, Victor let a moment of silence pass.

"Before you became a part-time security guard and a part-time actor," Victor said, "you were a policeman. A poor one, I'm told, but still you must have instincts. You know danger. I'm part of an international organization. I repeat. An international organization. Once you do what you need to do, your children will be safe as long as you forget this ever happened. Do we understand each other?"

The actor stared at Victor for a moment, and then nodded.

"Good. Why did you kill Valentine?"

"I didn't kill him. The boy did."

"In self-defense? Valentine attacked him?"

"I don't know how it started. How it went down. When I first laid eyes on them, the kid was stabbing the vic in the throat. Just like I told the cops."

Victor could sense when a man was lying. He'd been a liar and a thief his entire life. And he was certain the actor was telling the truth. At least on this point.

"So what did you lie about?" Victor said.

"What makes you so sure I lied?"

"Because I know the boy. And he wouldn't kill unless he was provoked. If you want to see your children again, you better tell me about the lie. The lie you told the police that might end up getting you in trouble."

The actor's eyes widened with surprise.

"Yes," Victor said, patting him on the shoulder. "I guessed. Of course I guessed. It was about money, wasn't it? Valentine was carrying something valuable and you took it. You had to have it, because you need the money. Part-time security guard. Part-time actor. Full-time financial misery."

The actor took a few breaths as though summoning his courage. He tried to speak but burst into a fit of coughing instead.

"Your throat is dry," Victor said. "That's to be expected. We can help you." He turned to the Gun. "Get this father of two a glass of water."

The Gun brought a glass of water. The actor drank half of it.

"The benefits of the truth aside, we may need to modify the script a bit after all," Victor said. "You may have seen Valentine attack the boy. The good news is you're obviously a fine actor. I'm sure you'll be convincing. Now, what did you steal from the dead man?"

CHAPTER 41

THE GENERAL PACED IN THE HOSPITAL WAITING ROOM. ALL these years he'd fantasized about being single again, free to bed whatever minx he wanted. Now, the thought of actually losing his wife horrified him. She was his constant companion. The woman who celebrated his successes as though they were her own and convinced him his failures meant nothing. She was the mother of his children. The queen of his manor. The only experience in life that fulfilled him as much as his wife's mere presence was the hunt.

The hairdresser said she'd called for an ambulance as soon as his wife began clutching her heart and wincing with pain. But the ambulance took ten minutes to arrive. Ten minutes. One thing was certain, the General thought. If his wife died, the men in that ambulance would die, too.

His cell phone rang.

"They went from their hotel to a car rental," Saint Barbara said. "As soon as they went in the office, our man bribed an attendant and made sure he put a GPS tracking device in the trunk of their car. From there they drove to Zarvanytsia."

"Zarvanytsia? For what, to pray?"

"Not sure. Our man had to keep his distance. By the time they got there, the woman and her brother had probably been there for ten minutes. Our man caught up with them as they were leaving the Pilgrimage Center. They went into a church together, and then left."

"Sounds like a typical tourist trip to the holy site."

"Except for one thing."

"What's that?"

"The brother went into the church wearing a priest's cassock. But he came out wearing his street clothes."

"He was dressed as a priest, you say?"

"Yes."

"Disguise?"

"I think so."

"Did our man see them talk to anyone?" he said.

"No. They went straight to the car."

"Then they must have talked to someone at the Pilgrimage Center. But why would the brother disguise himself as a priest?"

"So he could approach anyone without suspicion. No one would suspect a priest of having an ulterior motive."

"Where are they now?"

"Back at the hotel."

"They didn't check out. Good. That means she didn't find whatever or whoever she's looking for."

"We have a lead on who that might be."

"Speak."

"When she was here last year, she met a botanist in Chornobyl."

"How do you know this?"

"The deputy minister of the interior told me. A man by the name of Kirilo Andre needed help to find him."

"Kirilo Andre. I know that name. He was the lead investor on the Black Sea energy project. He vanished last year. His daughter inherited everything. What is this botanist's name?"

"Karel Mak."

"Let's see what we can find out about him. Maybe that's who she's trying to find. Maybe that's why she went to Lviv and Zarvanytsia."

"Maybe she already met with him."

"Then why didn't she check out of the hotel?"

"Good point. If we can get a step ahead of them I'm sure we'll be able to steer them where we need them to go."

"For your sake, I hope so."

A doctor entered the waiting room with a dour expression on his face. The General didn't bother telling Saint Barbara to keep him informed. He hung up.

"How is my wife, Doctor?"

"I'm sorry. We did everything possible."

The General staggered to a chair and collapsed. He'd gotten what he wished for, he thought. He'd lost his soul mate, his conscience, his link to normal society.

For years he'd thought he'd have mixed feelings. That he'd miss her but would also be secretly excited about the freedom that awaited him. But it wasn't so.

Instead, he sat in the chair and sobbed. His sole comfort was the knowledge that he still had one true passion to pursue. Fortunately, his friends from the Zaroff Seven had listened to his pleas and empowered him to be the one to deal with Nadia Tesla.

And make amends for the one that got away.

CHAPTER 42

NADIA SECURED THE SERVICES OF AN EXPERIENCED CAVE guide through the Leopolis Hotel. The concierge vouched for him. Still, Nadia insisted on interviewing him over the phone. He was a global explorer who'd done work for *National Geographic* on cave explorations across three continents. He had a website with pictures to prove it. In his mid-forties, Nadia thought, with the smile of a twenty-one-year-old. A purist. A dedicated outdoorsman with no visible connection to any private or government security service. The odds he was on the payroll of whoever was following them were low. Also, he was intimately familiar with the Priest's Grotto.

The guide picked them up in his jeep at the hotel on Thursday at 6:00 a.m. He'd balked about the time but Nadia wanted to get an early start. Every moment that passed brought Bobby closer to the inevitable verdict of life in prison. There was no time to waste.

The Priest's Grotto was located one hundred forty-five miles from Lviv. They drove east to the city of Ternopil and south toward the village of Strilkivtsi. Marko sat in the front with the guide. Nadia absorbed punishment from worn shock absorbers in the back seat. They passed mile after mile of wheat fields and farms.

When they got near the village, the driver guided the jeep off the road. He stopped on a knoll overlooking a green field surrounded by a tree line on all four sides. It stretched hundreds of yards in each direction. Clusters of wildflowers and bushes sprang from valleys and sinkholes where water gathered.

The guide said the cave was officially known as "*Ozero*," the Ukrainian word for "lake." Locally, however, it was called *Popowa Yama*, or the Priest's Grotto.

"It's the largest of the caves that make up the Gypsum Giant," the guide said, as he unloaded their supplies from the back of the jeep.

"Gypsum Giant?" Marko said.

"The Ukrainian system of natural caves. Not to be confused with the Caves Monastery in Kyiv, which was built by men. Five hundred fifty kilometers long. Second longest cave network in the world."

Marko whispered in Nadia's ear. "What's with all the underground action in this country?"

"Maybe life has been less than kind above ground," Nadia said.

"The Gypsum Giant is a crystalline structure," the guide said. "The crystal cracks like glass. So you have precise arteries but with jagged edges. That means we know where we're going but it can be dangerous."

They put on yellow overalls, helmets with chinstraps and mounted headlamps, knee pads, and elbow pads.

"Are we really going to need these pads?" Marko said, as he worked one over his forearm.

"Probably not," the guide said. "But in case your friend has gone farther than most folks, it's best to be prepared."

The guide handed each of them a knapsack containing two flashlights, spare batteries, bottled water, a pocket knife, a variety of plastic bags, a candle, a lighter, a roll of toilet paper, and an empty jar with a seal.

"The original entrance to the cave is filled with weeds and debris. We'll use a secondary entrance instead."

They hiked a hundred yards to a patch of shrubs and small trees. A shaft protruded four feet above ground. The guide strained to lift a manhole cover. Nadia and Marko peered inside.

Rusty metal pipes formed a ladder that disappeared into a black hole. A sense of dread gripped Nadia. She remembered her experience evading Kirilo Andre in Kyiv's Caves Monasteries. She didn't like tight places a quarter mile beneath the Earth.

The guide shined the light. "The ladder is made out of gas pipes," he said. "There are three of them. Each one is two meters long. So we will go down one at a time, about six meters deep. I will be last. I will close the cover."

"Can't you take the lead?" Marko said. "I'll go last. I'll close the entrance."

"I can't let you do that," the guide said. "I need to know you're both on solid ground before the cover is closed. If I go first, I can't be above ground to help you in the unlikely event something goes wrong."

Nadia lowered herself onto the first horizontal pipe and descended into the shaft. She hugged the ladder as she stepped down, her face almost kissing the dirt between the rungs. The Caves Monastery in Kyiv had a staircase. A year ago that staircase had felt like a portal into darkness. Now it seemed like a resort experience.

She focused on her breathing. Counted the rungs. Each pipe measured three meters. That was about three yards. Nine feet. Nine rungs per pipe. Three pipes. Twenty-seven steps down.

Marko's voice echoed down the shaft. "You counting in English or Uke?"

Nadia stopped. Her heart thumped in her ears. "What's the difference?"

"Numbers are a little longer in Uke. You'll make it down faster if you count in English."

The dialogue caused her to lose count. She swore under her breath. Took a deep breath and continued. When her right foot touched ground she lifted it and dropped it again. To make sure she wasn't imagining the sensation.

She stepped forward into a passageway. The walls were wide enough for two people to walk side-by-side but the ceiling was only four feet high. She had to stoop.

"Done," she said, looking up into the light.

"Move into the cave," the guide said. "So nothing falls on you."

So *no one* falls on her, Nadia thought.

Marko descended next. After he joined her in the cave, the guide closed the shaft behind him.

Darkness enveloped them. They took turns aiming their headlamps at each others' knapsacks and removed their flashlights. The guide scurried down the ladder with frightening speed, sliding down the last pole without touching a rung.

"Our destination is the "*Khatki*," he said.

"*Khatki*?" Nadia said. "The Ukrainian word for 'little cottage.'"

The guide pulled out his flashlight. "That's where the families lived."

"What families?" Marko said.

"The ones that hid from the Nazis," the guide said.

He took off before Nadia could ask questions. She and Marko followed. Shards of crystal hung from the ceiling. Gypsum crystal covered rocks. Water rolled down walls. Nadia brushed aside a sense of claustrophobia.

The cave's height gradually increased until they could walk upright. They weaved their way a hundred yards through a labyrinth of passageways to an open area. It was the shape of a diamond and the size of a living room. Beyond it the floor of the cave pitched upward and the ceiling soared. The forward chamber's soaring height created the illusion that the outdoors lay ahead.

"We'll rest here for a moment," the guide said. "Drink some water."

They took off their packs, sat down on rocks, and drank from their bottles.

"People hid from the Nazis in here?" Nadia said.

"Three Jewish families," the guide said. "Thirty-eight people. They spent three hundred and forty-four days under ground. They had three separate living chambers. A ventilated cooking chamber. They lit candles for only a few minutes a day so they wouldn't be seen."

"How did they get supplies?"

"They found a water supply in a chamber of the grotto on the east side. This cave is called 'ozero' for a reason. As for food, a Ukrainian farmer kept them alive."

"A Ukrainian farmer? A gentile?"

"Yes. He brought food to designated places outside the cave at pre-arranged times. Weekly, for almost a year. Until one day when the men went out to get the food and there was none. Instead there was a piece of paper. On the paper was a message. The message read: 'The Germans have gone.'"

"What happened to the families?" Nadia said.

"When they stepped into daylight for the first time, a four-year-old girl asked her mother to extinguish the candle. It was too bright for her eyes, she said. She was so young she'd forgotten daylight. The families ended up in displaced person camps in Germany. Then they went to Canada and America and started their lives all over again."

Nadia enjoyed a rush of adrenaline. She sipped her water, replaced it in her knapsack, and stood.

"Let's go," she said. She held the map in her left hand and a flashlight in her right. "Which way?" she said to the guide.

There was only one direction to go. Nadia marched onward.

Marko and the guide sprang into action.

"Hey, Nancy Drew," Marko said. "What the heck?"

The guide took the lead. Nadia and Marko followed him for another ten minutes.

The guide stopped in front of a cracked rock. The fissure was no more than six inches long.

"In other parts of the caves, the cracks are so wide they can swallow a person," the guide said. "Always watch your step. The scientists have done studies on the cracks. They are as much as two and a half kilometers deep. You fall. You die."

Nadia and Marko followed the guide deeper into the cave. They rounded a corner. Light came from an opening on the right side of the cave. Nadia heard a rustling noise. The sound of metal sliding against metal pierced the silence. It was the racking noise a semi-automatic pistol made when the sliding mechanism was pulled back and released to put the first bullet into the chamber.

Marko glanced at Nadia. She made a gun with her right hand. He nodded. She assumed he understood the signal meant someone had loaded the gun in the adjoining chamber. Instead, Marko reached down to his pant leg and removed his own pistol.

"Where did you get that?" Nadia mouthed.

In the glow of her headlamp, a glint shone in his eyes.

He had a gun. Somehow, her lunatic brother had procured a gun in Ukraine. Where? Kyiv? Lviv? Not Zarvanytsia, that's for sure. And from whom? Not the concierges at their two fine hotels. Then she remembered. She'd left him alone at the café in Lviv after she'd lost the man with the pointed chin.

Her concerns about how he'd gotten the gun and the risk he'd assumed in getting it gave way to relief. Marko knew how to use a gun. They both did, courtesy of their training during summer camps.

The guide's eyes widened when he saw the gun. Marko stepped in front of him and shut off his headlamp. He edged along the wall closest to the chamber. When he got near the entrance he squatted down to his knees. Took a deep breath. Nodded at Nadia to let her know he was going in. No discussion, no hesitation. He was going in. It was just like Marko, she thought. She wanted to help him. Pull him back. But toward what end? They had no choice. They needed to find Karel. And there was no way for her to share the risk. He was the one with the gun.

He pivoted into the doorway. The light illuminated him. Legs spread wide, both hands on the gun. He stretched forward and glanced in each of the near corners. No one there. He disappeared into the room.

The guide tapped Nadia on the shoulder. "Guns in the cave?" he said. "Not allowed. We must leave now."

Nadia shook her head. Put her finger to her lips.

Marko came out of the chamber. "Clear," he said. "I don't know what we heard but it wasn't from this room. It must have been an echo."

The guide eyed the gun in Marko's hand. "Who are you people? And this friend of yours who's caving? Why would he have a gun?" The guide stepped back. "No guns in the cave. I'm leaving now. Are you coming or are you staying?"

"We're staying," Nadia said. "Go to the car and wait for us there. That way we can still get back to Lviv and you're not in danger. If you see someone else coming out of the cave, you can take off without us. I promise I'll make it worth your while for waiting. Fair enough?"

The guide thought about it, nodded, and took off.

She followed Marko into the chamber. They aimed their headlights at each of the four walls. One of the walls featured cracks in the form of an upside-down horseshoe. Nadia aimed her light at the floor. Crystal dust shone in the light, scattered over rocks. A ledge protruded from one of the side walls. It was slightly higher than knee height and wide enough to accommodate a seated person. Something glittered beside it.

"Over here," Nadia said. She picked up a shiny blue fountain pen with gold trim. The pen was open. The cap was secured over the base. "This doesn't look like something from the 1940s." She pressed it against her yellow sleeve. Blue ink spread through the fabric. "Someone was here—"

"Drop the gun," a man said in Russian.

He stood in the entrance to the room, a gun in his right hand and a flashlight in his left. He also wore a headlamp. The light from the latter two overwhelmed Nadia's equipment and rendered her blind.

"Do it," the man said, waving the gun. "Do it now."

Nadia thought she recognized the voice the first time. The second time she heard it left no doubt.

"Karel, it's me," she said. "It's me, Nadia."

"Who are you? What did you say? Are you trying to trick me? I said put the gun down."

Nadia switched to English. "Marko, put the gun down."

Marko didn't lower his hands.

"Marko, it's him. It's Karel."

"How can you be sure?" Marko said.

"Nadia," the man said in Ukrainian. "Nadia-*Panya*. Is that you?"

"Of course it's me. What can I say, Karel. It was animal attraction. You knew I wouldn't be able to stay away forever."

The man approached. He kept his gun aimed at Marko. His flashlight continued to blind them. When he got to within three feet, he aimed it at the floor.

Wiry Einstein hair. The pale complexion, sunken face, and frail physique of a prematurely aged man. Large knapsack on his back. He lit up when he recognized Nadia. Stuffed his gun in the canvas belt cinched around his narrow waist.

"My God," he said. "It is you."

He stepped forward and hugged her. He held on a little longer than another acquaintance might have. Nadia didn't mind. She expected it. He'd done the same thing when they said goodbye outside reactor number four in Chornobyl last year. She had been sure she'd never see him again.

Nadia introduced Marko to Karel. Marko put his gun back in the holster around his ankle.

"We heard you load your gun," Nadia said. "But when Marko came in you were gone. How did you get out of here?"

Karel nodded toward the side wall with the horseshoe-shaped crack. "That's actually a hole in the wall. The people who hid here during the war found a rock and chiseled it to close the opening. It was their escape route in case they heard the Nazis coming. It leads to a series of secondary passages that extend along the outer edge of the cave. Very narrow. Some treacherous passes. I circled around to confront you."

Nadia showed him the pen. "Yours?"

He snatched it. "A gift from my friend Arkady Shatan. You remember. The scientist I told you about." He glanced from Marko back to Nadia, as though making sure it was okay to speak of Arkady in front of him. "What news of the formula? I've been watching the papers. Trolling the Internet for a headline that you've changed the world."

Nadia laughed. "Please, Karel. The gig is long up. You don't have to play along anymore. Obviously I know the whole thing was a ruse. Obviously there was no formula."

He frowned. "No formula? That's nonsense. Of course there was a formula. Of course there *is* a formula. I showed you the slides. How the cells regenerated. I showed you the wolves. How they kept coming back for the water treated with the formula."

"You made all that up."

"I made nothing up. You must not have searched the locket properly. It must be there under your very nose but you must not be able to see it."

Nadia stood flabbergasted. The formula for a radiation countermeasure had been a hoax. Or so she had thought. The last thing she expected from Karel was a heartfelt assertion that she was wrong. That it existed. And yet, here he stood before her, trembling with urgency.

"You must search it again," Karel said. "Where is the locket?"

"In an envelope. With Adam's other personal possessions. In jail."

"In jail? Adam? This can't possibly be. For what?"

"Murder."

"Murder?" Karel mumbled under his breath. "I must be having a nightmare. But no, I'm awake. That's complete nonsense. That boy would never hurt anyone. Life is too precious to him. Whom did he supposedly murder?"

"A young British businessman named John Valentine. But he was born in Russia. He was actually named after his father. His father's name was Ivan Valentin."

"Valentin." Karel's frown deepened. "Why is that name so familiar?" His eyes widened. A look of recognition turned to horror. "Valentin. The Zaroff Seven—"

Light filled the doorway.

"Don't move," another man said.

Nadia recognized him. It was the rawboned man who'd helped retrieve their bags from the thieves in Lviv. Her headlamp illuminated his rifle. He held the barrel with his left hand. A piece of jewelry glittered in the light from his ring finger. It was the same ring Valentin had worn in his family portrait.

Karel pulled the gun out of his belt and lifted it. Two loud thumps followed. Karel's head exploded.

Nadia dived for the floor. Her headlamp slipped off her head. She killed her flashlight. Marko did the same. He rolled atop her, pulled out his gun, and fired two bullets into the light at the doorway. The room turned dark. Pain wracked Nadia's eardrums.

Marko slid to the side wall. Fired another shot where the light had been. The man with the rifle had retreated out of the room. Marko put the gun in his overall pocket and slid the rock aside to reveal the hole in the wall.

"Go, go, go," he said.

Nadia scampered through the hole into a narrow walkway. The walls of the cave pressed tight against her torso. She had to stand up sideways to get her legs out.

"Come on," she said.

But instead of crawling through the hole, Marko began to slide the boulder back in place.

"Run," he said.

"No," she said. "You come, too."

He ignored her. Instead he sealed the opening.

Nadia heard more gunfire followed by silence. Then a man's voice. She couldn't make out the words. There was a measure of reason about it, as though he was trying to coax someone into obeying his order. She heard a deeper voice answer. Marko, she guessed. Voices and footsteps. More men entering the room.

He surrendered, she thought. They would keep him alive to find out what he knew. Which was nothing except that some group of men called themselves the Zaroff Seven. Jonathan Valentine's father had been one of them. Perhaps the rawboned man with the same ring was another. Somehow Bobby had gotten mixed up with them in Chornobyl, where the senior Valentin travelled every year.

They would be coming for her any second. She needed to move. Marko was resourceful, she told herself. He'd find a reason for them to keep him alive. Then he'd find a way to escape.

Still she couldn't bear to leave him. She knew they'd be pushing the boulder aside momentarily but how could she leave her brother alone?

Nadia focused on her breathing. Tried to think of an ingenious strategy to save him.

A single muted *thump*. The unmistakable sound of a gunshot.

Marko, she thought.

Light trickled in through tiny cracks in the sealed door. Then voices. Closer. Much, much closer.

Nadia's heart pounded in her ears. If she didn't do something, they were going to kill her. She was going to die.

The voices became more animated. The boulder moved.

They'd killed Marko and were coming for her.

A sense of impending doom gripped her. Move, she told herself. Move.

Nadia aimed her flashlight forward. Made note of the curve in the wall and the jagged edges in the floor. Shut the flashlight.

Hugged the wall and disappeared into the darkness.

CHAPTER 43

J OHNNY STOOD FACING BOBBY AS THE GUARD GUIDED HIM into the visitor's room. Usually he preferred to sit across the table from his client so he didn't appear to be an authority figure towering over him. So they could look each other eye-to-eye and on the level. But Bobby had been anything but on the level with him since he'd landed in Rikers Island. And now Johnny had the advantage he'd been hoping for. Forcing Bobby to look up at him would emphasize he had the upper hand.

The means with which he'd obtained his advantage was a source of constant guilt requiring liberal doses of rationalization. After Victor Bodnar called him with his news about the witness, however, he pushed aside the guilt. The witness had modified his original statement. As a result, everything had changed. If Johnny could get Bobby to retract his confession and tell him the truth, the DA would drop the murder charge. That much was certain. And if Johnny could prove self-defense, he had a real chance of getting the kid off completely.

The bad news was that keeping Bobby's true identity a secret would get more complicated. But that had to be of secondary importance to a lifetime in jail, didn't it? Johnny imagined Nadia's reaction to his uncovering the truth about what happened that night. To seeing the charges against Bobby reduced and ultimately dropped. He pictured the look in her eyes. Johnny savored that image.

"What about Nadia?" Bobby said, as soon as the guard closed the door behind him.

"She was all right as of this morning," Johnny said. "Time difference. We traded messages. That's all I know for now."

Bobby relaxed once he heard Nadia was safe. He rocked gently back and forth in his seat. Johnny knew from his prior visit that if he glanced under the table he'd find the boy's right foot tapping away furiously. He'd never returned to being the apathetic kid since Johnny had showed him the picture of old man Valentin. From the moment of his outburst that Nadia would be killed if she dug into Valentine's past, Bobby's demeanor had turned into suppressed rage. He really was a short Ukrainian fuse ready to blow. And now Johnny had the match.

"So here's the news," Johnny said. "The witness who saw you kill Valentine? He went to the cops yesterday afternoon and changed his story."

Bobby's eyes shot up.

Johnny leaned over the table. "Oh. Have I got your attention? Turns out the witness saw Valentine come at you with a knife. He saw you defend yourself with your screwdriver. Then he saw you walk away. We know you went to the police station to turn yourself in. That much was true. But from then on, he didn't tell the police everything. And neither did you."

Bobby blinked.

"Remember when I showed you a picture of the victim? His hand was curled as though someone had pried something from his fist. Turns out that's exactly what happened. Valentine was carrying a knife. Just like you said. A hunting knife. An expensive hunting knife. And that's not all. He was also carrying a compact briefcase. He probably dropped it when he went for his knife. You know what was in that briefcase. Care to tell me?"

Blood seeped into Bobby's face.

"A Sauer 202 takedown rifle with sound moderator. You know what a takedown rifle is?" Johnny paused. "Neither did I. It's a rifle that can be disassembled without tools. You know what a sound moderator is? It diffuses the source of the gunshot. So it's harder to tell what direction the bullet was coming from. What do you say to that?"

Bobby put his hands on the table. Moved his lips but didn't say anything.

"There's something else." Johnny paced in front of him. "There was another item of interest in the briefcase. A detailed map of a very specific part of New York City. It's called Hart Island. You know Hart Island, Bobby?"

Bobby closed his fists.

"No? Then let me tell you about it. It's a small island at the easternmost part of the Bronx in Long Island Sound. It's about a mile long and a quarter mile wide. Over time it's been a Civil War internment camp, a psychiatric hospital for women, and a base for Ajax missiles. Now it's the largest tax-funded cemetery in the world. About two thousand people who die in New York City are buried there every year. People with no names, no families. Stillborn babies. Dismembered body parts of murder victims that can't be identified. There're about forty of those per year. No one's allowed on the island except the people that conduct the burials. Ironically, that's Rikers Island prisoners. How about that, huh? Can't make that stuff up. No press is allowed. Ever. The ferry that runs from City Island to Hart Island is controlled by the city. Even family members have to apply for a pass from the prison system."

Johnny walked around the table and knelt down on one knee beside Bobby. Now the kid was looking down at him. Johnny lowered his voice to a near-whisper. Channeled as much compassion as he could muster into his expression.

"Hart Island is the darkest place in New York City," Johnny said. "It's a forbidden zone. There's no one there but the dead.

Why would a young real estate executive from London be carrying a takedown rifle with a sound moderator, a hunting knife, and a map of such a place? Why did you agree to meet him there? Why did you have no choice but to kill him?"

Bobby's knuckles turned white. His faced turned eggplant. For a moment, Johnny was concerned the kid was going to need medical attention. Then Bobby took a deep breath and exhaled slowly. By the time he was done, all the tension seemed to have seeped out of him.

"I want to see Iryna first," he said. "Then I'll tell you everything."

CHAPTER 44

NADIA SQUEEZED THROUGH THE CAVE'S PASSAGEWAY. IT curled into a semicircle around the inner chambers. She had to shuffle sideways, left arm by her side, right arm raised and parallel to the floor. Her hand gripped the flashlight. Her back scraped the wall. She heard the sound but felt no pain. The overalls were amazing. Then she remembered. The overalls weren't scraping the walls. She was wearing a backpack. The backpack was scraping the wall. The backpack was the problem.

She stopped, lowered her right arm, and tried to shimmy out of it. The backpack slid halfway down her spine and got stuck. Nadia pulled on the straps. The backpack wouldn't budge.

Light flashed behind her. Rock scraped against rock. The boulder, Nadia thought. A voice. The man with the rifle. No. Two voices. Two men. Entering the passageway.

Shit.

Nadia pushed off against the front wall and tried to compress her backpack's contents. Plastic cracked. The water bottle, she remembered. Half-empty. She straightened. Pressed against the front wall, face turned sideways. Slipped the pack off her back.

Light bounced off the walls behind her.

Footsteps. Coming.

She grabbed the knapsack by the strap with her left hand and powered forward. She turned the light on. Caught a glimpse of the next twenty steps. Turned it off. Five steps. Ten steps. Fifteen steps. Twenty steps. Flashed the light again.

A solid crystalline wall stood in front of her. Three more steps and she would have smashed her face. A crawl space at the bottom of the wall.

Light flashed forty feet behind her. Closing.

Nadia flung the knapsack into the narrow passage. Dropped to her hands and knees. Shined the flashlight into the crawl space. Saw air beyond the knapsack. Slithered into the opening and pushed forward.

The air thinned. Sweat trickled into her eyes. Crystalline dust drifted into her nose. She tried to suppress a sneeze but to her horror, couldn't. It didn't matter if she made noise, she realized. They were right behind her. They knew exactly where she was.

She crawled on her elbows and knees. Pushed the knapsack ahead. Kept the flashlight pointed at an angle to illuminate the ceiling and the tunnel. Considered the possibility the crawl space would end. Imagined being shot from behind, or dragged out by her legs. Or beaten with the butt of a rifle. Gritted her teeth and banished the thoughts. Crawled for twenty body lengths. Twenty-one, she counted. Twenty-two.

Light shone behind her. Voices.

The crawl space opened. Nadia scampered out of the tunnel. Stepped to the right, away from her pursuers' line of vision. Turned in a circle and made a sweeping motion with her flashlight. Cast an arc of light at her surroundings.

The ceilings soared. Solid walls surrounded her on three sides. The fourth wall provided the only possible escape. It featured a narrow passage that gradually widened the higher one climbed. At a height of thirty feet, a human being could slip through the passage, Nadia guessed. But there was no floor. Just a crack below where the two side walls met. The only footholds were the two walls that defined the passageway.

Nadia turned the light off. Her eyes had adjusted to the dark. She could see twenty feet in front of her. She stashed her flashlight in her pocket. Slung the knapsack on her back again. She considered leaving it but decided she might need the lighter, water, and batteries if she got stuck overnight. She scampered up the left wall. She'd scaled fifty-foot trap rock ridges in the hills of Litchfield County. Climbed up cliffs twice that height on the Appalachian Trail. Sturdy crystalline crevices provided decent toeholds and perches. It was child's play, she told herself. Child's play—

"Stop or I'll shoot," a man said in Russian.

It was a different voice. Not the rawboned man from Lviv. It was the other one. The man who'd been following them. The one with the pointed chin.

Nadia took a running start and leaped into the crevice between the walls. She spread her legs. Reached out with her hands. Her feet landed at odd angles against the two walls. Her right ankle turned in. She slipped. Started to fall. Pressed hard with her right hand against the wall to keep from falling. The rock stripped skin from her hand.

She winced. Regained her balance. Propelled herself forward, legs straddling the parallel walls. Crystal shards scraped her hands. She kept her knees bent to exert maximum force. She covered five, ten, twenty, yards.

The walls ended. Nadia found herself perched on a cliff. She had to be more than twenty feet high. She couldn't see the ground below. She reached for her flashlight.

Light shone behind her. Headlamps.

"I see her," a man said.

Nadia didn't have time for the flashlight. She found a toehold and descended down the cliff. The slope eased. Nadia ran down the final twenty feet. At the bottom of the cliff, a long horizontal strip of crystal protruded from the floor before giving way to a flat surface. Nature had honed it to a sharp edge. Momentum carried Nadia toward the crystal. By the time she saw it, there was no way she could stop.

She leaped. The running start carried her four or five feet past the jagged edge. Her right foot landed on a stone instead. She turned her leg. Lost her footing. Fell to the ground.

A straightaway awaited her ahead. Nadia ran. She managed fifteen strides before the gunshot exploded. The noise was deafening. She stopped in her tracks. Waited for the pain.

None came. He'd missed.

He'd also taken his sound suppressor off, Nadia thought. As though he wanted to make noise. It occurred to her that if they wanted to kill her they would have done so by now. It seemed as though they wanted to capture her instead.

"Stay where you are," the man with the pointed chin said.

He waited until the rawboned man with the rifle appeared behind him. He was limping. He took one look at the cliff and stopped. He aimed his rifle at Nadia. The man with the pointed chin descended down the cliff.

Nadia eyed the sharp strip of crystal. With any luck he'd trip and fall headfirst onto it. She realized her odds were low. The man kept coming though, arm extended, gun pointed at Nadia. He gathered momentum as the cliff became manageable. Broke into a slow trot as Nadia had done. She held her breath. He didn't appear to see the strip of crystal.

But then at the last second he looked down, as though his instincts had alerted him to possible danger. He leapt. It was a weak jump off one foot only, and the back foot at that. But it was enough to clear the razor's edge that Nadia had been hoping would take him down.

He sailed over the crystal and disappeared beneath the earth. A scream filled the air. It grew more distant with each second but its echo continued. It seemed to last forever.

Nadia remembered the guide's warning about fissures in the floor. Fissures large enough to swallow a human. She realized she must have leapt over the hole to avoid the sharp rock.

The other man was equally transfixed by his colleague's fall. Nadia didn't waste time. She hurried along the passage toward the entrance to the cave. Kept her flashlight on. Didn't turn back. The rawboned man with the rifle was injured, she thought. He couldn't keep up with her.

She stopped after ten minutes to consult her map. Oriented herself, and hurried on to the original cave entrance.

A ray of light. A collection of small rocks and boulders obscured the opening. Nadia tossed them aside. Daylight streamed into the cave. So did the sound of rain. She cleaned out dry sticks, leaves, and branches. A large pile of animal dung appeared fresh. From her experience, it looked like it belonged to a bear. She looked around again. No animal in sight.

She slipped through a circular opening and emerged on a mound of grass. Rain pelted her. Nadia stayed low and looked out. The field looked familiar but the other entrance to the cave was nowhere in sight. She crept around the mound and glanced in the opposite direction.

An old Range Rover was parked a hundred yards beside the main entrance to the cave. Her guide's car was gone. Fog obscured the Rover's windows. Someone was inside, she thought.

Nadia sat and waited. Stuck her hands out to let the rain wash the blood away and clean her wounds. Marko had been talking. Then she'd heard the thump. And not another sound from Marko.

He was dead. He had to be dead. It was only logical, and yet she couldn't contemplate the thought. A sense of loss paralyzed her. Marko had just reached the point in his life where he was comfortable with himself. He wasn't drinking. He'd discovered contentment and joy. She sat there trying to imagine a life without him and couldn't fathom it. And it was her fault. He was here on her behalf.

She sat in a quiet stupor for ten minutes until a noise rousted her. The rawboned man with the rifle emerged. She was shocked how quickly he made it out given how badly he'd been limping. Ex-military, she thought. He looked like it, and moved like it, too.

Rain pummeled him. He slipped the rifle off his shoulder and looked around. Found the Range Rover. Sealed the lid to the cave and limped over to the vehicle. He opened the passenger's side front door and lowered his head to speak to someone inside. The driver, Nadia thought. A few seconds later he opened the rear passenger door.

Marko stepped out of the Range Rover.

He was alive. A sense of euphoria swept Nadia. It left her giddy.

He had a bandage on his head. His hands were cuffed in front of him. The man with the rifle took him by the arm and directed him to the front passenger seat. Even put his hand over Marko's head to make sure he didn't bump his wound on the way in.

Marko carried himself with a fearlessness that belied his situation. He even stopped to say something to the man with the rifle before climbing in the front seat.

Another pair of men must have followed the two she'd encountered, Nadia thought. Perhaps they'd gone to search the other *khatki*, or the water source on the opposite side of the Gypsum Giant. They probably had shortwave radios. As soon as they heard shooting they must have come running. From there they took Marko to the car while the other two pursued her.

The thump must have been a warning shot. Followed by a rifle butt to the head.

Marko was alive.

Nadia's joy was short-lived. Karel. She'd put him out of her mind. The image of his head bursting open flashed before her eyes. His final words rang in her head.

Valentin. He knew the name. There was a connection between Bobby and Valentin. It involved something called the Zaroff Seven.

And one more thing. It was so unbelievable as to be laughable. But Karel hadn't wavered in his conviction. Not for a moment.

The formula was real.

CHAPTER 45

N ADIA WAITED FOR THE RANGE ROVER TO DRIVE OUT OF
sight. After ten more minutes to make sure they didn't double back, she walked five miles in the rain to the village of
Strilkivtsi. Along the way, she sipped water from the bottle in her
knapsack and considered her discoveries.

Karel had insisted the formula was real and was contained in
the locket. But if it wasn't on a piece of microfilm inside the compartment where was it? In a steel capsule within the body of the
locket? Or was it etched somehow? That sounded more likely.
The thought had never occurred to her before because the contents of the locket had proved it was all a ruse. Or so it seemed at
the time. But wouldn't that have been just like her uncle to hide it
so well?

Then the painful question dawned on Nadia. Did Bobby
know? Had he been lying to her the entire time? And where was
the locket? In jail, she suspected, with Bobby's other personal
possessions. He never took it off his neck except to sleep.

Her thoughts turned to her brother. If her pursuers wanted
Marko dead, they would have killed him in the Priest's Grotto.
But they didn't. That meant they had a use for him. Maybe they
wanted to see what he knew. More likely they wanted to use him
to get to her. Nadia wasn't sure why but that's what her instincts

told her. Alerting the authorities about his abduction could backfire. Her pursuers could change their minds and decide keeping Marko alive wasn't worth the risk of being found. If she notified the American embassy in Kyiv they would seek help from the Ukrainian police. They had a less than sterling reputation for integrity.

No. Frightening as it was, Nadia's optimal course of action was to wait. She had her cell phone. Marko knew her number. Soon she would get a call, and her pursuers would reveal themselves and their motives. Both were tied to Bobby's past, Ivan Valentin, and his son's murder. They'd begun following her as soon as she started asking questions about Valentin. She was sure of it. In the meantime, she took small comfort in knowing that Marko could take care of himself.

Nadia paid a seamstress's son five hundred *hryvnia* to drive her from Strilkivtsi to Lviv. It was the equivalent of sixty dollars. She listened to her voice mails during the trip. One was from Johnny. There had been a break in the case against Bobby. The witness had changed his story. The victim had been carrying a rifle and a hunting knife. The witness was broke. The rifle and the knife were worth money. The latter had an ivory handle. He'd taken them both for the money. The victim was also carrying a map of Hart Island. Johnny said it was a public cemetery. Nadia vaguely remembered reading an article about the burial of homeless people on an island. It was a place one needed a permit to enter.

They arrived at the Leopolis ten minutes past noon. New York was seven hours behind. That meant it was 5:12 a.m. Too early to call a friend, she thought. Unfortunately she had no choice. She called Paul Obon, bookman and source of knowledge on all things Ukrainian. She indentified herself and apologized for calling so early.

"Who is this?" he said.

"It's Nadia, Mr. Obon. Nadia Tesla. Your favorite customer."

He muttered her name under his breath as though making sure he wasn't dreaming. "Nadia? What time is it?" His voice trailed off. A second later he sounded awake. "What's wrong? Something must be wrong."

"No. Nothing's wrong. But I need your help. It's urgent."

"Nothing's wrong. And yet you're calling me at home at five fifteen in the morning. Should I be frightened for you?"

Nadia considered her words. "No. You should be frightened for the other guys."

"Oh. Oh, dear."

"I need you to put your glasses on and get a pen and paper."

"If I didn't have my glasses on, I wouldn't know what time it was. Hold on." The bed creaked. A drawer opened and closed. He took a deep breath and exhaled. Not with exasperation but anxiety. Like a man preparing to take on a crucial assignment. "One of the detriments of bachelorhood is the absence of family. Did I ever tell you that? Now, how can I help you?"

"I need you to find out everything you can about something called the Zaroff Seven. It might be a private club or society of some kind. Ivan Valentin was a member, so it's Russian, for sure. That's all I know."

"I'm getting up now. I have some reference books in the store that might be helpful. And my computer is there. I'll call you back as soon as I have an answer."

Afterward, still dressed in overalls with open wounds on her hands, Nadia called Johnny. He answered on the first ring.

"You're awake," she said.

"Always. You got my message."

"Incredible news. Why did the witness change his story? Did he give a reason?"

"His conscience, I guess."

"That's incredible news."

"What about your end?"

Nadia told him what happened at the Priest's Grotto.

"What can I do to help you from here?" Johnny said.

"Keep your phone on. What about Bobby?"

"He said he'd tell me everything. Which should happen today. But he wanted to see Iryna first."

Nadia thought for a moment. "He said that? That he'd tell you the truth but he wanted to see Iryna first?"

"Our boy's in love."

"Yeah. But he sees her all the time. It makes you wonder. The witness recants. He's going to tell you the truth. But he wants to see her first."

"Why? What do you think he wanted to talk to her about?"

"What if I told you the locket did possess a formula," Nadia said. She could hear her voice trembling. "What if I told you it wasn't inside the main compartment. What if there's another compartment, or it's inscribed or something like that."

"Where did that come from?"

Nadia told him what Karel said before he was killed. "What if Bobby figured it out at some point?"

"It's possible."

"I wonder if that's what he was talking to Iryna about."

"Why would he tell her and not you?"

"Because he's in love. And he has trust issues. We weren't exactly getting along perfectly. Me needing to build my business. Him needing to be a teenager. The notion he told her and not me pains me to no end. I'd rather not think about it. All I'm saying is we have two agendas now."

Johnny didn't answer right away. It was as though she'd lost him.

"Johnny? Two agendas?"

"What? Oh. Right. Two agendas. Yes. Bobby and the locket."

"Call me as soon as he tells you the truth."

Nadia took a hot shower and put bandages on the cuts on her hands. Afterward she called room service. She ordered Grand-mother's mushroom broth, Carpathian chicken kebob, and *varenyky* stuffed with poppy seeds for dessert. Guilt gnawed at her conscience after she placed the order—were they even feeding Marko?—but hunger and anxiety prevailed. She drank the broth, ate half the kebob, and polished the dessert plate clean.

An hour later her phone rang. Nadia couldn't believe Obon had found her answer so quickly. When she glanced at the number calling, however, she didn't recognize the number.

It was the woman from the Orel Group. The one who had met her with the chauffer at Boryspil Airport.

"Mr. Simeonovich would like to know if you're available for dinner tonight," the woman said.

"No," Nadia said. "I'm sorry. I'm afraid I'm not in Kyiv. I'm in Lviv."

"Lviv is a short helicopter ride for Mr. Simeonovich. He is twenty minutes away. He would be pleased to pick you up at your hotel at eight p.m. If that is convenient."

"I'm afraid it's not—"

"Mr. Simeonovich would like to present you with a check for your services. He also said something about a bonus. Would eight p.m. be convenient?"

The thought of enjoying a gourmet meal while Marko was being held captive didn't whet her appetite. Still, Nadia thought, if her pursuers called she could excuse herself and leave right away. In the meantime, a client should be shown the proper respect and a girl had to eat.

"Yes," she said. "Eight p.m. would be fine."

CHAPTER 46

NADIA'S CALL SHATTERED WHAT LITTLE INNER PEACE JOHNNY had managed to find since allowing Victor Bodnar to discover the witness's identity. There was no doubt about Victor's motives now. He wanted the locket. That didn't mean he knew for certain it contained a real formula. Something might have caused him to suspect this was the case. Career criminals had instincts that way. Especially thieves.

Bobby had the locket. Bobby was in prison. The locket was in prison. To get the locket, Victor had to get Bobby out of prison. Thus the offer to help the witness remember what happened the night of the murder. Just as Johnny suspected, the old man was playing him the entire time. Help those who helped him. What a load of crap. He knew it when he heard it.

And yet he still went along with it. For obvious reasons. He wanted Bobby out, too. And as long as the witness was telling the truth—which he seemed to be—Johnny had convinced himself he was within his moral boundaries. Maybe the witness had stretched the truth a bit at Victor's request and suggested Valentine had drawn his knife first, but that's probably what happened. Johnny was still an ethical warrior. The underdog defending the underdog.

What a pack of lies. Once a man compromised his ethics and let a thief into his life, the criminal's most likely course of action was to burrow deeper inside. Victor Bodnar would do anything to get that locket. And if he was motivated by leaving his daughter and grandchild some wealth before he died, he was twice as determined. He seemed like a wise old man who never resorted to violence but that too was a lie. He'd killed his cousin. He'd kill again. If it was in his best interest and there was no alternative, Victor Bodnar wouldn't hesitate to kill again.

Not two agendas. Three agendas. Bobby, the locket, and Victor Bodnar. In that order. Persuasion, protection, negotiation. These were his forte. He had to persuade Bobby to tell the truth and the DA to release him, protect the locket, and negotiate a settlement with Victor. He had no choice but to succeed at all three objectives.

He was the one Nadia trusted the most.

CHAPTER 47

THE RESTAURANT AT THE LEOPOLIS HOTEL IN LVIV WAS called Lev, which was the Ukrainian word for lion. But the predator was sitting opposite her at the table, Nadia thought. Simeon Simeonovich wore a black pinstripe suit cut in a European style to hug his athletic frame. He sat with such perfect posture Nadia found herself arching her back to make sure she didn't slouch.

Regardless of the circumstances, a current of electricity surrounded her whenever Nadia was in his presence. Even now, with her mind on Marko. She had yet to figure out if that was a function of Simeonovich's wealth, power, or his understated personality. But it was an interesting question, and she would have liked to explore it further. Under different circumstances.

"My girlfriend likes to order for me," he said, as they perused the menu. "What do you think?"

"I think she's your girlfriend for a reason."

"For starters?"

"For starters, she's obviously gorgeous and socially skillful. That was clear when we met on your yacht. But perhaps the real allure is that you like the company of a strong woman. One who can make the proper choices for you."

He looked up from the menu. "No. I meant, for starters. As in appetizers. What looks good?"

"Oh." Nadia buried her head in the menu. "They have caviar." As soon as she blurted the words she saw the price per person. It was a thousand *hryvnia*. More than a hundred dollars per person. Even worse, it was the most expensive item on the menu. Not that he couldn't afford it, but a polite guest wouldn't have suggested it.

"Perfect," Simeonovich said. "What about the main dish?"

"Meat or fish?"

"You don't know?"

Nadia studied him. He showed no emotion. "Your girlfriend would order the T-bone. It's the best cut of beef on the menu. Standard oligarch fare. But I recommend the sea bass filet."

"Why? Less cholesterol?"

"No. More nostalgia. For a man with roots in Siberia. Fishing capital of Russia."

His eyes twinkled. He called the waiter over and ordered their dinner, a bottle of ice cold vodka to go with the caviar, and a white Burgundy wine for the entrees.

"Where is your brother?" Simeonovich said. "I meant it when I said he was welcome to join us."

"Thank you. He's out with a friend."

"He has friends in Lviv?"

"Marko makes friends wherever he goes."

"You're very close, yes?"

"We were very close. Growing up. He was my big brother. Then we drifted apart. I went to college. He went . . . wherever. When we got back in touch we realized we don't have that much in common."

"Except that you're family. What more can two people have in common?"

"He saved my life once."

"This is interesting. Tell me more."

"We were both part of PLAST, the national Ukrainian scouting organization. It's big in America. It was especially big when Ukraine was part of the Soviet Union. Our parents wanted to keep the Ukrainian language and customs alive. PLAST was a way to cultivate a Ukrainian-American community. There were weekly meetings but summer camps were the focal point."

"Did you enjoy them?"

"No. I hated them. And the closer to eighteen you got, the more brutal they became. It was a strange mix of socialization, cultural brainwashing, and survival training. We had Vietnam veterans teaching us hand-to-hand combat in a green field with the priest and the *babushkas* from the kitchen watching. Then the counselors would set trip wires all over the hills and wake us up for maneuvers in the middle of the night. Trip the wire, you stood guard the next night."

"I'm not sure you should complain. Look at you now. There's a strength and resilience about you. When I visit America, I don't see it so much. Your society has become too rich. Your children are spoiled."

"I don't have any children."

"You know what I mean."

"I don't disagree. The most coveted merit badge was the survival badge. It had to be earned. It was reserved for older scouts, kids fourteen and up. But my father, in his infinite wisdom, decided that his daughter had to be the youngest girl in America to pass the test."

"What was the test?"

"Three nights alone on a wilderness range called the Appalachian Trail."

"Alone? At age twelve?"

"You have to understand these were Ukrainian immigrants. Many of the older people had suffered the Nazis. Everyone had lived under Soviet oppression. They knew a different way of life.

In their minds, only the strongest survived and proper training had to begin at an early age. Plus, unbeknownst to me, I wasn't alone."

"Of course. Your brother was guarding you the entire time."

"Which didn't help when my fire went out and some animal ran over my sleeping bag. Or when rain poured through my lean-to and I caught a fever. Or when a hiker broke his ankle and his brother came looking for help."

"What did you do?"

"I made a splint out of two sticks, a stretcher out of two tree limbs, my poncho, and what rope I had left, and pointed them in the direction of the nearest town with my compass. Cell phones were luxuries back then."

"When did your brother help you?"

"A pair of hikers kidnapped me. A man and a woman. Turned out they had a history of doing unpleasant things to children. Marko stalked us. Circled around and got ahead of us on the trail. Jumped out of a hollowed-out tree and took them out with a club he'd carved out of wood. Carried me on his back six miles to safety."

Simeonovich studied Nadia. She felt her cheeks burning, her heart pulsating against her chest. She couldn't tell if he was regarding her with respect, compassion, or dare she think, something more. Whatever it was, though, it felt like a positive vibe.

"I take it back," he said.

"What? That all American children are spoiled?"

"No. That there's no greater bond than family."

Nadia's phone buzzed. She checked the number. Obon.

"Would you excuse me?"

She stepped out into the foyer and returned Obon's call. He picked up on the first ring.

"I have your answer," he said. "A group of senior Russian Chekists—administrators at the highest rung of Soviet authority who reported directly to the Politburo—formed a cabal in 1992.

They formed this club to pool their resources so they could profit from the fire sale of Soviet companies. The larger the underlying entity, the more power it had to accumulate vouchers or bid for shares. It was a common tactic among *apparatchiks*. There were seven of them. They had special rings made. Gold with an onyx inlay. But it's not the number three that you saw in the middle. It is the Cyrillic letter Z. They're similar, as you know. In this case, the jeweler took the hard edges off the Z for stylistic purposes. In the process he made it look like a three."

"What's the significance of the 'Z'?"

"The origin of the club's name was based on something else the men had in common. They were passionate hunters. Have you ever heard of a short story called 'The Hounds of Zaroff'?"

Nadia searched her memory. "No."

"It's the story of a big game hunter who gets shipwrecked on an island owned by a Russian Cossack. It was published under a different name in America."

"What was that?"

"'The Most Dangerous Game.' In the story, the big game hunter becomes the hunted. He must kill the Cossack to stay alive. The Cossack's name was Zaroff. The 'Z' is for Zaroff. They called themselves the Zaroff Seven."

"How did you learn all this?"

"I found them in a book about Russian hunting societies circa 1999. Posing in the Yakutia Republic beside a Siberian bear. Six men and one woman. Vanity trumped prudence. They couldn't resist seeing themselves in print."

"A woman?"

"Yes."

"That's interesting."

"I placed a call to a friend who was a secretary for a man in Yeltsin's cabinet. She said they had a reputation for ruthlessness. They sent enough dissidents and enemies to the *gulags* in Siberia to pave the Road of Bones themselves."

"If I give you my e-mail address, can you scan the picture and send it to me?"

"I'm afraid all this technology is beyond me. But Boris, the university student who works part time for me, can probably do that."

"Do you think you can get names to match the faces?"

"I'll try."

Nadia thanked him.

When she returned to the table, the caviar and wine had arrived.

"Everything all right?" Simeonovich said.

Nadia sat down and smiled. "Yes. Why do you ask?"

"You looked very serious when you came back into the dining room."

"That's what people used to say when I was growing up."

"That you looked too serious?"

"No. Is everything all right."

"Behind every serious face is a child who wishes she'd had more fun growing up."

"She?"

Simeonovich piled some caviar on a piece of toast. "He. She. We are similar, you and I."

Nadia laughed. "I'm sorry. I don't see that."

"You're thinking about money," he said. "You shouldn't. Money doesn't define the man. But now that you've brought it up." He pulled an envelope out of his pocket. "Here's a check for your work. A billing rate of four hundred and seventy-five dollars per hour for twenty-two hours worked. Plus a bonus of four thousand and change to make it an even fifteen thousand dollars."

Nadia envisioned real estate tax and tuition bills getting paid. "That's very generous but what's the bonus for? I didn't do anything to deserve it."

"You did everything to deserve it. But did you hear what you said? That's what we have in common."

"What? Earning more than we expect on a deal?"

"No. Distrust of the person on the other side of the table."

He handed Nadia the envelope. She took it. Nadia usually savored a sense of accomplishment whenever she got paid but this time she experienced something more. A greater sense of pride. One of the richest men in the world had just paid her. And he'd paid her more than he owed her.

"I don't distrust you," Nadia said.

"But you don't trust me either."

Nadia considered his words. "They're not the same thing, are they?"

"No. They're not. Why are you here in Lviv? It has something to do with the boy, doesn't it?"

"No. I'm sightseeing with my brother."

"Now that's insulting. I deserve a better lie than that."

Nadia smiled. He was right. He deserved a better lie. But he'd caught her unprepared, and it was too late now.

"If you trust me with the truth," he said, "if you tell me what you're looking for, I can help you."

It was tempting, Nadia thought. The resources. The power. "Why?" she said.

"Why trust me?" he said.

"Why do you care?"

He stared at her. His face softened. He kept staring. Nadia felt her breath shorten.

"Obviously it can't be that I'm fond of you. After all, I barely know you."

"Obviously," Nadia said.

"This man Valentin. And his friends. They have a less than savory reputation in some circles. They are remnants of old Russia. Of the Soviet Union and the lawless transition that followed. If I were to get some evidence of criminal acts, I could put a stop to them. I could make them pay for prior sins."

"What sins? What criminal acts?"

"Oh, so now you are curious?"

Nadia shrugged. "You brought it up. I'm just asking."

"Rumors. Myths. It's hard to separate them from reality sometimes. One wouldn't want to libel a fellow countryman, especially a group that together is every bit as powerful as I am. But if a man had evidence . . ."

He's Russian, Nadia reminded herself. And he could be lying. The living members of the Zaroff Seven could be friends of his. She remembered her uncle Damian's final words to her. *With foxes we must play the fox.*

"I have no idea what you're talking about," Nadia said. "But I'll certainly keep my eyes open during the rest of my stay."

Simeonovich sighed. "You do that. Now, have some of this caviar. If you won't trust me, at least let me feed you. Before you go back out there among the wolves."

CHAPTER 48

THE CALL CAME LATER THAT NIGHT AS SHE LAY AWAKE IN bed pretending sheep were counting her.

A man with an endearing voice. The kind that sold flowers to women at the hospital to supplement his income during medical school.

He spoke proper Ukrainian. He apologized. Said it was a big misunderstanding. They'd lifted the wrong man. They had no business with her or with Marko. They'd mistaken them for some other Teslas.

He put Marko on the phone. Her brother sounded wonderful. Healthier and more sober than ever. One of his abductors was a woman, he said. A real looker. Vanessa from Odesa. She had a university degree with dual majors in nursing and massage. She loved motorcycles, green cards, and America. Her life ambition was to marry a strip club operator with a trigger temper. Nadia imagined how happy their mother would be when she heard her son was engaged. And to a proper Ukrainian beauty no less.

Then the endearing man delivered the good news. Nadia was right. There was a connection between Bobby and Valentin. It would illuminate the events the night of the murder and prove beyond a reasonable doubt that Bobby was innocent. The man didn't get into the all-too-important specifics but promised an explanation so convincing the judge would release him immediately. With the court's apology.

The endearing man said he had one last question before hanging up. Had she conquered her ethnic bias and accepted the billionaire's Russian heritage? Did she realize he was smitten with her? Had she made the proper decision to go for it?

Nadia scolded him. That was three questions, she said.

No, the man said. They were all the same question.

Yes, Nadia said.

Yes, she was going for it?

Yes, they were the same question.

The torrent of good news lulled her to sleep.

She awoke an hour later, in the heart of darkness, to the sound of the real phone ringing, whereupon she received a simple set of instructions consisting of nine words. It was delivered by a gruff and somber man speaking course Russian.

Then he hung up.

CHAPTER 49

L AUREN DEBATED WHETHER TO APPROACH JOHNNY TANNER
or Iryna first.

She considered Johnny. Her odds of coaxing the truth about
Bobby's background from his lawyer were zero. The probability
she'd get him to slip up about Nadia Tesla's current location was
no better. The man was a defense attorney. Confidentiality defined his livelihood. He woke up suspicious. He distrusted authority and people who asked questions. Attempts to trick him
would be a waste of time or worse. They could jeopardize her life.
She didn't know who Victor Bodnar was but her gut told her he
and his twin protégés were dangerous men. Johnny Tanner had
spoken to him as though he knew him. The risks of approaching
him outweighed the benefits.

Lauren imagined paying a visit to Bobby's girlfriend, Iryna,
at the bakery in Brighton Beach where she worked. She'd studied
the girl's Facebook page. A classic beauty. Not too Slavic the way
some Russian girls looked, with sunken faces and narrow eyes.
She looked like the innocent type who loved to bake cupcakes
and watch hockey. Pictures lied, though. And girls lied. Lauren
wondered about her real personality, her true motives. She had a
genuine hankering to find out, except her gut told her that was a
waste of time, too. At the first mention of Bobby or Nadia, Iryna

would clam up right away. To earn the girl's trust, Lauren would have to pose as a person of authority. Like a cop. And she was still rational enough to realize that was more likely to land her in jail than glean any information.

She was also concerned that Victor Bodnar had dropped the girl's name. It was as though he was encouraging Lauren to go see her, which told Lauren she should do otherwise. It didn't smell right. She had an eerie sense he was trying to manipulate her.

The answer was neither. She shouldn't approach the lawyer or the girlfriend. Both visits were losing propositions. There simply had to be a better plan of action. There had to be a more promising source of information.

A mother, Lauren thought. A mother was the best source of information about anyone.

Lauren found the address in the White Pages. She drove 120 miles to a small town in central Connecticut called Rocky Hill. She pulled into an old condominium complex in the late afternoon. Parked in a small lot across the street from a corner unit.

She rang the doorbell. The curtain over the front door window parted. Lauren felt a person's eyes upon her. The front door cracked open. A chain prevented it from swinging wider.

An elegant woman with short gray hair opened the door. Lauren recognized the family resemblance.

"Mrs. Tesla?" Lauren said.

"Yes?"

"Nadia's mother?"

"Who are you?"

"I'm Lauren Ross. Nadia's friend from New York. I'm sure she's mentioned me to you."

"How could she mention you to me when she never calls me? You'd think a daughter would call her mother at least once a week."

"Well, she's been busy. What with the trial and all." Lauren lowered her voice. "I know the boy's story. I know he's from

Ukraine and he got into the country through Alaska. I know about Bobby."

"You know about Adam?"

Lauren hesitated. "Yes. I know all about Adam."

Nadia's mother frowned. Gave Lauren a once-over. By the time she was done she was glaring. She'd blown it, Lauren thought. The hesitation had cost her.

"I don't know who or what you're talking about," Nadia's mother said. "Good night." She swung the door shut. A bolt slid into place. A door chain rattled home.

Lauren returned to her car.

Adam, she thought. Bobby Kungenook was the boy's alias. His real name was Adam. Forty minutes and thirty-two miles later a question occurred to Lauren at a rest stop on the Merritt Parkway.

What were the odds his last name was Tesla?

CHAPTER 50

N ADIA CHECKED OUT OF THE LEOPOLIS HOTEL THE NEXT morning. She took the #170 express train departing Lviv at 7:00 a.m. It arrived at Kyiv Central Station at 11:55 a.m. That left her with four excruciating hours to kill before meeting with the men who had Marko.

She ate lunch at Varenichnaya #1, a restaurant that specialized in Ukrainian dumplings. She'd eaten there last year, when she arrived in Kyiv for the first time. They offered twenty different kind of *varenyky*. She ordered three filled with potato and farmer's cheese, and two stuffed with black cherries. She dabbed sour cream on the potato and cheese dumplings, and spooned cane sugar onto the cherry ones. She ate as slowly as she could to savor every bite. The meal distracted her. For those fifteen minutes she was able to leave the real world and relive what few pleasant childhood memories she had. *Varenyky* were a cornerstone of those memories. Whenever her mother made them from scratch, her father never shouted at the dinner table.

After lunch she walked a few blocks to Saint Sophia Cathedral. Aesthetics and religion drove her to the destination. A campus of white buildings covered an entire city block. She sat outside on a bench and stared at the cathedral. Green and gold cupolas topped a maze of turrets. A man once told her green was the color of genius and gold was the color of dreams. Nadia wasn't sure about that, but the architecture soothed her soul almost as much as the comfort food. She'd been an altar girl growing up. When in trouble, we return to the sanctuaries of our childhood, she thought.

Inside, she studied frescoes and mosaics from the eleventh century. With an hour left, she kneeled down in the church and prayed. She prayed for Marko and Adam—it wasn't right to use his false name in a place of worship—and for her parents, too. She prayed for Johnny and that there was one good Russian oligarch among the lot of them, and that he might be a man she knew. She prayed she'd survive the night.

Kyiv Central Station. 4:00 tomorrow. White Lexus. Wear pants.

Those were the nine words. Those were her instructions. It was the latter two words that struck fear in her heart but also gave her hope. The need for pants suggested physical exertion. She couldn't imagine any other reason for the order. Exertion implied action. Action meant she and Marko would have a chance. Otherwise they would have let her wear a skirt and killed her at their leisure.

She returned to the train station at 3:55 p.m. and waited in front of the entrance. Five minutes later a white Lexus SUV with tinted windows pulled in. A young driver—at least six-foot-six—climbed out of the car and opened the rear passenger door. Nadia walked up to him. He cracked a smile to reveal four golden front teeth and bowed like a gentleman. He took her bag to stow in the storage area and motioned for her to sit in the back.

Nadia slid into the back seat. The rawboned man from Lviv sat beside her. She wondered if he was one of the Zaroff Seven. If not, he surely worked for them.

"Welcome," said the rawboned man. He smiled, too. "Seat belt, please."

The driver climbed back inside the car. He pulled into the exit lane and waited for a gap in the traffic.

"Where are we going?"

"We are going to a place where all your questions will be answered."

"Is my brother there? Where is he? Is he all right?"

"Your brother is fine. You must realize. If we wanted to kill you, you'd be dead by now. I know that you have many questions. About Ivan Valentin. About his son. We want to give you the answers you're looking for. But on our terms. In our theater."

"What terms?"

He pulled a translucent orange prescription vial out of his jacket pocket. Handed it to Nadia. There was no label on the vial. It contained a single pill. He unscrewed the cap to a bottle of spring water and offered it to her.

"The price of admission," he said.

"To what?"

"Our theater."

"What theater?"

"You know what theater."

Irradiated trees, buried homes, and an abandoned Ferris wheel flashed before Nadia's eyes. She stared at the pill with fear and revulsion. If she took it, she might awaken permanently incapacitated or prepared for torture. Taking the pill was insane. And yet, she knew she had no choice.

"You want answers? Take that pill and you will get all the answers you want. It's a form of benzodiazepine. Like the Xanax so popular in America. You will wake up in a few hours in perfect health. You have my word as a gentleman."

"Why is the pill necessary?"

"You'll find out when you wake up. You must trust me. I know that's very difficult, but if we wanted to harm you that would have already happened. Don't you agree?"

Words from the mouth of Karel's killer and Marko's kidnapper shouldn't have reassured her, yet for some reason they did. "Where will I wake up?" she said.

He smiled. "In the front row."

She opened the vial. Let the purple pill slide into the palm of her left hand. If she thought about it too much, she might lose her nerve. She remembered Marko slugging her abductors with his makeshift club on the Appalachian Trail.

A person is defined by her actions. Make your own decisions, and be accountable for them.

She popped it into her mouth and washed it down with water.

At first she didn't feel anything. Five minutes passed. The Lexus glided along a main thoroughfare. Another five minutes passed. Still she didn't feel any different. If Nadia had been able to focus she might have recognized the street. But she couldn't. The drug wasn't working. She didn't feel sedated. If anything she felt more agitated.

Panic gripped her. What had they tricked her into taking? A chemical had entered her bloodstream. What was it? She glanced out the window.

A sidewalk. A smattering of pedestrians. If she opened the door and jumped out, people would hear her scream for help. Someone would come to her aid. Maybe there was a cop nearby.

She found the latch to open the door. Considered reaching for it but changed her mind. She sank deeper into the leather instead. Stretched her legs their full length. Everything was going to be all right, she told herself. This is what she had to do. All she needed was to rest her eyes for a moment. If she rested her eyes, she'd have enough strength to overcome any obstacle.

Her eyelids pressed together. She drifted asleep.

CHAPTER 51

SATURDAY MORNING DEVELOPED IN SLOW MOTION FOR Johnny. The water in his shower took five minutes to heat up and the line for coffee at the gas station wound out the front door. Traffic snarled. The guards at Rikers kept joking around while he stood waiting for someone to sign him in. Nothing happened quickly enough. That was because today was the day. Today was the day the kid would fess up and give Johnny the ammo he needed to make Nadia's dream come true.

As soon as the guard brought him into the room, Johnny could see the apprehension in Bobby's face. Only the kid knew exactly what Johnny was about to hear. And by the tension in his eyes and the tightness in his lips, Johnny knew it was coming from a place he'd tucked away and hoped to never revisit. This was going to be some serious shit he was about to hear. Unlike anything he'd ever heard before in his life. He could feel it in his gut. And after eleven years of representing career criminals, his gut rarely deceived him.

They sat opposite each other at the table. Johnny put his briefcase beside his chair. Not on the table. He wanted nothing but clean slate between the two of them.

"To understand what happened on Hart Island," Bobby said, "you have to understand what happened in Chornobyl first."

He didn't pronounce it the way Americans did. He didn't call it Chornobyl. He softened the consonants. Put the accent on the third syllable. "Chor-no-BEEL." Proper Ukrainian, Johnny thought. Ukrainian, Russian, English, didn't matter. The word rolling off a person's tongue never failed to creep him out. It was the name of a place where a lot of people died without any violence. Without ever seeing the enemy that killed them.

"What happened in Chornobyl?" Johnny said.

Bobby took a deep breath. "It was about two years ago. I was fourteen going on fifteen. My best friend and I were stealing from the dead. We did that sometimes. When we had to. For the money."

"Stealing from the dead? What does that mean? You were robbing graves?"

"Yeah. But not the kind of graves you're thinking of. Vehicle graves. Equipment graves. Buried houses."

"What?"

"When reactor number four blew up in 1986, it snowed in Chornobyl and the villages beyond. The wind carried it all the way to Belarus. Except the white stuff wasn't snow. It was radioactive dust. So the Soviet government evacuated the village and bulldozed everything. They buried cars, trucks, tractors, ambulances. They buried the bulldozers with new bulldozers. They even buried the houses closest to the power plant. Then they set up a perimeter thirty kilometers around the village and called it the Zone of Exclusion."

"And you dug this stuff up? Radioactive stuff? What, car parts? Engine parts and stuff like that? Are you serious?"

"It was called scavenging. And it was a big business in Chornobyl. You see, by the year 2000, most of the radioactive particles were no longer dangerous. Except for strontium and cesium. They're going to be a problem for another hundred years. They get blown around by the wind. End up mostly in wet areas. Which is why we avoided water."

"But if these graveyards were sealed for twenty years, how do you know these two substances—what are they called again?"

"Strontium and cesium."

"Right. How could you be sure the first thing you touched wasn't covered with them back from the time they buried it?"

"You couldn't be sure. You could never be sure. It's a risk we took for the money. That's how hard money was to come by. And me and my friend weren't digging up the graves. The graves were already dug up."

"What do you mean already dug up? By who?"

"Other scavengers. People were scavenging by the 1990s. They didn't care if there were still twenty different particles that were still radioactive. Who knows how many hot parts made it to Kyiv, got fit on taxis, trucks, and cars. That's how hard life was. We were scavenging what the other scavengers couldn't get."

"You said 'we'. 'We were stealing from the dead.' Who's 'we'?"

Bobby's eyes watered instantly. Johnny had never seen the kid show any emotion before. The sight unnerved him. Made him see his client for who he really was. Just a kid.

"My friend and me," he said.

"Who was your friend?"

"Eva. She was sixteen going on seventeen. We both had the same guardian. Her uncle. I didn't live with my father. You know the story. He lived alone off the grid. I lived with my hockey coach. Coach was Eva's uncle. She lived with him, too. He would drive us to a hole in the perimeter fence and we would sneak into the village. When we were running low on money. He drank a lot. And gambled."

"So what time of year was this?"

"It was late fall. Like spring only colder."

"And the two of you were scavenging. In the daytime?"

"Never. Always at dusk. So there was some light to work but not so much we stood out. By the time it was pitch black out we'd be hiking back to the car with whatever we found."

"So what happened?"

"We were in an open pit by the red forest. Farm equipment mostly. We were both thin but strong. We could get deeper into the graveyard and get into tighter places than the other scavengers. I crawled though the hood of a tractor—someone had scavenged the entire engine piece-by-piece—to get to the harvester that was buried beneath it. The harvester still had most of its engine. I thought I could get the starter. Starters are worth good money. But I had to invert myself to get in and I accidentally kicked the piece of wood holding the tractor's hood up. It closed behind me. Locked me in. I had my screwdriver, my wrench, and my pliers in my pockets, but I dropped the screwdriver and I couldn't get the latch open without it. I kept banging but Eva was gone. First I was worried I wouldn't get out. Then I started worrying about her."

"How did you get out?"

"Eva came back. She thought she'd seen someone in the forest and she went to higher ground to get a better look. She had a crowbar. We always took turns going in. Whoever stayed up top had the hacksaw and the crowbar."

"So she pried it open?"

"Yeah."

"And you got out?"

"Yeah."

"And then what?"

Bobby took his eyes off Johnny and stared into space. "Then the gunshots started."

CHAPTER 52

NADIA WOKE UP GROGGY. SHE WAS STARING AT A CHALKBOARD. A clanging sound reverberated inside her head. Her vision cleared as the fog gradually lifted.

It wasn't a chalkboard. It was the sky. A charcoal sky at dusk. She was lying on her back, she realized.

Her nose detected a faint smell of petroleum. Not gasoline. Oil, she thought. The incessant banging in her head continued. She wondered where she was.

Nine words.

The rawboned man from Lviv.

A purple pill.

A bolt of euphoria ripped through her. She was alive. She was conscious. She pushed herself upright. Her arms. They functioned. She flexed her leg muscles. Her quads tightened. She cleared her throat. Said her name. She could speak. The man who'd given her the pill hadn't lied. It was just like Xanax—

The Zone. She was back in the Zone.

As soon as she saw the irradiated forest to her left there was no doubt. Nadia knew where she was. She remembered her final exchange with the rawboned man from Lviv.

Where will I wake up?

In the front row.

The front row to what?

The theater.

What theater?

You know what theater.

She was here for a reason. Something hammered at her temple again.

Adam. The link between Valentin and Adam. The reason Adam killed Valentine. That's why she was here. And Marko. Good God. How could she have forgotten? Marko was here somewhere. And what was that goddamn noise?

Nadia sprang to her feet. She stumbled. Tripped over something laying beside her. A crowbar. Why was she lying near a crowbar? Beside the crowbar was a flashlight. Nadia picked it up and took three steps.

Ten feet in front of her lay a pit. The pit was filled with vehicles. Old Soviet cars, buses, military jeeps. It was a cemetery for dead cars. She'd driven past it on a bicycle in the night during her visit to Chornobyl last year. The top layer of vehicles had been stripped clean. Rusty and discolored bodies were all that remained. In some places, however, a second vehicle lay hidden beneath the first one where the cars were small.

She heard the banging noise again. Now it didn't sound as though it was in her head. It sounded as though it was coming from beyond.

More banging. Nadia caught a glimpse of something moving in the pit. The noise and the movement had taken place at the same time. The noise was coming from the pit.

"Marko," Nadia said.

A muffled reply from beneath the pile of stripped vehicles. Nadia couldn't make out the words but she recognized the voice. She picked up the crowbar and moved to the edge of the pit.

"Marko," she said.

A trunk rattled. The muffled voice sounded again. It came from an old Soviet car lodged beneath a hollowed-out Datsun.

Nadia took the crowbar and checked the pit for water. She remembered her lesson from Hayder, the scavenger she'd met last year. Strontium and cesium settled in moisture. Her boots were going to get contaminated. They were probably already hot. But her hands. Her flesh. She could not let her hands touch water. Otherwise she'd absorb more radiation in a second than was healthy in one year.

She shined the light into the pit, saw the ground was dry, and climbed through the hollowed-out Datsun. She yanked the trunk open with the crowbar.

Marko lay curled inside.

"You all right?" she said.

His voice sounded raspy. "Sure. Like a day at the spa. Get me out of here."

Nadia pulled him out of the trunk. Marko groaned as he straightened.

"How long were you in there?" she said.

He checked his watch. "About two. No. Closer to three hours."

Nadia crawled out of the pit. Marko barely squeezed through the Datsun. He looked unsteady as he hoisted himself onto the edges of the frame. A woman or a child could negotiate the graveyard easier than a grown man, she thought. She reached out with her hand. He took it. She yanked. He stepped out of the pit onto solid ground.

A muted rifle shot cracked the air.

They ducked.

Metal clanged against metal. A bullet ricocheted among the cars in the pit.

They looked around.

"Which direction?" Nadia said.

"Can't tell. Sound suppressor."

"You see anyone?"

"Not yet."

They swiveled around, backs to each other.

Nadia spied a glint on the horizon. A man was taking aim with his rifle.

"There he is," Nadia said. "Go."

They ran.

A second gunshot rang out.

Nadia clenched her teeth as she ran, waited for the onset of pain. It didn't come. She glanced at Marko. He was catching up quickly. The bullet had missed him, too.

They sprinted onto an asphalt road. Grass, weeds, and small shrubs sprouted from its cracks. The path took them out of the hunter's line of sight. The forest shielded them. They continued running hard for twenty yards. Then they jogged side by side.

"Why did they go to all this trouble?" Marko said.

"Good question," Nadia said.

"Why did they kidnap me and lock me in the trunk of a car in a vehicle graveyard. Why Chornobyl?"

"Why give me a pill and have me wake up here?"

"Why is a man with a rifle shooting at us?" Marko breathed heavily. "Almost feels like a game."

The phrase struck a chord. Nadia remembered Obon's description of the origins of the Zaroff Seven. "Yeah. The most dangerous game."

"What do you mean?"

Nadia told him about the Zaroff Seven and the meaning of the name.

"And the Cossack in this story hunted a man?"

"Correct."

"So you think these guys are hunting us?"

"Maybe."

"Why? You mean for sport?"

"Who knows? They think Bobby killed Valentin's son. It could be about revenge and sport. They knew I wanted answers about Valentin and his son, and their connection to Bobby. The man said if I took the pill I'd wake up and get the answers. It's as though they are giving us the answers now."

"How's that?"

"I'm not sure. But if we stay alive, we might find out."

They stopped at a curve in the road.

"Which way?" Marko said.

Nadia glanced at the irradiated trees on the right. Remembered her previous travels along the road, the layout of the village.

"This is the road to Pripyat."

"Pripyat?"

"The city that was built to house the workers at the power plant. A couple of miles away from Chornobyl Village. It's a ghost town. I was there. There's a cultural center, a theater, a hotel. A Ferris wheel that was never used. It's dark and totally desolate. It leads to the opposite end of the Zone of Exclusion, furthest away from the formal entrance. It's perfect for us."

"Escape and evasion," Marko said. "Rule number one. Stay away from the hay barn."

Nadia recalled the rules of survival. "Right. The hunter could have set us up any way he wanted. Why point us this way?"

"Because he wants us to make a run for the hay barn."

"Why?"

"Because he's got a buddy there waiting for us."

"Then we better go the opposite way."

Marko shot her a glance. "You want to run toward the hunter?"

"We're going to loop around behind him."

Forest surrounded the road on both sides. Nadia veered left into the woods. Marko followed. Darkness fell upon them. They slowed to a march.

"Twenty minutes for our pupils to adjust," Marko said.

"We don't have twenty minutes. I'll shine the light every ten seconds so we can see straight. How many guys did you see?"

"One old guy. Looked like a Russian aristocrat. The ex-military guy who saved our bags in Lviv. And the driver. Basketball player with the eighteen karat mouth. They called the old guy General."

"Those two picked me up in Kyiv."

"They must have put me in the trunk first."

"Okay. We know the score. There's three of them."

Nadia knew that the forest sprouted in groves in and around Chornobyl. She was certain they were somewhere between the power plant and Pripyat. Soon the grove would end and the reactors would appear on the left. The only question was how far away they'd be.

The second rule of escape and evasion was speed. They needed to put as much distance between themselves and their hunter as quickly as possible. They took long strides, but every two minutes they veered off course to divert the hunter from their tracks. They left behind a complex and circuitous path. This was the third rule. Camouflage one's tracks.

Rule number four concerned scent.

"We have to worry about dogs?" Marko said. "Hunters use dogs."

"No," Nadia said. "A hunter loves his dogs. Think of the moisture, how much radiation they'd pick up. They'd be dead in a month."

Wolves howled in the distance. Something large rustled to the right. Based on Nadia's experience last year, it might have been a boar, one of the poachers' favorite targets. More than one had ended up in a Kyiv restaurant over the years. There were also a variety of wild cats and previously extinct species. Man's absence had prompted the Zone to become one of the largest wild preserves in the former Soviet Union.

Nadia kept waiting for a light to flash behind her. The hunter would surely be following. But it never happened.

They emerged unscathed at the edge of a field. Two smoke-stacks towered above six nuclear reactors half a mile away.

Sweat covered their faces. Nadia felt invigorated. The pace was comparable to her jogging speed. Her lungs filled and contracted. Marko appeared to be laboring.

"Let's run to that boulder and take a break," she said.

They stayed low and ducked behind the far side of a three-foot tall rock.

"We need to get past the power plants to a path the scavengers use," she said. "But to get to it, we have to cross the cooling pond."

"As in radioactive cooling pond?"

"Yes. It hasn't been decommissioned."

"How the heck are we going to do that?"

"Rowboat. They keep them on both sides of the pond."

"But what if the boat tips over?"

Nadia glared at him. "Next question?"

"After we get across, then what?"

"We keep going to the black village first. It's close. A kilometer away."

"Black village?"

"Some houses were left standing. Some squatters came back to live there. Our uncle was one of them."

"But he died."

"His live-in housekeeper didn't. She has bicycles. It's the squatter's favorite mode of transportation. And she has a gun."

Marko's eyes widened. "Now you're talking."

They jogged around the power plant. From their vantage point, the road to Kyiv was north of the plant. The plant's entrance was on the west side of the road. They were approaching from the south. A fence surrounded the reactors. There were six of them. Reactors five and six were only partially built. Reactor four was the one that had exploded. It stood entombed in a metal sarcophagus.

Light spilled from the power plant to the field. It illuminated their path enough for Nadia and Marko to see rocks, stones, and puddles. The cooling pond ran along the front of the power plant and wound its way north beyond the reactors. Nadia guided Marko to the far corner of the plant. Two rowboats were tethered to a steel buoy.

They climbed into one of the boats and rowed toward the opposite shore. Marko sat with his back to their destination. Nadia rowed looking forward. After an initial awkwardness, they fell into a rhythm. Water lapped the sides of the boat. A five-foot-long catfish swam by them. The pond was famous for its population of mutant catfish. The scientists who wanted to decommission the cooling pond had no idea what to do with them.

When they arrived at the opposite shore, Marko stepped out of the boat onto an embankment. He lifted the oar out of the boat and placed it on shore. Then he helped Nadia climb onto solid ground.

"What's with the oar?" Nadia said.

"Rule number five."

"Never leave a tool behind."

"You never know when it'll come in handy."

They hustled through a patch of evergreens. Light from the power plant shined from behind them. Nadia emerged onto the street. Marko crept up beside her.

A man with a rifle stood with his back to her, twenty-five yards away. He was looking left at the main road in front of the power plant. As though he'd expected them to sneak in along the inner perimeter of the power plant, not via the cooling pond. It was the six-foot-six driver. He gradually turned in a circle to keep a lookout in every direction. His line of sight started to align with the forest—

They darted back into the woods. Nadia motioned for them to continue along their original path. If one of the hunters was in Pripyat as she assumed, and the second one was covering the main road, that left only one man unaccounted for.

Nadia and Marko walked for ten minutes to distance them-selves from the hunter. They turned left at a cluster of brush and crept up to the side of the road again. Nadia peered around a tree trunk in the direction they'd come from.

The man was still there. Nadia had counted their steps so she would know how far to double back. She guessed they'd put two hundred yards between them and the hunter. His silhouette was framed by the arc of the power plant lights. She and Marko would be much darker from his perspective, but they would still be visible.

She told Marko the plan. They squatted side-by-side, waited for the hunter to turn their back to them, and raced across the street. Once they were in the woods, Nadia took the lead. She shined her flashlight to get oriented. Turned it off. She continued to do so every fifteen steps or so, aiming the light downward. Dense evergreens provided thick cover. The hunter on the road was behind them now. There was no risk he'd see the flashlight's glow.

Marko followed close on her heels, oar in hand. They were experienced hikers. They both knew the distance they needed to cover. Marko trusted that once they retraced their steps through the woods, Nadia would know the way to the black village. He bounded with confidence. Didn't ask questions. There was no need to. It was as though they were communicating without speaking.

They emerged on a trail with two tracks wide enough to ac-commodate a car. Weeds, grass, and small shrubs covered the middle. It had been a dirt road for vehicles, Karel had told her. Now it was a path for bikes and motorcycles.

They marched for three quarters of a mile until they came upon a cluster of abandoned homes. Farther down the path they came upon a small gray house with a thatch roof. The windows were blacked out but a light shone under the front door.

Nadia had been inside the house last year. This was where Karel took her to meet her uncle before he died. It was here that she met Oksana Hauk, the *babushka* who took care of her uncle and managed the house.

Nadia suspected the *babushka* was still inside. Some residents of Chornobyl had returned to their houses even though law forbid anyone to live in the Zone. They loved their homes, lives, and properties. This is my home, the *babushka* had said. My health is my business.

Stakes marked the vegetable garden beside the house. The ground had been tilled in preparation for seeding.

Nadia didn't need to remind herself that people in abandoned homes in a black village didn't hear knocks on their door in the night. She pressed her mouth to the edge of the door. Knocked three times, paused, and knocked three times again. Like Karel had done last year.

"*Pani* Hauk," Nadia said, addressing her formally. "*Babushka*. It's Nadia Tesla. From America. You remember me. I came here with Karel last year. Nadia Tesla."

Nadia counted to five. Prepared to knock again.

A bolt slid open on the other side of the door. Then a second one. Nadia felt Marko's hand on her back. He pulled her aside so she wasn't standing in the doorway. Moved to the opposite side himself.

The door opened.

A familiar voice spoke her name. Rosehips, gravel, and grit. "Nadia?"

Nadia recognized the voice. She stepped to the front. "*Babushka*."

Nadia's voice faltered before she could finish the word. As soon as she saw the *babushka*'s face, Nadia knew she'd miscalculated. The *babushka* looked sturdy and resilient as ever, but the sparkle was gone from her eyes. In its place was a look of dread.

Footsteps behind them.

Marko whipped around, oar in hand.

The rawboned man from Lviv pointed a rifle at them. It had a long curled magazine at the base. It didn't look like a weapon a hunter used to kill an animal. It looked like a weapon a soldier used to kill another. Nadia remembered how he'd smiled at her when he'd given her the purple pill. He wasn't smiling now. In fact, he wasn't exuding any emotion at all. He simply looked efficient, albeit with a slight limp.

"Drop the oar and get in the house." His tone was quick and curt.

Marko dropped the oar. Nadia stepped into the kitchen. Marko followed.

Two lanterns lit the room. The *babushka* stood beside the wood-burning brick oven.

A tall and distinguished man entered the kitchen from the hallway that led to the bedroom. He had a palpable air of entitlement about him, and a hunting rifle with a scope slung over his shoulder. He cast a look of disgust at Marko and then brightened as he measured Nadia.

"Yes," he said. "Your head will look quite nice among my other trophies. Quite nice, indeed."

CHAPTER 53

J OHNNY COULD SEE THE ANGUISH IN THE KID'S FACE. ALL
this time Johnny thought Bobby's conscience was eating him
up about the Valentine killing. But in fact an altogether different
event persecuted him. Something that happened two years ago
on the opposite side of the world, in a place everyone had heard
of but no one wanted to talk about.

"Gunshots?" Johnny said. "Who was shooting?"

"The hunters."

"What hunters?"

"The hunters that were there to hunt men."

"What men?"

"Criminals. If a man is in trouble with the police, the Zone is
a good place to hide out. No one lives there, except for the squatters. There's no law. Just the animals. What could be a better
place to hide?"

"Who were these hunters?"

Bobby shrugged. "I don't know. Coach told me later they
were powerful men. Men who could do whatever they wanted."

"And had they done this before?"

"There were rumors but we never believed them. When
they spotted me and Eva from a distance they assumed we were
scavengers. Scavenging and poaching in the Zone is illegal. A

scavenger is a criminal. That made us no better than the other criminals they were hunting. So they shot at us with their rifles."

"And what happened?"

"They missed. We got away. We ran from the village to Pripyat. It was dark there and we knew the way out of the exclusion zone. We didn't come in via the main road, though. We came in through the forest. When we saw the car parked behind the cultural center—there are no cars in Pripyat—we knew."

"There was another hunter waiting for you."

Bobby nodded. "We turned back, cut into the forest and hiked two kilometers back toward the power plant. There are only two places along the perimeter for a scavenger to escape. One path starts at Pripyat. The other one starts on the other side of Chornobyl, half a kilometer before the main entrance to the power plant. That's how we got in. That's how we needed to get out."

"You and Eva."

"When we doubled back, we snuck inside the power plant so we didn't have to cross the cooling pond. There's an opening in the fence. A person can sneak through. That way you walk along the cooling pond on the inner bank. By the reactors. You don't have to cross it. But when we looped around toward the far side of the plant, another hunter was there waiting for us with a rifle. She was the lookout for the cooling pond. We caught her by surprise by coming along the inner perimeter."

"She?"

"One of the hunters was a woman. She pointed her rifle at us and told us to put our hands in the air. She looked confused. She said, 'You're not criminals. You're children. What are you doing here?' When we didn't answer, she told me to show her what I had in my knapsack."

"What did you have in your knapsack?"

"Gear shafts from a tractor. They look like darts made out of iron. When she saw them she got angry. She said, 'Who put you up to this? You poor things. They're not going to care. Because you're scavengers. Don't you see? My husband and the others. They're not going to care that you're children.' And then she said, 'Go. Run.' But it was too late. Eva had pulled a knife out of her back pocket and was charging her, trying to catch her by surprise. It was reckless and stupid but that was Eva's way. Eva was fast. Very fast. It all happened so quickly. There was no time to think. The woman did what any person would have done if someone with a knife charged them."

"She squeezed the trigger," Johnny said.

Bobby nodded.

"And?"

"Nothing happened."

"It was a squib." Johnny heard the relief in his own voice.

"When the rifle didn't fire, all three of us were surprised. None of us understood what had happened. Especially not her. So before she got her senses back, I ran up and shoved her as hard as I could. She wasn't expecting it. She went flying backward. The rifle fired into the sky as she fell backward—"

"Delayed discharge," Johnny said. "Not a squib. Hang-fire."

"As she fell backward headfirst into the cooling pond."

CHAPTER 54

N ADIA AND MARKO STOOD AGAINST A WALL IN THE KITCHEN. The same picture Nadia had seen last year hung behind them. It was a picture of a boy in skates holding a hockey stick on a frozen pond. It was the same picture her uncle had sent her mother. It was the first snapshot of her cousin, Adam, she had ever seen.

The *babushka* stood between the oven and a portable cabinet. To her left, the rawboned man from Lviv held his assault rifle pointed at Marko and Nadia. The man they called the General sat in a narrow chair, rifle by his side.

He pulled a radio transmitter out of his pocket. "The game is over. I repeat. The game is over. Report to base camp. We'll be there shortly."

Three men answered sequentially in the affirmative.

Nadia and Marko exchanged glances. They'd thought there were three men. But there were five. The two in the house, the one they'd encountered on the street, and two more. They had both scavenger trails staked out, Nadia thought.

"Once you've hunted the human," the General said, "nothing compares. If you tell a person that, they'll say of course, the target has a chance. The truth is all prey has a chance to survive. If hunting were easy, there would be no sport in it. Men wouldn't hunt. What's different with a human is the tactics change. The hunt becomes cerebral on both sides. And that elevates the stakes of the game. And its rewards. For instance, today I hunted you successfully without hunting you at all. I knew what you were going to do. I knew where you were going to go. Can you imagine how gratifying that is?"

"How did you know where I was going?" Nadia said.

"I was in charge of clean-up and security at the power plant in 1986 after the explosion. After Ukraine proclaimed independence, they put me on a retainer as a consultant. There are very few people left alive who lived through that first month and can provide an eyewitness account to everything that happened. In my capacity as security consultant, I see every application for special entry into the Zone. Last year a man named Kirilo Andre received entry on the basis of national security from the deputy minister of internal affairs. There was a mention of an American woman, and a criminal thief named Damian Tesla in the report. Kirilo Andre has since disappeared. But I was able to locate his driver. He told me they went to see a house in a black village where an American woman was rumored to have been. From there it wasn't hard to find the house. The house with bicycles. And weapons."

He walked over to the square wooden table beside the stove. Picked up a cleaver from a block of knives. "Sharp weapons," the General said. He reached behind the table and pulled out an old rifle. "And dull ones."

Nadia suppressed her dejection. That was the rifle she'd wanted. It had belonged to her uncle. The *babushka* had used it to kill the two deranged hunters who'd been sent by the Soviet government to Chornobyl after the explosion. Radioactive dust had landed in pets' fur and the government had decided to exterminate them. This particular pair of hunters had derived too much joy from their mission. The *babushka* heard of their abuses, invited them for a drink, and shot them dead. Then she buried them in her root cellar.

Nadia stared at the General. "He said I'd get answers about Ivan Valentin if I took the pill," she said, nodding toward the rawboned man from Lviv. "He said I'd get the answers in your theater."

"And you did. We just gave you all the answers. You just don't realize it yet."

"I don't understand."

"What usually happens in a theater?"

"Someone puts on a show."

"Exactly. Actors re-enact a familiar scene."

"You hunted my brother and me. That was a re-enactment? Of what?"

The General smiled.

Nadia pictured Bobby helping another boy out of the trunk of a car, just as she had helped Marko. The General had recreated the circumstances under which Bobby had met Valentin, or his son. That meant the General had hunted Bobby.

"You hunted scavengers?" she said. Simply looking at the man filled her with loathing. "You hunted children?"

"Children? We never hunted children. We hunted criminals. Men evading the police. Scavengers stealing radioactive automobile parts and selling them to cab drivers in Kyiv. Poachers killing boar raised on radioactive water and selling it to restaurants in Kyiv."

Nadia imagined Bobby with a friend of his from school. "And if two of the scavengers happened to be boys?"

"They weren't. They were a boy and a girl, but they were both teens. They were old enough to know right from wrong. And besides, they were children from the Zone. We were doing them a favor by trying to kill them. No one wants to be around their deformities. Normal men and women don't want to marry them. You say I'm a beast for saying so but I'm just admitting what everyone else is thinking. And we don't need a society of deformed people, do we?"

Nadia could sense Marko tightening beside her, exercising restraint so as not to say something that would get them shot.

"What was the connection between Adam Tesla and Ivan Valentin?" Nadia said.

"The boy killed his ex-wife."

"Impossible."

"He pushed her into the cooling pond." The General explained how three members of the Zaroff Seven stumbled upon Adam and his friend scavenging and the pursuit that followed. "She inadvertently drank some of the water and died five months later. She was an agent provocateur with the KGB before he married her. 'My honey trap,' he used to call her."

"How did Valentin's son fit into all of this?" Nadia said.

"Valentin's son had come home from America and had come along for the hunt. He saw the boy and the girl through his scope. He was the one who fired the initial shots. In that way, he was culpable in his mother's death. If he were a better marksman, his mother would still be alive. But he wasn't. So he took a vow of vengeance. His father tried to find out who the two children were but wasn't successful. Then the boy's picture turned up in a newspaper in New York. Something about him beating a professional hockey player in a race on skates."

"Not *a* professional hockey player," Marko said. "The fastest professional hockey player on skates in the world."

"Congratulations," the General said. "Maybe there's a pond outside the prison where he'll be spending the rest of his life. Young Valentin promised his father to avenge his mother on his deathbed."

Nadia noticed the *babushka*'s right hand curling around a broomstick. Nadia tapped Marko's foot.

"And why bring us here?" Nadia said. "Why go through all this trouble when your men had ample opportunity to kill us in Kyiv or Lviv?"

"You are the boy's cousin. You are his guardian. You have to pay for his sin. It is a matter of honor that his death be avenged. As for the method, the vehicle graveyards are empty. There's nothing left to steal. Chornobyl is changing. Nature is gradually healing itself. Thus there are fewer and fewer criminals to hunt. So I brought you here, tedious as the arrangements were, for the sport of it. To recreate the scene and make amends for the one that got away."

"There are still poachers," Nadia said.

"But they have rifles," Marko said. "What fun would that be? A fair game."

The General glared at Marko and started to reach for his rifle.

"What about the rest of the Zaroff Seven?" Nadia said.

The word "Zaroff" distracted him. He forgot the rifle, nodded at the rawboned man from Lviv instead. That made two of them, Nadia thought. "The Valentines are gone. The remaining five of us decided this could not go unpunished. The two of us happily volunteered for the mission."

"Is Simeon Simeonovich one of them?" The question rolled off her tongue. Nadia had no reason to suspect him. But she didn't trust him completely, either. Maybe she was constantly looking for validation he was a good man.

"That arrogant child? I don't even like being in the same room with him. He's a disgrace. He doesn't know the real Russia. He doesn't appreciate that it's Russia's destiny to recreate the Soviet Union. To take back the so-called independent states and make them her own again."

Nadia could hear Marko cringing beside her. A moment of silence passed.

"I have a question," the *babushka* said.

Everyone in the kitchen glanced in her direction with shocked expressions. No one was expecting her to speak.

"You said you were in charge of clean-up and security here," she said. "Were you the one who brought the pet hunters?"

The General laughed. "Pet hunters? What are you talking about, old woman?"

"Someone sent pet hunters from Kyiv to kill the pets. Was that you? Are you responsible for my dog's death? Did you send the butchers? The ones who drove around in trucks guzzling vodka and giving each other points for running over turtles?"

The General appeared incredulous. "We had to evacuate the entire village. What did you want us to do? Let radioactive animals act as agents to spread the poison?" He laughed. "Old woman, you're a proper little Ukrainian peasant, aren't you?"

"Yes," the *babushka* said, showing no signs of having been insulted. "And you're a proper Soviet bastard."

She whipped the broom handle around and smashed both lanterns. Glass cracked. The lanterns crashed against the stone oven. Kerosene spilled. A flame erupted.

"Fire," said the rawboned man from Lviv.

Marko leaped at him. He grasped the rifle with outstretched hands. The rawboned man pulled the trigger. Marko's momentum pushed the barrel of the gun toward the floor. A shot rang out. The bullet went into the wooden floor.

The General stood. He straightened his rifle. Nadia charged. She reared her right leg back and snapped her foot into his groin. He screamed. Doubled-over. Nadia grabbed his rifle. Tried to rip it out of his hands. He struggled to breathe but maintained his grip.

A flame flickered in the corner of her eye. Nadia pulled. He wouldn't let go. She pulled harder. His grip strengthened. She pulled her right hand away and punched his nose. A groan escaped his lips. He fell back. Fury crossed his face. He used his backward momentum to rip the rifle out of Nadia's hands. He fell to the floor, gun in his hands—

A deafening blast.

Nadia turned. The rawboned man from Lviv lay on the floor with a hole in his chest. Marko was sprawled beside him. The fire spread toward them.

A second blast.

Nadia turned back. The General collapsed. Blood spurted from his neck. A third shot. A hole appeared in his stomach. His eyes were open. He held his neck, gasping.

The *babushka* stood by a portable cabinet pointing a handgun, flames flying around her, still aiming at the General.

"This gun belonged to one of your pet hunters," she said. "Now you will die by the bullets you gave them."

She walked up to him and fired a fourth shot into his forehead.

Marko coughed. Smoke filled the kitchen. Nadia helped him up.

The *babushka* opened the front door. Nadia and Marko grabbed the rifles and hurried outside. The *babushka* told them to follow her to the back of the house. The white Lexus was parked around the corner from the garden.

"You must take their car and go," the *babushka* said.

Nadia checked the ignition. "No keys," she said.

Marko ran back into the house. He came back ten seconds later coughing, keys in hand.

Smoke oozed from the chimney and the window sills. There was no brush surrounding the perimeter of the house. No trees overhanging. The house would burn down but the fire wouldn't spread.

"Where will you go, *Pani* Hauk?" Nadia said.

"I have some friends. Other squatters. They are close by. I will stay with them tonight. Tomorrow we will return and collect the bones. My friends have a root cellar, too."

"Can we drive you there?" Marko said.

"No. It's not too far down the road. Maybe there's a flashlight in the car."

The trunk contained Nadia's suitcase, bag, and two knapsacks filled with hunting paraphernalia including ponchos and canteens. Marko fished a flashlight out of one of them. He handed the *babushka* the flashlight and one of the knapsacks.

"How is Adam?" the *babushka* said. "Does he love America?"

"Yes," Nadia said. "He loves America."

"And do Americans love him back?"

Nadia realized that by now he'd told Johnny the truth. Whatever the details, he had to have been defending himself when he killed Valentin's son. And now she knew why.

"They will, *babushka*. They will."

CHAPTER 55

J OHNNY PICTURED A WOMAN WITH A RIFLE FALLING BACKWARD
into water she knew to be radioactive.

"Eva and me," Bobby said. "We didn't waste time. Once the woman fell in the water, we took off into the forest. We knew the rest of the hunters would be coming once they heard the shot. Because there was only one shot. But there were two of us. They'd want to know what happened. They may have had radios to communicate but she wouldn't be able to answer. And sure enough, before we could take ten steps I heard a man's voice shouting for us to stop. He must have been on his way to her already."

"Valentine's father. That's how you recognized him from the picture."

"Yes. He didn't even raise his rifle because he was running to help his wife."

"How did you get out of the Zone of Exclusion?"

"We figured they'd be expecting us to head for the scavenger trails. So we didn't. We hiked to the main entrance instead. Last place they'd be looking for us. We climbed up a pair of trees that gave us cover but let us see the checkpoint. So we could see every vehicle that came in and out. An ambulance came flying in about half an hour after we got there. Went flying out ten minutes later. We stayed hidden until the car we saw in Pripyat left the Zone."

"When was that?"

"The next day. In the afternoon. A young man and an old man."

"Valentine and his father," Johnny said. "They hunted you through the night."

Bobby nodded. "I didn't know their names at the time."

"I thought your father lived in an abandoned house in Chornobyl," Johnny said. "Why didn't you go there?"

"I didn't want to lead the hunters to him. Squatting is illegal. Squatters are criminals."

"They might have killed your father. What happened to Eva?"

"She died nine months later."

Johnny detected the sadness in Bobby's eyes. "I'm sorry."

"She had thyroid disease," Bobby said. "She left school early one day. She didn't come home. Neither did Coach. Three days later Coach came back and told me to prepare for a funeral. She was gone. Sometimes it happens quickly. I didn't even have a chance to say good-bye."

"How did Valentine find you in New York?"

"He saw my picture in the paper and the YouTube video of my race against the Rangers in Lasker Park last year. He called me while I was with Iryna one night at her cousin's bakery in Brighton Beach."

"He must have been in London. Promised his father to avenge his mother. Made the call then. How did he get your number?"

"It's on my Facebook page."

"Facebook? You didn't hide it?"

"Not until after he called. I'm an American. I wanted to make friends. I wanted to be like everyone else."

Johnny shook his head. Foolish kid. "What language did Valentine speak with you?"

"English."

"Did he identify himself to you?"

"No. All he said was that he knew me from Ukraine. That he knew who I was. Which was funny."

"Why?"

"Because he still called me Bobby. You'd figure if he knew who I was he'd have called me Adam. No matter. He said he'd be calling with instructions for us to meet the next day. That I was to follow those instructions to the letter. That if I didn't or I told the police or anyone else about that call, he'd have Nadia and me killed."

"So what did you do?"

"What do you think? If it's not for Nadia, I'm not here. So I did what I had to do to protect her."

"Which was?"

"I followed the instructions. A man picked me up in a boat at South Street Seaport. It was starting to get dark. He looked like a fisherman. He took me to an island nearby. From the angle of his approach, it looked about one and a half kilometers long, half a kilometer wide."

"And this was Hart Island."

Bobby nodded. "I didn't know what it was called until I got to prison. People talk about it here. The fisherman dropped me off at one end of the island. He gave me an envelope. Said everything would be explained in the envelope. Then he took off."

"He have a Russian accent, this fisherman?"

"No. He was American. He looked like a random guy. Someone for hire."

"What was in the envelope?"

"A letter. It said, 'Welcome to Hart Island, the forbidden burial ground of New York City. In the daytime, it's off limits to everyone except the prisoners who do the burials. In the nighttime, it's off limits to everyone. It's a place New Yorkers can't visit without special permission. It's a place no one likes to talk about. Sound familiar?' Then he told me who he was. That he'd had me in his sights, that he'd missed, and that as a result I'd killed his mother. He said only one of us was going to leave the island alive. The one who survived was to bury the other in one of the mass graves in the potter's field. He said he was arriving at the southern end of the island at that very moment, and by the time I read his signature the game had begun."

"And the boat's gone by now, right?"

"One of them is."

"What does that mean? There was more than one?"

Bobby shrugged. "As soon as I read the note, I knew Valentin had to have a boat waiting. Whether he had a man with him or not, I wasn't sure. I was guessing not, that he was doing this alone. Out of some Cossack sense of honor, and to keep his witnesses to a minimum. But there was no way he was waiting to call someone to come pick him up if he managed to kill me. He wasn't going to put his fate in someone else's hands. And he wasn't going to risk any delay. I knew I wouldn't have. I knew there had to be a boat."

Bobby's father had been a notorious con man, famous for his misdirection. If plotting was genetic, the kid had inherited his father's insight into human behavior.

"You had to be suspicious when you came?" Johnny said. "Did you bring any weapons? Anything at all to protect yourself?"

"I had my screwdriver and my flashlight. I always carried my screwdriver and my flashlight. And I brought a bat. A baseball bat. Louisville Slugger."

"Better than nothing," Johnny said.

"I wouldn't have known how to get a gun if I wanted one. It didn't matter. I don't like guns."

"So you're alone on an island with a guy intent on killing you. He has a high powered rifle and a hunting knife. You have a screwdriver and a bat. You have no way of leaving the island except swimming. Are you a good swimmer?"

"I don't know how to swim. The end of the island where I got dropped off was open fields. There were a couple of monuments, but mostly it was one huge field. It turned out this is the northern end. They started the cemetery there, and they're working their way south as they run out of room. There aren't any headstones. Just mass, unmarked graves. But when I looked north I could see buildings and trees. And so I understood right away. I'd landed in an open field with no cover, while he was starting out with places to hide. To survive, I had to even the playing field. To even the playing field, I had to use the only advantage I had."

"Which was?"

"Speed. My father once told me that most people are right handed, so when there's a choice to be made between a left and right entrance—say, to a cinema—seventy percent of people choose the right one. Valentine's right was my left. So I ran up the far right side of the island as fast as I could. There was a tree line and some buildings in the center of the island. I ran toward some brick buildings. I ran for about half a mile. Maybe a little more. Two and a half minutes, maybe a little less. There was no way Valentine could have been moving as quickly. No way. I knew that."

"The only question was whether he was playing the game fair or not."

"It didn't matter. I needed to run for cover no matter what. There's a main road that goes up and down the middle of the island. Then there's a web of abandoned streets around. Grass growing through cracks. Just like the Zone. The first building I ran into must have been a place where they stored records. There were stacks of files. All over the place. Thousands of them. The second one was a chapel. The third one was a shoe factory. That's where I hid."

"In a shoe factory?"

"That's what I thought it was. Turns out it was part of a woman's psychiatric hospital. Something to keep them occupied while they did their treatment. There was a huge room filled with shoes. Huge. Every color and type of woman's shoe you could imagine. They were piled more than a meter high. I took off my left basketball shoe and buried it in the pile far away from the door. And I put it in a place where it would have lined up if a person was hiding under the shoes."

"That's why you were wearing one shoe when you showed up at the police station."

Bobby nodded. "I waited outside along the north side of the building, back against the wall. I could see north, east, and west. There was no way he could approach me without my seeing him. Unless he went into the building coming from the south."

"And you'd hear him coming."

"I did hear him coming. Once he went inside I could hear him moving through the shot-out window. The room with the shoes was at the back of the building. Once he was halfway in the building, I knew he'd go through the rest of it. And I knew once he saw the man's shoe sticking out he'd spend some time lining up his shot. Then he'd have to plow his way through the shoes to see if he'd killed me. So I slipped away really quiet."

"Slipped away? Slipped away to where?"

"The southern end of the island. My mission was to get past him and stay out of his line of fire. If I got past him, then I could use my speed to get to his boat."

"And he had a boat?"

"Yes. A little power boat. He had it tied to a fence post on the south end shore. I took it to South Street Seaport. It had a glove box. Like a car. In the glove box was the rental agreement for the boat."

"Which had his name and address."

"It did. I took the subway to the Meatpacking District where he lives. What I'd done by escaping from Hart Island was give myself the element of surprise. And the last thing Valentine would be expecting was to run into me on the way home. So I found his apartment. I waited in a dumpster in an alley on a street that was the shortest route from the subway. Odds were high he'd have to pass it on the way home from the subway."

"What if he'd taken a cab?"

"Then I would have been out of luck that night. But eventually he would have passed that dumpster. And I'm patient. I learned patience in the Zone, especially the night with the hunters. Eventually I would have gotten my chance. But I got lucky. He took the subway that night. It's what I would have done. A cab leaves a trail. And he already did that with the two boat rentals."

"And then what?"

"I surprised him. He had just enough time to pull his knife out to defend himself but then I tackled him. I used my screwdriver and that was it."

"So technically you pulled your screwdriver first?"

"No. He aimed his rifle on me on Hart Island first."

"Good point."

Johnny's conscience eased. If Victor Bodnar had convinced the witness to stretch the truth and swear that Valentine had drawn his weapon first, it was the truth in spirit.

"What happened to the bat?" Johnny said. "The bat you took to Hart Island?"

"I was actually hiding in the dumpster. I needed both hands to get out. To go up and over the top. There was no way I could have moved as fast as I needed to and gotten the bat out. I forgot all about it and left it there." Bobby took a deep breath and exhaled.

Johnny reflected on what he had just heard for a moment. "So you didn't have a date with Iryna."

"No."

"And that's why your only call from prison was to her. To tell her to back up your story you were meeting in the Meatpacking District on a date."

"Yes. To hide the part about Hart Island, for fear someone connected to Valentine from Russia would come after Nadia."

"Why would you be concerned about that? How did you know Valentine wasn't just acting on his own?"

"I didn't. But when you grow up in Ukraine, you understand that powerful men work in packs. There's never just one of them. They're all tied together, and they all have connections to the government. So I had to be careful and assume the worst. I had to assume someone else might come after me and my family. And Nadia's all the family I have."

The kid sounded sincere. His comments, heartfelt. "I'm going to do my best to keep your real identity a secret," Johnny said. "Nadia's been digging into Valentine's background. If she found any evidence that he was a nutcase, a reckless guy with a history of violence, that'll help. Where's the letter you got when you landed on Hart Island?"

"In the Long Island Sound."

"Good. Let's review the truth, or our best guess of what it was, and then what we're going to tell the district attorney. Truth first. Valentine saw your picture or video on the Internet. Probably the Gáborik race in Lasker Park. He went to the hockey game to see you in person. He probably followed you before and knew Iryna was your girlfriend, or maybe he figured it out from Facebook. Maybe he hadn't talked to his father yet, didn't have the orders to avenge his mother's death. He just went to the hockey game angry and lost his cool. Then maybe he spoke with his father on his deathbed. Maybe not. Either way, he accepted responsibility to kill you. Then things got serious. Events occurred the way you described.

"The district attorney doesn't need to know any of that. All he needs to know is that Valentine hit on Iryna, she told him to take a hike, and he got pissed off. She said number four was her boyfriend, and he confronted you after the game. Why? Because he had that kind of personality. He called you from London and said he would hurt your loved ones if you didn't agree to meet. You met outside his apartment. He pulled a knife, things got ugly. That part is true, mind you. We won't get into any of the rest unless it becomes necessary. I'll bet his boat rentals were cash transactions. He might have had to show ID but there's no credit card record. No one's going to find out about them unless they go to the docks looking for them."

"Will they send me home?"

Johnny detected a strange note of reluctance. "Let's see what Nadia found out about Valentine. Maybe she learned some things that will help convince the DA he had a volatile personality. You do want to go home, don't you?"

Bobby dropped his chin. Stared at the floor for a moment. "I don't deserve to go home. I killed that woman. She was a good person. Not like the other hunters. She wanted to help us. It's my fault she's dead. I deserve to go to jail."

His comment caught Johnny off guard. All this time he'd thought the kid had remained mute strictly to protect Nadia. In fact, his motives were more complex.

"It was an accident," Johnny said. "Her husband and friends were shooting at you and your girl. The woman was pointing a rifle at you. You did what you had to do. Nothing that happened was your fault. Do you understand me?"

Bobby continued looking at the floor.

"And let me tell you something else. Look at me when I'm talking to you."

Bobby looked up at Johnny. Guilt shone in his eyes.

"You may be the smartest guy in this room or any other, but that doesn't mean you're the wisest. Wisdom comes from suffering. Take it from someone who's experienced and seen his share. It's easy to forgive other people because you have no control over their actions. The hardest thing is to forgive yourself because you have control over your actions. You must forgive yourself right now for what you think you did. If you don't, you'll be miserable the rest of your life, and you'll make everyone else miserable, too."

Bobby thought about this for a moment. Then he took a deep breath and exhaled slowly. "Thanks," he said. "Thanks for everything."

"Don't mention it, kid."

"How is Nadia? Where is Nadia?"

"I honestly don't know."

"Is she okay?"

"I hope so." Johnny cleared his throat. "Listen. I have to shift gears for a second. Your freedom is my main focus, I promise you, but Nadia told me to ask and if I don't she'll be upset with me."

Bobby raised his eyebrows.

"The locket," Johnny said.

The emotion drained from Bobby's face.

"Nadia got some intelligence in Ukraine that suggests there might be more to it than you all originally thought." Johnny studied the kid's expression but he remained inscrutable. "That make any sense to you?"

He kept a straight face.

"Because if it does, and it's with your personal possessions, it would be good to know ahead of time before you get released." Johnny considered telling him Victor Bodnar might try to steal it from him, but didn't want to alarm him yet.

Bobby thought about it for a moment. "Yes, and yes."

"Yes there might be more to it, and yes it's in an envelope with your personal possessions?"

"Yes."

"Okay. Then we may have a little bit of a problem—"

"Victor Bodnar."

Johnny's jaw dropped. He studied the kid again but he was giving him nothing now. He was his father's son once again.

"How did you know?" Johnny said.

"Iryna." Bobby shrugged. "She told me everything without saying a word."

CHAPTER 56

MARKO GOT BEHIND THE WHEEL. NADIA NAVIGATED FROM memory. She'd travelled on one of the scavenger trails last year in an old Soviet military supply truck.

An alarm sounded once they crossed the main road onto the path that led to the trail. Nadia guessed it was the fire alarm at the power plant. There had to be a fire truck on the premises. Nadia saw flames in the side view mirror coming from the direction of the *babushka*'s house.

Marko drove twenty miles through the woods. They didn't encounter the driver or the other hunters. They'd abandoned their posts per the General's instructions. The trail was wide and well-worn by truck tires. Marko spun the wheel to avoid trenches, eased the throttle when the trail wound around trees. The SUV's suspension absorbed dips, bumps, and sudden turns. They emerged out of the forest on the main road to Chornobyl three miles past the checkpoint. From there it took them a little over an hour to get to Kyiv.

The navigation system was in Russian. It included a directory of destinations. Nadia programmed it to take them to the Intercontinental Hotel. When they got there, they circled the property and parked two blocks away. Wiped down their fingerprints out of paranoia, took Nadia's luggage, and walked to the hotel.

They got one room with two double beds so they could protect each other. Although the General and the rawboned man from Lviv were dead, they assumed they might be at risk out of sheer prudence.

It was 12:07 a.m. by the time Marko posted the DO NOT DISTURB sign on the door. Nadia checked her e-mail. Obon's assistant had forwarded the picture of the Zaroff Seven. It was a black and white photo of six men and a woman standing around a large bear. Nadia recognized the General and the rawboned man from Lviv. They looked twenty years younger. Beside them stood Valentin, his hair darker and face fuller. An attractive woman pressed against him, undoubtedly his first wife. Nadia didn't recognize the remaining three men. Although the General had told her Simeon Simeonovich wasn't one of them, she still felt relieved he wasn't in the picture.

New York was seven hours behind. That made it 5:07 p.m. Nadia called Obon and thanked him for the e-mail.

"The other three men are similar in stature to Valentine," Obon said. "They're all junior oligarchs, all still alive."

He read their names to Nadia. She wrote them down but they meant nothing to her. Afterward, she thanked him and hung up. She told Marko what she'd learned.

"The General told us he took this responsibility on himself," Marko said. "Didn't sound like the other three were in on it at all."

"Agreed," Nadia said.

"And it'll take some time for them to find out what happened. We should be able to get out of the country."

"But even if we do, bottom line is there are three more guys out there, who may or may not care about revenge."

Marko shrugged. "It's not neat and tidy, is it?"

"No it is not."

"Life rarely is."

Nadia called Johnny. She got voice mail but he returned her call immediately. They exchanged updates. Between the two of them, they knew everything now, Nadia thought. Except for one thing.

"What about the locket?" Nadia said.

"He found some markings under the gilding. He thought it might be chemical compounds of some sort."

"Who else knows?"

"No one."

"Not even Iryna?"

"He says no."

"Do you believe him?"

"He told you he'd never lie, didn't he?"

"Johnny. Do you believe him?"

"Yeah," Johnny said, without hesitation. "I believe him. Iryna doesn't know anything. She's not a concern. When are you coming back to New York?"

"New York. I used to think of it as the rat race. Now it's sanctuary. I miss it so."

"It misses you."

She told him she'd call back with flight information as soon as she had it. After hanging up, she took a shower and fell asleep while Marko watched local news to see if there was a report on the fire in Chornobyl.

At 7:00 a.m. she dialed the cell phone number Simeon Simeonovich had given her. Perhaps he could expedite their departure from the country.

"You didn't call the office," he said. "You called my personal cell phone. I don't say this often. I'm flattered."

"That makes two of us since you gave me the number in the first place."

"I'm pleased to hear your voice. Did your trip to Lviv reach a satisfactory conclusion?"

"Yes. Very much so."

"Good. And did you discover something that might help you with the boy's case?"

"Yes. I'm optimistic."

"Outstanding. Then to what do I owe the pleasure of this call?"

"I need to leave Kyiv this morning. I was hoping you might put in a call and ease the way with Immigration."

Simeonovich paused. "The Orel Group simplifies entry and exit to and from the Independent States for its contractors. Unfortunately, your assignment ended. So it would be inconsistent with our corporate policy for the Orel Group to act on your behalf."

"Of course." Nadia cringed. "I shouldn't have asked. It was unprofessional."

"But if there were prospects for us to do business again soon, that might change matters."

"Oh?"

"Yes. I'm always considering acquisitions. I've been looking at a small coal company in the U.S. The stock has gotten killed. I'm scheduled to be in New York City next week. Would you be interested in discussing it over dinner?"

"I'd have to check my schedule but I might be available."

"I may need help with the menu."

"That could possibly be arranged, too."

"Call my assistant with your flight information. She'll arrange VIP." He softened his voice. "Until the day we meet again."

"Yes," Nadia said, savoring that familiar electric current over the phone. "Until that day."

After she hung up, she saw Marko staring at her, head propped up on a pillow.

"Are you going to be dating a Russian guy?" he said.

"No. I'm not dating anyone. I'm going to have a business dinner with him. That's all."

"Didn't sound like business to me. You realize if he steps out of line I may have to kick some ass."

"Of course."

He nodded, satisfied. Then turned serious. "And if I didn't say it, thanks."

"For what?"

"For coming back for me. You're a good sister."

He'd never said anything like that to her. Ever. If she thought about it any more, she feared she'd show her emotions, which was unthinkable. She burst into motion and started packing.

"Don't be ridiculous," she said. "It was a purely selfish act. If you're gone, who's going to protect me?"

"You got that right, Nancy Drew."

CHAPTER 57

THE GUN DROVE THE TOWN CAR AROUND THE SAME BLOCK slowly three times. Tall lamps cast circles of light at the street corners. Victor admired Johnny Tanner's home. It was an old English style house made of stone. It even contained a turret that looked like a rook. Victor had to hand it to the lawyer. He didn't look like a man of good taste, with his slick black suits and that horrific ponytail. But here he was, living the American dream.

"This is one of the best neighborhoods in Elizabeth," the Ammunition said, reading from the screen of his cell phone. "It's called Westminster."

Victor grunted. "That's no surprise. You see a beautiful building or taste good food in America, more often than not you can thank a foreign country. Like England."

The Gun parked behind the house, a block away. Victor and the Ammunition walked to the front door. The Gun went to the back of the house.

The Ammunition rang the front doorbell. A curtain parted in a room to the left. He rang the doorbell again. The door swung open and Johnny Tanner appeared.

He looked shocked. He glanced quickly in each direction as though he was afraid someone would see Victor on his stoop. "What do you want?"

"You have a beautiful home," Victor said.

"Thank you. I bought it at an auction. Why are you here?"

"I'd love to see the inside," Victor said.

"And I'd love a summer house in Spring Lake."

"Would you rather I talk with Nadia when she returns instead?"

Johnny let them in. Victor and the Ammunition followed him into a living room. It was filled with small furniture built in another century for smaller people. Victor saw dollar signs. He couldn't help it. He was a thief.

"You have some beautiful things here," he said. "I didn't know you were a collector."

"I'm not," Johnny said. "This stuff came with the house."

Victor and the Ammunition sat down on a red velvet couch. Johnny slipped into a small chair the shape of a half-circle. He wore blue jeans and sparkling white tennis shoes. Sneakers, Victor thought. In his own home. Victor cringed. No foreign country deserved thanks for such a complete lack of class. That was America's creation.

"Since you're here," Johnny said, "I might as well be hospitable. You guys want coffee, tea? Something stronger? I've got bourbon. And vodka."

Victor was taken aback by the offer. He studied Johnny. Noticed his hands looked red and clammy. This was not a man who lost his cool easily. Victor knew from experience. Johnny was anxious because he knew why Victor was here. He was nervous because he did indeed have the locket. Best to let the evening develop slowly. In Victor's experience, patience was a prerequisite to a non-violent resolution. And the pursuit of non-violent resolutions was the single biggest reason he was still alive today.

"Since you're offering," Victor said. "Coffee will be fine."

Johnny glanced at the Ammunition, who shook his head.

A fourth voice rang out. "I'll have a Coke if you have one." The Gun appeared in the hallway. "You should keep your back-door locked. Nice neighborhood, but it's still Elizabeth."

"It was locked," Johnny said.

The Gun put his hands on his hips. His sports jacket opened up to reveal a gun in his waistband. "Huh. Somehow I walked right in."

Johnny took a deep breath and regarded the twin with a mixture of respect and concern. "I don't have Coke. I have Diet."

"Coca Cola Light? That's for girls. I'll have coffee instead."

Victor nodded to the Ammunition. The three of them went into the kitchen. Johnny described how he'd bought the house from a bank after the former owner was sent to prison for embezzlement. Victor wanted to interrupt him but couldn't find an opening to say a word. Johnny simply wouldn't shut up. No surprise, Victor thought. He was a lawyer.

The water came to a boil before Johnny was finished. He fixed two coffees and a tea for himself. Victor and Johnny sat down at the kitchen table. The Timkiv twins stood, one near the hallway leading to the front door, the other blocking the way to the back door the Gun had jimmied open.

"You know why we're here," Victor said.

"I do?"

"Yes. I could see it in your face as soon as you opened the door."

Johnny pretended he didn't know what Victor was talking about. Victor stayed patient. Let him deny his accusation five times.

"One last time," Victor said. "You know why we're here."

Johnny took a breath. "The locket," he said.

"Good. Where is it?"

"You know where it is. In an envelope with Bobby's other personal possessions waiting for his release."

Victor sipped his coffee. It was good and strong, the way he liked it. "I don't think so."

"No?"

"No."

"Then where is it?"

"Here. In your home. Or in a safe place of your own choosing."

Johnny laughed. He sounded nervous. "That's ridiculous."

"Of course it is. That's what makes it so brilliant. The boy knew he was going to meet Valentine, didn't he? That's my guess. He must have known his life was in danger. And he knew the locket might be priceless after all. So did he wear it the day he ended up killing Valentine in self-defense? Of course not. The last thing he wanted was for the locket to fall into someone else's hands, or simply be lost. So he sent it to you through the mail for safekeeping instead. He knew you from his journey to America. He knows you're the man Nadia trusts the most. In fact, he probably knew odds were high he'd either be dead or might need a lawyer. Making you an even better person to trust with his most priceless possession."

"That's such a load of garbage I don't even know what to say." Johnny turned serious. "You didn't come up with this on your own. Who told you this?"

"I only act on impeccable information," Victor said. "That's all you need to know."

"Impeccable information means an impeccable source."

Victor chuckled. "Are we going to dance all night? You know me. You know how I work. Do I need to remind you the pressure I can bring to bear to make you speak the truth?"

"No," Johnny said. Victor was certain he was thinking of Nadia. "You don't have to remind me what kind of man you are."

Music started up on a radio. It was a song about a preacher's son named Billy Ray. Johnny reached into his pocket and pulled out his mobile telephone. Victor realized it was a phone call, not a radio. Johnny touched the phone and started reading the screen.

"Stop," Victor said. He extended his hand. "Make it loud so everyone can hear."

Johnny held both hands up, phone in his right. "It's not a call. It's a text."

"A text?"

"A written message."

Victor snapped his fingers. The Gun stepped forward and took the phone from Johnny's hands. He read whatever was written on the screen. Then he frowned, glanced at Johnny, and handed the phone to Victor.

The message consisted of two words.

It's done.

Victor checked to see who sent the message but he didn't see a name. Just a random string of numbers and letters.

"What's done?" Victor said.

Johnny didn't answer.

"Your laundry?"

"No."

"A transaction related to the boy's case?"

Johnny considered this for a moment. "I guess you can say that."

"I'll ask you one more time. What's done?"

Johnny leveled his chin at Victor. "You're done."

Victor laughed. "Really."

"Yes. Really."

Victor nodded at the twins. The Gun headed for the foyer to look out the front window. The Ammunition stepped to the rear to check the back door.

"You have less than two minutes," Johnny said. "You might still have a chance if you make a run for it now."

"Who am I running from?"

"Now."

Victor smiled. "Let me give you some advice, Johnny."

"What's that?"

"Never bluff a thief."

"I'm not bluffing."

Victor studied Johnny. Light perspiration dotted his forehead. Was he sweating because Victor and the twins were in his house, or because he was waiting for some plan to come to fruition?

"Impossible," Victor said, the word escaping his lips accidentally.

"Not only is it possible. It's done."

The twins returned.

"Nothing," the Gun said.

"The back's clear, too," the Ammunition said.

Johnny glanced at his watch. Some gaudy black thing with a face the size of a manhole cover. "The cops will be banging on both doors in less than a minute. This is your last chance."

A sense of apprehension seized Victor. It was an alien feeling, one that came to him in rare moments of self-preservation. The sensation infuriated him, as it suggested he may have been duped, which was the most horrific thought he could imagine other than his daughter or grandson getting injured. Who could have duped him? The ponytailed one? Impossible.

"Do you play chess?" Victor said.

"No. But I played checkers as a kid."

Relief washed over Victor. "Then I give you my congratulations. You had me doubting a second ago. You actually had me considering leaving your home without the locket. You had me scared. That is not an easy feat. Nicely done."

"Thank you," Johnny said. "But I can't take credit for all this. I had help."

Engines screamed in the distance. Victor thought his imagination might be running away from him. The noise grew louder. Victor glanced at Johnny with disbelief.

Johnny had one foot stuck outside the table in case he needed to make a move. Victor realized the abomination wasn't wearing tennis shoes because he was an American slob. He was wearing them in case he needed to run. In the unlikely event his plot was foiled and he needed to fight.

The Gun ran to the front window. The Ammunition checked out the back door.

"Cops," they said.

They ran back into the kitchen. Both of them had their guns bared. They pleaded with their eyes for instructions.

Victor offered them a soothing expression and motioned for them to put the guns on the table.

He turned to Johnny. "How did I miss this?"

"Once, when Bobby was out on a date with Iryna, she went to the ladies' room and left her cell phone on the table. Bobby checked the address book. There was a phone number for a Rotciv Randob."

"Rotciv Random," the Gun said. "I know that name. Rotciv Random's battle number three was a Super Mario game."

"I said Randob," Johnny said. "Not Random."

"Rotciv Randob," Victor said, "is Victor Bodnar spelled backwards."

"Bobby knew who you were from the year before. When you and your cousin Kirilo—the one you murdered in the butcher shop basement—chased him around the world. And once he saw your name spelled backward in her phone directory, he knew Iryna belonged to you all along."

Tires screeched. Doors opened outside.

Victor said, "You seem to have forgotten the role I played in getting your witness to speak the truth."

"Who's going to believe you? I'm not going to back up your story. The witness sure isn't. It's your word against ours. And who are you exactly? Are you even a proper citizen? I never shared anything confidential with you. If one of your boys took a look at one of my files while I was in the men's room, that's not on me. You came here tonight to threaten me. To extort my client's private property. I'm protecting myself and my business."

Someone pounded on the front door. "Police."

Johnny stood up.

More pounding, this time on the front and back doors.

"You realize this isn't over," Victor said. "I survived the *gulag*. I will survive American prison."

"Ten to twenty is a long time," Johnny said. "Good luck with that."

Victor thought of Tara and his grandson. Then he remembered his own words, the ones he'd spoken. If he'd survived the gulag, he could survive an American prison. But survival wasn't enough. He'd be damned if he spent his last days in a prison cell away from his family. He needed to escape. Was that even possible? Everything was possible, he reminded himself, especially for a man who could disappear by standing sideways.

Ten to twenty years implied he was about to be accused of a serious crime. But he'd never serve a year. He didn't know how or when, but he'd make his escape.

And then he would seek compensation from those who'd put him behind bars. The ponytailed lawyer and the son of the best confidence man the Soviet Union had ever seen.

That's who'd outsmarted him, he realized.

A child.

Two members of the Elizabeth Detectives Bureau and Narcotics Unit interviewed Johnny. After they left, he called the James brothers and thanked them for their help. They'd purchased five ounces of heroin from one of their old suppliers on Johnny's behalf for nineteen thousand dollars. Then they'd planted the drugs underneath Victor's Lincoln Town Car the night before. Victor parked on the street, and at 3:20 a.m., most Manhattan side streets were usually empty.

Anyone caught with five grams of heroin in the state of New Jersey was charged with intent to sell. The cost had wiped out half of Johnny's savings excluding his equity in his house but it was a bargain. The only other solution he could conjure was killing the twins and Victor and Johnny simply couldn't contemplate it. He could rationalize putting murderers in a prison to protect Nadia. Couldn't he? But taking a life—any man's life—was an entirely different matter.

He had two double bourbons to calm his nerves before he went to sleep. As he drifted, he comforted himself by reviewing the to-do list that defined his existence. He'd vowed to protect Nadia by removing Victor from her life. Bobby had set up Victor by telling Iryna he'd mailed the locket to Johnny, which was a lie. It was with his possessions in jail. Check. He'd promised to secure Bobby's freedom. The DA wanted to talk. It was just a matter of time. Check. And he'd assured Nadia he'd find out the truth about the locket from Bobby. Check.

There was nothing left to do but get the girl.

CHAPTER 58

NADIA AND MARKO RETURNED HOME ON SUNDAY. MARKO drove home to Connecticut. Nadia dumped her bag in her apartment and burst into action. Her primary objective was to help secure Bobby's freedom. Her secondary objective was the locket.

Nadia called Johnny and told him everything she'd learned about Valentine's past. She presented her evidence in a way that would help Johnny persuade the district attorney that the dead man had been a sociopath. She recounted Headmaster Darby's stories of his horrific conduct at the Felshire School, and described his sordid relationship with his stepmother, Natasha. Both of those sources would verify that young Valentine had been self-indulgent and ruthless. He was also an avid hunter with his father's bent Cossack morals and quick temper.

The district attorney was not surprised by Johnny's revelations. He gave Johnny full discovery of the state's case. It turned out Valentine had been arrested twice since moving to New York. Once for assaulting a female passenger who pushed him to get onto a crowded train, and a second time for threatening to kill a man for not thanking him for holding a restaurant door open for him.

The Fordham hockey coach signed a sworn statement that he saw Valentine and Bobby collide in a hallway after a hockey game. Valentine reacted furiously, the coach said. The odd thing was that he appeared to have initiated the contact. Iryna corroborated the story after a brief discussion with Johnny, who offered to help her earn American citizenship as long as she stayed away from Bobby.

The district attorney wasn't sure which event incited Valentine—the girl's rejection or the bump with Bobby. It didn't matter. It was apparent that Valentine became obsessed with exacting a measure of revenge. He followed Bobby one night when he was going to meet Iryna for a date and attacked him. Bobby defended himself with the only weapon he had on his possession, a screwdriver. The district attorney asked Johnny why his client was carrying a screwdriver. Johnny responded with a sliver of truth. Bobby had been locked in a trunk as a child. The event had traumatized him, and he'd been carrying a flashlight and the tool that could have secured his release ever since. The kid had issues. Which of us was perfect? Johnny said.

That was the only part of Bobby's actual childhood that needed to be revealed. The witness saw the fight, watched Bobby walk away, and stole the knife and rifle. The latter showed the magnitude of Valentine's sickness. It was as though he was hunting a human being, the district attorney said. He'd prepared himself to shoot from a distance or kill at close quarters. The district attorney also admitted his star witness was not a bastion of integrity. He'd earned a poor reputation during his brief stint as a cop, primarily for abuse of power. He'd been asked to leave the force or face an investigation for accepting a bribe. The witness had been clean since then, though he seemed to live beyond his means as a part-time security guard and actor.

The district attorney dismissed the murder charge based on the self-defense law. The force the defendant used was immediately necessary. His life depended on it. The force used against the defendant was unlawful. Valentine was trying to kill Bobby. And the amount of force was appropriate. Valentine was trying to stab Bobby with a hunting knife. Bobby responded accordingly. It was unrealistic to expect him to not inflict potentially lethal damage.

Bobby Kungenook was scheduled to be released four days after Nadia returned from Ukraine. Johnny never mentioned anything about Hart Island. The only evidence that Bobby had been there was his left shoe. It was destined to remain in the factory among the women's shoes until the building was destroyed to extend the public cemetery. Bobby's true identity and the incident in Chornobyl with Valentine and his parents were never revealed. The only people who knew his real name was Adam Tesla were Nadia, Marko, their mother, and Johnny.

And Victor Bodnar. If he was still alive.

Nadia thought of the old thief as she leaned against Johnny's car waiting for Bobby to emerge from behind prison doors. She had an appointment with a radiobiologist later in the afternoon to review the chemical symbols inscribed in the locket. Johnny stood beside her.

"You know what's surprising?" Nadia said.

"What?" Johnny said.

"That Victor Bodnar didn't turn up during all this."

Johnny didn't say anything at first. "Victor Bodnar. Haven't heard that name in a long time. Why are you worrying about him?"

Nadia shrugged. "I'm not worrying. I'm just saying. I held my breath when he vanished last year, hoping he'd never turn up looking for some alleged debt for me to repay. For all I know, though, he may be back in Ukraine. Or he may be dead."

"Yeah," Johnny said, staring at the prison doors. "Could be either of those. Or maybe something else happened to him. Whatever the case, you don't need to worry about him anymore."

Johnny's confidence struck a chord with Nadia. "You know something I don't know?"

"Yes. I know that life is on the upswing for you now. You

should relax and enjoy it. Spend time with the people you care about. And care about you."

"Listen to you. Since when have you become so mellow?"

"Time passes. A man looks around and sees what and who are important to him." Johnny paused and looked into Nadia's eyes. "Am I wrong?"

Nadia smiled. They turned toward the prison doors. Smiling was a strange sensation. It wasn't a momentary reaction to something funny. It was a smile based on hope. The expectation of happiness. She couldn't remember when she'd last enjoyed the sensation.

"No," she said. "You're not wrong. You're right." She thought of Simmy Simeonovich, imagined choosing his entrée in a New York City restaurant. "Could you imagine me dating a Russian billionaire? I can't imagine what would be stranger. That he's Russian, or that he's so rich." She glanced at Johnny.

A shadow crossed his face. Nadia did a double take. Johnny? Jealous? Of someone who might want to date her? Preposterous. She'd met two of his girlfriends. They were to sex appeal as she was to the quadratic formula.

"Somehow, I think you'll get used to the money. As for the Russian part . . ." Johnny grinned. "Like I said. I think you'll get used to the money."

Nadia laughed, as much at herself as at Johnny's retort. Clearly her imagination had run away from her.

Johnny broadened his grin. Nodded at the prison doors. "Look," he said, stepping forward, away from Nadia. "Here comes our guy."

Bobby looked like he'd lost ten pounds and he'd never had any weight to lose in the first place. As he approached them he looked around. He appeared relieved that no one else was waiting for him. Media interest had faded since the initial headline. In New York, it usually did. There was always something more sensational on the horizon. Two reporters had showed up at court to hear the murder charge against Bobby had been dismissed. There would probably be a small paragraph in the local papers tomorrow.

An electronic barbed wire fence opened. Bobby exited Rikers Prison.

Nadia and Bobby walked toward each other. When she'd first met him in Ukraine, she'd put her arm on his shoulder and he'd pulled back. Told her never to touch him again. They'd hugged once at an emotional moment, when he'd revealed the contents of the locket. Otherwise, Nadia kept her distance so as not to upset him. Now, with a dozen steps left, they both picked up the pace. Nadia hugged Bobby without waiting for his approval. Bobby returned her embrace.

"Thanks," Bobby said, when they parted. "Thanks for getting me out." He gave Johnny and her an earnest look, blushed, and looked at the ground. As though he was embarrassed for everything that happened.

"You're welcome," Nadia said. She punched his shoulder. Waited until he looked into her eyes again. "You trust us now? You trust Johnny and me?"

Bobby reached into his pocket and handed Nadia the necklace and locket. "Here. You hold onto it."

Nadia glanced at the locket. An engraving stood out where some gilding had worn off. The etchings looked like chemical symbols. A sense of hope and power washed over her. Nadia put the locket in a small jewelry box and stuffed it into her front jean pocket.

"What do you want to do today more than anything else?" Nadia said.

"Eat, sleep, skate."

Johnny drove them back to Manhattan. He dropped them off on East Eighty-Second Street in front of Nadia's apartment.

Bobby stood to the side. Nadia walked over to the driver's side and motioned for Johnny to roll down his window.

"I can never thank you enough," she said.

"No problem. Just doing my job, you know."

"You're my hero, Johnny Tanner."

He smiled but in a detached way. "Let me know how that thing with the radiobiologist goes."

"You'll be my first call."

"Damn right." He took off.

Nadia walked over to Bobby and put her arm around his shoulder. They walked toward the front door. Pedestrians passed them in both directions along the sidewalk.

"Pizza or sushi for lunch?" she said.

"Both."

A pedestrian approached from the right. Nadia stopped to let her go by but she stopped as well. Nadia turned. It was Lauren Ross.

"Hello, Nadia." Lauren turned to Bobby. "Hello Bobby. Or should I say, Hello Adam. Hello Adam Tesla."

Johnny got as far as the George Washington Bridge before he remembered he was driving a car. His mind kept replaying a scene where a man carried Nadia to a bedroom. But it was some Russian billionaire, not him. His phone woke him up. A friend from the Elizabeth police force called to let him know Victor and the twins had been charged with intent to sell heroin.

Johnny made a pact with himself. If his phone rang and Nadia's number appeared, he'd let the call roll to voice mail. He'd only return the call if it were about business. There was another man in her life. It was his privilege to take care of her now.

Johnny stopped at a liquor store and picked up a six pack of Rolling Rock and a bottle of cabernet sauvignon to go with his steak. When he got home, he changed into sweats, watched Paul Newman in *The Verdict* on a DVD, and drank three beers. He marinated the steak but didn't open the wine even though he craved the entire bottle. Instead he waited until his phone rang and he heard Nadia's voice over the speaker.

She was back from her meeting, safe at home, she said.

Only then did he pour himself a glass.

CHAPTER 59

LAUREN READ THE SHOCK IN THE BOY'S FACE. NADIA DIDN'T look surprised by Lauren's appearance or the sound of the boy's real name. But then she'd been a cool customer when they'd had their only chat at the hockey rink between periods last year.

"Hi Lauren," Nadia said. "I'd ask how you've been but I suspect I know the answer."

"I'm sure you do," Lauren said. "I wanted to see you face-to-face to let you know I'm going to go live with my blog today. Whatever my reputation, I'm sure I'll find readers. Eventually someone in the mainstream press will pick this up."

To Lauren's surprise, Nadia smiled. "Have you had lunch yet? Why don't you come inside? We're going to order pizza."

"And sushi," the kid said.

A doorman opened the door. Lauren watched with amazement as they walked inside as though nothing had happened. Nadia glanced over her shoulder and motioned for her to come along.

Lauren wasn't sure what to do. She realized she'd been hoping for a confrontation. Lauren had ended up on a Russian island because of her own actions, but if Nadia had agreed to speak with her, none of that would have happened. And now Nadia was being nice to her. Why?

They took the elevator to the tenth floor. The apartment was a modest two bedroom with simple furnishings. Large windows provided ample daylight. Lauren was shocked by its brightness. The kid flew into his room. A few seconds later Lauren could hear the shower running behind the closed door. A bowl of colorful Easter eggs decorated with folk designs caught Lauren's eye on the coffee table in the living room.

"They're called *Pysanky*," Nadia said. "It's Ukrainian art. The designs are drawn by hand using bee's wax. My mother makes them. It takes a lot of patience." She paused. "Good things take time, Lauren."

"What's that supposed to mean?"

"I thought we had a great chat when we met last November. I thought we had got along well. I thought we had a lot in common."

"I thought so, too," Lauren said.

"Then what happened?"

Lauren couldn't contain her fury. "You're asking me what happened? Your friends sent me on a one-way trip to Russia that ended up ruining my life. That's what happened."

"I don't know anything about that. If something happened, it certainly wasn't at my request. Regardless, I'm sorry for your troubles. I'm not just saying that. I really am."

Lauren detected a note of sincerity, which was not what she was hoping for.

"What happened to our understanding?" Nadia said.

"What understanding?"

"I told you I'd give you an exclusive interview in June. It's only April. Why couldn't you wait?"

"Wait?" The question didn't make sense to Lauren. Of course she wasn't going to wait. Whoever got the story first would be the winner. "Why would I wait?"

"Because you said you would."

"I said I'd wait before I wrote anything. That didn't mean I wasn't going to investigate."

Nadia thought about this for a moment. "I assumed waiting meant waiting before you did anything, but I see what you mean. I should have been more explicit when I made a deal with you. So what is it you think you know?"

"I know he's not from Kotzebue. I know you brought him in from Ukraine via Russia via the Diomede Islands. And I know his name is Adam Tesla."

"How do you know that?"

"I visited your mother."

"Yeah. I heard. That was not cool."

Lauren shrugged. "Desperate times call for desperate measures."

"But my mother only told you his name was Adam. Who told you his last name was Tesla?"

"You and the kid did. About ten minutes ago. When you didn't say boo when you heard me say it. When you invited me into your home."

Nadia studied Lauren and shrugged. "You didn't need me to confirm it. You knew already." She rubbed her hands together. "I'm starved. How about you? I have to order. Bobby's going to be starving when he comes out—Oh. We use the name Bobby to keep things simple. So there are no slip-ups or confusion. Okay?"

Lauren wondered what the hell was going on here.

Nadia rushed to the kitchen and pulled out some menus. "I'm ordering a large pizza and a huge pile of sushi. Any favorites?"

Nadia placed two orders for food. Afterward, she poured them each a Diet Coke on ice. They sat in the living room. Lauren was confused. She thought she should be furious but she wasn't. She felt strangely comfortable with the woman she wanted to hate.

"Why the urgency for this story?" Nadia said.

"That's the business. That's journalism. You have to be first or you're dead."

"Were your parents in the business?"

The reminder of her mother knocked Lauren off balance. As it always did. "No."

"You went to law school, didn't you? You're an attorney by trade. Why did you get into journalism?"

"I was an intern in the Sports Network's legal department. One of the producers offered me an assignment to look into a college quarterback's alleged ties with a booster. I learned something about myself."

"What's that?"

"I like to dig. Especially when there's a wrong involved."

"Me too."

"And I like the race. The urgency. I like the need to be first to win."

"Why is that?"

The images flashed before her eyes for the zillionth time. The phone call from her father. *Your mother doesn't sound good. I'm in Florida. You should go take a look. Can you go take a look?* Richie pulling her back into bed, begging for a morning romp. He was gorgeous, irresistible, the man who could make her career. How could she say no? Then the detour. When she arrived her mother was lying dead on the sofa, a syringe sticking out of her arm. If only she'd taken her father's warning more seriously. If only she'd moved faster. If only she'd gotten there first.

"I don't know," Lauren said. "Must be how I'm wired." She considered Nadia's questions. "This is starting to sound like a job interview."

"Is it?"

"Yes."

"Funny you should say that. Because like I said, I thought we had a lot in common and got along real well. Bobby's going to be eighteen next year. The day that happens he's eligible for the NHL draft. He's going to need an agent. With your legal and sports backgrounds, I thought you might be interested in exploring the possibilities."

"Of what? Being his agent?"

"Yes."

"Me?"

"Yes. You."

Lauren sat dumbfounded. "This is a cruel joke, isn't it?"

"Not at all."

Lauren allowed herself to entertain the notion. "What would I do for the next year leading up to his graduation?"

"Build the foundation for your practice. Get the word out. You've got connections. Go to the games. Be seen. I have a friend from Russia who might be able to help. He's very powerful. Maybe he can find a promising Russian kid who doesn't have an agent yet and wants to play in North America. You never know what can happen until you get out there and give it a try."

Lauren thought about the idea some more. The pause allowed her to gather her senses. "This is all very nice. You invited me into your home. You're talking to me. I appreciate that. But as for this other thing, it's crazy. How do I know you're not just saying whatever you can to push me away? To buy time. He can't sign a contract until he's finished his amateur career. What assurances can you possibly give me?"

"That's easy," Nadia said.

"It is?"

"Sure. We can give you the truth."

Bobby came out of the shower with wet hair, a t-shirt, and sweats. They drank soda and talked. The food arrived in two deliveries. They ate pizza and sushi. Nadia told Lauren the truth about Adam Tesla's identity and their journey to America. The kid sat listening and eating. He never said a word.

"Now you know everything," Nadia said when she was finished. "Bobby came here for the freedom and the opportunity. The same way you have the freedom and opportunity to do whatever you want. You can go publish your blog. Tell the whole truth. Or you can join us. See where it takes you. You want to sleep on it, that's fine. All I ask is that you decide within a week and give us a heads up if you go the blog route so we can prepare ourselves. Because for sure Bobby will get deported back to Ukraine, and that's if they're even willing to take him."

Lauren agreed.

On the way home, an unfamiliar calm enveloped her. Her pace slowed of its own accord. She enjoyed sights and watched people. She'd lived in New York for eleven years but she couldn't recall when she'd been more content. She was no longer in a hurry. There was no one left to save. Her mother was in a better place and she had arrived at her final destination.

Fifteen minutes after she left, Lauren called Nadia on her cell phone.

"Tell me about this powerful Russian friend of yours."

EPILOGUE

N ADIA DIDN'T TELL LAUREN ABOUT BOBBY'S EXPERIENCE
with the Valentines in Chornobyl. She also didn't reveal that
the locket might actually contain a revolutionary formula. Neither one was relevant to Bobby's real identity, which was the
essence of Lauren's story.

Lauren's arrival wasn't a surprise. When Nadia's mother described the woman who'd come asking questions about Bobby,
Nadia knew it was Lauren. She could reveal Bobby's true identity
by publishing her suspicions. Even if her story were inaccurate, it
could lead to Bobby's deportation. Nadia had liked Lauren when
they first met, and crafted her solution based on instincts. It was
a risk but so was giving an illegal immigrant from Chornobyl a
new life in New York City.

After Lauren left, Nadia and Bobby went to the jewelry district on Forty-Seventh Street. She visited with a jeweler who'd
designed an amethyst ring, earrings, and a bracelet as gifts for
her mother over the years, back when she was gainfully em-
ployed and flush with cash. The jeweler removed the gilding
from the entire locket. The process exposed a web of chemical
symbols etched into the underlying metal.

Nadia's heart pounded as they took the subway uptown to
Columbia University. At 4:00 p.m. they met with Professor Eric

Sandstrom, a radiobiologist. Professor Sandstrom studied the symbols. Enthusiastic exclamations ended with disappointment.

The etchings consisted of the known formula for 5-Androstenediol modified to include a protein substance of some kind. 5-Androstenediol was a direct metabolite of the most abundant steroid produced by the human adrenal cortex. Its potential as a radiation countermeasure was discovered by the Armed Forces Radiobiology Institute, and later studied by Hollis-Eden Pharmaceuticals for acute radiation syndrome. Initial studies on monkeys were successful. 12.5% of monkeys treated with 5-AED died compared with 32.5% of those treated with a placebo. In 2007, however, tests were cancelled due to a supposed decline in success rates. Scientists reported that an additional protein complex was necessary to further modify 5-AED and make it effective. To-date, such a modification had not been discovered.

Professor Sandstrom concluded the etchings on the locket were promising but incomplete. It appeared that only half the essential protein was defined. There was plenty of room left on the locket for additional etchings. His first thought was that a scientist had conducted some experiments and had gotten marginally better results from additional protein substances that shared the identified composition, but the results were not conclusive enough for humans. His second thought was that the formula was complete nonsense, and the etchings had been added to make the locket's purported value stand up to a cursory inspection.

Three weeks and three days later, Nadia was working on a new project for the Orel Group at 10:30 p.m. at home when she heard a sound from Bobby's bedroom. It was more masculine than a shriek, but louder than a gasp. It propelled Nadia to her feet and sent her running to Bobby's door. He opened it before she got there. He looked either amazed or terrified, she couldn't tell which. He moved out of the way like a barefoot zombie to let her in.

"Computer," he said.

Nadia marched to his desk and looked at the picture on the screen. It was a photo of the necklace and the locket in the palm of Bobby's hand.

"Why did you take a picture of yourself holding the locket?"

"I didn't," he said.

"What?"

"I didn't."

"Then who did?"

"No one."

"I'm confused."

"That's not my hand. And it's not my locket. The necklace has smaller loops. The locket is more circular."

Nadia lost her breath. Bobby edged past her and slipped into his chair.

"There's another locket," Bobby said.

Nadia let the words sink in. "There's another boy," she said, as much to herself as to Bobby. "Is this an e-mail?"

"Just got it."

"Who sent it?"

Bobby scrolled to the message details. The sender's name was 'GenesisII26486.'

"Does that mean anything to you?" Nadia said.

Bobby shook his head. "No."

"Can you get any more information about where it was sent from?"

Bobby summoned the source information. Half a page of gibberish came up. Nadia couldn't make any sense of it. Bobby pointed at the screen with his pen.

Sender> Okuma-asahi.net.

"Asahi," Nadia said. "That sounds Japanese."

"Must be the local Internet provider."

Bobby searched. Asahi Net was, in fact, one of Japan's top broadband providers.

"What about Okuma?" Nadia said.

Bobby searched again. A Wikipedia page offered five subjects named Okuma. Nadia and Bobby scanned the list. Nadia stopped when she reached the fourth subject. She knew Bobby was transfixed by the same entry without even asking.

Okuma was the name of a Japanese town in the Futaba District. It was a city whose name was known in infamy around the world. It was the only place besides Chornobyl to experience a level seven nuclear disaster, according to the International Nuclear Event Scale. The message from the second boy had been sent from this location.

Fukushima.

ACKNOWLEDGMENTS

I am indebted to the many articles and books I sourced for historical context and setting. Among them were Mark Hollingworth's and Steward Lansley's *Londongrad*, and Peter Lane Taylor's *The Secret of Priest's Grotto.*

My sincere thanks to the following people for their invaluable assistance:

Professor Roman Voronka and Mykola Haliv helped with various matters Ukrainian, including editorial input and book reviews. They are the smartest and kindest men in any room. Kim Palmer, Pam Marra, Jeff Palmer, Mary Jane Cronin, Jim Cronin, John Jarosz, Eudokia Stelmach, Dan Simeone, and Bob Simeone spread the word. Thanks to Bob for also sharing his intricate knowledge of firearms. How lucky I am to call you family and friends. Olga Konuich, Lydia Gulawsky, and the other members of the Soyuz Ukrainok of Warren, Michigan, turned a conference call into a motivating experience. The Ukrainian Museum in New York City, Paul Stankus, Jud Ashman, and the entire Gaithersburg Book Festival provided generous hospitality. Kathy Ryan and Chernobyl Children International make wonderful partners and create an effective means for every reader to help save children's lives with the purchase of a book. My intrepid editors, Alison Dasho and Charlotte Herscher, shepherd a book to creation and kill the darlings within like nobody's business. The rest of the team at Thomas & Mercer including Alan Turkus, Terry Goodman, Jacque Ben-Zekry, Gracie Doyle and Paul Morrissey have supported and promoted this author beyond all reasonable expectations. For this I will always remain indebted to Daphne Durham, the high priestess of the Boy cult, and Andy Bartlett. My fierce and fabulous literary agent, Erica Silverman, remains my formidable and trusted partner and friend.

And, of course, I must thank my wife, Robin for her continued support and encouragement. Her husband will forever be the boy who got lucky.

ABOUT THE AUTHOR

O REST STELMACH WAS BORN IN Connecticut to Ukrainian immigrants and didn't speak English when he was a child. He's earned a living washing dishes, stocking department store shelves, teaching English in Japan, and managing international investments. In addition to English, he speaks Japanese, Spanish, and Ukrainian.